Dear Mom, Dad & Ethel

Dear Mom, Dad & Ethel

World War II
through the Eyes of a Radio Man

A Novel

Mark Stuart Ellison and Eli Ellison

iUniverse, Inc.
New York Lincoln Shanghai

Dear Mom, Dad & Ethel
World War II through the Eyes of a Radio Man

iUniverse books may be ordered through booksellers or by contacting:

iUniverse
2021 Pine Lake Road, Suite 100
Lincoln, NE 68512
www.iuniverse.com
1-800-Authors (1-800-288-4677)

ISBN-13: 978-0-595-31916-9 (pbk)
ISBN-13: 978-0-595-66444-3 (cloth)
ISBN-13: 978-0-595-76724-3 (ebk)
ISBN-10: 0-595-31916-5 (pbk)
ISBN-10: 0-595-66444-X (cloth)
ISBN-10: 0-595-76724-9 (ebk)

Printed in the United States of America

Contents

▼

PREFACE AND ACKNOWLEDGMENTS

The protagonist of this story is not a war hero. We have given him the pseudonym Don. Target practice excepted, Don fired his gun only once, and under the most unheroic of circumstances. He served in Western Europe during the Second World War as an Air Corps radio truck operator, a liaison between the lead pilot in a fighter squadron and an air traffic controller. His performance was unremarkable.

So why write a story about an undistinguished soldier?

Most of the millions of men and women who served in World War II did not receive medals or commendations, but, like Don, they did their best. The clerk, the driver, the nurse, the radio operator—all made major sacrifices in defense of their country. All were exposed to the hardships of military conflict: prolonged separation from family, lack of many civilian amenities, and, of course, risk of severe injury or death.

Considering his status, Don was very close to "the action." He made plenty of friends in the service, but buzz bombs and air raids were his constant companions. With one exception, he was always about five to ten miles behind the front lines. That exception occurred during the Battle of the Bulge, when he was right on the front lines, and American forces had to hastily retreat in the wake of an unexpected German advance.

Naturally, front-line soldiers—such as the infantryman, artilleryman, pilot, and aerial gunner—were in the greatest mortal danger. However, as the following pages demonstrate, you didn't have to be in combat to risk getting blown up.

This book defies easy categorization. Although it contains a substantial amount of historical information, it is not a history. It features considerable correspondence, but it is much more than a collection of letters. It is part love story, part comedy, and part tragedy. It is about an ordinary fellow's coming of age in an extraordinary time.

Most of this story is true. The letters to Don's family reproduced here are genuine. Pains have been taken to preserve their original syntax.

Some readers may find Don's concern with food obsessive. War veterans will not. Soldiers overseas frequently did not get enough rations, and when they did, the quality of their diet varied greatly. Thus, food was of paramount concern to all.

Don's letters included exhaustive details of daily life in his outfit. They covered a wide variety of topics, including air raids, prices, the black market, living conditions, and the fighter control and point systems. Within the minuteness of these details lies their beauty.

After being in a cigar box for over fifty years, some of the letters may have been misplaced. Despite the lost missives, Don was eternally grateful to his father for having preserved most of his mail.

Apart from the familial letters, anecdotes in this book—including Don's encounters with the English, French, Belgians, and Germans—are nearly all true. Some names, ranks, and physical descriptions have been changed to protect the anonymity of actual persons. In a few instances, factual gaps have been replaced with likely scenarios. The overwhelming majority of events, however, actually occurred.

We have endeavored to profile the lighter side of army life without losing sight of the fact that war is a deadly serious business. From the beginning of civilization, humor and romance have provided much-needed relief from everyday anxieties. In wartime, that need is at a maximum.

Our protagonist was no exception. In close encounters with women from four countries, he got around. Naive about war and sex before entering the service, Don received a thorough education in both subjects during his two years overseas.

We did our best in attempting to strike the right balance between humor and tragedy. This volume is dedicated to the unsung men and women who did the same while serving their country during a time of unprecedented peril.

Our sincere thanks to the following persons and organizations for their help in making this book possible: Paolo Zagaglia of PZCommunication, Andrimont, Belgium, for providing reference material on a timely basis and permission to reproduce photographs on pages 92, 96, 98, and 110 of *Vues d'une occupation et d'une libération: Verviers, 1940-1945* by Armand Ruwet, Copyright ©1994 by

Editions Irezumi, Andrimont-Dison, Belgium; Dr. Stanley J. Michalak and Henry Stremba, for commenting on the manuscript; The Imperial War Museum, London, England, for permission to reprint Photographic Image Nos. B5114 and BU 10769; Verviers attorney Roger Hotermans, for background information on Verviers and Stembert; London resident Tom Holloway, for background information on Covent Garden; and the Railroad Museum of Pennsylvania, Strasburg, Pennsylvania, for providing timetables for trains running between Chicago and Madison, Wisconsin in 1943. A very special thanks to the Belgian historian Jacques Wynants, who commented extensively on the manuscript and provided us with much documentation on wartime Verviers.

Mark Stuart Ellison
Eli Ellison

CHAPTER 1

▼

JUST THE THING
TO DO

I just had to. I'd made up my mind, and that was it.

The pressure to join up was overwhelming. I had seen plenty of technicolor movies of pilots and aerial gunners in their fantastic, brown leather jackets. Color films were still a novelty back then, and their surprisingly naturalistic tones made the heroic airmen even more vivid. Many of my friends were already in the service. Some were volunteers, others were drafted. I was a happy-go-lucky kid dying to fight the enemy. It was just the thing to do.

October 7, 1942 was exactly ten months after the attack on Pearl Harbor. In four weeks, I would be twenty. I was on the brink of manhood, and my country was calling. My name is Don Quix. This is my story.

I was born near Yankee Stadium on November 5, 1922 to Marvin and Michelle Quix. Though only mediocre in baseball, I had tremendous confidence in my abilities and enjoyed playing and watching games. I was too young to remember the Babe hitting his sixtieth homer, but I do recall seeing him steal second base at the end of his career in 1934. It was late in the season, and the hefty, thirty-nine-year-old Ruth had never been known for his speed. The pitcher ignored him, and thus failed to hold him on first.

My stealthiness was less constructive. When I was sixteen, my buddy Seymour said he could get my best friend, Normie, and me into a Yankees game without our having to pay the two dollars apiece for bleachers seats. Seymour snuck in, but an alert guard spotted him. The man chased Seymour, caught him, and had him arrested. Meanwhile, Normie and I took advantage of the officer's absence and were able to see the game for nothing. Seymour had made good on his promise, but at great personal cost.

At first, I lived in a thirty-eight-dollar-a-month, three-bedroom basement apartment, where I shared a room and small bed with my brother, Joe. My sister, Ethel, had her own bedroom, and Mom and Dad had the third.

When I was thirteen, we rose in the world. Dad rented forty-five-dollar-a-month digs on the third floor of a five-story walkup on Phelan Place. Joe and I still shared a room, but now we had separate beds. Thank God. I loved my brother, but for years, we'd been waking each other up every time we turned in our sleep. Being more active and restless than Joe, I suppose I was mostly to blame. In any case, for the first time in my life, I had a whole sack to myself. It felt wonderful.

Academically, I was an average student, although teachers said I had more potential. I did well in English, but poorly in music and art. Although I had little scientific bent, when puberty struck, biology became one of my favorite subjects.

Actually, my interest in the opposite sex predated my teenage years. I've never believed much in psychology, but I think that Freud would have found me intriguing. For example, during an English class when I was eleven, we had to read one of those fill-in-the-blank sentences out loud. I should have said, "He placed his hand over the brazier," a pan for warming coals, but a different phrase inadvertently flew out of my mouth: "He put his hand into the brassiere."

That innocent mistake earned me scattered chuckles among the boys, embarrassed grimaces from the girls, and a trip to the principal's office, courtesy of my buxom teacher. Although I do not remember having lustful thoughts about her, I must have had more than hot carbon on my mind.

Outside the classroom, I was cheerful and made friends easily. I was slow to anger but never let anyone take advantage of me. When bullies saw I wasn't frightened of them, they usually backed down. In the few instances when they didn't, I gave as good as I got.

Now, just shy of twenty, I was nervously pacing up and down my living room. It was cramped, but I easily dodged the coat rack, ottoman, and dining table. At the time of this writing, I am an eighty-one-year-old man, slow, heavyset, and ailing. But back then, I was wiry and broad-shouldered. I had jet-black hair and rosy, angular features. I didn't have a care in the world and fancied myself an immortal superman. If it wasn't for the two hammer toes on my left foot, I might have been an excellent runner. Unfortunately, my parents couldn't afford to pay for the corrective operation. Thus, by an accident of birth, I was relegated to the status of respectably fast. Still, I managed to be a decent half-miler on the high school track team.

Shifting gears, I slowly approached Dad. He was placidly sitting on an armchair by a window facing the retreating daylight, thoughtfully puffing on his pipe. A few feet to the right, an ancient grandfather clock stood against the wall and marked time.

My father was sixty years old, and we were a study in contrasts. I was a trim athlete, nearly six feet tall, with a full head of dark hair. Dad was five feet six, pudgy, and had receding, snow-white locks. He was quite sedentary, but occasionally we would enjoy a catch together. While my face was perpetually animated, often with a silly smile, his was owlish. My father was mild-mannered, had bespectacled, large, round eyes, and possessed a thoughtful reticence. Florid lips and broad shoulders were the only physical characteristics we seemed to share, though in recent years I have come to resemble him.

I stopped in front of Dad. I wasn't going to take "no" for an answer, but I still wanted his approval. A resident buyer for a department store, he had a high school education augmented by considerable common sense, a trait which I infrequently exercised.

When I was a sophomore in high school, my father stopped me from going out for football. I was upset but eventually realized he was right. At the time, I weighed less than 140 pounds and probably would have been slaughtered by mammoth linesmen. Now, four years later, I was going to expose myself to much greater danger.

"Dad, I've applied to join the Army."

My pop's brow furrowed slightly. Collecting himself, he removed the pipe from his mouth and looked up at me. A billowy cloud of white smoke wafted toward the ten-foot ceiling.

I impatiently waited for a response. The yellow rays of the late afternoon sun, streaming in through the westward window, gave my father a vivid glow. Each tick of the clock seemed painfully long.

Although Dad wasn't particularly sentimental, my words must have cut through him like a sharp knife. He had known for some time that this moment would arrive, but it was still much too soon.

"A wise man changes his mind, a fool never," he gently intoned, his bushy eyebrows rising. "Think it over, son."

"I already have," I shot back. Although I wasn't very introspective, I was usually considerate of other people's feelings, especially those of my family. Regretting my abruptness, I relaxed my frame, put a hand on my father's shoulder, and softly continued, "Don't worry, Dad. Besides, as a volunteer, I can pick my branch of service."

That meant only one thing: the Air Force.[1] And I wasn't joining alone. Normie was enlisting with me. It was just the thing to do.

Risking your life to serve your country is the ultimate gamble, but I would take many more chances over the next three years.

My application was approved in less than three weeks. On October 26, 1942, I left the relative comfort of my working class home to begin a wartime odyssey which continues to fascinate me nearly six decades after it ended.

CHAPTER 2

▼

YOU'RE IN THE ARMY NOW

It was 2 a.m. and pouring outside. I was one of forty recruits sleeping soundly after a long day at Camp Upton, New York. We had done a hard calisthenics workout, run the obstacle course, and jogged many miles.

There were ten four-man tents, with a cot for each private. The cots consisted of a canvas mattress with loops through which wooden posts were threaded. They were probably less comfortable than my Bronx bed, but because I was so physically active and tired at the end of the day, I never really noticed the difference. I was happy to be away from home for the first time in my life; I was making new friends from all over the country; and I was thoroughly enjoying my adventure. At this point, it seemed to me like extended summer camp, but not everybody shared this opinion.

The wind was kicking up, ruffling our green shelters. Suddenly, the sergeant barked, "Everybody up!" With muttered curses, fledgling soldiers forced themselves to dress and staggered out to the formation. Unperturbed, I merely yawned.

Jeez, this must be awfully important.

Within seconds, we were all soaked to the skin. The sergeant was ready. He was going to introduce us to some awesome military logic.

"Somebody stole my light bulbs!" he hollered. "And anybody who steals your light bulbs will steal your money. You're all going to stand in this downpour until the thief comes forward and confesses."

Nobody moved. Struggling to stay awake, we were shivering and drenched. Ten minutes passed, and no one admitted to this fiendish crime. Another five minutes went by. Still no takers. My clothes were sopping wet and heavily pasted to my body. My toes were swimming in my shoes. Finally, the sergeant capitulated.

"Okay, go back to bed. But keep one eye open to watch your wallets 'cause we got a crook living with us."

I tumbled back into dreamland as best I could, having learned the inner workings of a seasoned military mind.

*   *   *   *

Soon I got shipped down to Miami Beach, Florida and was billeted in the Barbizon Hotel. It was December 1942, and what better place to be? Even so, I couldn't help reminiscing about the train ride I had just taken.

Once we hit Dixieland, the weather became uncomfortably hot. Several of us spotted a shining oasis on board: a water fountain. I rushed over to it, only to find a mirage, for it was disgustingly dry. I pressed hard on the button, but zip. Not even a trickle. With parched lips, I sullenly walked back to my seat.

GI after GI went over to the fountain, only to be infuriated, and with the favorite retort, "son of a bitch," delivered a karate kick to the side of the car. Ten feet away, I viewed the frustration and repeated disappointments. The recruits would approach the alleged water source with great anticipation, only to return to their seats thirstier than ever. Then something unusual happened.

There were some civilians on board, among them, a short, slight man with a grizzled beard, who had tossed some fiery spirits down his gullet in the club car. This unassuming little fellow wobbled over to the fountain for a cool chaser. He pressed the button. Although no liquid sprayed upward to his lips, he was so inebriated that he actually believed ice-cold, spring water was sliding into his mouth and soothingly trickling down his throat.

Having quenched his thirst with phantom refreshment, the drunk sauntered back to his seat with a big, happy grin on his face. He was the only satisfied customer on board.

*   *   *   *

Each morning, we had required calisthenics on the beach in front of the Barbizon. I felt sorry for the few forty-somethings, sweating profusely as they tried to
do deep-knee bends and push-ups. They couldn't push up very much, and whenever they tried, they would plop heavily back into the sand. When running, they
had to stop frequently to catch their breath. Their hearts were painfully pounding
inside their chests, and the drill sergeants showed no mercy.

"Hey, no stopping! I don't wanna see any slouches here. If you got too much
beef on you, we'll work it off."

By contrast, I was exhilarated. For years, I had been doing calisthenics every
morning at home. Ever since I could remember, I had been running races around
the block and playing stickball and basketball with friends in the neighborhood.
Thus, the military workouts were only slightly more challenging than my daily
activities in the Bronx.

During one of these morning rituals, the drill sergeants asked for boxing volunteers. Everyone who signed up would be exempt from regular calisthenics.
Most of the men remained in formation, but I and a dozen others stepped forward.

After putting on gloves, we were paired off for two-minute bouts. Four large
wooden posts connected by heavy twine formed a makeshift ring in the sand.
There, two at a time, we tried to beat each other's brains out. The first fighters
swung mightily and hit nothing but air. The second match featured two bloated
giants who got so entangled in the ropes that they nearly choked each other to
death. Three more equally unimpressive matches followed. A usually impassive
drill sergeant turned away from the ring and began writhing with silent laughter.

I was one of two fighters remaining. The other was Bill Diamond, who stood
a husky six feet two inches tall. At five eleven, I looked the underdog. We started
off slowly and stiffly, warily feeling each other out. Bill threw the first punch. I
quickly rose to the occasion, answering each of Bill's jabs with my own, and my
greater speed enabled me to slip punches more effectively than my opponent.
After the first minute, we were warmed up and really going at it. I was having so
much fun that I was slightly upset when time was called. The exchanges were
even, and neither of us was hurt.

A civilian promoter had been watching our exhibition with great interest.
When we exited the ring, he put a hand on each of our shoulders and asked,
"Hey, how would you boys like to fight in Flamingo Park on Friday night?"

I couldn't believe my ears. I had just put on boxing gloves for the second time in my life. The first was when I squared off against a playmate in a street fight on Phelan Place at age ten. Now I was being asked to participate in a real, live boxing match—in front of twenty thousand screaming soldiers. My buddy, Jack, was at my side, egging me on.

"Flamingo Park! Hot Dog! Go on, Don," he urged.

"Oh, I don't know."

"Why, you'll have more fun than a frog in a pond."

Jack Spring was a twenty-two-year-old Georgia farmer. Although he was six feet three inches tall, he weighed no more than I. His curly red hair, prominent cheekbones, and deep-set, blue eyes gave him an unconventional, wild look.

A neophyte soldier who exuded an affable, nervous energy, Jack had already earned a reputation as a prankster. His repertoire included lighting newspapers on fire while people were reading them, putting whoopee cushions on seats, and shaking hands with joy buzzers. Anyone else attempting these antics would have wound up with a bloody nose, but Jack had the rare ability to make people like him despite his childish and unpredictable behavior. Perhaps it was his infectiously sunny disposition that prevented the other fellows from retaliating against him, or maybe deep down, they just knew his heart was in the right place.

Jack and I shared similar interests, including sports and women. We quickly became fast friends.

My optimism soon overcame my inhibition. Tempted by the challenge of physical competition, I simply couldn't resist. "Hell, I'm in the Army. The sky's the limit," I eagerly replied. "Might as well give it a shot."

"That's the spirit!" exclaimed Jack.

"I'm game," concurred Bill in a deep baritone.

The next day, Bill and I met with the promoter to finalize arrangements. There was one slight hitch: the weigh-in scale was broken.

The promoter lost no time in solving the problem. "You guys look about the same weight," he observed. "I guess it'll be okay."

Everything was set for Friday night. Bill and I were slated for the first bout of a ten-fight program. All contestants had been examined by a doctor, but I unintentionally went one step further. As part of an unrelated medical checkup a few days earlier, I had received a tetanus shot. Signs hyping the event were plastered all over the hotel. All fighters would receive a steak dinner as compensation for their efforts.

By Thursday, I was brimming with over-confidence. In preparation for my pugilistic debut, I had boxed for a grand total of three minutes.

It was afternoon, and I was in the hotel lobby listening to a health lecture with the other recruits. The speaker posed a question: "How many prostitutes are diseased?"

Quizzical murmurs buzzed through the audience. Jack and I looked at each other and shrugged. Dead silence followed.

"All of them!" shouted the lecturer. This was the Army's way of telling its personnel to stay away from hookers.

While the orator droned on about the horrors of venereal disease, I began to perspire profusely. I was bored with the monotonous discourse, but instead of feeling tired, I was agitated. Something was wrong.

"What's the mattah, pal?"

"I feel like shit, Jack. I think I'm real sick."

"Come on, boy. Let's get you upstairs."

I took off my wet shirt and slumped onto my cot. Jack touched my forehead.

"Dayem! Yer burnin' up."

"I think I'll be all right if I can just sleep it off. Gotta fight tomorrow night."

"Fight? You crazy? You got a 102 fevah, if Ah evah saw one. No donnybrooks for you, Donnybrook. Stay put. Ah'll get the nurse."

The nickname stuck. Because of the two-minute spar with Bill Diamond, my fellow GI's dubbed me "Donnybrook."

Influenced by the syphilis speech, I was afraid I had contracted some dread disease. My worry was unfounded. I had never been with a woman, let alone a prostitute. So far, my lengthy conversations with Jack about the opposite sex had been confined to the hypothetical.

The cause of my illness turned out to be a reaction to the tetanus shot. I had to spend several days in the infirmary, forcing cancellation of the eagerly anticipated "Battle of the Century."

I soon learned that Bill Diamond outweighed me by thirty pounds, a fact which would not have troubled the civilian fight promoters in the least. All they cared about was how much money they were going to make. The weigh-in scale had been broken for months.

CHAPTER 3

▼

MADISON

At the outbreak of the Second World War, Madison, Wisconsin, with its verdant, rolling hills and grasslands, already had an entrenched reputation as "America's Dairyland."[2] Named after James Madison, the fourth President of the United States,[3] the city began importing milk cows from England in the 1830's.[4] By the mid-1860's, cheese factories dotted the countryside.[5]

During winter, the mercury typically plummets to 20°F,[6] and single-digit weather is frequent here.[7] At this time of year, the ground is blanketed with forty inches of snow.[8] In this climate, I had my first radio course.

With a population of 67,447,[9] Madison in the early 1940's was a city in transition. Although its industrial base was rapidly expanding, it continued to retain its intimate, small-town character.

For nearly a hundred years prior to my arrival, Madison had been home to a major university[10] and a well-developed railroad system,[11] but the pace of industrialization greatly accelerated after World War I. In 1919, Bavarian immigrant Oscar Mayer expanded his specialty meat business into Madison, where instant success led him to choose "America's Dairyland" as his corporate headquarters.[12] The French Battery and Carbon Company was founded here in 1907,[13] and by the mid-1930's, had become corporate giant Rayovac.[14] My base, Truax Field, established in 1942, was one of the largest Army Air Force training centers in the country, housing up to thirty-five thousand soldiers.[15] It was named in honor of

Lieutenant Thomas Leroy "Bud" Truax, a Madison pilot who was killed when his plane crashed into a California mountainside on November 2, 1941.[16]

Despite this technological upheaval, Madison continued to possess qualities of a simpler time. Even in the early 1940's, few homes had electric freezers,[17] and Schoep's ice cream[18] was still being sold out of corner drug stores.[19] Madison's four glacial lakes, which delighted generations of skaters, were home to the Winnebago Nation.[20]

Mindful of the area's Native American heritage, Leonard J. Farwell, a young Milwaukee businessman and future Governor of Wisconsin, had given the lakes their Algonquin Indian names around 1850.[21] Closest to Truax, the largest, "Mendota," means "great."[22] "Monona," directly to the east, means "beautiful."[23] I would work with a Native American soldier toward the end of the war.

The World War II years were the tail-end of Madison's era of front porches and picket fences.[24] Since housing starts were negligible during the Depression and World War II,[25] the residences I saw were built no later than the 1920's. They were charming single family homes framed in banks of lily-white powder on neat, tree-lined streets, where people on wicker chairs would chat on their front porches and greet passersby.[26] Some had swings[27] where children rocked and lovers wooed. It was a soft, delicate atmosphere of quiet beauty. Colorful picture postcards attempted, but never quite succeeded, in capturing its natural appeal.

Unfortunately, I seldom had time to enjoy the town. On one occasion, however, I had the privilege of spending an entire afternoon at a local farmer's home, along with Jack and other recruits.

It was a large, three-story Victorian structure, surrounded by well-manicured hedges. The enormous living room, with its oak-paneling and plush, brown carpeting, conveyed the very essence of country opulence. Large, gilt-framed paintings of rustic life hanging from the walls complemented a fireplace full of crackling logs. A mahogany dining table filled the room's center, while a chandelier resembling delicately-trimmed icicles shaped into a birthday cake seductively dangled overhead.

There was much merrymaking and good cheer as we relaxed over drinks before lunch. Then the maid walked in with an enormous tray of food. We made a bee-line for the table and dug in.

Despite the camaraderie and great chow, I couldn't keep my eyes off the maid. She was certainly no great beauty. She had a chubby face, a big nose, and a powerful-looking jaw—a real hayseed sort of gal.

Although her visage was coarse, she looked the model of propriety. Her conservative black-and-white uniform was neatly buttoned up to the neck, and her brown hair was tied back in a bun. She seemed the picture of Miss Prim-and-Proper, except for one thing: she was blushing uncontrollably.

Her cheeks were so flushed that I thought she was drunk. I confidentially leaned over to my buddy at the table.

"Psst. Jack. What's with the maid?"

"How do you mean?"

"Her face is like a rose in full bloom, and we're not even quarter-tanked."

"That milkmaid? She's not crocked."

"Not crocked? She looks like she's going to burst out like a wild hyena any second now."

"She's perfectly sobah, Donnybrook."

"Bullshit. I'll bet you twenty bucks she couldn't count to ten."

"You'll lose."

"Why?"

"See, Ah was ovah heah early this mornin', before the rest of y'all."

"What the hell for? Breakfast with the roosters?"

"No siree. Ah didn't have any breakfast. Ah had Jane instead."

*   *   *   *

Madison was an airman's culinary dream. Even on base, the food was great, with plenty of good-tasting milk. But a stout GI got greedy on the chow line, overloading his mess kit with five slices of white bread. Then he spread himself out on an empty table. An alert officer spotted the mound of nourishment on the enlisted man's tray and sat down directly opposite him.

"Are you going to eat all that food, soldier?"

"Yes, sir," was the weak reply.

"Well, I'm going to sit here to see that you do."

The soldier stuffed his belly until his mess kit was empty. The Army let us fill up, but didn't want food to be wasted.

We went to radio school at all times of day and night. To accommodate our busy schedules, we sometimes ate meals at ridiculous hours. Once we had frankfurters at 3 a.m.

We were learning the basics of being radio operator mechanics as part of the Control Net System. It was an intricate chain of command under which a controller in an operations block would communicate with the lead pilot in a group of five fighter planes. Included in the system were receiver and transmitter trucks spaced miles apart from each other. The vehicles were deliberately arranged this way so that if one unit was destroyed during an air raid, a replacement could immediately be sent in, thereby avoiding any interruption in communications.

We erected seventy-five-foot antennas on the highest ground available to receive and transmit the strongest possible signal. A homing device would bring lost pilots back to base. With three trucks strategically placed, each taking a bearing on a straying flyer, we could determine his exact location from a crisscross pattern at the operations block and direct him accordingly.

Unwinding after an evening class, I took in a movie with a couple of friends. When the show ended, we schmoozed outside the theater for awhile. During the conversation, I made the mistake of uttering the word "homer," a reference to an aerial direction-finding station. A male lieutenant leaped at me.

"Are you in school now, soldier?"

"No, sir," I sheepishly replied.

"Well don't use any words you use in school when you're not in school. Those words are classified."

"Sorry, sir," I sputtered.

Humiliated, I walked back to the barracks in silence. The lieutenant was justified in chastising me because the Control Net System was indeed on a highly secret list, but I still thought that the only reason the officer balled me out was to impress his date, a curvaceous, redheaded nurse of equal rank.

There was always some tension between officers and enlisted men. Sometimes it involved the friendly rivalry of a ball game. At other times, it was the usual resentment of people with little or no power who felt imposed upon from above. During my service, I would experience both varieties.

At Truax, calisthenics and sports were a scheduled part of the activities. I played on two basketball teams. One was for students only, and the other was open to all military personnel. Contact with officers outside of social or athletic events usually meant trouble, a reality with which I would soon become familiar.

But sometimes officers could be very helpful. If you played your cards right, they could even help you bend rules. For example, I hated going out on the obstacle course, especially in the winter when it was always covered with ice. So I wrote the following note and placed it in the suggestion box:

January 3, 1943

Dear Colonel Dicer,

I am attending radio school at the base here and playing basketball on both the base team and the school team. I feel I am keeping in great shape and getting plenty of exercise, along with my duties in school, and was wondering if it were possible for me to be excused from the obstacle course.

Pvt. Don Quix

Pleasantly surprised, I found the following reply on my cot a week later:

January 10, 1943

Attention Private Quix:

Since you are being very active in basketball several times a week and maintaining good grades in the radio courses, it will not be necessary for you to continue using the obstacle course. You are to be excused.

Col. Chuck Dicer
Commanding Officer, Truax Air Field
Madison, Wisconsin

I was elated. On the frigid mornings when the rest of the men were slipping, sliding, and groping their way through the obstacle course, I would pack my duffle bag with gym shorts and amble over to the heated basketball court. There, I'd practice foul shots, throws from the outside, and layups. I was only a mediocre player, but I enjoyed the sport and always worked up a good sweat.

One afternoon, while I was in the corridor outside class, an announcement came over the loud speaker: "As of now, all radio students have been promoted to privates, first class."

My classmates and I were justifiably jubilant. However, our instructors were mortified. They were still privates. This, of course, was unfair, but the Army Air Corps was never a democracy and often worked in mysterious ways. We may have merited higher rank because we were being shipped overseas into a war zone, but so were infantry and artillery men, and they weren't given automatic stripes. Still, these ratings were coming directly from the Washington brass, and they were in charge.

CHAPTER 4

▼

HIGH-PRICED FUN

Bored with base routine, I, Jack—and a mutual friend named Ken—yearned for some big-city entertainment. We were set on visiting Chicago, but to do so, we would need passes. These were usually given out at noon on Tuesdays, and required the holders to return within twenty-four hours. There were rumors that radio men would be shipped overseas within the next few weeks, and we knew this was our last chance to visit a major American city during the war.

Just as there was a civilian black market to circumvent rationing of essential consumer items, the military had its own procurers of unauthorized material. Through the grapevine, we learned that a Corporal Jenkins had access to blank passes which could be ours for five dollars apiece. I volunteered to close the deal.

I met Jenkins at the hangar shortly after Monday evening mess. This dimly lit place was filled with parked planes and devoid of people.

"Corporal Jenkins?" my voice echoed down the hollow chamber.

A short, stocky fellow in a mechanic's suit tumbled out of a nearby B-17. His large, coarse hands were full of grease. Jenkins took a puff on his stubby cigar before crushing it against the ground with his heel. He looked up at me with an impassive expression.

"Who wants to know?"

"I do, Corporal. My friends and I are having some trouble getting passes, and I heard you might be able to help us out."

Jenkins furtively glanced around and motioned me toward the B-17. We clambered up the belly of the aircraft.

"They're five bucks apiece."

"No problem."

"How many do you need?"

"Three."

Jenkins extracted a wad of blank passes from the breast pocket of his rumpled work clothes and peeled off the requested quantity. After returning the balance of his stash to its hiding place, he held the goods in his left fist.

This guy was really giving me the creeps. I was getting more nervous by the second, but I didn't let on.

"This your first time doing this, PFC?" asked Jenkins.

"Yeah," I cooly replied.

"Then listen up. You pay for these, they're yours. Fill 'em out any way you like. They're the real thing. I don't deal in counterfeits. But there's always a chance you can get caught. When you leave here, I never saw you. Got it?"

"Yeah. No problem."

I pulled out three five-dollar bills, and Jenkins handed over the passes. The deed was done.

My mission accomplished, I bounded out of the aircraft and quickly exited the hangar. Once outside, I stopped to wipe the sweat off my forehead and exhale in relief. Then I returned to the barracks and distributed the passes to Jack and Ken.

Each of us happily completed his ticket to freedom, filling in an expiration date of "Wednesday noon." Better yet, by leaving early Tuesday morning, we could extend our vacation a few extra hours. Things were looking up.

Though pleased that the transaction went smoothly, I still felt a gnawing sense of unease. I had a sudden urge to take a shower.

Determined to squeeze in as much fun as we could, we allowed ample time to catch the eight o'clock run out of Madison. We had planned this trip carefully and didn't want to take any chances on missing our train.

We arrived right on schedule at Chicago's Union Station at 1:21 p.m.[28] and found the Main Concourse buzzing with activity. Many thousands scurried about, while concessionaires profited from the brisk traffic. Numerous redcaps dutifully toted luggage. The station was at full capacity:[29] up to one hundred thousand passengers and three hundred locomotives were passing through its confines each day.[30]

Moving through the Concourse, we were touched by numerous displays of patriotism. Huge, multicolored banners hawking war bonds loomed overhead, surrounded by Allied flags of comparable size.[31] Their beauty was enhanced by the yellow rays filtering in from the ninety-foot, skylighted ceiling.[32] A photographer offered to take our pictures for free. I was skeptical.

"That's real nice of you, pal, but where's the catch?" I asked.

"Ain't no catch," the photographer replied. "Anyone fighting for Uncle Sam deserves a break."

"Sounds good to me," opined Jack. "You know what they say 'bout gift hosses, Donnybrook."

"Yeah, but I'm not used to getting something for nothing."

"Well, where Ah come from, you were glad to have two dollars in yer pocket. You gotta stop bein' so cynical, Donnybrook, an' trust folks once in a while. The man's makin' a contribution to the war effort, an' we're it."

"I suppose you're right," I reluctantly admitted. "What about you, Ken?"

"Gentlemen, I never refuse free gifts. Snap away, Mr. Flashbulbs."

Ken Jackson was very different from Jack and me. He possessed neither my athleticism nor Jack's extroversion. Short, slight, and cerebral, twenty-five-year-old Ken was an electronics whiz. Instead of playing ball, he got his childhood kicks out of tinkering with household appliances. He never attended college, but was well-read on many scientific and lay topics. We often wondered why he hadn't been assigned to an outfit that could make better use of his abilities. Though stiffer in social situations than the two of us, Ken shared our strong desire for women.

Although he expected to see other soldiers in this teeming metropolis of over three million,[33] Ken was surprised by the number and variety of military personnel in the station. Every third or fourth person was in uniform.[34] Young men and women in army olives and navy blues flitted by. His alert eyes followed the passing WAC's[35] and WAVE's,[36] whose smart skirts blended well with their neat, white blouses. I drew up alongside my five-foot four-inch friend and became similarly occupied.

"What y'all lookin' at, boys?" teased Jack.

"Nothing," Ken and I chorused.

"Well, nothin' looks pretty darned good to me, too."

Our photos taken, we continued on our way. Still inside the station, we stopped at a concession stand for chili dogs.

"You know, these are a Chicago specialty, Donnybrook," observed Jack between munches.

"What does a country boy like you know about Chicago?"

"Mah daddy took me heah for the World's Fair when Ah was a kid. Stayed the whole week."

"I was here for a lot longer than that, Donald," confided Ken.

"I thought you're from New Jersey."

"I am. But I was an army brat. My father got moved around quite a bit when I was young. I lived here for about a year."

"You guys know this place," I observed, "so you can lead the way."

We walked briskly out into the cold February air,[37] intent on doing the town. Fortunately, "The Windy City" didn't live up to its name. Instead, the weather enhanced our cheerful mood. The sun was shining through a cloudless sky with nary a breeze.

Over the next several hours, we hopped bright-red, double decker buses, disembarking at various points of interest along "the Loop." For a while, we meandered around the downtown skyscrapers. The structures passed quickly: the sleek, cubic geometry of the Chicago Board of Trade Building; the champagne bottle shape of the Carbide and Carbon Building; and the Chicago Building on State and Madison, the "World's Busiest Corner."[38] But we began to tire of the congestion and moved on to more open space. I was more enthusiastic than my buddies about marching in the cold.

"Come on, don't go soft on me now, guys," I complained.

Jack hugged himself tightly. "Ah don't know, Donnybrook. Ah'm a Georgia man. Ain't used to this. It's freezin' out heah."

"You don't really know a place until you've walked it."

"You nevah liked exercisin' in the cold before. Why you startin' now?"

"A brisk walk on a nice day is fun. The obstacle course isn't."

"Twenty-five-degree weather is a little uncomfortable," Ken opined, "but it's not any colder than Madison. I'll walk for a while."

"Dayem! Outvoted by a coupla Yankees."

Even on vacation, we felt a strong military presence. With armed services personnel of all bars and stripes walking the streets, Truax seemed simultaneously close and distant. This didn't mean that we felt stifled. On the contrary, free of base constraints, we were in high spirits, letting off steam while watching fellow soldiers work.

From Grant Park we cheered sailors training on two aircraft carriers anchored on Lake Michigan. We saluted a crew on the Navy Pier, and the sailors returned the greeting. Our boots crunching against the snow as we negotiated the Wacker Drive Esplanade, we enthusiastically waived to the destroyer escorts, landing craft, and frigates traversing the Chicago River. Moving past the monumental sculptures, we experienced pride in being a small part of living history. These activities may appear trite to today's readers, but we had a great time doing them.

With the sun fading and the wind growing, Ken suggested hot soup and sandwiches at Walgreens.[39] Despite the cold, we couldn't resist topping off our meal with the chain's famous "double rich chocolate malted milk."[40] By 7 p.m., we were in the Rush and Division Street entertainment district.

"Hey, let's jump on the Elevated an' go ovah to the South Side," Jack suggested. "They've got some real jazzy clubs ovah there."[41]

Ken objected. "If we were staying over, I'd be all for it, but since we have limited time, I think we should stay close by."

"There's Kensy, always playin' it safe."

"There's Jack, always trying to screw up. We can only stay a few hours. If we start running all over the place, we could miss the Madison run. And if we get back late, we'll be AWOL."

"Guys, let's not get bent outta shape over this," I interceded. "Let's walk a few blocks. Something hip's bound to turn up."

While bar hopping, we came across a place interestingly named O'Leary's. It was a brown, oak-paneled, barn-shaped structure, capped with the golden head of a cow. Inside was a traditional tavern: brown wooden counter; bar stools; brass spigots with white, porcelain-coated handles dispensing beer; and a generous stock of spirits. Torch-shaped fixtures flickering subdued, red light upon the white stucco walls added an intimate touch.

After polishing off a pitcher of beer, we sauntered over to a pictorial display near the bar. Each frame was a piece of Chicago's checkered history: Van-Gogh-style fireballs enveloped the city's skyline in an artist's rendering of the Great Fire of 1871;[42] a tan-colored lithograph displayed the first Ferris Wheel during the "World Columbian Exposition" of 1893;[43] a photo of slugger "Shoeless" Joe Jackson of Chicago Black Sox infamy showed him sitting cross legged amongst a pile of baseball bats;[44] a picture of a *Tribune* headline announced the "St. Valentine's Day Massacre" of 1929;[45] and a publicity shot of a famous "fan dancer" caught her in a seductive pose during the 1933 World's Fair.

I stopped in front of the last picture. With one knee to the ground, a beautiful, blonde woman wearing nothing except high heels was coyly concealing her front with an enormous, circular fan. The bottom of the photograph read "1933: A Century of Progress Exposition." Jack sauntered up to me and put a hand on my shoulder. We were both a bit tight.

"Now, that's what Ah call progress! An' the exposition ain't bad, eithah. You know who that is, Donnybrook?"

"I dunno, Greenjeans. Your long-lost sister?"

"No, that there is Sally Rand,[46] one of them risky dancers from the World's Fair, right heah in Chicago."

"Risqué," Ken corrected.

"Whatevah. She was the headlineah. Couldn't wait to see her."

"Did you?" I asked.

"Well, Ah was only twelve. Mah daddy was a very stern man. Wouldn't let me go."

"Let me guess. You went anyway."

"Mah parents had their hands full with mah three brothahs an' three sistahs. So Ah gotta way from 'em all an' bought a ticket. Ah was kinda tall for mah age, so the usha didn't say anything. Got right in."

"So how was the show?"

"Very nice, but kinda frustratin'. Sorta like puttin' a delicious meal in front of a starvin' man an' not lettin' him eat. But that ain't all.

"Ah got quite a shock when the show ended. The lights went up, an' who d'ya think was sittin' nexta me? Mah daddy. He whupped me pretty good that night."

"Sounds like you paid a high price for a tease that didn't deliver," I observed.

"Sure, today it would be bullshit. But back then it was worth it. Ain't every day a Georgia fahm boy gets to see a big city show like that. Hey, Ken! You remembah Sally Rand?"

"Absolutely. She used to recite this little ditty. How did it go?"

Jack began the following doggerel in a loud, singsong voice, with Ken joining in for the last two lines:

> Now you see it,
> Now you don't,
> Maybe you'll see it,
> Maybe you won't.

The three of us burst out laughing, but we were interrupted by the bartender.

"Hey, fellas. I know you wanna have a good time, but keep it down. We're trying to run an intimate establishment here."

Jack approached the bartender in an unusually sedate manner, making a conscious effort to minimize his Southern accent. He furrowed his brow.

"Pardon us, sir. My buddies and I are on leave, and sometimes we get carried away."

"No problem, soldier. Just try to keep it down."

"Fine. Right guys?"

Ken and I nodded our heads in bemused agreement, wondering what our comical friend was up to.

"Good," Jack continued in a cold sober tone. "Because I have a serious question for you, bartender."

"What's that?"

"Where are the broads?"

Smiling and shaking his head, the bartender gestured to a narrow, blue curtain at the end of a short corridor. "You'll find everything you want in there."

Mirthfully sputtering like fools, the three of us negotiated the route.

"Jack, you should win an Academy Award for that," Ken complimented. "You sounded just like a Northern gentleman."

"Well, hangin' around two Yankees all day is bound to rub off some."

We entered a nightclub capable of holding about two hundred people. Small, circular tables, each with a miniature candle encased in translucent, red glass, filled the front half of the room. At the rear, a small, illuminated stage looked out upon a crowded dance floor. A light blue cloud of smoke pervaded the area where a five-piece band performed.

We quickly found partners. Having taken a number of lessons at Arthur Murray Studios, I was very comfortable. Jack was okay. Clumsy Ken couldn't keep up with the music.

A black man bearing a striking resemblance to Louis Armstrong stood center stage, belting out a "hot" jazz number on his trumpet.[47] He subtly swayed back and forth, cheeks puffing away with enjoyment at every note. Occasionally, the musician would creatively use his mute. A white clarinetist playing the more traditional "I Only Have Eyes For You" followed, inaugurating a musical war between "cutting edge" and "smooth" sounds.

With beads of sweat dripping from my forehead, I sobered up with the rhumba, swing, and fox trot. On unfamiliar numbers, I improvised. I went through several partners over the next hour but couldn't convince any of them to join me for a drink. Frustrated, I decided to take a breather and return to my fellow soldiers. They were already sitting at a table full of beer and whiskey.

"What's up?" I asked. "You two look quieter than Grant's Tomb."

"I made a bet with Jack that he couldn't behave himself the whole night," quipped Ken. "I'm surprised he's winning."

"How did you guys make out?"

"If we'd made out, we wouldn't be sittin' heah," lamented Jack.

"Cheer up, fellas," I offered. "We've still got a lotta night ahead of us, and I hear there's a show starting in a few minutes."

An insipid female vocalist belted out standard tunes: "Boogie Woogie Bugle Boy," "Don't Sit Under The Apple Tree," "Give My Regards To Broadway," and, for geographical correctness, "Chicago, That Toddling Town." Her technique was adequate, but her voice lacked fire.

Jack yawned and stretched his arms. "That trumpet playah was mighty good, but this babe's puttin' me to sleep."

Then the stage went dark. The footlights snapped on with a drum roll. An announcement came over the microphone: "Ladies and Gentlemen, please welcome Emerald." The red curtains parted, revealing a new band and a fetching female vocalist.

She had wavy, dark red, shoulder length hair and wore a green-sequined gown. An overhead spotlight replaced the footlights. She began to sing.

Her mellifluous alto was spellbinding. Her figure was stunning. Ken and I were instantly hooked on "When Irish Eyes Are Smiling."

"Emerald" performed for another forty-five minutes. Thunderous applause followed each song. An intermission ensued.

"Wow," I blurted, rubbing my eyes as the houselights above us came on.

"She sure got mah Irish up," concurred Jack. "An' Ah ain't even Irish."

"Neither am I, but they say there's a bit of blarney in everyone."

"Ah'll drink to that," Jack intoned, downing a boilermaker. I matched him.

"Not bad for a Jewish boy from the Bronx, huh?"

My grandfather was a rabbi. A Russian immigrant who settled in South Carolina, he did not live to see my birth. Although he diligently instructed my father in Judaism, when Dad grew up, he moved north and proceeded to live a largely secular life. Marvin Quix did not encourage his children to study religion, and they were not observant. Within two generations, tradition had been completely diluted.

"Ah gotta take you down South some day, Donnybrook. Get some real moonshine in ya."

"Whew! This stuff's really starting to kick in. I usually don't drink this much."

"C'mon, live it up. The sky's the limit."

"No, I'm gonna lay off for a while."

"Dayem, yer no fun."

"Hey, where's Ken?"

"Who knows? Maybe conversin' with Einstein… Well Ah'll be."

During intermission, Ken had somehow managed to approach the headliner. He was animatedly conversing with her, exuding an air of confidence unfamiliar to us.

"Look at that," I said. "He's bringing her over."

"Didn't think that egghead had it in 'im."

"Don, Jack. This is Marie. Her stage name is Emerald," Ken began.

"Hello, ma'am. Mah name's Jack, but mah friends call me Greenjeans. That is, except for mah buddy Ken heah, who could nevah get used to usin' nicknames."

"*Je ne comprends pas* [I don't understand]," Marie uncomfortably replied.

"Marie doesn't speak English. She's a French expatriate," Ken explained.

"Talk English, Kensy. Ah barely graduated high school, so don't go usin' them fancy words on me."

"She's from France. She left her country just before the German occupation."

"Her voice has shamrock written all over it," I countered. "I'll bet she's from Dublin."

"You'll lose, Donald."

"Why?"

"Don't you see? She knows the words but doesn't know what they mean. She's a professional singer, so she studies accents. This is the only way she can make a living here."

"Damndest fool thing Ah evah heard."

"Jack, please. There's a lady present," cautioned Ken.

"You just said she doesn't undahstand English, so what difference does it make what the fuck Ah say?"

"C'mon, Jack," I scolded. "Ken's right. That's no way to talk in front of a lady. She might not understand what you're saying, but she can probably tell from the tone of your voice that it isn't nice. Besides, she might understand curse words."

Jack hesitated. With a wry expression, he turned to Marie and apologetically waved his hand. "Sorry, ma'am."

Ken pulled out an empty chair. "*Asseyez-vous, chanteuse excellente* [Sit down, excellent songstress]," Ken began in flawless French. She hesitatingly complied, and he quickly took the seat closest to her. "*Marie, je voudrais vous présenter mes deux amis, Don et Jack* [Marie, I'd like to introduce my two friends, Don and Jack]."

Having studied French during my first two years of high school, I reached back half a decade, searching for the right words. It was uncomfortable, almost painful. Here I was, trying to impress a beautiful Frenchwoman with my rusty language skills which were never very good.

"*Bonsoir, mademoiselle,*" I began in a heavy American accent. After clearing my throat, I continued, "*Vous êtes très belle, et vous chantez très bien* [You are very beautiful, and you sing very well]."

"*Enchantée, monsieur, et merci,*" replied Marie, holding down a nervous giggle.

Stripped of the power of language, Jack cracked a stiff smile, tentatively waving to the vocalist at the opposite end of the table. She reciprocated with a composed "*enchantée.*"

The liquor continued flowing, and the conversation grew more familiar. Ken, with his superior language ability, did most of the talking. I tried to compete, but was no match for my fluent friend, and, Greenjeans, totally out of his element, started fidgeting with his drink. Sensing Jack's restlessness, Ken, judiciously translating, involved the farmer in just enough conversation to pacify him while ensuring Marie's attention—and affection—focused on the man who spoke the best French.

Marie was a little tight now. Her cheeks were flushed, and she started playing footsie with Ken underneath the table. He proposed a toast.

"To beautiful Marie, the best singer in all Paree," he began. Then he dropped to one knee, and, switching to French, continued, "*Oh, ma chérie, ta beauté fait frapper mon coeur avec le désir le plus extraordinaire* [Oh, my dear, your beauty makes my heart pound with the most extraordinary desire]."

"*Arrêtes* [Stop]*! Tu me gênes* [You're embarrassing me]," she vainly protested, nearly choking with hilarity. Then she grew quiet, listening to the mounting earnestness of Ken's diatribe. The rich romanticism of his voice contrasted powerfully with his impassive visage. He paused and gestured at all the right places. Several people at nearby tables pricked up their ears. Even Jack, who didn't understand a word, looked on in silent admiration.

Ken was on a roll. "*Tous les langues du monde ne peuvent pas faire justice à toi* [All the languages of the world cannot do justice to you]. *Mais j'essaierai* [But I will try].

"*Les cheveux tous rouges m'enveloppent comme un feu d'amour, mais ils sont aussi tendres que la soie* [Your red-hot hair envelopes me like a fire of love, yet it is soft as silk]. *La peau est aussi délicieuse que la crème fouettée; la chair, douce comme le miel* [Your skin is as delicious as whipped cream; your flesh, sweet as honey]. *Les yeux brillent plus forts que les astres* [Your eyes shine brighter than the stars]. *C'est la raison que je ne peux pas vivre sans toi* [That is why I cannot live without you]."

Ken's admiring mini-audience approved with claps and hoots. Marie planted a wet kiss on his cheek.

"Great speech, buddy!" I cheered.

"Ken, you sound like a despr'it man," quipped Jack. "You didn't propose, did ya?"

"Good grief, no. My girlfriend back home would kill me."

Ken got up off the floor and returned to his seat next to Marie. I sat at her other side, slightly farther away. She tapped me on the shoulder.

"*Vous vous appellez Don, oui* [Your name is Don, right]?"

"*Oui, mademoiselle.*"

"*Donnie?*"

"*Non, seulement Don* [No, just Don]."

The corners of her mouth turned upward in a mischievous grin. "*Il faut que je reviens à travailler* [I have to go back to work]. *À bientôt* [See you soon]!"

Marie exited through a small door at the side of the stage. When the curtains went up, she began:

> Oh, Donny Boy,
>
> The pipes, the pipes are calling,
>
> From glen to glen and down the mountain side...

She sang for another hour. Though disappointed that I hadn't aroused amorous feelings in the chanteuse, I consoled myself with at least having won some of her affection.

It was past midnight, and the evening was winding down. Marie came by the table dressed in a heavy overcoat, apparently ready to leave.

"*Bonne nuit, messieurs* [Goodnight, gentlemen]. *Visitez encore* [Come again]," she cheerfully intoned. Marie rounded the table, stooping to give me and Jack a peck on the cheek. She did the same for Ken, but then hesitated and whispered in his ear for several seconds. Then I noticed something unusual.

Even in emotional situations, Ken's facial expression changed very little. That was why his corny French speech had been so entertaining. With a deadpan delivery, he could be funny without resorting to Jack's vulgar bravado. The slightest tilt of his head or flaring of his nostrils could be very effective. That's why I was startled by Ken's reaction to Marie's innocuous kiss. It was momentary but unmistakable. Ken reflexively jerked his eyebrows upward, as if someone had jabbed a small needle into his hand. Nobody would have been shocked by that kind of a sendoff, least of all, poker-faced Ken.

"I didn't know you were fluent in French," I began.

"My father fought in France during the First World War. He met my mother in Paris."

"No shit? You're half French?"

"I guess you could say that. But my mother became an American citizen when she married my father, and I was born in the States." Ken glanced at his watch. "I hate to run out on you guys, but I just forgot something very important. I promised to look up an old friend while I was here. Be back in a little while."

"When?" I asked.

"An hour or so. Why don't you fellas hang around here? The band will be playing for a while, and the bar's still open."

"Okay. Just remember, we've got a train to catch."

"Enjoy yerself, Kensy," Jack said, screwing up his eyes.

An uneasy silence descended upon the two of us remaining at the table. Jack spoke first.

"Now, you know he ain't goin' to check up on an old friend."

"Sure he is. Ken's friend is about twenty-five years old and has red hair to die for. They go back hours."

"Just checkin' to see if we were both on the same wavelength."

"When did you first suspect?"

"The way them eyes of his bugged out when she kissed 'im."

"You noticed that too."

"Donnybrook, Ah may sound like a hick, but Ah ain't stupid."

"Nobody in this outfit is stupid, Jack. We're learning some pretty technical stuff. I mean, you don't have to be an intellect like Ken to pass the radio classes, but you can't be dumb either. You've gotta know some basic math. You have to be able to understand the books and the lectures."

"Math is not exactly one of mah strong points."

"Not one of mine either. But we'll get through it all right."

"Well, Ah'm sure that egghead shootin' his rocks off—God knows where—will be at the top of the class. Even when he's tanked, his mind's sharper than a razah. One hair nevah outta place. Hell, it's hottah in heah than one of them Brazilian rainforests, an' he didn't even crack a sweat. Ah tell ya, 'tain't human." Jack paused, moved his bloodshot eyes closer to mine, and whispered, "Ya know what Ah think? He's a robot, one of the Ahmy's latest experiments. Imagine that.

Maybe that's the war of the future. Men won't fight anymaw. They'll let machines do it for 'em."

"You'll always need people," I retorted. "Machines are overrated. There's been talk for years about death rays that can knock out pilots. It'll never happen. All that stuff's a bunch of Buck Rogers crap."

"Don't undahestimate scientific ingenuity."

"Greenjeans, the only reason you started this conversation is because you're jealous."

Jack grew uncharacteristically serious. For a moment, the mask had dropped. "Ah actually admire old Ken. He's smart. He's hittin' a home run with a woman tonight. His daddy's probably some kind of a war hero travelin' all ovah the world. Wish Ah had one like that. Someone to look up to. Mah daddy, he's just a paw Georgia farmah."

"Don't sell yourself short, Jack. We all have problems. I'm sure Ken's had it harder than you think."

"Ah ain't sellin' mahself, period. Just tryin' to get through this war in one piece. Don't need to be a hero. Don't wanna prove anything. Just wanna serve mah country some. Do mah job. That's all. What 'bout you, Donnybrook? What d'you want outta this war?"

"The same things most guys do. Serve my country, see some action, and do some good. No, better than good. Do the best I can. I guess I'm more ambitious than you. In fact, I took a test on base a while ago."

"What faw?"

"There was a sign on the bulletin board for 'Airborne Forces.' Maybe they want pilots. Or bombardiers. If they pick me, I'll be on my way to getting up in the air."

"So you wanna fly?"

"If I can. Don't you?"

"Ah'd rather stay on the ground. Ah mean, Ah'd love to get up into an airplane sometime. Especially one of them open cockpit ones, with the wind whippin' all aroun' you. But Ah got mah hands full with these classes. Mah brain's tired."

"Well, the test I took wasn't academic. It was physical."

"You mean runnin' obstacle courses an' stuff?"

"Tougher than that."

"Then Ah certainly wouldn't be interested. Do enough manual labor on the fahm. But, just outta curiosity, what did they make you do?"

"We did wind sprints up and down the gym for about ten minutes. Then we did pushups until we couldn't do anymore. I think I did a hundred and fifty-something. There was some weight lifting, and we had to drag a sack of grain—"

"Enough! Ah'm gettin' tired just listenin' to you."

"Okay, I'll spare you the details. But let me tell ya, it was hard as hell, and I'm not sure I even passed."

"Don't sweat it, Donnybrook. You passed. Ah know you. When you set yer mind to somethin', you get it done no matter what." Jack paused for a moment. "So you really wanna fly?"

"Yeah."

PFC Spring banged his fist on the table in enthusiastic assent. "Then go to it, boy! Blast them Gerries outta the sky."

"If I do make it, I wonder what my family'll say. My mother'll probably have a fit."

"You worry too much, Donnybrook. Ah'd trust mah heart more than mah head. Ah nevah worry 'bout what othah people think."

"I can see that."

"Speakin' of family, do you have any brothahs or sistahs?"

"Yeah. One brother and one sister."

"They oldah or youngah than you?"

"My brother's older, and my sister's younger. I'm the middle child."

"It's good to be in the middle."

"How do you figure that?"

"Ah'm the youngest of seven kids, an' believe me, 'tain't no fun bein' the baby. You get hand-me-down clothes. Yer opinion don't count for nothin'."

"I guess your family's a lot different than mine. I always had a lot of respect for my kid sister. Even when she was small. She's seventeen now. Seems like we always listened to what she had to say. I mean, she's no genius, but she has a lot of horse sense. You know, mature. Practical."

"What's her name?"

"Ethel."

"She pretty?"

"Very."

"Sounds like mah kinda gal. Can Ah date her?"

"You ask me that again, and I'll kill you."

"You evah get laid, Donnybrook?"

"No. Did you really do that maid?"

"Hell, yes. And a few othahs besides. But let me tell you, friend, 'tain't what it's cracked up to be."

"You, Mr. Lump-In-His-Pants, trashing sex? I don't believe it."

"Now don't get me wrong, Donnybrook. Ah didn't say Ah don't like sex. Just that it's usually not that heavenly thing that the movies talk 'bout. Look heah." Jack scooped out a handful of roasted peanuts from the bowl in front of him. "Sex is like one of these. Ah've raised lots of 'em. Healthy. Cheap. You can make hundreds of products from 'em. You eat one. It tastes great, an' you have anothah. Soon you can't stop, an' you've finished a whole jar. Fine, but the next day yer constipated. Too much of a good thing can be bad."

"I suppose. But what about nice girls? I mean, really nice girls. You ever meet one of those?"

"Now yer talkin' 'bout somethin' completely diff'rent. Ah know a nice girl. Huh name's Bonnie. Kinda like yer sistah. Pretty, down to earth, an' hoss smart."

"What happened?"

"We went togetha for the last two yeahs of high school. We've been on again, off again. Ah've been tryin' to save enough money to buy mah own fahm. You see, Ah'm the last one in the nest. Ah was thinkin' then maybe Ah could get back togetha with huh an' make huh a propah offah."

"Well, don't wait too long."

"'Spose yer right. Ah heah she's fixin' to marry someone else. Yep. Nice girls you marry. The othah kind, you fuck."

"Why can't you find a nice girl that fucks?"

"Then she's not nice anymaw."

"I don't believe that."

"Believe anything you want, Donnybrook. Just let me give you a little bit of advice. When you do get laid, nevah take a bath with a woman."

"Why not? It sounds like good, clean fun."

"Ah did it once. Hated it. Too cramped. Now maybe Kensy there can have a good time in the tub with his French pastry tonight, but guys like us aughta stay cleah."

"So what do you suggest?"

"Take a shower instead. And anothah thing. Don't be fooled by all them Hollywood movies 'bout girls rollin' around in the hay in some barn. Most of 'em prefur a good mattress in a comf'table room. Hay can be irritatin'."

"I'll remember that next time I meet a girl in a barn."

"One last thing. Nevah kiss an' tell. If you got somethin' goin' with a babe, keep yer mouth shut. Otherwise you'll be finished. No woman wants to be thought of as a whore, even if she is one."

"You just told me about Jane."

"She don't count."

"Why not?"

"Ah was talkin' 'bout girls you got somethin' goin' with. Ah'll probably nevah see Jane again."

"This is starting to get complicated."

"Women are complicated."

Jack ordered more drinks. I demurred.

"Don't you think you should take it easy on the sauce, Greenjeans?"

"Donnybrook, Ah walked in freezin' cold for you today an' gave up mah chance to go to the South Side. Now Ah'm doin' what Ah want, an' Ah wannna get plastahed."

"Okay, but I don't want to be carrying you outta here this morning."

"Don't worry. Ah can take care of mahself," Jack replied, cheerfully downing a shot of whiskey.

There were only six couples on the floor, and I decided to join them. While Jack proceeded to drink himself into oblivion, I found a dancing partner and tried working off the effects of the alcohol. I had drunk less and could hold my liquor better than the farmer.

When Ken returned, the band was packing up. I was alertly sitting at my seat, holding vigil over Jack, who was passed out on the table.

"Bombed again," Ken surmised. "Come on. Let's get him up."

We tried to sober the Georgian, plying him with coffee and getting him to walk a few steps, but it was no use. So Ken and I dragged our semi-conscious companion into a taxi and headed for Union Station. We caught the 7:25 a.m. train[48] to Madison and chatted while Jack slept.

"Gosh, he even snores loud," Ken began.

"You know Jack. He overdoes everything."

"Yeah, but I kind of admire the big guy. Sure, he makes a fool of himself sometimes, but at least he's not afraid to be himself. My father's all spit and polish. There wasn't much kidding around when I was growing up."

"Your dad still in the Army?"

"No. He just retired. Another career man pensioned off. Colonel."

"That's a pretty high rank. Do you want an army career?"

"Nope. We had a whole discussion about that, my father and I. He said the Army would make a man out of me. I'm a man already, and I don't need to prove anything. No, I'm just here to help out Uncle Sam for a while, and then I'll return to civilian life."

"You should go to college."

"I'll have to pay for it myself, and right now, I'm just about broke."

"Hey, how did it go tonight?"

"None of your business," Ken angrily replied. "Look, Donald. Jack's private life may be an open book, but I don't like discussing mine."

Attempting to defuse my buddy's unexpected hostility, I held up my hands in mock surrender and chuckled. "Okay, okay. Don't get so upset. I was just asking about your visit with that old friend of yours."

"Oh yeah. I did say that, didn't I?"

"You sure did."

"Well, sorry I snapped at you, but I still don't want to talk about it."

A few moments of frosty silence followed. I broke the ice.

"Guess your dad had it pretty rough in the First War."

"Second Battle of the Marne in '18.[49] First Division.[50] He doesn't discuss it much. It was very bloody."[51]

"Your dad okay now?"

"He got some shrapnel in his leg just before the fighting ended. That gave him a slight limp, but otherwise he's fine."

"You know, all the guys wonder why you're not in another unit. I mean, with your brains, you should be designing engines."

"I'm not the genius everybody thinks I am, Donald. First of all, I don't have the training to design engines. I don't even have a college diploma. On a good day, I might make a decent electrician, but I wouldn't want that."

"Why not?"

"Look. We all took an aptitude test before we were assigned, and this is where the Army put me. Being a radio man isn't a bad job, and it's pretty darned useful. I'm not about to argue with the Washington brass. I might tick them off. And then, who knows? I might wind up on the front lines. Besides, you're a pretty swell bunch of fellas, and I wouldn't want to leave you." Ken paused, and with a wink, added, "Maybe I can swipe a spare crystal set to tinker with when I get bored."

"See, Ken. Even you've got a little larceny in you. I think you and Jack have a lot in common."

"Go to sleep, Donnybrook."

"Hey, that's the first time you called me that. I thought you didn't like nick-names."

"Well, there's a first a first time for everything. You seem to have gotten used to it, so I thought I'd surprise you. I don't want to be too predictable."

"Taking a page from Greenjeans over there?"

"Yeah. I'm trying to get some sleep."

We had all finally drifted into a restful slumber, gloating over our success in outsmarting the Army. Arriving at Madison on Wednesday morning at 9:30,[52] we had a leisurely breakfast in town and entered Truax just after 11 a.m. True to plan, we'd made the customary deadline with nearly an hour to spare. Unfortunately, we were in for a rude awakening.

Shortly after our departure, the base commander had ordered a special curfew. Passes were restricted to twelve hours. Therefore, anyone leaving on Tuesday was due back by midnight the same day, instead of the usual noontime Wednesday. Rather than familiar banter from fellow servicemen, we were greeted with notes on our beds to "report to the first sergeant immediately." We'd been AWOL for over eleven hours.

Worse, during my absence, I had been among twenty enlisted men ordered to gunnery school for training on aerial bombers. The other selectees had left at 9 a.m. that morning.

The three of us shuffled into the first sergeant's office with bowed heads befitting guilt-ridden AWOL's. First Sergeant Abatelli was big, muscular, and dark-haired. He had a pug face that never seemed to relax. His hands resembled suitcases; his fingers were like baseball bats. If he ever grasped your palm, your bones were sure to crack.

Despite his intimidating demeanor, Abatelli was a square guy who didn't bother you if you followed orders. But if you crossed him, there was hell to pay. Anyone who didn't toe the line caused him extra work, and then Abatelli would get dressed down by the CO.

Abatelli was the top kick, the highest-ranking noncom at Truax. He served as liaison between the enlisted men and the officers, but he was buried in piles of paper and had no time to counsel errant airmen. With his workload, he was never in a mood to take on the extra burden of incurring the CO's wrath. We were facing a predator primed for attack.

"No more passes for you jerks and plenty of latrine duty," Abatelli menacingly growled. Then he hit us with both barrels.

"Where the fuck were you guys? I treat you well, give you every conceivable break, give you passes. Now you screw up. You screw yourselves. You screw me!"

he roared. "Do I have to take shit from the CO because you louse up? You know the rules. Don't I have enough crap here? Do I have to run after you guys and wipe your behinds and make excuses for your mistakes?"

Steamed out, the first sergeant rested his elbows on his cluttered desk and exhaled into his clasped hands. After a long silence, Abatelli regained his composure. But he wasn't finished yet. "Oh, by the way. The CO wants to see you."

Major McDonnell was snarling. "You guys are no better than if you were in the German army," he bellowed in disgust.

During our escapade, McDonnell had been promoted from captain to major. He was someone you rarely saw and really didn't want to see, because if you had an audience with him, you were in hot water. The silver-haired major was six feet five, trim and sinewy, with a torso resembling a steel cage. He had penetrating, blue eyes that seemed capable of reading a person's innermost thoughts. "Old Man McDonnell's got x-ray vision," everyone would joke. People used to say that all he needed was a cape and tights.

We feared the worst. The major peered down at us. His words were brief and on target.

"If I ever have to call you clowns into my office again, I'll kick your butts so hard you'll regret the day you were born."

We were in huge trouble. At the time, I believed our mistake was that we got caught, but our real error was that we violated military rules. Phoney passes were fairly common, but bad behavior can never be justified by its prevalence. With the perspective of time, I have come to realize that although not all regulations are fair, they exist for a purpose, and you violate them at your peril.

But in early 1943 I was twenty-one years old and exuberantly reckless. This was my most costly lapse in judgment during the war. I would continue to game the system, but I had my limits. I was part Eddie Haskell and part Wally Cleaver, the schemer and the all-American boy.

There was one bright spot to the nasty aftermath of our trip: my radio job was secure. The Air Corps had to have everyone well-trained and ready for duty overseas. The Control Net System was top priority.

Despite my disastrous, unauthorized furlough, my ambition remained intact. An urgent notice was circulating on base. Pilots were needed badly, and applications were available. I applied.

Unfortunately, my effort was wasted because Major McDonnell never submitted my paperwork. My fate was sealed: I would never fly. Although I escaped court-martial, I would always remember this episode with profound regret. A few hours' fun in Chicago cost me my only chance to live out a cherished military fantasy. I wanted to be a pilot, should have been an aerial gunner, and was now grounded forever.

I sure wish Ken had been that lucky. He was transferred to a demolition unit.

CHAPTER 5

▼

OVER SEAS

We were on the move. After finishing the basic radio course in Madison, my outfit was shipped to Tomah, Wisconsin Air Base for advanced training. We'd been attending classes for only a few weeks when an announcement came over the loud speaker in the school hallway: "All students in the advanced course are now promoted to corporal."

We were elated, but, once again, our instructors remained privates. The furious protests of the teachers fell on deaf ears.

Newly-promoted, Jack and I soon found ourselves in Orlando, Florida. I was amazed to see twenty- and twenty-one-year-old airmen sporting captain's, major's and colonel's bars on their collars. These were the surviving combat pilots.

The sight of young, high-ranking officers in flight jackets weighed heavily on me. I gazed upon them with admiration and shame. Yet even the pain of recent, self-inflicted wounds couldn't cloud my sunny disposition for long. I refused to dwell on past mistakes. It was time to move on.

Our unit had about three hundred men. Most of the officers were former pilots. Summer was in full swing now, and members of the 888th Fighter Control Squadron were practicing with their transmitter and receiver vans in small Florida towns, including New Port Richey and DeLand. We worked in clusters of three to six men and slept in field tents. The heat was staggering. In DeLand, my group found relief by renting hotel rooms for three dollars a night.

Shortly before Labor Day, the 888th was shipped to Taunton, Massachusetts. In Florida, the hot weather had sapped my strength, but once exposed to the cool, dawn breezes of New England, I enthusiastically bounded out of bed each morning. With our squadron continuing to roam throughout the Northeast, I was ready for action.

Though there was tension among us because of our impending shipment overseas, I managed to enjoy a lighthearted moment. An officer entering my tent one morning was doing a head count, checking names and serial numbers. Five of us were present, but there were six cots. Jack Spring was on guard duty. We provided our names, serial numbers, and Jack's name, but the officer was still missing Jack's serial number. I piped up.

"Corporal Spring's serial number is 12187693."

The officer jotted down the missing information and left. Frank Angelo, who had a space next to mine, stared at me in bewilderment.

"How the hell do you know Jack's serial number?"

"I just know it," I casually replied.

"I can hardly remember my own eight serial numbers! And you can rattle off Jack's!"

Angelo walked a few feet, shook his head, and muttered to himself in disbelief. Over the next several weeks, he frequently expressed great admiration for my powers of recall. I wasn't worthy of his praise, but I never revealed my secret. An astute observer might have labeled it the "Roving Eye Trick." While the officer was questioning the others, I positioned myself in a spot facing Jack's cot, underneath which sat a duffel bag bearing the stenciled inscription "JACK SPRING #12187693." Thus, despite what Angelo related to his grandchildren decades later, I did not have a photographic memory.

Angelo, a short, dark-haired twenty-eight-year-old, was a former seminary student. Although he had long ago abandoned the idea of becoming a priest, he remained devout, sleeping with a small Saint Anthony tethered to his cot.

His religious training earned him some good-natured ribbing. Whenever a soldier came back from a hot date, he'd go up to Angelo and say, "Bless me, Father, for I have sinned." Whenever Angelo returned from a date, someone would invariably greet him and ask, "Father, have you sinned?" And with a cheerful nod, he'd wrinkle his aquiline nose and reply, "None of your goddamned business."

*　　　*　　　*　　　*

Now it was time for the real thing. I was among many hundreds of GI's jammed onto the *Tristan Dalton*, a Liberty ship bound for Europe, and soon I was puking my guts up. I compounded my seasickness with two critical errors.

My first mistake was that I didn't eat anything. When I tried to vomit, only green gook came out, and I wound up with a sore belly. Secondly, instead of getting fresh air on deck, I lay nauseated in my bunk for days.

Finally, I ventured out of the hold. My legs were wobbly, and I reflexively averted my eyes from the bright sunlight. Grasping the railing tightly, I slowly ascended the stairs. The irrepressible Jack Spring ran over to greet me.

"Ya look a little punch drunk there, Donnybrook."

"Don't start, Jack. This is the first day I've been able to keep anything down."

"You look paler than the whites of mah eyes. C'mon, siddown."

I compliantly plopped myself onto a stray crate amidships. The briny air pleasantly coursed through my nostrils. My head began clearing, and my vision rapidly adjusted to the outdoors. Jack broke the silence.

"Ah miss Ken."

"Yeah. Me, too."

"You still miffed 'bout losin' out on gunnery school?"

"Who wouldn't be? I had a chance to be in combat, and I blew it."

"Do you have any ideah what the life span of a ball tee gunner is? Yer cut loose aftah twenty-five missions, but most fellas don't survive fifteen.[53] They're sittin' ducks in that glass bubble up there. You gotta have balls to be in the ball turret."

"I've got balls. Don't you?"

"Cut the crap. You know what Ah mean."

"Yeah. I suppose you're right."

"You bet yer ass Ah'm right. Stick with Fightah Control, Donnybrook. Like you said, bein' a radio man's an important job. You might not be a dead hero, but you can still make a difference on the ground."

"I know, but I just—"

"Hey, lookee heah!" With an explosive movement, Jack leapt into the air and gleefully tossed a one-dollar bill into the ocean. "Bone voy-age!"

"You nuts or something?" I scolded. "That's two trips to the P.X."[54]

"Well, Ah hadda do somethin' to get you out of that stupor of yours. You look better already. Nothin' like a good shock to get the blood flowin'."

"Jack, you're one of a kind."

"Ya know, Ah once read somewhere that you can't stay down in the dumps long if you look up."

I gazed upwards and smiled. "The sky's the limit."

"Now that's the spirit, buddy."

Within a few days, I developed sea legs. I now frequented the deck, dipping and rolling with waves rising twelve feet over the bow. Soon I was my usual self again. I started to enjoy the saltwater smell and the sound of swells crashing against the hull. The navy food wasn't bad either.

The ship was part of a huge convoy ringed with protective destroyers. During the evening, someone had fallen overboard, but the crew couldn't stop to rescue him. They weren't going to endanger the mission for one man. It was too risky, and they had a schedule to keep.

All ships were blacked out to maintain secrecy. We were traveling in complete darkness, and depth charges were constantly dropped to destroy any submarines lurking below. Monstrous mounds of water rhythmically burst forth from the ocean. In the midst of this roiling turbulence, the heart of naval warfare beat strongly. Kapow! Kapow! Then the unpredictable occurred.

In order to identify herself, a lumbering Red Cross hospital transport, passing in the opposite direction, was painting the sky brighter than Yankee Stadium during a twi-night double-header. The humanitarian vessel lit up the entire convoy. Cover had been blown. A frantic ensign aboard the Liberty ship radioed his Red Cross counterpart: "Turn off your goddamned lights!"

With merciful quickness, the hospital ship complied and darkness was restored. There were no further incidents.

Now that my health had returned, I lost no time writing home. "Homesick" was never part of my vocabulary, but I was anxious to assure my folks that I was well.

All outgoing V-mail was read by an officer who affixed his censor's stamp to the upper left-hand corner of the sender's stationery. For security reasons, exact locations could not be revealed. I contributed to the editing by maximizing the cheerfulness of my letters. They were factually truthful, but they never included morbid details. I didn't want my parents and sister to worry.

Younger readers may at times find my letters formal, but most people wrote that way in those days, and when I was writing to my family, I was on my best behavior. Spoken language has always been more colloquial than written communication, and the contrast is even greater between writing to parents and speaking to friends. We use different voices with different people. An extreme example was Eddie Haskell, the wiseguy character in the 1957-63 television sitcom "Leave It

To Beaver," who was a stuffed shirt in front of Mr. and Mrs. Cleaver, and a very smooth talker with his peers.

Don Quix
Fighter Control Squadron #888
APO 4781
c/o Postmaster
Sept. 14, 1943

Dear Mom, Dad & Ethel,

I am writing this letter while en route to my destination. Our trip has been far from a pleasure cruise, as you might well imagine. After the initial two days of seasickness, I gradually accustomed myself to the rocking chair motion and got along fine.

They had movies on board daily, but no World Premiere ever played before a house that was more densely packed per square inch. There is a P.X. on board, and cigarettes sell at the abominable price of 45 cents per pack.

Food thus far has been fairly good sometimes, and terribly bad most times. We have two meals daily, and occasionally they serve sandwiches at bed-time. There is a library here, but picture yourself in Times Square on New Year's Eve, yanking out a book, trying to read a few snatches. I've gotten more than a usual quota of sleep.

Love,

Don

Sept. 17, 1943

Dear Mom, Dad & Ethel,

You should have received a previous letter describing part of my recent voyage, and this letter is now being written to you on solid ground some-where in England. The food is good, and living conditions are excellent. We've already come in contact with English people, and although first impressions are not always sound, I doubt if my opinion of them will be altered in the future. They are extremely polite and amiable.

The salaries here are pitiful. One driver told me he works 100 to 125 hours per week and is paid something equivalent to $35. The Labor Board specifies time-and-an-eighth for overtime, and the most technical receive slightly higher than manual labor in the United States.

The post here has inconceivable items of entertainment, for which we are grateful. There is a Red Cross Club, which puts on shows frequently. They also sell sandwiches, coffee, etc.

Right now we are having one hectic time trying to learn the respective values of English coins and notes. We got some athletic equipment today and had a swell game of ball. I am going to try to get in touch with Wally shortly.

Hope you are all well. As for me, as usual, I feel great. Please send me Joe's address.

Love,

Don

Wally Gold was a good friend of mine from the Bronx. He was the first of a group of teenagers who played baseball, basketball, and football together. Wally was also the first of my buddies to be sent overseas.

He was a dark-haired six-footer, very articulate and self-confident. Wally wanted to be a doctor, but like most of his peers, could not afford medical school. He took any work available because jobs were scarce.

When Wally got shipped abroad, I concocted a plan to keep him from feeling lonely. All the boys would write letters to Wally and hand them over to me. Then I would fit them into an album to be shipped overseas.

In early 1942, before entering the Air Corps, I bumped into Wally's mother on Phelan Place in the Bronx. In a letter to his mom, Wally had written "ETO" as part of his address. ETO stood for European Theater of Operations, but his mother had a different interpretation. Looking me straight in the eye, she exclaimed with maternal pride, "I think Wally is helping to plan the invasion!"

*   *   *   *

How different can two brothers be? Plenty. Although nearly two years older than I, Joe was drafted several months after I joined the service. We did physically resemble each other: we were both five feet eleven inches tall, dark-haired, and slim. However, we had little else in common.

Joe was sedate and serious. He wasn't athletic, and, therefore, didn't socialize with my friends. He had been a member of Arista, a high school honor society; was elected class secretary; and was graduated with honors. It wasn't surprising that Joe didn't associate much with my friends, who would rather have been on a baseball diamond than in a library.

I was always a bit of a hell-raiser. Joe, by contrast, had been conservative since childhood. He knew where he was going, walked a narrow path, and was successful in most of his endeavors. Mom always used to say, "You two boys are like Cracker Jacks and spinach."

Though we kept separate company and displayed few overt signs of affection, we still cared deeply about each other. Toward the end of the war, I would mount an anxious search for my big brother, Joe.

When I couldn't see him, I tried to find some childhood friends who were serving in the London area. Thoughts of them brought back many good memories.

Oct. 15, 1943

Dear Mom, Dad & Ethel,

I expect to go to London in the very near future. Once again, they have changed the system on passes, and as soon as I figure it out, I can make plans. Trying to see Wally and Seymour.

Love,

Don

Seymour Levy ranked among my closest friends. After that brush with the law at Yankee Stadium, he had developed into a young man of excellent character.

Seymour was very organized and had been the coach of an amateur baseball team in the Bronx. He eventually succeeded in getting a bunch of us into a league.

Our youthful, trim coach was an enterprising fellow with a take-charge personality. At age twenty-three, he was already part-owner of a sporting goods store. Seymour's passion was baseball, and he had been the driving force behind the team's formation. I, on the other hand, had no talent for management and was mostly a pinch runner and hitter.

We were all buzzing with excitement when our grey pants and shirts, striped in blue and yellow, arrived at Seymour's store. He had a back room furnished as a clubhouse for us. Now each all-star hopeful would proudly wear the name "Comets" across his chest.

We were really charged up when we trotted out onto the diamond in our classy uniforms. A healthy-sized group of spectators filled the stands.

The opposition watched in stony silence as we took to the field. The shortstop whipped the ball over to first base with pinpoint accuracy. The practice double-play execution, short to second to first, was flawless. However, there was one slight problem. Although dazzling during warmup, the Comets fizzled when the game actually got underway.

Our team finished the season in last place with one win and eight losses.

In London, I never did get to see Wally, but I did meet Seymour. During our night out, we took in some terrific theater.

Oct. 24, 1943

Dear Mom, Dad & Ethel,

You will probably receive a card of sights of London soon after you receive this letter. This past week, I had a 48-hour pass and decided to see the town.

If anyone ever questions the worthiness of Red Cross institutions, just send them around to me. As usual, we had comfortable beds with clean sheets and pillow cases.

Then the Red Cross furnished us with a pair of free tickets to a sellout show, "Hi Di Hi." We were also entitled to go backstage and chat with the comedians, Allen and Flanigan. We thought British humor was different from American humor and discussed it with them. We had a good belly laugh when they told us that they were originally from, of all places, Brooklyn, N.Y.

The show is in ways similar to "Sons of Fun," with the performers sometimes seated in the audience and then jumping from your midst with a gag
line. In one scene, some beautiful dancers came down off the stage and
sought partners from the audience. One asked me to dance, and the girl I
was with insisted that I comply.

There were about ten girls and ten fellows from the audience. We joined
hands and ran up and down the aisle. They brought us on stage, and we
formed two concentric circles, one revolving around the other. The men
then took off their jackets and handed them to the girl in front of them.

The girl's circle moved in one direction, and, we, in the outside circle,
moved in the opposite direction. Then Allen, the comedian whom I had
seen backstage a short while ago, halted us, and we took the coat of the
girl directly in front of us. Now, naturally, we don't get the same coat
back. There were American soldiers, British soldiers, and civilians of all
sizes and shapes. It was comical to the audience when I tried to squeeze
into a civilian's coat and a Britisher put on an American jacket.

So, all in all, we had a great time in London.

Love,

Don

It was in London that I had my first amorous, wartime encounter. My inexpe-
rience showed.

A few buddies and I were dining at a delicatessen when a voluptuous redhead
with great cheekbones and bewitchingly blue eyes sat down at our table. She
turned out to be the waiter's wife.

"My husband seldom takes me out to nice places," she lamented.

I felt an almost irresistible current of sexual electricity emanating from her.
The conversation wasn't much, but she was a real turn-on. The nonverbal signals
were unmistakable. She repeated several cycles of flashing me a coquettish smile,
looking down in feigned embarrassment, and fanning herself as if overheated. Yet
when we finished eating, the raven-haired beauty abruptly departed. Perplexed, I
left with the others shortly afterwards.

You can imagine how shocked I was to find her waiting for me on the street.
Sensing an incipient liaison, my friends abandoned me.

"Wanna go somewhere?" she asked.

Part of me did, but I had serious reservations. Doctoring military passes was a
world away from committing adultery. I was barely out of adolescence and had

minimal competence in dating. Being out with a beautiful, married woman was light years beyond my imagination. My parents would have skinned me alive if they knew I was even considering such a proposition. I thought hard, an exercise which did not come naturally. After a few seconds, I decided to put the ball back in her court.

"Walk around the block and make sure you want to do this," I said.

Without uttering a word, she sauntered off, and I never saw her again.

My missteps with wartime women didn't end there. During another visit to London, I made a date with an unattached British girl, and I planned to take her to a movie at 1 p.m. She showed up early.

"I can't stay because I have an appointment with the Labor Board," she explained. By giving advance notice, this young lady had been unusually honest with me. Soldiers and their dates were constantly standing each other up.

"Thanks for coming down and letting me know," I replied. Satisfied with her explanation, I blithely shrugged my shoulders as she walked away.

With some time to kill before the movie started, I got friendly with a slim, blonde usherette from the theater and made a date with her for that evening. Earlier that day, I had purchased two tickets for the 1 p.m. showing of "For Whom The Bell Tolls" and had them in the inside pocket of my jacket. It was still early, and I decided to take a stroll.

When I returned, I was surprised to find that the movie was completely sold out. Because my original date had canceled, I now had in my possession a cherished, extra ticket. Over a hundred people were lined up, and many of them had to be turned away. After gloating over my good fortune, I addressed the restless standees.

"Who wants a ticket to the show?"

All hell broke loose. The footrace got underway, and in the lead by a kneecap was an attractive brunette in her early twenties. I took her hand and led her into the theater. We hit it off well and enjoyed the movie. At the end of the flick, she conspiratorially leaned over in her seat and whispered, "Look, I can call my mother and tell her I won't be home tonight."

Most GI's would have given their stripes and medals for this invitation, but remembering I had already made a date with someone else, I politely declined. "Thanks, but I've made other plans."

Appalled by my refusal, the young woman indignantly stormed off. Anxious to honor my prior commitment, I then proceeded to rendez-vous with the blonde usherette. She never showed up.

Man, was I a greenhorn! I'd started out with two girls—one of whom had wanted to sleep with me—and wound up with none. Still, there were a couple of bright sides: I was gaining useful experience with the opposite sex, and I'd have some spare cash to spend another time.

Oct. 31, 1943

Dear Mom, Dad & Ethel,

A number of reports that reached me when I was in the States said that England is a place where you spend very little money. This is far from the truth because you spend a pound quicker than you spend a dollar. Back home, a pound is $4.03. The reason appears to be that everybody here knows American G.I.'s are well-paid in comparison to English soldiers. Like Good Samaritans, they want to relieve you of this burden of being laden down with all this money.

Transportation is a problem in England. When we go out, sometimes events necessitate our remaining until the wee hours of the morning. There are no trains or buses running after midnight.

However, everything is running smoothly for me.

Love,

Don

Dec. 1, 1943

Dear Ethel,

Just received your letter, and, like yourself, cannot understand why you haven't been receiving my letters.

In reference to Nancy, I don't write her anymore, so unless you want to call her for your own interests, don't communicate with her on my behalf. That is something that is over and done with, and only your reference gave it a rebirth.

Feeling swell.

Love,

Don

I had met Nancy through another GI who was her cousin. I began courting her by mail, and then started seeing her in the Bronx while on furlough from basic training. We were hitting it off pretty well and often spent six hours a day hugging and kissing.

"Oh, it must be love," Nancy's mother once remarked.

That was it. I felt pressured. For a time, I continued to date Nancy. Then things cooled down for reasons I couldn't remember, and we drifted apart.

By contrast, I had very strong memories of my sister. I had always been very close with Ethel. Now, caught up in a seemingly endless war thousands of miles from home, I often thought of her.

How's she doing? She must be quite a woman by now. Who knows? Maybe she's getting married. If she is, I'd sure as hell like to be there.

Ethel was a striking brunette, about five feet four inches tall, with dark eyes and sensuous lips that frequently curved upward into a genuinely sweet smile at just the right moment. I was never sure exactly how tall she was because the size of her heels varied with the occasion. She had particular shoes for school, family affairs, parties, and hot dates. The more romantic the event, the taller she grew.

Even though I had three years on her, I never thought of Ethel as a kid sister. Ever since I could remember, she always seemed very capable. Her wavy, shoulder-length brown hair was impeccably coiffed. She wore cheerfully embroidered outfits that were neat and perfectly color-coordinated. Her royal-blue scarves gave her a classy look that distinguished her from most of the local girls. She dressed modestly, but not prudishly. Ethel was extremely well-organized but never a schoolmarm.

In speech and manner, she was a bit more refined than the rest of the family, but she never spoke down to people. I was very proud of her.

Because of her attractiveness, Ethel was never alone. Guys were always calling for dates, or just stopping by to say hello. Her articulate and friendly demeanor easily won people over. She had a knack for shedding light on a problem, removing the extraneous cobwebs, and then proceeding to render a solution.

Once she double-dated with her girlfriend, Betty, who seemed uncharacteristically rude. Sensing that Betty liked Ethel's date better than her own, Ethel, who wasn't particularly enamored with her male companion, had just the cure for Betty's ailment. She filled me in after administering this remedy. Here's what happened:

"Betty, let's not let a couple of boys ruin our friendship. You seem to like Bruce a lot, and he's been making eyes at you all night."

"Ethel, no, really—"

"Yes, really. You can have Bruce, and I'll go home with Phil. Bruce is nice, but he doesn't mean that much to me."

"Boy, you're a pal. My other friends would die before giving up a hunk like him."

"Oh, there's plenty of fish in the sea. They seem to wash up on shore all the time."

To be sure, Ethel and I had our differences. After all, she was still a teenager. And like any adolescent, she had her moods. For example, she would be emotionally distant, usually because of some boy, and then complain that I didn't talk to her enough. But these episodes were rare.

When it came to creative writing, she knew her limitations. In elementary school, she'd sometimes ask me to lend a hand with her English compositions. Once I helped her with a story on women in sports and didn't think I had done a very good job of it. I was surprised to see Ethel's teacher a few days later.

"Don, have you ever considered becoming a writer?" Mrs. Johnson asked.

"No, ma'am."

"Well, I think you should. Ethel read her composition about Babe Didrikson in class today, and it was one of the most interesting stories I've ever heard. She said that you gave her the idea."

That was Ethel, never missing an opportunity to share credit for something well-done.

CHAPTER 6

▼

BATTERED BUT
UNBOWED

It was 1940, and the world was on fire. With brutal efficiency, Hitler's armies swept across Europe, occupying Poland, Hungary, Rumania, Norway, the Netherlands, Belgium, and France.[55] The Germans called their onslaught *blitzkrieg*—"lightning war" (57). Amidst this menacing shadow of tyranny, Britain, led by her bulldog prime minister, Winston Churchill, remained a beacon of steadfast hope.

Hitler offered Churchill peace in exchange for acceptance of Nazi domination of Western Europe (98). Churchill refused. A fierce, sustained aerial bombardment of England ensued (98). The Battle of Britain had begun.

Churchill had taken stringent measures to prepare the civilian population. He ordered the evacuation of one-and-a half-million women and children from the cities (98). Enforced blackouts began (98). People started carrying gas masks (98), and hospitals readied for hundreds of anticipated victims (98).

Unfortunately, the British military were poorly prepared. At the outset of hostilities, they had only 704 serviceable aircraft—including 620 small Spitfire and Hurricane fighters (98). By contrast, the Germans commanded 1,392 bombers and 1,290 fighters (98).

On August 15, 1940, Hitler unleashed a one-thousand-plane assault upon England (98). On the twenty-fourth, the Luftwaffe began concentrating its attacks on London (98), specifically targeting civilians (99). By the time night bombings began on September 7, the Royal Air Force had lost nearly one-quarter of its pilots (98).

Still, the RAF managed to hold its own. Despite losing 915 fighters defending their island that year, the British managed to down 2,698 German aircraft (99).

Because the bombings were intended to break the spirit of the people (99), London became an irresistible German target. The city was much more than Britain's capital: it was the very nerve center of the nation. With nearly three-and-a-half-million inhabitants,[56] it had almost seven percent of the country's population.[57] Among London's other assets were Parliament; the United Kingdom's largest port; the Bank of England; the commercial districts of Fleet and Lombard Streets; and an enormous cultural infrastructure.[58]

September 7, 1940 marked the beginning of what Londoners called "the Blitz."[59] By January 1941, the number of nightly visitors to public air raid shelters had swelled to one million.[60] Places of refuge included store basements, coal holes, and church crypts (4). Reports described conditions there as "medieval" (4). Most of these places lacked toilets, water, light, and heat (4). Rats, filth, and dampness were common (4). Ten buckets served as latrines during a night in a stifling brewery cellar crammed with over one thousand people (4).

Worse, many desperate souls crowded under railway arches (4). These hideouts were extremely dangerous because their aboveground locations made them prime military objectives (4).

While Luftwaffe planes pounded the surface of London, its people found the safest havens within the city's subway system or "tubes." Constructed an average of over 60 feet underground,[61] stations were nearly impervious to bombing (303). Many were much deeper. At Hampstead, for example, platform depth reached 192 feet (111). Because of the great distance below street level, the Otis Elevator Company had installed 140 "lifts" or elevators before the tubes opened in 1907 (115).

Depth was a major factor in saving lives. All tube casualties directly related to bombings occurred in stations less than 35 feet underground (303). The worst single incident occurred on October 14, 1940, at Balham, where 68 people were killed and seven million gallons of water flooded the tunnels (303-4). The death toll in other shallow stations was more modest. A total of 152 civilians died because Nazi bombs hit subway shelters (304). All of these fatalities occurred during the Blitz (304), which continued unabated until the summer of 1941 (298). Then Hitler turned his attention eastward toward the Soviet Union (298).

One very bright spot during Britain's bleakest days was the performance of its fighter control system. The British credited Fighter Control as the single biggest factor in the successful defense of London in 1940, when the Luftwaffe was at peak strength.[62] In this regard, Americans owe their brethren across the Atlantic a great deal. RAF radio men tutored many of their "Yank" counterparts.[63] In fact, shortly after setting foot on British soil, every soldier in the 888th began attending several weeks of lectures and hands-on training at RAF bases.

Ironically, the worst carnage in the London Underground was only indirectly related to an air raid. It happened at the Bethnal Green station in the East End on March 3, 1943,[64] about six months before I arrived. Civilians on the street panicked after hearing anti-aircraft fire about a mile away (305). At this time, the station was only partially complete (305). Among its shortcomings was a poorly lit, wooden staircase without a central bannister (305). When a frightened mob pushed its way down the entrance, 173 people were trampled to death (305). This tragedy prompted the British government to improve lighting on the tube stairwells (305).

Fortunately, such accidents were rare (305), but at least one sleeping shelterer was killed by a train after rolling onto the tracks (305). The authorities quickly remedied this hazard by painting white boundary lines (305) four and eight feet from the edges of the platforms (299).

The government had not always been so accommodating. When war broke out in Europe on September 3, 1939, Whitehall announced that the tubes could not be used as air raid shelters (298). However, Londoners ignored this regulation once the Blitz began. People flocked to the subways in droves, and there was no stopping them (298). About 177,500 civilians slept on the platforms during the night of September 27, 1940 (299), and an average of over 138,000 shelterers stayed in the Underground every night during October (299).

During the first days of the Blitz, conditions in the tubes were similar to those in other public shelters. The atmosphere was chaotic (299); the air was foul; and there were no bathrooms at platform level (299). People sprawled haphazardly on the ground (298-9), sleeping on rugs or pillows alongside their most precious possessions (299).

There was, however, one important difference from aboveground shelters: the stations were much safer. Nothing else the government had to offer provided comparable protection against bombing (298). The tubes also insulated people from the noise of explosions, allowing them to sleep (298).

Living conditions gradually improved. Portable toilets arrived at the end of September 1940 (299), making the air more tolerable (299). In November, a

sophisticated sewage system further improved sanitation (300), and medical personnel worked the platforms. Food service was fully operational by December 9
(300), and by late February 1941, nearly all stations had three-tier bunks (300).
A ticket system for regular visitors brought order (300). Some tubes had recorded
music, live concerts, their own newspapers—and even libraries (300). Life in the
Underground wasn't heaven, but it provided safety and sustenance for millions.

The government soon raised wartime tube use to the level of a high art. Two
miles of unfinished Central Line tunnels became an aircraft component factory
(301) employing round-the-clock shifts of two thousand workers (301).
Churchill and his War Cabinet often met at the obsolete Down Street station
(301), and in late 1942, the Goodge Street tube shelter became General Eisenhower's headquarters (302). Others became hostels for British and American
troops (302).

When the Blitz ended in July 1941, the shelter population dramatically
dropped to a nightly average of ten thousand (301). In 1942, it bottomed out at
between three thousand and five thousand (301). However, due to renewed
bombing, the number of shelterers had sharply increased by the time I arrived in
1943 (301).

I've included these statistics because they will help you better understand the
environment in which I found myself, but, at the time, I was only vaguely aware
of them. In fact, tube shelters were the farthest thing from my mind when I was
walking the streets of Covent Garden with Jack late on a cold, foggy Saturday
afternoon in December. We were on our way to a social at the Royal Opera
House, which had been a Mecca Dance Hall since 1939.[65]

Covent Garden was a major fruit and vegetable market whose history dated
back to the Middle Ages,[66] when Benedictine monks sold produce to Londoners
from their "Convent Garden."[67] In the late seventeenth century, it was already a
fashionable district filled with coffee houses and theatres.[68] By the mid-1800's, it
had grown to thirty acres.[69]

Now enshrouded in wartime danger, the place had a subdued dreariness. Jack
and I picked our way through discarded cabbage stalks and old sacks. We noticed
sandbags piled against office windows as protection from bombing.

"Jeez, what a smell!" I exclaimed with some irritation. A hard day's work, the
weather, and the surroundings had momentarily taken the air out of my sails.

Jack stopped chewing on the wad of gum in his mouth and gave me a puzzled
look. "Ya know, the problem with you city boys is that you all spend so much
time indaws that you can't appreciate fresh air."

"My idea of fresh air's a ballfield in the Bronx."

"You gotta broaden yer horizons, boy. Ah love a good ballgame too, but what's wrong with the smell of cabbage? It's good, natural produce. Kinda reminds me of a mahket Ah used to go to in Albany."

"New York?"

"No. Georgia."

I grinned and put a friendly hand on Jack's shoulder. "Well, the girls in the dance hall have gotta smell better than this."

"That's what Ah like 'bout you, Donnybrook. Yer an eternal optimist."

＊　　　＊　　　＊　　　＊

We arrived at the Opera House at dusk. Passing the cloak rooms, I smiled at two female usherettes dressed in eighteenth century costumes, including white wigs.[70] Their only concession to modernity was above-the-knee skirts.

Mecca Cafés, which leased the House, didn't use bouncers (14). Instead, the company relied upon the tact and charm of its all-female staff to maintain order (14).

Opened in 1858, this was actually the third Opera House constructed on the same site.[71] The first and second, which respectively held performances beginning in 1732 and 1809,[72] were both destroyed by fire.[73] When Hitler invaded Poland in 1939, all theaters in London were ordered closed.[74] Thus, the Opera House, which was open almost every night during the war (17), became a major source of entertainment.

"Good evening, ladies," quipped Jack in a good, haughty English accent. "I'd really love to chat, but I must be off to tea."

The liveried young women looked at each other and giggled. One of them piped up.

"You'll only find the hard stuff in there, Yank."

I playfully pointed an admonishing index finger at Jack. "Better watch out. I think they're wise to you, Greenjeans."

"Guess the American uniform gave me away. Let's go inside."

In renovating this old theater, Mecca had sought to maintain its dignified atmosphere while satisfying the plebeian tastes of ordinary soldiers (17). The result was a living anachronism. The wartime owners had installed large circular parquetry and a modern bandstand (17). The original ornate balustrade around the stairway, stretching from the dance floor to the Victorian-columned Grand Tier,[75] contrasted sharply with the throngs of quick stepping servicemen and women.[76]

I estimated the size of the crowd at fifteen hundred. The manager told me that I was right: ticket sales indicated that the hall was filled to its official capacity of fifteen hundred dancers (18). What I didn't know was that this limit was often exceeded by several hundred (18), and, therefore, this was slow for a Saturday.

"Wow. You wouldn't think there'd be this good a turnout on a night like this."

"Well, Donnybrook, looks like the Brits ain't so stuffy aftah all. Jumpin' an' jivin's the best antidote for bad weathah. See ya later, Yank."

Jack exchanged his chewing gum[77] for a brunette dancing partner, while I, contented for the moment to take in the scenery, sidled up to the crowded bar. I ordered a beer from one of the barmaids, whose black uniforms and white collars made them easily identifiable. I mindlessly gazed up and down the hall, alternately admiring the cute, young usherettes in their nifty short skirts and the twirling silver spheres overhead. Then I felt a gentle tap on my shoulder.

When I turned around, I saw a mischievous-looking English girl with short auburn hair smiling at me. She was tall enough to stare me straight in the eye, yet looked awfully young.

"Would you like to dance?" she shouted above the band and an ocean of chattering voices. Her accent was educated, with a glibness and confidence beyond her years.

"Sure," I replied, "but first I think we'll have to fight our way onto the floor."

"That's all right by me. I'm quite used to that sort of thing by now."

"Say, what's your name?"

"June Carver."

"I'm Don Quix."

"Hello, Don."

"Well, June, you're one heck of a warm sight on a cold winter evening."

"That's what I like about Americans. Direct and to the point."

Pleasantly surprised by her forwardness, I took June out on the dance floor for a fox trot. She was my equal in energy and stamina, and we kept on swinging for another six numbers.

"You're a real pro at this," I offered.

"What do you mean by pro?" asked June, screwing up her eyes.

"I mean you're dancing swell."

"Why, thank you, Corporal. I knew you couldn't possibly be referring to anything else."

"How old are you?" I asked, distorting my face with a facetious scowl.

"Old enough."

"For what?"

"Anything."

Now I knew I had a real live one. "C'mon. Level with me."

"All right," she reluctantly confessed. "Sixteen."

I gulped hard. Great. The girl of my dreams had turned out to be jailbait. I struggled to convince myself that I could stop short of going to bed with her. She was just too good to pass up.

"Sixteen?" I repeated, my voice drifting into an uncomfortable falsetto.

"Yes. Is that a problem, Corporal?"

"No, I—"

"Because if it is, then I'll leave."

"No, no. No problem at all." I paused to collect my thoughts. "You here alone?"

"If you mean to ask if my parents are about, the answer is no. They're away for the weekend."

Good. One less thing to worry about.

"Isn't it past your bedtime?" I teased.

"No, but you could tuck me in if you'd like."

Our blossoming tryst was shattered by an unfamiliar sound. It was simultaneously dull and shrill. For a split second, I thought I was being treated to some hot, new instrumentation. Then it dawned on me: it was the wailing of sirens. Yet only when I heard the booming concussion of falling bombs did I fully understand what was happening.

Jeez, it's an air raid!

A pall of silence abruptly descended upon the dance floor. June and I got separated in the confusion. The lights went out, and the ground shook violently. Antiaircraft guns angrily opened up in reply.

Several minutes passed before the "all clear" sounded. I was worried, but most people seemed anxious to continue dancing. Someone explained to me that air raids had by now become a familiar part of the landscape. The Luftwaffe be damned, the Brits were going to enjoy their entertainment.

The lights snapped back on, and the music resumed. It was just another typical evening in London.

Although I never saw June again, I considered myself lucky. I was several miles from the point of impact.

✳   ✳   ✳   ✳

It was nearly 11 p.m., and the Opera House had just let out for the evening.[78] Jack and I were on the street, plotting our next move.

"Don't sweat it, Donnybrook. There's plenty more where she came from."

"Yeah, but she was throwing herself at me," I argued.

"So what d'ya wanna do now?"

"I dunno. Maybe take in a movie. I hear 'Stage Door Canteen'[79] is playing somewhere around here."

"Bore-ing! Let's go to a club. Ah know just the place."

"Okay. As long as you don't get too loaded. I don't wanna be scraping you off the…Shit, here we go again!"

Gerry had not yet finished with Mother England that night. The air raid sirens were wailing anew, louder and shriller than ever.

"Let's get the fuck outta heah!" shouted Jack.

"Where?" I asked.

We looked at each other and simultaneously blurted, "The subway!" In the glare of searchlights and the distant, reverberating explosions, we made a bee-line for the tubes.

I was slightly ahead when we reached the entrance to the Covent Garden station. There, we merged with a large group of civilian and military personnel.

The crowd moved quickly and calmly down the stairwell. I recognized the blue uniforms of RAF men, but, oddly enough, did not see any soldiers in American olive drabs. Enmeshed in the center of this human phalanx far from home, I felt small and out of place.

We were shepherded into the lift by an authoritative-looking, middle-aged man in a dark poncho. "Step lively now," he barked. The harshness of his voice was tempered with a mundane, almost familial quality. "You know the drill. Careful boys, mind the women an' children now."

"All aboard!" cried the grizzled lift operator. The elevator's metal gate swung closed, and the car began its descent. Covent Garden was the deepest station on the Piccadilly Line.[80] The ride down to platform level ordinarily took about a minute, but every second seemed that long. A young RAF lieutenant struck up a conversation with me.

"You new around here, mate?"

"My outfit's been here about a month," I replied.

The lieutenant's informal tone immediately relaxed me, but I was surprised that a British lieutenant would even talk to an American corporal. British sergeants were treated like demi-gods by their subordinates, and there was an even larger status difference between officers and noncoms. Mirroring the class-based structure of the United Kingdom's larger society, each of these groups had separate mess halls and latrines.

We squirmed to shake hands.

"Don Quix."

"Pete Kingsley. These are my buddies Pat, Mike, and Davy." The soldiers pleasantly nodded. "You'll have to excuse them for not shaking hands. They're big fellows, and they don't want to accidentally knock anyone about."

"This is my buddy Jack."

"How are y'all?"

A little girl tugged on Jack's trousers. "Excuse me, sir. Are you a cowboy?"

"No, honey. Why'd juh think that?"

"Because you talk like one."

We all burst out laughing, but our mirth was short-lived. The lift had stalled in the middle of the shaft. There was a creak and a bounce, and then the lights went out.

"Mummy, I'm scared," the girl said in a hushed, frightened tone.

"Nothing to be scared about, dearest," a young woman's voice replied. "Just a power outage. It'll be over soon enough."

The lights went back on, but the lift remained stuck.

Pete looked over at me. "Nervous, mate?"

"Nah." Of course I was, but my macho mind wouldn't let me admit it.

"You look like you've never been down here before."

"Oh, we've used the subways—I mean, tubes—a few times. Mostly to go to dances, but never like this."

"This your first air raid, then?"

"Yeah."

"Ah guess you could say we're a coupla virgins," quipped Jack.

We all started laughing again.

"Careful, there's a woman and child present," facetiously cautioned Davy.

"Don't get him started—," I began. I was interrupted by a creak and a hum. With full power restored, the lift continued its descent.

"Platform level!" cried the operator. The gate swung open, and everyone poured out.

"So long, Yanks," said Pete, as Jack and I parted from the British airmen.

The public address system broadcast the usual alarm, followed by an announcement : "Now hear this! Now hear this! This is an air raid. Keep calm, and follow any broadcast instructions or directions of station personnel. Please stay in the station until the all clear has sounded. Do not lean over the edge of the platforms, and stay behind the white lines. Thank you."

Although lighting in the stairwells had improved after the Bethnal Green disaster, the stations were still dreary. In 1942, the government cut lighting on platforms and trains to a third of prewar levels[81] in order to save five thousand tons of coal a year (307).

"Ah guess we won't be doin' any heavy readin' down heah," observed Jack.

"I don't remember you ever doing any heavy reading," I retorted. "Look, Greenjeans, I'm gonna try to get something to eat."

I passed a woman porter sweeping the floor. Although she was plain-looking, her outfit was attractive. Female porters and ticket clerks had been working the tubes since September 1940 (308). At first, they wore white dust coats and ugly grey kepis (308), but now they were sporting nifty blue tunics, slacks, and berets.

The lights may have been dim, but I could still see that the station was clean. I noticed several women diligently scrubbing the ground in front of a row of three-tiered bunks. It was said that many treated the area around their beds as their own doorsteps (300).

I could almost feel the weariness on the faces of the men, women, and children I passed. They were full of quiet resignation. Early on, the government had developed a "code of behaviour"[82] for tube shelterers. It was almost universally obeyed,[83] and few people complained.[84] I admired these British civilians for their level-headed discipline during this scary time.

My stomach growling, I walked up to a red vending machine advertising miniature chocolate bars. Its coin slot was huge by American standards. This was no accident. The British had designed their mechanical confectionaries to accommodate their enormous pennies. I dropped one into the machine. Nothing came out, and I couldn't get my money back.

It must be broken. No, wait... Jeez! How could I be so stupid? Of course there's no candy in the machine! There probably hasn't been for years. Oh, well. Guess I just made a cash contribution to old Mother England.

Rationing of staples was critical to the war effort. Meat was rare, and candy was virtually non-existent.

Listening more closely now, I caught snippets of conversations. Most, but not all, station dwellers were working class folk. People from all walks of life were united by fear and anger toward a common enemy. They would rather have been elsewhere, but after eating and sleeping together for extended periods, they had become almost a family.

Class distinctions had begun evaporating at the outset of the Blitz. In November 1940, the Duke of Kent and Lady Louis Mountbatten, dressed in nurse's uniform, visited shelterers at the Piccadilly Circus station during a Monday night air raid.[85] Three years later, there was still privation, discomfort—and a wonderful egalitarianism.

"I say, would you mind not playing that harmonica?" a distinguished-looking old gentleman requested.

"Sure thing, Gov'nor," cheerfully responded a middle-aged man in overalls.

A matronly woman with a smudged blouse was hauling a small, ruddy-faced boy under each arm. "Do that again, and I'll box both your ears," she scolded.

A white-bearded man with rumpled, thinning hair was tucking in his young granddaughter. "At least we got bunks now," he explained. "A few years ago, the train doors would open during the evening rush, and the people coming out would have to step over everyone on the floor."

"What's a rush, Grandpapa?"

An athletic female porter was chatting with an office worker. "My husband's been fightin' fires over at the East End for three bloody years. One more night ain't gonna make a bit o' diff'rence, God willin'."

Standing dangerously close to the edge of the platform, a little girl cradled a doll in her arms. Brilliantly blue-eyed, she looked about six years old and had curly, shoulder-length blonde hair. It was the child who had been afraid when the lights went out in the lift. The doll slipped out of her hands and fell onto the tracks.

"Dolly, Dolly!" shouted the girl. She dropped to her knees, reaching out across the seven-foot drop in a vain attempt to retrieve her inanimate companion.

"Be careful, honey!" I warned. Then she lost her balance.

"Amanda, no!!!" screamed a young woman rushing toward her. It was her mother, the lady who had comforted the child in the lift. She was only a few feet away, but her unnaturally heavy body was moving too slowly. She wasn't going to make it. The girl's legs flew upward, and she began falling headlong toward the cold steel.

I lunged for her at the last instant. I must have blacked out for a second or two, because the next thing I remembered was opening my eyes and seeing Amanda dangling over the tracks. Half of my body was jutting over the edge of the platform, and I had her by the ankles. With a quick exertion of energy, I drew her up in a sweeping motion. Amanda landed seated in my arms. Though briefly stunned, she was unhurt. Her fitfully sobbing mother embraced her. Rising from the ground, I shook my head in disbelief and exhaled loudly.

By now, a small crowd had gathered. Hearty applause followed. I looked up and recognized the four RAF men I had just met.

Pete tapped me on the shoulder. "Great catch, Yank!"

"Hear that clapping? You're a bloody hero!" added Pat.

"You've made quite a splash, Corporal," concurred Mike.

"Dove like a regular paratrooper, he did," offered Davy.

"Quit flattering me, guys. I'm no paratrooper, and I'm certainly no hero. Just happened to be in the right place at the right time."

"A modest Yank," Pete observed. "Fancy that!"

The four Brits burst out laughing.

By now, the mother had recovered her composure. "Gentlemen, would you mind not carrying on here? My baby was almost killed just now, and I am not amused."

"Pardon us, madam," answered a contrite Pete. "We were just letting off some steam."

"Sorry. We meant no disrespect," added Davy.

Mike and Pat silently tipped their hats, and the four RAF men gave ground.

The woman addressed me. "Thank you, Corporal," she softly intoned. She was about thirty, blonde, and very attractive. Her heavy, unbuttoned overcoat revealed that she was also very pregnant.

"You're welcome, miss—I mean—ma'am," I stammered. "You've sure got your hands full."

"And another's on the way."

"How far along are you?"

"About eight months."

"You know, those fellas didn't mean any harm."

"I know, but it's been quite difficult lately. We got bombed out of our home…"

"Very sorry to hear that."

The woman nodded, and I paused uncomfortably. "Is your husband in the service?"

"Yes. He's a major in the RAF."

"A flyer?"

"Yes. He would have been much nicer to those boys than I was. He's an easy-going sort of chap."

"I guess you miss him."

"Indeed I do. I just hope he'll be back in time to see his second child born. Do you have a name, Corporal?"

"Don Quix, ma'am."

"Elizabeth Higgins." Elizabeth removed one of her discolored white gloves, and we shook hands.

I really felt sorry for this lady—and admired her. Here was a pregnant mother who had truly come down in the world. She was obviously well-educated and had probably lived in a nice house. Now she was homeless, worried about becoming a widow, and had to raise two children without a father. She could have been killed when her home was bombed, and just now almost saw her daughter die. And she was handling it all very well.

Elizabeth gently, but firmly, took her little girl by the shoulders.

"Amanda, you must never run away from Mummy like that again, and you must never walk near the edge of the platform. Do you understand?"

"But, Mummy, I've got to get Dolly. She's still down there."

"We'll get you another Dolly. Now, Amanda, you must promise me—"

"No, no. I want this Dolly."

I piped up. "Your mom's right, Amanda. You almost got hurt real bad. What if I buy you a—"

"No, no. I want Dolly." Amanda was inconsolable. She began to cry.

Jack had been close enough to see the aftermath of my fateful catch. He took me aside.

"What in blue blazes she ballin' 'bout?"

"Her doll fell on the tracks."

"So what are you, huh doll-keepah?"

"Greenjeans, she was about to fall over the edge of the platform."

"An' you caught huh?"

"Yeah."

Jack scratched his head, turned away, and then back toward me. "You mean, this kid woulda bought it if it weren't for you?"

"Probably."

"An' she's ballin' ovah a fuckin' doll?"

"Yeah. She's a little kid, Jack."

"Dayem! Where Ah come from, huh mothah'd give huh a good lickin', an' that'd be the end of it."

"Well, they do things a little different here."

Amanda was still crying.

"Look, Donnybrook, Ah can't take this anymaw. Gotta do somethin'."

"Don't do anything," I asserted, while grabbing hold of Jack. "I've done enough for both of us. Let her mother handle it."

Jack slithered out of my grasp. "Don't worry. It'll be all right."

Lanky Corporal Spring walked up to Amanda and got down on his knees. "Listen, honey," he began softly. "Ah'm gonna get yer Dolly for ya, but first you've gotta promise me one thing."

"What's that, Mr. Cowboy?"

"That you stop that God-awful cryin' an' be good for the rest of the night. Deal?"

"Deal."

"Put it there, partner." Amanda put her small hand around Jack's oversized fingers.

"What are you gonna do?" I asked.

"Get the doll."

"Are you nuts or something? That drop's deeper than an orchestra pit. You've got a live third rail, and a train can come any time."

"Be back quicker than a grasshopper."

Because of his long legs, Jack didn't have far to drop. Amidst gasps from several startled onlookers, Jack leaped onto the tracks, scooped up the doll, and clambered back up onto the platform.

"Heah you go, honey."

"Amanda, what do you say to the man?" prodded Elizabeth.

"Thank you, Mr. Cowboy." Amanda kissed him on the cheek.

I turned to Pete. "I save her life. He saves her doll, and she kisses **him**. Go figure, Lieutenant."

"Kids are a queer lot. I've seen stranger things in this war."

Just then, a wail came over the loud speaker, followed by an announcement: "Attention! Attention! The all clear has sounded. You may return to your homes. Only ticket holders may bunk for the night. Limited service will continue according to schedule."

A moment later, a four-car train labeled "Tube Refreshments Special" lumbered into the station.

"Why, that's odd," remarked Pete.

"What?" I asked.

"Grub trains usually don't come this late. Delayed by the bombing, I suppose."

Pete was right: the train was very late. It was one of six[86] departing each day at 1 p.m., spending about thirty seconds at each shelter station to unload refreshments and take up the previous day's refuse (300). Food was warmed up at "feeding points" by electric ovens and boilers, and distributed to shelterers, who brought their own utensils in the early morning and mid-evening (300).

Moving among the huddled masses, young women clad in green frocks and bright red kerchiefs handed out dinner.[87] Some poured tea from giant pots (6); others warmed babies' bottles (6). Nearby, a female accordionist performed a soothing rendition of "Good Night, Sweetheart."

Even on corporal's pay, I had plenty of spare change, a good thing because I could never fully master the British monetary system. Today, all Her Majesty's subjects have to remember is that there are one hundred pence ("p") to the pound. The euro, which the government continues to resist at the time of this writing, is similarly straightforward. But during the war, things were much more complicated.

Before 1971, the penny was abbreviated "d," for denarius, a common coin of the Roman Empire, whose value had fallen to about one penny at the time of that society's demise.[88] Wartime Londoners had to know that there were 12 pennies in a shilling ("s"), also known as a "bob,"[89] and 20 shillings to the pound.[90] Then there was the farthing (1/4d.), the "ha'penny" (1/2d.), the thruppence (3d.), the sixpence (6d.), the florin (2s.), the half-crown (2s./6d.), the crown (5s.), and the sovereign (a 1-pound gold coin).[91]

Because of my relative affluence, and the complexities of the English monetary system, I never bothered counting the change I received. By contrast, UK soldiers always counted their pennies. While British enlisted men were financially compelled to order cider at the local pub, Americans could afford hard liquor. Thus, it was easy to see how His Majesty's subjects developed the first prong of their epithet for the U.S. military: "overpaid, oversexed, and over here."[92]

I browsed the modest assortment of tube refreshments. Tea was 1d. a cup; buns and cake were 1d. apiece; a meat pie was 1½d.; and a packet of biscuits was 2d.[93] Apples went for 1½d., and chocolate bars for 2d.[94] The latter two items infrequently graced the menu and were unavailable that evening.

Propped against the wall beside the red, circular logo of the London Underground, I munched the standard fare. For me, it was just a snack, but for many of the shelterers, it was their only meal since morning.

"What's that?" asked Jack.

"Totally unidentifiable," I replied. "But it's not bad."

"Guess Ah'll ask for some unidentifiable."

A British corporal overhearing us antagonistically remarked, "It's a bloody meat pie. Hope it meets your approval, Yanks."

"I said it wasn't bad," I answered. Offended, I got in the man's face. "And I don't remember asking your opinion."

"Well, you got it anyway."

Before we could square off, Jack took me aside. "C'mon, Donnybrook. It ain't worth it."

"Butt out, Jack. He's an asshole."

"So he's an asshole. It still ain't worth it."

I sighed noisily. "Yeah, I guess you're right."

Jack walked up to the British corporal. "Look, friend," he said. "Let's not get bent outta shape ovah a buncha bullshit. How 'bout savin' some energy for the folks we're supposed to be fightin'?"

"He should have more respect," protested the Brit.

"Respect for what? Some grub? What the hell are we talkin' 'bout? Lookit. Mah friend don't know squat 'bout meat pies, an' you don't know squat 'bout chili dogs. Yer even."

Nonplussed, the British corporal grunted and walked away.

From a discreet distance, I watched Elizabeth and Amanda play house with the salvaged doll. I gingerly approached them.

"Guess you're all set for the night, ma'am."

"Yes, quite. Thank you, Corporal Quix. But please don't call me ma'am. It makes me feel old."

"Sorry, ma'am—I mean—Mrs. Higgins."

"You can call me Elizabeth... Ohhh!"

"What's wrong?"

"I'm not sure. I think it's—Oh my God!"

"What?"

"Owwww!!"

Elizabeth doubled over in pain.

"Mummy, what's the matter?" asked Amanda.

"Don't worry, ma'am. I'll get some help." I convinced Jack to stay with mother and daughter.

"Whaddya want me to do?" asked the bewildered farmer. "Ah don't know nothin' 'bout women's problems."

"Just keep 'em company. Besides, the kid likes you. Tell her some cowboy stories."

"Oh, yer a barrel uh laughs."

"C'mon. I'll be back in a coupla minutes."

"Dayem!"

"Thanks, Greenjeans."

I began running around the station like the proverbial headless chicken. Breathless, I approached a clerk at the ticket booth.

"Is there a doctor around? There's a sick woman on the platform."

"Calm down, soldier. I'll fetch the medic."

"Medic? The lady needs a doctor!"

"We'll get who we can, mate. This isn't New York General, you know. We'll fix 'er up fine. We've been doing this a long time."

They sure were. The Underground medical staff was very busy throughout the war.[95] Babies were born on subways, and there was a constant stream of minor ailments and injuries.[96]

When I got back to the platform, I found a small, solicitous crowd gathered around Elizabeth and Amanda. Jack, with the help of a few Good Samaritans, had managed to get the pregnant woman into a bunk, and I was lucky enough to get hold of a full-fledged doctor.

"Step aside, now. Give us some room, please!" shouted the physician. His white beard and thick spectacles made him look older than his sixty years. The doctor took off his heavy plaid overcoat and opened his black bag.

"How often have the contractions been coming?" he asked.

"Every couple of minutes," answered an exhausted Elizabeth.

"This soldier tells me you're about eight months along. Is that right?"

"Yes, doctor."

With quiet efficiency, the old man listened to Elizabeth's stomach and took her pulse and blood pressure. He pursed his lips and coolly sighed.

Half-delirious with pain, Elizabeth began thrashing about and sweating profusely.

"Please try to keep calm, madam. It will all be over in a few moments."

Jack, sensing Amanda's fear, gently led her away from Elizabeth's bedside. "Now don't you worry, honey. Yer mama's gonna be all right." He produced a shiny, gold-plated air force pin. "Now, Ah think this would make a mighty fine braid for Dolly's hair. Don't you? By the way, have you evah been to a rodeo?..."

Everyone knew exactly what was going on except me. "What is it, doc?" I asked.

"Her timetable appears to have been accelerated by the stress of tonight's events."

"What?"

"She's in labor."

Once again, onlookers began encroaching. "Never seen the likes o' this," remarked a smirking teenage boy to his mystified companion. "'Ang in there, missus!" cheered a ruddy-faced woman.

A subway official in a blue uniform took charge. "Move back, the lot of you!" he bellowed. "The last thing this woman needs is a bloody audience."

The crowd dutifully complied.

The official looked at me. "You too, soldier," he commanded.

But before I could leave, the physician overruled the transit worker. "No, that's quite all right, sir. He's with me."

"I am?" I murmured in bewilderment. The blue-uniformed man did not hear my query.

"Very good, doctor," the official said. Satisfied that the situation was under control, he strode off.

Elizabeth was still tossing and turning. I was getting squeamish.

"Listen, doc, I think I'd better get going," I said.

"Stay right here, my boy. I need your help."

"Don't you have nurses for that?"

"We're short-handed tonight."

"Gee, I'd really like to help, but what can I do? I don't know anything about this stuff."

"You can start by holding her legs still. I can't work and keep her from moving at the same time."

I looked doubtful.

"Come on, soldier. You've seen bullets and bombs, haven't you?" the doctor coaxed.

"Well, actually—"

"Then why should this bother you? You're a young fellow. Haven't you ever seen a woman's legs before?"

"Yeah, sure, but not like this."

Overcoming my uncomfortableness, I grasped Elizabeth's ankles.

"Good. Now get her knees up and plant the bottoms of her feet against the bedding," directed the doctor. "That's it. Now, madam, can you hear me?"

No response.

"Madam!"

"Yes," was the weak reply.

"We're almost done. Take a deep breath. Relax. Very good. Now, when I say three, I want you to push."

"Holy Jeez," I whispered. I wondered whether Churchill, during any of his "blood, toil, tears, and sweat"[97] speeches, had ever thought of babies being born on the subway.

"We can do without your colorful comments, soldier," the doctor quietly admonished.

"Sorry, doc."

The old man raised his voice. "One. Two. Three!"

Elizabeth's screams segued into the cries of a newborn. Another life had come into being in the bowels of war-torn London.

A matronly woman helped clean the baby and wrap it in a blanket. The doctor looked over at me. "Okay, we're done here, soldier. You can go."

"No, wait," I demurred. "Can I—"

"Well, I suppose you've earned it. As long as the mother doesn't object."

Elizabeth nodded her assent.

I gently cradled the infant, amazed at the miracle I held. Then I walked to the head of the bed and placed the child beside its mother.

"It's a boy," I said.

Elizabeth looked simultaneously pleased and embarrassed. "I know. But I didn't expect him so soon," she softly intoned.

"I guess the major really missed out."

"A small casualty of war. We'll catch up."

"I'm glad everything worked out okay."

"Thank you for everything, Don."

"Good luck to you, Elizabeth."

It was about a quarter to midnight. I felt I had lived an entire lifetime in less than an hour.

The last train of the evening was approaching the station, a welcome sight for two American corporals wanting quick transportation to the outskirts of the city and in no mood to start looking for a ride. Before boarding, Jack and I took one last look at mother, daughter, and baby—three dimly illuminated figures happily huddled together in their bunks.

"Ah guess we did good tonight," Jack opined.

"Yeah. We did good."

*   *   *   *

On the trains, the sound of ATS girls brazenly singing their favorite song always brought a smile to my lips:

> Roll me over,
> In the clover.
> Roll me over,
> Lay me down and do it again.

Although sympathetic to the plight of the tube shelterers, I preferred to focus on London's more positive qualities. The war had not shut down the Rogers Corner Restaurants. These were spacious, warm establishments featuring violinists whose sweet sounds calmed the mind and enriched the spirit. And my mouth watered at the sight of street vendors hawking pungent fish and chips rolled up in newspaper. What a glorious treat at a reasonable price!

*   *   *   *

Until now, I had seen only London's West End, which was relatively affluent and touristy. The East End was poorer, grittier,[98] and sometimes more colorful, but a place where visitors rarely ventured. With some time to kill before an evening shift, I wandered into this working class district.

I began my self-tour near the battered St. Paul's Cathedral. In September 1940, the Cathedral's High Altar was saved from a delayed-action explosive by a heroic bomb disposal unit, only to be destroyed during an air raid the next month.[99] Fortunately, the main structure was undamaged.[100]

During the Blitz, the East End was the Luftwaffe's favorite punching bag. Many of the twelve thousand dead and sixteen thousand seriously injured civilians were from this part of town.[101] A large number of them had leaned against buildings for protection and were blown through windows.[102] Because most bombs exploded upward, the majority of pedestrians wounded were hit above the waist (4). They soon learned to drop quickly to the ground at the first sign of danger (4).

Fires were everywhere. As a precursor to their attacks, the Germans dropped flares and incendiaries to light up their targets (1). Then they'd let loose with the "heavy stuff" (1).

On November 6, 1940, a second "Great Fire" hit London.[103] Many tube stations in the East End were vulnerable to bomb damage, either because they were not deep enough, or because they intersected with gas and water mains which exploded on impact.[104] The stops at Whitechapel and Balham were hit. A lot of people drowned at Balham (238).

I made my way along the narrow, yellow streets[105] off Whitechapel Road. I bought some fish and chips on Wentworth Street. This was London's Jewish quarter. With its peddlers, pushcarts, and closely-packed stores, the area reminded me of Manhattan's Lower East Side, which I had visited once or twice before the war.

Still, there were major differences. There was less food here than in Manhattan, and I was intrigued by the cockney accents. Before going overseas, I thought the English were stuffy and aristocratic. Though somewhat vulgar, these coarser voices seemed refreshingly down-to-earth.

"Aaoooow, step right up 'ere, mate. Everything's a bob," shouted a stubbly housewares vendor.

A matronly woman was arguing with a merchant over bread. "Why, 'tain't fresh!" she stammered. Before she could walk away, the brawny salesman thrust a long, thin baguette in front of her and retorted, "Well, 'ow'd ya like a taste o' this, Mum?"

Although offended by the man's language, I was in an unfamiliar place, whose ways I did not understand, and decided not to get involved. I was hungry, but I didn't buy a farthing's worth of stuff from that s.o.b.

I made a wry face in front of Spitalfield's Synagogue. "You'll never catch me in there," I murmured.

As a pre-teen in the Bronx, I had dutifully gone through the rote exercise of Hebrew School. I read from the siddur without understanding a word of what I was saying. From this experience, I gleaned subliminal messages: fit into the mold; go through the motions; be nice; obey and respect your teacher.

The rituals seemed superfluous, the moral lessons obvious. From a very young age, I instinctively knew that in order to be treated fairly, you had to extend a helping hand to others. I didn't know Scripture, but the Golden Rule was my bible. This was the Wally Cleaver in me. He was constantly fighting with Eddie Haskell.

Mom kept a kosher home, but I had a taste for non-kosher foods, among them: bacon, sausage, ham, and pork chops. So whenever I ate out, I had whatever I wanted. In the Army, I got along with people of all religions and enjoyed a variety of ethnic foods, including Italian, Chinese, and Russian.

Religion had absolutely no bearing on my personal relationships. I celebrated Christmas with my army buddies and enjoyed their holiday songs. During that time of year, I would help decorate trees and kiss women under mistletoe.

The streets of the East End were oddly subdued. There were plenty of people around, but something was missing. Then I realized I hadn't seen any boys or girls.

At the beginning of the war, Churchill ordered the evacuation of children and young mothers from the East End to the English countryside,[106] but eighty percent of them had returned by April 1940 (236). Once the Blitz began, they were promptly re-evacuated (237).

I made my way past the bombed-out buildings near the waterfront, thinking how lifeless everything was without kids. My daydream was interrupted by a dirty soccer ball flying at me from a side street. I caught it.

I turned the corner to investigate. There were several children playing in the rubble. Some were imitating soldiers, using long sticks as mock rifles and a broken-down wheelbarrow for a jeep. The soccer ball was their crown jewel.

A grimy-faced urchin about ten years old ran up to me, and I threw him the ball.

"Thank you, sir," said the boy, smiling through a missing front tooth.

"Don't mention it, kid. Hey, tell your friends to stick to soccer instead of war."

"Yes, sir."

I shook my head in amazement. This was no place for little boys and girls. They should have been playing on a nice ballfield, somewhere clean, with wide open space and good equipment. Where were their parents? It was dangerous out here. There were glass shards, sharp rocks, and who the hell knew what else. Maybe unexploded bombs. The kids seemed happy enough, but what lessons were they learning?

The sunny day had turned overcast, and I could hear the bleating of foghorns along the Thames River. Broken concrete and shrapnel crunched heavily beneath my boots. Here, under heavy bombing, docks, warehouses, bridges, railroad tracks—even entire streets—had vanished (237).

An emaciated pit bull lay lethargically beside a small cat outside an apartment building. Too weak to chase his natural enemy, the dog emitted high-pitched yelps. Exhausted, he grew silent. An enormous black cockatoo with red cheeks[107] suddenly appeared in an open ground-floor window. It pierced the silence with cackles of "Ack-ack!"

Startled, I instinctively clutched the light carbine strapped to my shoulder. I was close enough to feel a light breeze from the bird's agitated wing-flapping. Relaxing my frame, I laughed loudly, wondering whether he was spontaneously trying to imitate anti-aircraft fire or if his owner, in a bizarre display of wartime humor, had taught him that weird sound.

I spotted a longshoreman near a serviceable dock. Short and muscular, this fellow had a curly, grey beard sprouting from beneath his black flannel jacket and seaman's cap.

"Excuse me, sir," I began. "Do you know where I can get some fresh oranges?"

The longshoreman looked at me as if I were insane. "Oranges? Are ya daft, man? Ain't no oranges 'ere.'Aven't ya 'erd? There's a war goin' awn."

Indeed, rationing in Britain had been phased in between 1940 and 1941.[108] By 1943, a civilian was limited to a weekly allotment of less than one pound of fresh meat, eight ounces of sugar, and four ounces each of bacon and ham (65). These items were sold only in designated stores (65). Non-essential foods, including salmon, dried fruit, and biscuits, were governed by a more flexible point system (65). Though subject to strict price controls (65), staples such as bread, fish, and potatoes weren't rationed at all (65).

Fresh fruit, on the other hand, was extremely hard to find. Bananas, an imported product, were non-existent (65). Oranges were rare (65). They were occasionally found at the front of long lines (65), where disputes were frequent (65).

But I wasn't ready to give up. "Do you know where I can get any?" I asked.

The longshoreman scratched his beard. "Ya might try a pub[109] a few blocks from 'ere."

"Are we talking black market?"

The longshoreman playfully clapped me on the shoulder with his heavy, calloused hand. "Do ya think I'd ever suggest such a thing to an honorable soldierin' man?"

"Yeah, I do."

The grizzled dock worker answered with a great guffaw. "I'm beginning to like you, Yank. Blimey, I'd pegged ya for a straight-laced sorta bloke, but I see yer a reg'lar chap. The pub opens at eight. I'll point ya in the right direction. Just ask for Jake in the back room."

"Thanks, but I'll be on duty then. Any place else I can try?"

The old man scratched his beard again. "Hmmm. Ya might try Covent Garden on Saturday mornin'. Never go there meself, but I 'ere that's where ya might get some good deals.[110] The place is kinda empty then, but yer a fit lad. Looks like you can 'andle yerself. Just keep that carbine close to ya."

Back home, I would never have considered such a thing, but England's black market had a better reputation than its American counterpart. Organized crime did not dominate the British underground economy as it did in the United States (68-9). Unauthorized entrepreneurs tended to operate independently, and most people tried to abide by the government's rationing system (68-9). Not known for gluttony, the average UK civilian bought just enough on the black market to survive (68-9).

"I think I'll pass, but thanks anyway," I said.

"Got cold feet, 'ave ya?"

"Well, I like oranges, but not that much. I won't starve."

"Ain't that the truth. Good luck to ya, me lad."

I began my long walk back to the West End. By dusk, I had St. Paul's in sight, which I often used as a landmark from the other side of town. I had great respect for that cathedral. It had withstood vicious Nazi pounding, and its dome reminded me of the Capitol Building in Washington, DC.

The thickening fog was obscuring my vision, and I wanted to reach the St. Paul's tube station before dark. Soon I wouldn't be able to see at all. To avoid Luftwaffe targeting, London had blacked out its gas-lit streets, and the miasma threatened to render my flashlight useless. Still, something was better than nothing, so I decided to turn it on.

Except for an occasional barking dog, the area was silent and deserted. I had started the day wanting to take a leisurely stroll about town, and now I felt like a cop walking a dangerous beat.

Then came voices and heavy breathing outside the front entrance of a tenement. I focused my beam in the direction of the noise and illuminated a young American GI in an amorous encounter with a local girl. That was just the comic relief I needed. I smirked, flashed the "V for Victory" sign, and saluted before moving on.

The fog began to lift. Soon I could see street signs: Cable Street, City Road, Goswell Road. Then patches of sky—just in time to witness an airborne spectacle. A huge, powerful British searchlight had trapped a Heinkel HE-111H-6 bomber. Soon there were ten bright beams zeroed in on the bandit. From the ground, the craft resembled a miniature toy replica. The lights crisscrossed, locking onto the target. RAF fighters were approaching. It was a classic textbook interception. Gerry was about to be blasted out of the sky.

It didn't seem real. I had to keep reminding myself that this was no model airplane or special effect in a movie. There was a flyer up there who wanted to kill people on the ground, and there were other pilots who were to trying to kill him before he could complete his deadly task. I cleared my dry throat.

Suddenly all the searchlights snapped off. Above the clearing fog amidst the London twilight, the Heinkel had found a lucky star. The anti-aircraft gunners, leery about hitting their own planes, were ordered to desist. The British pilots then lost sight of their quarry. Against all odds, the enemy had escaped.

*   *   *   *

Even when undamaged by bombing, small towns like Felixstowe bore scars of war. Located on the English coast ninety-two miles from London,[111] Felixstowe, with its sunny beaches and spas, had become a fashionable resort by the 1890's.[112] Its famous pier, constructed in 1905,[113] boasted a half-mile-long tram route with landings for paddle steamers.[114] But during the war, it was cut in half to prevent enemy landings.[115] This once-bustling area went into a period of decline from which it did not emerge until the 1950's.[116]

The venerable Landguard Fort, the only one to repel a full-scale invasion attempt of England in 1667,[117] was once again put into service. In 1940, it was converted into a barracks and plotting room, then retrofitted with six-pound guns and fixed-beam searchlights.[118]

Unfortunately, my fellow radio men and I saw little of Felixstowe. Working in remote areas outside of town, our only opportunities to see the village were during train and truck rides. Most of these excursions were short hops to and from dances. Occasional glimpses of lush farmland, majestic bluffs overlooking the North Sea, or an eerily quiet pier, was the extent of my experience with this community.

*   *   *   *

On an overnight trip from Felixstowe to London, three buddies and I spotted a Land Army girl standing on the train platform. She was part of a contingent of seventeen-year-old female civilians. They wore green uniforms but were too young to enter the regular army. Working on farms, these young women had obtained employment which dovetailed nicely with the color of their garments.

The girl was stunning. The four of us stared and tipped our hats as she passed.

More daring than the others, I ambled over to her and said, "Hi." That was all it took to break the ice. We boarded the train together, locked in pleasant conversation.

English trains had separate, cozy compartments seating six, and things were heating up inside one of them. With female companionship kindling, I envisioned my trip to London being more enjoyable than I ever thought possible. The enforced blackout didn't hurt either—especially since this Land Army girl wasn't wearing a bra.

"I get off at the next station," she announced. "I've got to go visit my mum."

"Can't you go to London and see her on the way back?"

"No, that's not possible. She's expecting me now."

I quickly jotted down her name, Dawn Garrison, and the address of the farm where she worked. It was within easy walking distance of camp.

I had barely finished putting the pen back into my pocket when Dawn tightly grasped my hand for several seconds. The hum of the locomotive slowed to a putter. Approaching the station with a breathy hiss, the train stopped at the platform. Dawn opened the compartment door, and before exiting, turned to flash me a final, inviting smile. Then she was gone.

My hopes of a wild weekend in London dashed, I was momentarily disappointed. However, my optimism soon overcame my dejection. I decided to see Dawn when I returned to my outfit in Felixstowe. Her farm was close enough.

A week later, I paid her a visit. A plain-looking Land Army girl answered the door.

"Dawn's not here tonight," she said. "Would you like to take a walk?"

"Okay," I replied with a shrug.

I wasn't the least bit interested in this young woman and only wanted to be polite. Her personality was no more attractive than her appearance, but I made the best of the situation and found beauty in the countryside.

I enjoyed the feel of the hard earth against my feet as I traveled the bare wheat fields and apple orchards. They looked majestically sad under the pink sky of the post-harvest. When I got slightly ahead of the girl, I happily paused and watched the sun set, savoring the crispness of the late autumn breeze. We walked for an hour, but talked little. Then I left.

I returned a week later. This time, Dawn was there, but her reception was far from cordial.

"You went out with my girlfriend," she pouted. "I never want to see or talk to you again."

"I was just trying to be friendly," I protested. "Nothing happened. We just talked."

"I don't care."

It was useless. Dawn wouldn't listen. The harvest was over.

But not for long. In a very short time, I would acquire carnal knowledge. Like my buddies, I'd have my share of failures, but there were many Mays and Junes in my future.

For the moment, I contented myself with the realization that the plain girl was jealous and had set me up. Pining over Dawn was a fruitless exercise. "Her loss," I opined, as I headed back to base.

I returned to my outfit a little wiser. My confidence had been tempered with a touch of humility. I still had a helluva lot to learn and remembered that famous book *What Men Know About Women.* Inside, all the pages were blank.

Writing on them wasn't one of my priorities. I went out with girls for a good time and had no intention of becoming romantically involved. By nature, I was a lighthearted, lusty fellow, not a profound lover. If females became a problem, I could do without them. My more serious thoughts—to the extent I had them—were reserved for my closest buddies. I was anxious about a pilot friend of mine who had recently earned his wings.

Dec. 12, 1943

Dear Mom, Dad & Ethel,

Jerry just received his flying equipment, and he must have been up several times by this date. He's been doing book work up until this time, but now he'll actually find out whether he's got the makings of a flyer.

The new place I am in now is favorable in many respects. Town is nearby, and last night I got my first glimpse of it. I don't believe it is as large as the last town we were at, but I manage to get around.

Last night we witnessed a typical English dance. Before each dance, they announced what type of dance it would be: fox trot, waltz and—excuse me—quick step. That's when cutting in is permitted. All over England, Yanks are breaking one tradition after another and almost making the traditions obsolete.

To illustrate some other variations: in the U.S. the tax on jewelry is 10%; in England it's 100%. If you buy a $50 watch here, it costs you $100.

Love,

Don

Jerry was another pre-army chum of mine from the Bronx. He, Normie, and I had been very tight as teenagers. We would often sit and chat on the front steps of tenements on Phelan Place. Another of our favorite hangouts was a brownstone on Billingsley Terrace near University Avenue. The buildings were a fifteen-minute walk from NYU's uptown campus. The campus featured the Hall of Fame, which contained busts of famous historical figures.

We would trek up to NYU in the evening, when we could lie on the grass and listen to the melodious music of Goldman's Band. The concerts were free and well-attended. It was a very safe place. There were no muggings or fights. With a backdrop of violins, trumpets, and clarinets, the atmosphere was perfect for relaxing and dreaming of the future.

We were sixteen, and the three of us would stroll up to the campus in the afternoon with a couple of fifteen-year-old females. The girls, Irene and Myrene, were buxom, blonde twins. They usually wore white, knitted sweaters which made them all the more enchanting.

By modern standards, we were incredibly ignorant about sex, but no more so than the typical teenage male of the day. There was no internet, HBO, or *Playboy*. A little fondling, hugging, and squeezing was considered "making out."

Once a seventy-year-old gardener tending the lawn spotted us in action. Planting himself nearby, he watched us awkwardly press our bodies together. His lined jaw dropped, and his lips curved upward in a mischievous smile.

"Don't mind me," chirped the old-timer. "Please continue."

No clothes were ever removed. Getting naked was much too advanced for us. But whoever could work his hands under those white sweaters was the envy of every kid on the block.

Chagrined by the gardener's comment, we abruptly halted our sexual experiments. The spell had been broken, and we decided to call it a day.

My friend Jerry was about five feet seven inches tall, with dark hair and a pleasant face. He wasn't particularly fond of school, but was happy whenever he could get his hands on a baseball. He was a good batter and had an excellent throwing arm.

Jerry was a square shooter and very articulate. He wouldn't have hesitated to cut off his right arm for a buddy in need. But he never pulled any punches; he always spoke his mind.

While Jack Spring was my best army pal, Normie was my closest civilian friend. About Jerry's size, Normie Friedberg, with his frizzy, blonde hair and ready smile, was a diamond in the ruff. Two months younger than I, Normie lost his mother when he was a small child, and his father couldn't take care of him.

He spent most of his youth in an orphanage in Pleasantville, New York. During his teens, he lived with an aunt in the Bronx. By then, he had already become a talented trumpet-player.

Like me, Normie had his wild side, but he also had a level head. He had a reputation in the neighborhood for stopping brawls. Walking on Tremont Avenue, he once came to the aid of a passenger and his family being assaulted by a cab-driver.

I would often mentally compare my two best friends. They were so similar, yet very different. Both were good-hearted peacemakers, but Normie was more settled than Jack. Before joining the Army, Normie had a terrific, steady girlfriend and a good job at an interior decorating firm. Jack's life plans were up in the air, and he was more unpredictable.

I hadn't seen Normie since leaving home. While I was tending Air Corps radios in Europe, Private Friedberg was touring the States in a military band. We wouldn't see each other until the end of the war.

Although I wrote home sparingly about Normie, I thought of him often. He was a true friend, someone who would help me regardless of any inconvenience to him. He was the type of person whom I could call at any hour of day or night, a fellow who would visit frequently when I was sick, or travel thirty miles to shovel my car out of a snowbank during a blizzard. He performed the last of these favors for me one winter during the 1960's, but I'm sure he would have done it in the early forties had the need arisen. My fond recollections of Normie Friedberg kept me in good stead as 1943 drew to a close.

Dec. 25, 1943

Dear Mom, Dad & Ethel,

Today is Christmas Day, and everyone is trying to make the holiday spirit as warm and gay as possible. The mud here is getting unbearable, and this resulted in the importing of a bed of straw over which a metal mat was laid. It's not the best looking rug in the world, but as far as we are concerned, it is a marvelous addition to our newly-formed community.

This morning, at formation, we were informed that we could participate in something which is truly a luxury in these parts. Showers are now set up, and a lorry (excuse me, truck) will make trips to this H_2O this afternoon. It will be the first shower in quite a while.

[We would usually bathe by emptying our canteens into our metal helmets, and, with a little soap, treat ourselves to what was affectionately called a "whore's bath."]

At the same formation, we were given the good news that we are free this afternoon. Exactly what there is to do in the way of recreation is very minute, but we can rest up and take it easy.

For Christmas Day, turkey is on the menu. For noontime chow, and, in a few minutes, the clanking of mess kits, plus the equivalent of stampeding hoofs, will be audible. In England our appetites are none the less smaller, and we are still the chow hounds we always were. For our holiday treat, we are supposed to be allotted one pound of turkey per soldier, which is a generous portion. The officers also managed to get us some kegs of beer, so we should have a merry session.

Feeling great and hope everybody is okay.

Love,

Don

Dec. 26, 1943

Dear Ethel,

The fact that we are out in the field, away from our base, entitles us to a certain laxness in the way of regulations to make up for the many disadvantages that confront us. I now have a seven-day beard growth, and a buddy of mine has the same project of pride. We are now awaiting a sunny day to take some closeup pictures of our House of David qualifications. It sure feels good to give our faces a rest away from the razor. We aren't permitted to go to town and thus don't come in contact with the civilian population.

Love,

Don

Dec. 30, 1943

Dear Mom, Dad & Ethel,

Today two of us walked into town in search of a newspaper. The fellow with me spotted some cakes in the window of what appeared to be a shop. An elderly lady and a young boy were standing in the doorway of the place that now received our attention. We asked if this was a bakery shop. It turned out that we weren't by a bakery shop, but that this was actually their home.

We were talking with them for a few minutes when a girl dressed in the A.T.S. uniform of the British army came out and her dad also. In a short while, we were invited into their house for tea and cake. We talked with them for quite a while on every conceivable topic. It sure felt swell to be inside a neat, comfortable home for a change. We were enjoying ourselves so much, and were so engrossed, that we lost track of time and almost missed our noontime chow. Now that would have been a calamity!

Feeling great.

Love,

Don

Jan. 6, 1944

Dear Mom, Dad & Ethel,

Received a flock of letters from you today, plus a couple from Ethel, and one from Joe. In all, it totaled about thirty letters, and it was a swell pack to be waiting for me upon my arrival back in camp. We hadn't had any mail in quite some time, and the pile that greeted each of us well satisfied our wildest hopes.

Back from our recent expedition, we just got paid. After reading our mail and making replies to them, we really want to go to town and have a whale of a time. Tomorrow we will be concentrating on digging up our remaining clean clothes, if any, and then bringing them out to be pressed, if we can find a presser.

Concerning my stay in England thus far, I've been fortunate in having three luxuries: ice cream, two glasses of milk, and champagne.

Received a letter from Joe about spending some time in Washington. I also received some letters from Normie. He's okay, but like the rest of us, he wants this thing over with.

As usual, I'm in excellent condition, and the few minutes I spent exercising each day when I was at home didn't hurt any.

One thing I'm glad didn't happen to me around Christmas time. A lot of fellows received Christmas cards instead of letters. If you want to see a look of disappointment, watch a fellow open up an envelope and find a card there when he's expecting a beautiful letter. It's the difference between hand-made and machine-made.

In one edition of Reader's Digest that you gave me a subscription to, they stated that hotdogs and similar dishes were preferred by army personnel. That is a lot of first class bunk.

Love,

Don

Jan. 16, 1944

Dear Mom, Dad & Ethel,

We had chicken for lunch today, and it was real tasty. At noon some officer got a brilliant idea about the mess lines. So he had us wait on lines of a different arrangement. I've seen experiments of this sort in Wisconsin, and the result here was no different. His attempt to speed up the chow lines resulted in a general mixup, with lines running every conceivable way—including into each other. I suspect that by tomorrow morning we'll go back to our original way.

Our school tent blew down due to a strong wind yesterday. So we now hold class above the mess hall.

Love,

Don

Jan. 27, 1944

Dear Mom, Dad & Ethel,

Today we had our examination. Part was written, and part was oral. I am quite sure I did all right. Our orders call for completion of the course tomorrow at noon. I'm not certain whether we'll return to base Thursday or Friday.

Am following up anxiously the present postwar plans in reference to college. I'm dead set on going. As the Bill stands now, it sounds fairly generous.

Feeling good and hope you feel the same.

Love,

Don

Feb. 1, 1944

Dear Mom, Dad & Ethel,

I haven't had any mail for quite some time from anybody, and I'm quite sure it's because we are working with this other outfit.

Last night I saw the Jack Benny Show live. There was Ingrid Bergman, who is beautiful; Martha Tilton, who really knows how to sing; and Larry Adler, whom I don't believe has an equal with the harmonica. It was a first class performance, and I'm glad I didn't miss it.

They're still shuffling us around as if we were hearts, diamonds, spades, or clubs, and we are still in that uncertain state. Chow is a little better than fair.

I'm feeling fine, but I sure hope that I start getting some mail soon.

Lots Of Love To All,

Don

The only stars at my next location were in the night sky. I was now stationed in a forest about twenty miles from Felixstowe. Here, I worked in one of several transmitter trucks housing six-foot-high radio units. The trucks were situated on the highest possible elevation to ensure optimal transmission. They operated twenty-four hours a day.

A transmitter sat on the floor in the back of each truck. The tall tower had eight dials and a slit for inserting a crystal.

I always began my eight-hour shift in the transmitter truck by taking a telephone call instructing me to use a particular frequency. I would then locate the correct crystal and adjust the transmitter accordingly, rotating the dials to specific positions. When I first started training, it took me several minutes to accomplish this task, but, by now, I could do it within thirty seconds. In this way, we established a line of communication between a controller in an operations block and a lead pilot in a group of five fighter planes.

Frequencies were changed on a moment's notice. After fielding a call, I would immediately re-tune my set to conform to the new orders. The lead pilot would then send a message back to the controller through a receiver truck.

Receiver units were much smaller than transmitters. Radio technicians in receiver trucks sat on benches monitoring and transcribing conversations between lead pilot and controller. A ledge protruding from the unit served as a desk for writing. All fighter control technicians got to work in both types of vans.

Twice a week, those of us who had worked a day shift would pile into vehicles bound for an evening dance at a Felixstowe hotel. At about 11 p.m., we would be taken back to our field tents. Although Felixstowe was technically off-limits to non-British personnel, the rules were skirted, and we got in.

Here, I met a gorgeous, blonde, British WAAF. I had seen her working on a radio van near camp a few days earlier. Her name was Sally.

Sally had soft green eyes, a petite nose, and a radiant smile that showed she enjoyed life to the fullest. A man could get snow-blind looking at her white teeth. That night, she looked especially desirable in an electric-blue-sequined gown. Sporting a playful, mischievous expression on her face, she sauntered about the dance hall, flirting with various uniformed men and infuriating their dates.

I soon came under her spell. After having her in my sights for awhile, I knew this fun-loving girl was for me. Sally beat me to the punch.

"Where have you been?" she coquettishly inquired.

"I've been here all the time, waiting for you," I replied.

We introduced ourselves. A few fox trots later, our relationship was firmly cemented, but a pang of squeamishness seized me.

"Wanna go upstairs?" I tentatively suggested.

"I thought you'd never ask." Sally clasped my hand. "See you soon, love."

I grasped the cold metal with the enthusiasm of a child who had just won an unexpected award. A thousand delicious, little pinpricks began etching a serrated outline on my sweaty palm. After several seconds, I released my grip and triumphantly looked down at Sally's room key.

My reaction was similar to the startled look on Ken's face that night about a year earlier in Chicago. Marie must have snuck her key into Ken's hand right before she left O'Leary's—the same way Sally put hers in mine. Pretty sharp ladies!

Before going upstairs, I had to adjust my next day's work schedule. Jack Spring was happy to oblige.

"Greenjeans, I think I got something going here. Can you work the eight to four shift for me tomorrow morning? I'll work your four to twelve."

"You got it, buddy," assented Jack with a wink. "Ovah an' out."

Rearranging work shifts was commonplace and didn't require an officer's approval. As long as the vans were in continuous operation, the commanders were satisfied.

I located Room 212, inserted the key into the door, and opened it. Inside was a neat, comfortable space equipped with a queen-sized bed.

My knees buckled. To a lowly corporal accustomed to field tents and bunk houses, this chamber was a veritable cornucopia of the senses. The white sheets were imprinted with a floral design of bright reds, yellows, and blues, on top of which lay a matching, down quilt. Thinking that I'd died and gone to GI heaven, I fancied myself a four-star general.

Rapidly stripping to my undershorts, I gleefully jumped into bed and got under the covers. I tried to lay still, but my eager legs were twitching with nervous anticipation. I began fumbling with a rubber.

Jeez, I don't know why I can't get this crap on. I've practiced with it a thousand times. First time jitters, I guess. Oh, what the hell. I'll get it later. First things first. Conversation and foreplay before screwing. Relax, Don. You've hit the jackpot.

Five minutes later, I heard a gentle knock at the door. It was Sally.

"Undressed already, are you?" she delightedly inquired. Without further ado, Sally disrobed and slipped into the sack. After a flurry of kisses and caresses, we paused for a brief chat.

"Can you imagine?" she pouted. "Captain Sweeney wanted to go out with me. The man's married and has two children at home in America. I wouldn't want to be his wife, the two-timing cheat."

I nodded in agreement. *That Sweeney's certainly a cad, but, you, my dear, are a hypocrite.* For several seconds, I'd been admiring the engagement ring on Sally's left hand.

Although I condemned her criticism of Captain Sweeney, I never considered Sally a slut. In those days, an average fellow could walk into just about any pub, and after a few minutes of small talk, start getting physical with a woman. But these gals weren't prostitutes or nymphomaniacs. All over war-torn Europe, women were starving for affection. They were lonely, often ill-fed, and afraid of dying in air raids. In many cases, wives and fiancées hadn't heard from their men in months—even years. Women who, before the war, wouldn't think of looking at someone else, reconsidered after the bombs started falling. For all I knew, Sally's intended might have been a missing or captured soldier. While on foreign soil, I never judged her, or any other woman's lifestyle.

Soon we were devouring each other. For five minutes, the bed squeaked fast and furiously. Our sustained, rhythmic panting rapidly reached a crescendo, followed by somnolent sighs. Our libidinous aria over, we grew silent, and I settled down to the most peaceful sleep I had experienced since joining the Army.

The next morning, after enjoying a wonderful breakfast, Sally and I shared a cab ride back to our respective camps. During the drive, we made plans for a future rendezvous.

I couldn't get enough of her. For a naive Bronx boy who barely knew the meaning of the word "petting," making love was very intoxicating. It was like Jack's peanuts: the more you had, the more you wanted—and it was one helluva break from base routine.

Feb. 7, 1944

Dear Mom, Dad & Ethel,

Today was the second consecutive day we were treated to one of the rarest delicacies: oranges. I ate them slowly and carefully, as Maxwell House advertises, "Good to the last drop."

To give you an idea how much we like our present setup, I'll quote from a fellow who was out on a 48-hour pass and just got back: "I missed camp these two days and couldn't wait to get back."

Hope you are all okay.

Love,

Don

At last, I had gotten my coveted oranges. They were the best I had ever eaten, not because of their quality, but for their scarcity. I never appreciated such small comforts until I had lost them, and could only imagine how the lady in the tubes felt when she was bombed out of her home.

Feb. 12, 1944

Dear Mom, Dad & Ethel,

Your package containing the watch and moccasins came in today, and Joe's box of chocolates also arrived. Boy oh boy, is that watch a honey! It even has these illuminated numerals—which will be very useful during the blackout.

The moccasins are beauties, although they are a trifle large. I guess they are supposed to be like that, though. I just glanced down at my feet and noticed that I still have on my G.I. shoes, and since my day's work is completed, it's time to relax and take it easy. So I interrupted this letter and changed into my moccasins. You see? They are already being put into practical use, and, believe me, they feel nice and comfortable. Wow, what luxury! Thanks again.

But it's the watch that gives me the greatest joy. It was one pain in the neck heretofore, asking this person and that person what the current time was. Honestly folks, you're treating me as good as any son anywhere could ask to be treated, and I do appreciate it. Everything I've asked for I've gotten. By God, all of you are swell.

With these chocolates, I've gotten a million new friends already. It's something we haven't had in a long time. I guess the censor who reads this letter will pay me a visit tomorrow when he reads that I've received some chocolates.

I also received a few letters from you, and I sure was glad to learn everything is okay. Incidentally, send me some more chocolates, if possible.

In your letter, you state that I'm making everything rosy for your benefit. I know it's difficult for you to believe that I'm continually enjoying myself at dances and shows, but truthfully, Dad, I'm not holding a bit back from you. You know that I can't possibly describe my work to you.

Love,

Don

Dad was wise to me. He knew I was in more danger than my letters revealed, and I knew he knew. However, as my correspondence suggested, my job had the feel of civilian employment. I usually worked quiet, eight-hour shifts in a skilled position. Still, I was a soldier within earshot of combat and subject to the vicissitudes of war, but unless I wanted to scare the hell out of my parents, there was no use in discussing death and destruction. Even if I'd been inclined to dwell upon those topics, they were heavily censored, and, therefore, unlikely to appear in my missives.

Writing home was a safety valve. It was a good way to get my mind off the reality of my situation, but I never lied to my parents. I just tinted the truth with joy. That was easy. A natural optimist, I believed a protective force hovered over me. Any bullet or bomb aimed in my direction would surely curve away.

Yet I wasn't religious in the traditional sense. I shunned temple and didn't observe most religious holidays. My spirituality consisted of a secular moral code which directed that I always try to do right by people.

When it came to affection, I loved my family but never verbally expressed those feelings. Although unaccustomed to revealing their emotions, my parents and siblings harbored equally warm sentiments toward me.

As for chocolate, I was never a big candy eater, but privation prompted my buddies and me to relish something no longer obtainable. Once I overheard a GI voice some confidential information: "If you send a dollar to the Hershey Company, they'll mail a box of chocolates to a soldier overseas."

Rumors such as these abounded, and I was skeptical. "Oh, it's only a buck. What the heck!" I sent the dollar and forgot about it.

Two months later, when I was expecting a package from home, another parcel arrived. My eyeballs almost flew out of their sockets when I unpacked a carton containing twelve Hershey bars. We had a rollicking good snack that evening.

Feb. 14, 1944

Dear Mom, Dad & Ethel,

I went for a walk in a nearby town and bought three wooden hangers for myself. They were reasonable, one shilling apiece (20 cents).

Stockings of any sort are just plain luxury. Here you see many girls going around bare-legged, suffering from windburn.

Tomorrow I believe I'll go to an A.T.S. (similar to our W.A.C.S.) dance. Everything here continues to be the closest thing to perfect.

Love,

Don

Feb. 16, 1944

Dear Mom, Dad & Ethel,

I know Dad's birthday is March 10th, and I don't know if I'll get the opportunity to send him a card, but, nevertheless, do have a happy birthday, Pop. I've sent you a little souvenir from England, and I hope you can make use of it. It will probably arrive around the 25th of March.

I chopped a bit of wood today, and it feels good to do some physical work. I still insist that country folk got city people beat when it comes to living.

Feeling swell.

Love,

Don

Feb. 17, 1944

Dear Mom, Dad & Ethel,

Tonight I am going to an R.A.F. show. There is a good friendship being built up between British boys and girls and ourselves. Social activities, such as the one this evening, tend to bring us closer to one another and add another link onto the ever-growing chain of friendliness.

The proximity of their camp to ours, plus our lack of facilities—since we are living in tents—make it very important that we remain on excellent terms with them. Things have now reached such a closeness that their weekly functions are posted on our bulletin board.

Feeling great.

Love,

Don

Feb. 24, 1944

Dear Mom, Dad & Ethel,

We were shorthanded on K.P.'s this week, and our bunch drew cards to see who the unfortunates would be. I was one of the luckless soldiers, and thus my occupation for the day was mainly cleaning pots and pans.

Last night I went to the cinema (movies). I went as early as possible (7 p.m.), but already a short line had gathered. However, nobody ahead of me wanted to take a 50-cent seat, so I took it and gained admittance in short order. I guess money makes a difference. The other seats were 25 cents. You can well imagine what difficult financial condition these people are in when they are willing to wait in a long line for a savings of 25 cents.

It should be chow call very shortly, and you know my appetite is none too small. Feeling 100%.

Love,

Don

Feb. 27, 1944
Cpl. Joe Quix
Elkins, West Virginia

Dear Joe,

Was in London over the weekend and had a grand time. Saw "Madame Curie," which I enjoyed very much, and "Hostages." Had kosher meals at restaurants I found. They were excellent. Stayed at a hotel two nights, rode around in cabs and subway trains, ate in nice places, and just did anything to suit my fancy.

Almost got stranded coming back last night. Was on my way home when I changed trains and found that the next train to our camp was at 5 a.m. I started walking a distance of 10 miles, but a cab fortunately came along.

Staying in tonight, but tomorrow will spend the evening with a British lass.

Best Wishes,

Don

March 4, 1944

Dear Mom, Dad & Ethel,

Your package just arrived, and the candy was a complete surprise. The fact that the candy came from Addie Vallins brought back many pleasant memories, for, as you know, it is located next door to Book Art, where I used to work. It's too bad you can't send malted milks through the mail.

Today we had something for breakfast that we haven't seen since arriving in England. We had sunny side eggs, the kind hens lay. The kind you have to crack open.

The subscription to the Reader's Digest came through, and I certainly am glad that I requested that magazine. It makes the rounds here, and everybody enjoys it.

We had a special treat, Southern fried chicken, but, unfortunately, our regular cook is on leave. The chicken was a little tough, and it tends to prove that the cook's role is just as important as the food itself. It was a little disappointing that they had to mess up a meal that generally is very satisfying. Now I finally found out why they call it a <u>mess</u> hall.

We were awaiting an officer on an inspection team, but he failed to show up.

We had a British soldier visiting today. I showed him a Sunday edition of The New York Times. He said, "I've seen thick newspapers before, but never in my wildest imagination dreamed of a paper of such a size."

I'm in excellent shape, and everything continues to be rosy red, but I do wish the regular cook comes back soon.

Love,

Don

Addie Vallins was a superb candy shop in the Bronx on 161ˢᵗ Street near Gerard Avenue, a ball's throw from Yankee Stadium. Their homemade ice cream and candy were extra special. So were their malted milks and ice cream sodas. Patrons could choose from a variety of delicious, fanciful whipped cream designs. All had the artistic touch of a master chef.

Book Art, Inc. was a book, card, and record store of excellent reputation. I had worked there when I was seventeen, a year after my graduation from Clinton High School. I was graduated early because I had been placed in a rapid advance class in the ninth grade. Soon I regretted being out in the working world at such a tender age. My salary was a modest fifteen dollars a week. For a year, I dutifully opened and closed the store every day, waited on customers, and rang up sales. But when my bosses decided to reward me with a "generous" one-dollar raise, I knew it was time to quit.

Still, my memories of the store were pleasant. My eyes almost popped out of their sockets when I was asked to wait on Myrna Loy, and there were plenty of laughs. I was practically rolling on the floor when a partner named Rick chased a couple of adolescent boys off the premises. After ogling a buxom young woman, one of the teens had unfortunately remarked, "Wow, I'd sure like to get hold of a pair of those!" The woman was Rick's wife.

Though understandable in this instance, such a display of temper was very unusual for Rick. His behavior was generally much more subtle. With a wicked sense of humor and a keen appreciation for the nuances of language, he was perpetually bemused by the human condition. Rick particularly enjoyed demonstrating how most people are poor listeners. I observed one of these demonstrations when Mrs. O'Hara visited the store.

Mrs. O'Hara, a portly, middle-aged redhead with a cherubic face, was a long-time patron of Book Art. She was always buying cookbooks. This time, she had more than food on her mind. Her mother had been ill for some time, and she began to prattle on about the lurid details.

Standing at the counter with his hand resting on his chin, Rick patiently listened for several minutes. Then he nonchalantly remarked, "Well, I hope it's nothing trivial."

"Oh, no, not at all," replied Mrs. O'Hara in her perky Irish brogue. "But thank you for your concern."

Then there was Nora Anderson, a statuesque honey-blonde. She was four years older than I and a part-time stock clerk at the store. Four years is a large age difference at that point in life, but, looking back, I know she had a big crush on me. Nora would always wait until I closed up so I could walk her home. I enjoyed her company, but, at the time, had no idea that her intentions were romantic.

What I remember most about Book Art is the peaceful solitude of the tall, hickory-colored stacks and the quiet friendliness of the customers. The lighting was bright enough for reading, yet still subdued. There was something reassuring, almost protective, about the store. It had the ambience of a school library, but was much homier.

Now I had to worry about shots. For the moment, they weren't the ones fired from a gun. They were those that come at the point of a needle.

Mar. 8, 1944

Dear Mom, Dad & Ethel,

Early this week, a medic paid us a visit to give us some injections. Attached to our pay book is our shot record. I looked for my pay book, but my search was futile. I envisioned the delightful thought of having to retake all my shots if my book could not be found. Today, just before going on duty, I undertook an intensive searching program, carefully checking all my belongings, down to the last parcel of dust. This time, my work reaped a reward in the form of the misplaced pay book, which is once again in the possession of its owner. Believe me, I am a much happier man this evening.

In perfect health.

Love,

Don

Mar. 14, 1944

Dear Mom, Dad & Ethel,

Today I received a letter from Joe in which he states he's fine and glad to be living under more civilized conditions for a change.

Sawed a bit of wood this morning, and now we have nothing left to saw. Supply is very low, and I do hope they send a truck out to replace this stack.

Yesterday I got a shot in the arm again, and I am up to date, for which I am thankful indeed. Our little home here is still the best we could hope for.

Love,

Don

Mar. 15, 1944

Dear Mom, Dad & Ethel,

I know it's hard to believe what a sweetheart of a deal we have right now. Most G.I.'s would be envious if they knew of our unusual setup.

This morning, while still in bed, we were debating whether to get up for chow or not. Finally, out of our midst came forth a pioneer who ventured to brave the cold morning.

We were still unwilling to follow his courageous example until a few minutes later—when he returned with two sunny side eggs and bacon visible in his mess kit. We jumped up and raced for the mess tent. Then we made toast on our potbelly stove and thus had, as the English would say, "a smashing breakfast."

There is a radio in an officer's tent on our site, and this morning we hooked up wires from his tent to ours, and being in possession of headsets, we merely don them on our heads and listen to the radio as if we had one in our tent. There was a British all-star program on this noontime, and I heard part of it, and this radio deal has sliced about 1,000 miles off our distance from home.

This Saturday evening we are throwing a party and dance for the R.A.F. in appreciation of the facilities they have placed before us on their premises. We've ordered beer, hired an orchestra, and really should have a grand time.

Love,

Don

Mar. 17, 1944

Dear Mom, Dad & Ethel,

Received a letter from you this evening. It is the first one in quite some time, and I am glad that everything is okay.

I've got a pass and don't have to be back until midnight tomorrow. I've already taken my room in town, and, consequently, am all set. Tonight I'll go to the dance at the hotel. They have a nice floor there, but occasionally the place gets too crowded. Tomorrow I'll go into another town and probably see a film or two. In the evening, we've got that program at the R.A.F. hall.

My buddy Ben finished this letter as follows:

Don has just run off to make the Liberty truck that goes into town every evening. Since he was good enough to act as my secretary a few days back, I'm finishing this letter for him. Don has a date with a very cute blonde. (I bet he would never tell you that!) He's become one of the gay-

est Lothario's we have in camp. I've just been called. So my temporary position as secretary must end now.

Love,

Don (per Ben)

Mar. 27, 1944

Dear Mom, Dad & Ethel,

For some reason, our present tent seems to be larger than the one we previously stayed in. Am with the same group of guys, and it doesn't look like they'll ever split us up unless something unforseen occurs.

The grounds here are much nicer than in our previous location. Green grass about an inch high serves as a colorful carpet. Everything is laid out nicer, and we seem to have a great deal more room.

The chow is very good, and we all notice in particular how spotless everything is here. They are a good deal stricter here, but when it pays dividends in neat and tidy mess halls, and latrines which are spic-and-span, we are more than willing to cooperate.

Our guns were a bit dirty and were in dire need of oiling. Having a little time today, I oiled several guns.

They have a bit of athletic equipment. I've noticed baseballs, footballs, bats, and gloves. Morning chow starts about 7 a.m. Nightlife is minimized here. We had a little too much of it at our last place.

The big, disappointing blow this week was that my furlough was canceled. Furloughs are not recognized here, and mine was supposed to start tomorrow. I had written Wally and Seymour and told them I would try to see them, but that is temporarily out of the question. Perhaps when I get a 48-hour pass, I'll try to look them up.

So far, the coal situation here is good. We've got enough for our needs, and, therefore, the tent is nice and warm.

We tried to bring the dog from our last location with us, but after we lured him into one of our trucks, someone spotted him, and we were compelled to release him.

I'll say good night now, until tomorrow.

Love,

Don

Mar. 28, 1944

Dear Mom, Dad & Ethel,

The biggest news today is that our A.P.O. number has been changed. Our new number is 895.

The past two evenings, we haven't received "Stars and Stripes," which is the daily army newspaper. There also appears to be a shortage of "V" Mail the past two evenings, and it has been necessary to do a wee bit of chiseling in order to get more than one sheet.

A lot of fellows are complaining that the British aren't too enthusiastic about giving us lifts along the highways. It brings to mind an incident that occurred about a week ago at our former camp.

I missed our return truck that night, and, along with another fellow, was trudging about 4 miles back to camp. An American jeep came along the road, and I blinked my flashlight intermittently. The jeep came to a halt. In the back of the jeep was a captain, and he looked us over. When he saw we weren't from his outfit, he ordered his driver to resume driving. We stood there dumbfounded.

That's how it goes sometimes. Can't win them all.

Love,

Don

Apr. 4, 1944

Dear Mom, Dad & Ethel,

The crossword puzzles you sent are certainly enjoyed. All the fellows are getting a kick out of them. I left the book around the other day, and when

I came back, I found about four fellows delightfully at work with them. So send me some more puzzles if you can.

I heard that my cousin Claire was having a baby soon. I must say that we all seem to be growing up mighty fast.

I'm in good shape, and I don't regret having enlisted.

Love,

Don

Apr. 7, 1944

Dear Ethel,

Just the other day, I mentioned you in my letter and was wondering why I hadn't heard from you in some time. Since you were wrapped up by the unexpected visit of a soldier on furlough, you are justly excused.

Pertaining to your fear that I might get serious with an English girl, you have no cause to worry. My night life has been cut down considerably, partly due to a slimmed opportunity to get out, and partly due to my own lack of enthusiasm. Ethel, when we go out here, we merely do so for a sort of diversion or escape from camp routine. Personally, I'd rather chat with the fellows than spend the evening with an unappreciative, cheaply-perfumed female.

Love,

Don

Apr. 14, 1944

Dear Mom, Dad & Ethel,

For several days I was out on detached service with a small group. No officer was with us, thank God.

But there was a drawback in that we couldn't get any mail censored. Therefore, our letters couldn't be mailed. We did a bit of cooking in our tent recently, and some veterans of outdoor life were able to give us a few pointers.

I am now back at base once again, and things are per usual. Feeling fine.

Love,

Don

Apr. 26, 1944

Dear Mom, Dad & Ethel,

Instead of the usual calisthenics program, three fellows and myself volunteered to do some running on a long distance scale. We all figured quite correctly that we can benefit more from these runs than from the routine exercises that we do daily.

Last night I went to town and saw a film. The lineup in the theater was comparatively small, and this was a break because we sweat out enough chow lines and P.X. lines in camp.

After the show we went to the Red Cross, and, naturally, there was a good-sized line for sandwiches and soda. The line moved surprisingly rapidly, and soon we were seated at a table with our snacks. The favorite G.I. chant is: "When I get out of this man's army, I'm not going to wait in another goddamned line as long as I live."

Love,

Don

May 16, 1944

Dear Mom, Dad & Ethel,

I'm getting to be quite skillful at making coffee. I drink coffee much more frequently here than at home because there is no milk available.

The other day I increased my allotment to you to $40 per month. It will start two paydays from now.

Everything here is pretty much the same, and the papers are being read with tremendous interest these days.

Hope you are all well, and say hello to our Southern relatives for me.

Love,

Don

May 19, 1944

Dear Dad,

Received your letter and sure am happy that Mother and Ethel are actually taking the trip south. It will be a good reunion for all. I guess the house will be pretty lonesome now.

The good news about the fall of Cassino was reported today. It brings us that much further towards victory.

In good shape.

Love,

Don

There were rumors of an Allied invasion of the European continent. I was concerned.

So far, I had lucked out. I pulled a generally uneventful eight-hour radio shift, and the dangers I faced paled in comparison with those experienced by infantry and artillery men.

My lifestyle was quite healthy. Living outdoors in a tent, I got plenty of fresh air. At this point, I was in the best shape of my life. Overall, the food was fair: sometimes good, sometimes miserable, but nearly always edible.

Still, air raids were frequent. By now, the sights and sounds were routine: wailing sirens, glaring searchlights, and massive pounding of antiaircraft fire. No bombs had come close to hitting any of the sites I occupied. At least until now.

CHAPTER 7

▼

NORMANDY

General Dwight D. Eisenhower kicked nervously at the cigarette butts on the ground outside his modest trailer.[119] He preferred the woods near Portsmouth, England (36) to the more comfortable lodgings of Naval Headquarters, just two miles away at Southwick House, because he wanted to be closer to his men (50-1).

Eisenhower commanded 3 million troops, 1.7 million of which were American (51). Fondly known as "Ike," he was immensely popular among Allied soldiers. He had the uncanny ability to work well with commanders of the various nations comprising his forces,[120] including Britain, Ireland, Canada, Poland, Belgium, Czechoslovakia, and France (490). This was not the aging, heart-attack-prone, American President of half a generation later. At this time, General Eisenhower was a tall, fifty-three-year-old Midwesterner endowed with virile charm. Even the Germans admiringly described him as having "an athletic appearance, full health and strength, a well-formed head and jaw showing great will,...a man whom his countrymen would call a he-man (490)."

It was a windy, cloudy Sunday afternoon, and the treetops were swaying.[121] With his upper body tensed and both hands in his pockets, Eisenhower marched in tight circles while chain-smoking (59). The Supreme Allied Commander had been up most of the night but managed to catch a few winks around 8 a.m. (36). Now, on June 4, 1944 (36), he was faced with the most difficult decision of his career: the timing of the Normandy invasion.

The weather had been ideal in May (20), but June began inauspiciously. Conditions in the English Channel were "the worst in twenty years (50)."

On May 17, Eisenhower had decided to invade on either June 5, 6, or 7 (56-7). At that time, meteorological forecasts indicated that two of three required elements would exist during those days. The first was a late-rising moon, which would initially provide cover of darkness and then illuminate drop-off points for pre-"H" Hour advance teams. The second was a low tide to expose beach obstacles (57).

While Eisenhower had been planning the invasion, Hitler had been busy erecting an "Atlantic Wall" for the defense of the continental European coastline (25). Among the planted obstacles were shoulder-high, six-pronged, wrought iron "spiders."[122] Enormous explosive-tipped logs rose from the sand (361). These booby-traps were submerged just below the surface of the water to inflict maximum damage on landing craft (361). By now, the Germans had planted over five million mines.[123]

Eisenhower originally planned for June 5 but had delayed the invasion twenty-four hours because of the foul weather (36). Vessels in transit were turned around. Now, on June 4, he would have a 9:30 p.m. meeting with his staff at Southwick House to decide whether to postpone again (59-60). It was a tough call, and the decision was his sole responsibility (56). If the invasion failed, the war effort might be set back years (53).

With nearly five thousand ships and over two hundred thousand men, the Allies had created a navy of unprecedented power.[124] If Eisenhower postponed again, the extra time needed to refuel convoys might prevent an attack on June 7 (58). Then he could still attack on June 19, when there would be low tide but no moonlight (58). His other choice was to wait until July, an option he later described as "too bitter to contemplate (58)." He knew it was virtually impossible to keep two hundred thousand briefed soldiers quarantined for several weeks without devastating morale and losing the element of surprise (58).

With military punctuality, Eisenhower, in immaculate, green uniform, entered the library of Southwick House at precisely 9:30 p.m. (60). The large room had Spartan furnishings: a few chairs, two sofas, nearly empty bookcases, and a table covered with sturdy cloth (59). Present were Eisenhower's chief of staff, Major General Walter Bedell Smith; Deputy Supreme Commander, Air Chief Marshal Tedder; Allied naval commander, Admiral Ramsay; Allied air commander, Air Chief Marshal Leigh-Mallory; and British General Bernard L. Montgomery (59-60). They were ready to hear the latest forecasts of three senior meteorologists (60).

Meteorologist Group Captain J.N. Stagg of the Royal Air Force predicted a twenty-four-hour window of opportunity: a new front of improving weather would begin arriving within several hours and last until the morning of June 6 (60-1). Then the weather would worsen again (61). It was a "barely tolerable period of fair conditions, far below the minimal requirements (61)."

A brief discussion was followed by a long silence (62). With hands together and eyes firmly fixed on the table, Eisenhower decided to move on June 6. "I don't like it, but there it is," he said. "I don't see how we can do anything else (62)."

June 6, 1944

Dear Mom, Dad & Ethel,

This morning a few of the fellows heard the news about the beginning of the invasion, and, naturally, it is the topic of most interest right now. Everything here is hazy, and we don't have a radio.

Am sure glad that it finally got underway. There's no doubt that the sooner we start this grandiose hammering, the sooner it's going to be over with, and the sooner we'll be home. However, let's not be too hasty and jump to conclusions.

Love,

Don

The invasion plans called for dividing the Normandy beachhead into sectors code-named, from west to east, as follows: Utah, Omaha, Gold, Juno, and Sword.[125] While the Americans took Utah and Omaha, the British and Canadians would arrive at Gold, Juno, and Sword.[126]

Omaha, over six miles wide, was the largest assault area.[127] It was sub-divided, from west to east, into portions with the following code-names: Charlie, Dog Green, Dog White, Dog Red, Easy Green, Easy Red, Fox Green, and Fox Red.[128] Behind Omaha's western third was a ten-foot seawall and one-hundred-foot cliffs.[129] Here, heavily armed German soldiers manned concrete bunkers called "pillboxes."[130] These were communication nodes fortified with barbed wire.[131] Other defenses included blockhouses and machine gun nests.[132]

In the wee hours of the morning, advance teams began dropping from the moonlit skies over Normandy. The experience of the 82nd Airborne Division was typical.[133] Only one of its regiments, the 505th, landed accurately (135). The Division lost sixty percent of its equipment overnight, including most of its radios, mortars, and ammunition (135). Paratroopers came down miles from their targets (136). Many drowned in areas flooded by the Nazis (136).

June 6, 1944 dawned with an overcast pall. The initial assault wave began hitting the beaches at 6:30 a.m., D-Day's "H" Hour.[134] Opposition was relatively light on Utah, Gold, Juno, and Sword,[135] but the men who survived on the remaining sector would forever remember it as "Bloody Omaha."[136] Renowned war correspondent Ernie Pyle later wrote: "It seemed to me a pure miracle that we ever took the beach at all…our troops faced such odds that our getting ashore was like my whipping Joe Louis down to a pulp."[137]

The 29th Infantry Division's 116th Regiment and the 1st Infantry Division's 16th Regiment comprised the first wave of assault forces on Omaha.[138] Attached to these regiments were sixteen teams of the Army-Navy Special Engineer Task Force.[139] The Task Force had one of the most important and dangerous assignments of the invasion (42). Its mission was to blast through beach obstacles blocking exits leading inland (42). One-half hour was allotted for this objective (42).

The time frame was ludicrous. Delays in transferring men and materiel from LCT's (landing craft, tanks) to LCM's (landing craft, mechanized) caused half the teams to arrive on shore at least ten minutes late (42). Only five hit their designated area; tides carried the others eastward (42). At least three had no support from infantry or tanks (42).

A member of one of these teams called "Professor" was a dear friend of mine. I pieced his story together from what little he and those who worked with him told me months later, and library research after the war.

At 6:30 a.m., one of many LCM's crammed with soldiers was chugging toward the coast. Each capable of carrying a tank, LCM's provided shuttle service from larger transports to the beaches.[140] They also carried pre-loaded, rubber rafts for moving demolition equipment onto dry land.[141]

There was a thick silence among a group of engineers. Their weary faces showed little emotion, but turgid feelings within each man rivaled the choppiness of the cold Channel waters. Several licked their lips, irrigating mouths dry with speechless uncertainty.

Most were heavily loaded with oversized packs.[142] Bangalore torpedo men carried two bandoleers of M1 ammunition, a pistol, fuse lighters attached to their helmets, and bangalore torpedoes strapped to their backs.[143]

The LCM kept getting swamped from enormous waves created by the fourteen-inch guns of the battleship *Texas* pounding the cliffs on shore. Except for a short corporal and a tall master sergeant, everyone aboard was seasick. The two men stood together in a half-crouch near the bow.

"You ladies waiting for an invitation to the prom?" barked the master sergeant. "We've got four inches of water in here. Get off your asses and bail!"

Aroused from their listlessness, the murmuring engineers dropped their vomit bags and anxiously began scooping liquid with their helmets. The corporal, a bangalore torpedo man, was about to pitch in when the master sergeant stopped him.

"Wait a minute, Professor," he commanded. "I wanna talk to you."

"Yes, sir," dutifully replied the corporal. He always got a kick out of his superior's calling him Professor. The master sergeant had gone to college, while the corporal was only a high school graduate.

Master Sergeant Ronald "Butch" Robinson had the usual tough exterior of a man of his rank. Beneath the surface, however, lay a gentler side. Butch worked his engineers hard, but he also knew when to relax and insisted they do the same. Occasionally, he would schmooze with the Professor and other lower-ranking soldiers over a few beers.

The men felt honored whenever Butch drank with them. He never let anyone forget his stripes, but he had a way of treating people with respect—even when he was chewing them out. A dark-haired, thirty-year-old with bulging biceps, he had once been an all-American quarterback. He earned his sobriquet in college. When he joined the military, only master and first sergeants called him Butch: soldiers of inferior rank wouldn't dare, and officers did not know him well enough for such an informality. Six feet four inches tall and 240 pounds, Butch was never sacked during his football career. Nobody knew why he never earned his bachelor's degree. Master Sergeant Robinson was the strongest, smartest, fastest man the Professor had ever known.

"Have you ever been to hell?" Butch asked in an uncharacteristically hushed tone.

"Sarge?"

"Damn it, Corporal. Doesn't anything move you? We're going into a fucking shitstorm and all you can say is, 'Sarge?'"

"We're all scared, Sarge. I guess I'm just less expressive than most."

"Then you're okay, Professor?"

"Fine."

"Good. That's what I wanna hear. Listen. Things are gonna get pretty crazy out there. I want you as close to me as possible."

"Sure thing… Sarge?"

"What?"

"Why did you start calling me Professor?"

"Don't you like that nickname, Corporal?"

"I like it fine. I'm just curious about how you chose it."

"I chose it, Corporal, because you're the best fucking engineer I've ever had."

"Gee, I always thought it was because of my glasses."

Butch smiled wryly. "No, Professor. It wasn't because of your eyes. It was because of your mind. Look around you. Most of these guys are puking their fucking guts out. Right now, they wouldn't know the difference between a cabdriver and a stormtrooper. Sure, they're all good men, and they give their best. I wouldn't expect anything less. But you're one of the few guys I can really count on. Lord knows why you're still a corporal. I've recommended you for promotion three times."

"I never knew that, Sarge."

"Well, now you know."

"Thanks. That really means a lot to me."

Butch drew himself up to his full height. "Okay, that's enough bailing!" he bellowed. "Gather round, and listen up." The engineers surrounded the master sergeant in a close huddle.

His voice softened slightly. "Well, just about everything that needs to be said has been already. You guys are well-trained, but nothing can prepare you for what's out there. Expect the unexpected. Things have been tough, and they're gonna get tougher. I'm proud of each and every one of you. Good luck, and God be with you."

A bleary-eyed lieutenant approached him. "Good job, Robinson," he said. "You've really whipped these men into shape."

Butch stiffly saluted. His face was dotted with droplets of water and perspiration. Several of them aggregated and began streaming down his right cheek.

"Thank you, sir."

"You all right, Robinson?" asked the lieutenant.

"Just peachy, sir."

*   *   *   *

The Professor took his General Eisenhower message[144] out of his front jacket pocket. It was a one-page pep talk distributed to all Allied soldiers just before the invasion. Several of his buddies had signed it, and he had intended to keep it as a souvenir. But now the missive was waterlogged, tattered, and hopelessly illegible. He stared at it a few seconds before tossing it overboard.

Hell began about one hundred yards offshore. Unknown to the Allies, Germany's crack 352nd Infantry Division was defending Omaha.[145] Butch's team arrived a quarter-mile east of Dog Green. Men here and on Fox Green saw the most vicious machine gun fire of the invasion.[146]

The inaccurate landing was not unusual. Recall that only five out of the sixteen Task Force teams hit their appointed sector.[147] Some combat units came in two miles off course.[148]

An artillery shell blew off the landing ramp. Six men spilled into the water. Those wearing flotation belts turned upside down.[149] The lieutenant who had congratulated Butch was shot between the eyes. Two buck sergeants were hit in the chest and died instantly. One fell backward onto the Professor. A bullet severed the chin strap on the latter's helmet, which disappeared into the surf as he lurched forward. The last thing he heard before hitting the waves was Butch yelling, "Stay with me, Corporal!"

Burdened with two bangalores, the Professor quickly sank to the Channel bottom. He was ten feet underwater.[150] Many men drowned under the weight of overstuffed packs on that day.[151]

Under the best of conditions, the Professor was only a fair swimmer. His ordnance tangled around him.

Stay calm. You panic, you're dead.

He hastily pulled a utility knife from a holster around his calf and freed himself. To further lighten his load, he discarded his boots. His glasses, miraculously curled around his forearm, were undamaged. He wedged them between his belt and pants.

Even without spectacles, he could see the blurry outlines of submerged, motionless bodies. The Professor spied the bubbly wake of bullets churning through the surf, miniaturized torpedoes foretelling death. He wanted to close his eyes, but his survival instinct forced him to witness the horror.

He began struggling to the surface. During his ascent, he saw several men fatally shot. The cold, dark water had a reddish tinge.

Hitting air, he reflexively gasped. After treading for about thirty seconds, the Professor had caught enough of his breath to put on his glasses. Disoriented, he began swimming away from shore. Starting and stopping several times, he couldn't find the right direction. Finally, he saw the smoky beach. He was about seventy-five yards from the water's edge.

It was low tide. Exhausted but unhurt, the Professor reached one of the exposed obstacles. He found a captain by his side.

"What unit you from, son?" the officer asked. Before the Professor could open his mouth, the captain was shot dead.

Shit, they're targeting officers!

The Professor was right. For example, seven minutes after landing on Omaha, only one officer in the 116th Infantry's A Company was still alive (68). That man was Lieutenant Elijah Nance, who was hit in the heel and stomach before reaching sand (68). Within ten minutes, every A Company sergeant was either dead or wounded (68).

An LCI (landing craft, infantry) carrying Twenty-Ninth Division commanders took a direct hit coming ashore.[152] Exploding, it spewed flames 150 feet into the air.[153]

Frantically paddling toward the beach, the Professor soon became winded again. His uniform was monstrously heavy; every stroke was a major effort. He floated on his back for a while, occasionally blowing into his shirt to increase his buoyancy. But he didn't tie it off properly, and the trapped air lasted only a few seconds. Through trial and error, he discovered that a slow, steady sidestroke best conserved his energy.

Wheezing heavily, he collapsed onto the sand and vomited. It was 7:30 a.m. His hands and legs were twitching uncontrollably. A bullet grazed his left knuckle. Another nicked his buttocks.

"Jeez!"

In a supreme act of self-preservation, the diminutive corporal forced his body into submission. With the tide lapping at his bare feet, he lay still, hoping that German sharpshooters would mistake him for a corpse.

All along Omaha, the chaos of the wee hours was continuing into the morning. Only two out of twenty-nine amphibious DD Sherman tanks, outfitted with floatation screens, made it ashore.[154] The others sank.[155] Disabled tanks deposited by landing craft were burning.[156] When naval missiles fell short, they hit Allied troops.[157]

Walking one-and-a-half miles along Omaha the day after the invasion, Ernie Pyle would describe the peculiar wreckage strewn along the water, including partly submerged barges, overturned jeeps, battered typewriters, telephones, office files, toiletries, clothes, rations, a tennis racquet, and "mysterious oranges."[158]

Task Force team engineers fared no better. Much of their equipment was either lost or destroyed, including nearly all buoys and poles for marking lanes.[159] Seven of eight navy personnel in Team 11 were killed when an artillery shell set off explosives in their pre-loaded rubber raft (42). Another shell hit Team 14's LCM, detonating munitions on deck (42). Nobody survived (42). Team 15 was dragging its raft ashore when a mortar activated its explosives, killing three and wounding four (42). When Team 7 was ready to clear a path, a landing craft smashed into the obstacles and set off seven mines, preventing the charge from being blown (43).

Explosives experts coming in at unexpected places worked wherever they landed (42-3). Late-arriving infantry moved through the demolition units, complicating their efforts (43). Combat soldiers frequently took cover behind obstacles, further delaying teams trying to blow them (43).

Machine gun fire raked the beach. Artillery shells pockmarked the coastline, flinging beige mounds into the air. The smell of explosives mingled with the stench of the dead and dying. Bodies littered the area.

An athletic soldier tried sprinting 150 yards[160] to the seawall and was quickly cut down. Fifty feet from the Professor, a private was screaming for his mother. His legs had been blown off above the knees, and he was clutching a mass of blue intestines below his chest. A mortar mercifully silenced him.

The corporal thought he was going mad. Then he had it out with himself.

Fuck it. If I die, I die, and that's it.

For several minutes, he watched the motionless figures washing up and back with the water. Men were making it up shore, but how?

His mind clearing, the Professor noticed that not all the soldiers lying at the shoreline were dead. Nostrils pointed upward, they moved with the surf, progressing inland with the tide.[161] Following their example, he spent two tense hours this way. Then he found he could move about a foot a minute without being noticed. Or so he thought. Slowly, almost imperceptibly, he turned onto his belly. Then he heard a loud crack. A shower of wood rained down upon him, and everything went dark.

When he regained consciousness, the Professor found himself pinned by an enormous log. He tried squirming his way out, but it was no use. There was one plus: a momentary lull in the action. A familiar voice barked at him.

"You all right, Professor?"

He looked up and saw Butch solicitously peering down at him. The master sergeant's shirt was ripped open, exposing his massive, heaving chest. He clutched a bangalore in his right arm.

"Forget about me, Sarge. I'm as good as dead."

"Cut the crap, Corporal. I'm not gonna stand for any of that defeatist bullshit. You'll live as long as I need you. I'm gonna get you out of here."

"That log's gotta weigh a ton. There's no way in hell you're gonna move it."

"I'm not giving up on you, Corporal, so don't give up on me. When I say, 'Go,' you go. Got it?"

"But—"

"Got it?"

"Yeah."

"I can't hear you, Corporal."

"Got it, Sergeant!"

"Now that's what I wanna hear."

Butch dropped his bangalore. Squatting, he grasped the huge slab pinning the corporal's legs. With a sudden exertion, he pushed upward on the log. The veins in his temples began throbbing, and the wood laboriously groaned. Two inches of space appeared above the Professor's thighs, followed by a primal scream: "Go!"

The small man joyfully clawed his way out from under the massive timber. Butch released his grasp, and the log slumped back onto the sand.

The Professor stamped his blood-stained feet. He had only minor cuts below the waist, but there was a wild look on his face. Gleefully jumping up and down several times, he shouted, "You did it, Sarge. You're fucking Samson!"

Butch pulled him to the ground and slapped him sharply. "Get hold of yourself, Corporal. I didn't get you out of there so you could go batty on me."

An expressionless sanity returned to the Professor's face. "Sorry, Sarge. It won't happen again."

"You all right now?"

"I can travel."

"Then let's get moving."

Butch picked up his bangalore, and the Professor swiped a helmet off a dead man. Running in a crouch through a deafening gauntlet of artillery shells and small arms fire, they reached the seawall.

They recognized five enlisted men from their team propped against the lumpy boulders.[162] Three were heavily bandaged. A dejected PFC had a sprained wrist. Butch approached a shivering staff sergeant who appeared unhurt.

"Santiago, what's happening here?"

No response.

"Santiago!"

Butch shook him by the lapels. Santiago slumped forward, exposing a bloody back. He had been hit by a shell and was dying fast.

PFC Rollins piped up. "The medic said it was a waste of time to work on him, Sarge. We've been pinned down here for hours." He forlornly held up a lone blanket. "We lost most of our equipment when our raft capsized."

Butch plucked the blanket from Rollins. Cradling the dying man in his arms, the master sergeant wrapped and gently laid him against the seawall. Then he removed Santiago's boots and flung them at the Professor.

"Put these on. You're no use to me barefoot."

Master Sergeant Robinson menacingly turned toward the PFC. "Rollins, I didn't have the luxury of coming in on a raft. I was too busy swimming with a goddamned bangalore torpedo! What the fuck's wrong with you? You've got a sprained wrist, and you couldn't spare a blanket for a dying man? Don't you think he's got a right to some comfort and dignity?"

"Yes, Sergeant," Rollins sheepishly replied.

"I want you to take an inventory of everything we have. Now."

There wasn't much: a few small tools, some pocket knives, several inoperative pistols, and a bangalore torpedo.

Butch slapped his thigh in disgust. "Shit. We can't even defend ourselves. Professor!"

"Right here, Sarge."

"You and Rollins go scout for more stuff. And for Chrissake, stay close to the seawall."

Butch pulled a small waterproof pouch out of his hip pocket. Inside was a map. While the master sergeant tried to figure out where he was, the other two able-bodied engineers began a dangerous scavenging operation. Their eyes smarting from noxious fumes, they trotted along the seawall, looking for corpses bearing serviceable equipment.

The area's lofty, steep rock formations provided ample advantage for the Germans. Under heavy fire, Rollins and the Professor didn't get very far. They returned with a meager stock: a loaded M1 rifle, a few extra cartridges, two grenades, and a canteen.

Butch pursed his lips in frustration. "That's it?"

The two men nodded affirmatively.

"Well, it'll have to do. Professor!"

"Yes, Sarge."

"Give those three wounded men a sip of water."

"What about us?" asked Rollins.

"Us can wait."

Just then, a barrage of bullets raked the seawall. The able-bodied soldiers flattened to the ground. Butch picked up the rifle and fired three angry shots up the slopes.

"Damn it. It's like pea soup out here. Can't see a fucking thing. But don't worry, we'll accomplish our mission."

"Mission!" snapped Rollins. "With all due respect, Sergeant, the mission's fucked. We don't know where we are. We've got almost no supplies, and most of our team's either dead, wounded, or missing."

The master sergeant viciously peered down at him. "I'll deal with you in a minute."

Butch crawled over to the three wounded men. "You guys'll have to wait to be evacuated. The rest of us will be leaving soon. I wish I could do more for you fellas. Good luck."

"Thanks, Sarge," replied a man with puss oozing from red bandages. The others, unable to speak, nodded in agreement.

The master sergeant motioned Rollins and the Professor out of earshot of the three incapacitated soldiers. "Rollins, I'm gonna let you in on a little secret. I don't know about any evacuation. As far as I'm concerned, those three men over there are dead. If you wanna join 'em, that's fine.

"You might have noticed, PFC, that staying alive here is a job in itself. Well, we're working overtime. If you come with us, you pitch in and quit whining. Otherwise, I'll have your ass court-martialed for insubordination. That is, if you make it out of here. Got it?"

"Got it."

"I didn't hear you, PFC."

"Got it, Sergeant!"

"Good. Listen up. Both of you. I think we're near an exit. I'm gonna have a look."

Butch made several attempts to breach the seawall, but, each time, had to retreat from enemy fire. "It's no good here. Let's move west."

They were about to depart when a bizarre scene caught their eyes. Fifty feet from the seawall, amidst throngs of frenetic soldiers, an infantryman was aimlessly walking up and down the beach. He would take twenty paces or so, and then reverse direction. Perfectly calm, he stopped to light a cigarette.[163]

"Hey, jerk-o! Hey, dumb-o!" yelled Butch. "Get down."

The master sergeant began crawling toward the wayward soldier. He was going to tackle him, but before he could get close enough, the infantryman was cut down. Butch grabbed the dead man's pack and rifle. The hail of bullets and bombs continued.

When he reached the seawall, he flung down the pack and rubbed his eyes. "Dumb asshole got himself killed."

He threw the Professor the dead man's rifle. The corporal rummaged through the infantryman's belongings. "There's nothing we can use."

"Then let's get the hell outta here," barked the master sergeant.

"Where are we going, Sarge?" asked Rollins. "We can't even get over the seawall."

"Well, we can't stay here. We've gotta keep moving and look for an opening."

Just then, ten well-armed men came into view. A tall, lanky fellow leading the group suddenly dropped to his knees. He aimed his rifle and fired.

An odd silence was broken by a loud scream. A German soldier began tumbling down the jagged, precipitous decline. Rolling with increasing speed, he bounced into the air several times before lifelessly thudding onto the beach. A machine gun nest had been temporarily knocked out.

The group's leader was a baby-faced PFC. None of the others—all privates—looked more than twenty years old.

"That's some mighty fancy shooting, soldier," Butch complimented. "Who are you guys with?"

"Fifth Ranger Battalion,[164] Sergeant. We had a pretty rough landing and got separated from our unit. Right now, we're just looking for a way off the beach."

"Just so happens, we've got the same idea. What's your name, son?"

"Dave Austin. My friends call me Tex."

"How old are you, Tex?"

"Eighteen."

"Good. We can use some young blood around here."

The two men shook hands. The others exchanged quick pleasantries.

"Any bomb guys in your group, Tex?"

"We're not explosives experts, but we have enough training to get the job done."

"Good. Right now I just need your marksmanship. With shooting like that, you can play on my team anytime. We'll hold the rest of your skills in reserve. Tex, you're with me and the Professor." Butch addressed the rest of the rangers.

"We're going over the seawall to look for an exit outta here. We'll blow what we can with this bangalore. The rest of you will hold your position."

"Request permission to accompany," interjected Rollins.

"Request denied. If we don't survive, you'll be the only demo man who can make another attempt. Okay, let's move."

The three men began clambering up the ten-foot seawall. Master Sergeant Robinson, bangalore in tow, was in the lead. He was followed by the Professor, with Tex covering the rear.

After a brief search, they found an unmanned exit. The trio walked slightly uphill for about thirty yards before being stopped by a mesh of concertina wire. While Tex covered them from a respectful distance, Butch and the Professor began assembling the bangalore.

The standard M1A1 bangalore torpedo was five feet long after assembly of two interconnected steel tubes.[165] It was filled with nine pounds of amatol and had four inches of TNT at each end.[166] Amatol, a mixture of ammonium nitrate and TNT, provided more complete combustion and less smoke than pure TNT.[167] Each end of the torpedo contained a fuse well, which could accommodate a primacord attached to a firing device.[168] A primacord was a lead tube with a core of PETN,[169] one of the most powerful high explosives of the day.[170] The firing device attached to the primacord on this bangalore was of the "pull" type, which was activated by removing two safety pins and tugging on a wire.[171]

"You guys finished yet?" shouted an apprehensive Tex. While Butch and the Professor were assembling the bangalore, the PFC had been trading increasingly nasty fire with an enemy that he couldn't see. The Germans were well-hidden in their lairs, and their visibility was further obscured by smoke from shells bursting nearby.

"I'm running low on ammo, Sarge!"

"Okay, Tex, we're done!" bellowed Butch.

The master sergeant and the corporal pushed the assembled torpedo under the wire. Butch removed the safety pins and raised his right hand. "You guys know the drill. It's a five-second fuse. When I say 'three,' you take off."

Immediately after the two men nodded affirmatively, Butch pulled the wire and shouted, "Three!" He was the first one over the seawall, followed closely by Tex, and, an instant later, by a struggling Professor. The five seconds had passed. Nothing.

"Damn it, can't anything work right today?" remarked an angry Butch. "Come on, Tex. We're going back to see what's wrong."

"That's crazy, Sarge," protested the Professor. "We barely got out of there alive. If that bangalore doesn't get you, the sniper fire will."

"I've got no time to argue with you, Professor. We started something, and I'm gonna finish it. And if I don't, you will. Got it?"

"Loud and clear, Sarge."

Throughout this conversation, the rest of the rangers were engaged in a fierce firefight. Two privates were hit. Butch and Tex dragged them to relative safety.

"Hold down the fort, Professor."

Butch and Tex disappeared over the seawall. With Tex covering him, the master sergeant raced to the bangalore. Just as he was approaching the torpedo, enemy fire severed the primacord.

Butch was going to order Tex to shoot the bangalore in an attempt to detonate it, but they were too close, and the gunfire was too heavy. "Let's get the fuck outta here, PFC." The two men quickly returned to the beach.

"What happened?" asked an agitated Professor.

"Nothing."

"Then what are we gonna do, Sarge?"

"You all right, Professor?" Butch asked.

"I'm fine. Why?"

"Because you're breathing harder than my asthmatic grandmother."

"I'm okay."

"Take a break, you look like hell."

"But—"

"Just get away from me and sit down. I'll call you if I need you."

Slithering several yards along the seawall, the exhausted corporal slumped to the ground. A deafening sound followed. The Professor had the odd sensation of being hit in the eye with a bowling ball.

He was knocked horizontal. Stunned, he lay silent for several minutes. His head was throbbing, and his right eye began swelling.

Rallying, the Professor slowly raised himself to a sitting position. His left lens was broken, and his right arm felt stiff. He noticed it was trickling blood. Just then, his left hand brushed against something round and hairy. It was Butch's severed head.

Reflexively recoiling, he tried to scream, but nothing came out. He struggled to get hold of himself.

Up until this moment, he had thought of the dead as nameless bodies. Now his commander, savior, and friend was gone. In an instant, this mid-twentieth-century Jean Valjean[172] had been blown apart. The war had suddenly become intensely personal.

Why him and not me?

"Where is everyone? Tex! Rollins! What's happening?"

The Professor felt a gentle hand on his shoulder. It was Tex.

"We've got three heavily wounded, two lightly wounded—and, as you know, one dead." Tex somberly paused. "I'm sorry about the master sergeant, Corporal. Want me to patch your arm?"

"You a medic, Tex?"

"No, but we've got a first aid kit, and I'm pretty good with bandages."

The Professor struggled to his feet. "Well, don't waste your talent on me. Use it on fellas that really need it. I've only got a flesh wound."

"We've already taken care of the others. Any orders, Corp?"

"Where's the rest of our ammo?"

"Over there." Tex pointed to Butch's headless corpse.

The Professor peered down at the two scavenged grenades sitting atop a rucksack. Slightly moist, they glistened under a half-sun.

"We're really fucked," croaked Rollins. "Fucked and trapped."

The Professor glared at him. "Tex."

"Yep."

"If Rollins opens his mouth again, shoot him."

A murmur of protests arose among the men.

"That's right!" shouted the Professor. "I'm in command now. So everyone shut the fuck up, and let me think."

Less than two hundred yards away, infantrymen were making progress up the slopes. Some were picked off, but others, finding cover in rocky folds and crags, steadily advanced.[173] A quarter-mile further off, troops outfitted with climbing ropes scaled Omaha's cliffs. Many had their lines cut and tumbled to their deaths. But the tide had turned against the Germans, and successful climbers began penetrating their defenses. Amidst sparse houses and coarse hedges, startled peasants began greeting their liberators, plaintively shouting: *"Ah, mon Dieu, ne nous quittez pas maintenant* [My God, don't leave us now]!"[174]

The Professor's small group knew nothing of these developments. They were among the numerous victims of battlefield "isolation," units typically unaware of nearby goings on.[175]

A few tense moments passed. Then the Professor got an idea.

"Tex, how's your arm?"

"I played a little minor league ball before I got drafted."

"Excellent. What was your position?"

"Left field."

"Well, Tex, today's your lucky day."

"Huh?"

"You're gonna use that fine arm of yours to throw one of those grenades and set off that bangalore."

"At this distance? Over that seawall, and with this smoke? You've gotta be kidding. That's a one in a million shot."

"You've got another for insurance. Which would you rather have, Tex? Certain death, or two in a million chances of getting off this beach alive? Look. We're in shallow left. It's the bottom of the ninth and two out. We're ahead 2-1, but the other team's got the bases loaded. Throw the ball home."

Tex pulled the pin on a grenade and heaved it over the seawall. Silence.

"Shit, it's a dud," he surmised.

"PFC, you're a bangalore torpedo man now. Know what a bangalore man does when he can't blow an obstacle?"

"I don't remember, Corp."

"Then let me remind you. He sacrifices his body on the wire and lets everyone else step over him."[176]

"Well, in that case, I guess I'll just have to blow it."

"Now that's what I wanna hear."

With a mighty grunt, Tex flung the second grenade over the seawall. A small bang was followed by a larger, concussing boom. The obstacle had been blown. A cheer went up among the men.

Rollins looked toward the water and smiled. "That's the most beautiful sight I've seen all day."

A destroyer had moved into position on the horizon and began blasting away at the slopes. The machine gun nest was demolished.

"Hey, we've got an exit open here," yelled one of the privates. The news quickly spread. Columns of men began streaming over the seawall.

A lone figure with an authoritative gait approached Tex and the Professor. It was Brigadier General Norman D. Cota, Assistant Division Commander of the Twenty-Ninth Infantry. Cota figures prominently in D-Day history. Fearlessly striding up and down the shoreline, he had spent most of the day exhorting his men to action.[177]

"Fine job, boys. I'll personally see to it that you both get promotions."

"Thank you, General," replied the corporal. "But begging the general's pardon, sir, I have a request."

"What is it, son?"

With two movements of his good arm, the Professor gestured toward the dead master sergeant. "We couldn't have done it without him. Can you make sure he gets a decent burial?"

"You bet."

Tears welled up in the Professor's eyes. His lips momentarily quivered, and then stiffened. He paused, took one last look at his shattered icon, and said, "Goodbye, Butch."

Tex and the Professor joined the crowd. The upward path was steep, but blissful compared with what they had already endured. It was now 2:30 p.m. Most of the survivors had been on the beach for over seven hours.

Later that afternoon, the Professor collapsed. Suffering from a concussion and exhaustion, he spent the next few days in a makeshift hospital before returning to duty.

Overall, the demolition Task Force had blown six complete gaps and three partial gaps through all obstacles.[178] Two were in the 116th Infantry's sectors, and four were on Easy Red (43). The Task Force suffered forty-one percent casualties that day, most inflicted in the first half-hour of the invasion (43).

Fighting around the Normandy area would continue for several weeks, but the Allies had a toehold they would never relinquish.[179] It was the beginning of the end of the Third Reich.

✳   ✳   ✳   ✳

At 4:30 a.m. the next day, June 7, an LST (landing ship, tank) was approaching Omaha near the town of Grandcamp.[180] LST's were among the most versatile vessels of the war.[181] Their spaciousness had many uses: floating hospitals, barracks, machine shops, and small landing craft transports.[182] This one was overloaded with about four hundred infantry and radio men, including myself and Jack Spring.

I was among the restless men milling around on deck during the wee hours. Few could sleep, but many stayed below, nervously awaiting the dawn of a busy day. However, having previously battled seasickness, I wanted fresh air.

Who knows? Maybe I'll get to see some action.

Standing amidships along the railing, I dreamily stared out into the void. A loud explosion shattered the silence. Mild shock waves reverberated throughout the craft. I looked over my shoulder and saw a flaming yellow cloud illuminating the Channel. A troop transport had struck a mine half a mile aft of starboard.[183]

Looking on in awe and fear, I witnessed the secondary explosions, followed by plumes of dark smoke.

By now, nearly everyone had clambered onto the deck, straining to get a look at what was going on. Powerless to help, we mournfully watched the transport turn upward and slowly descend to a watery grave.

I approached a crewman. "Hey, pal, how many men do you think were on that ship?"

"Can't say for sure, Corp. She looked like a Liberty. Those babies are supposed to hold five hundred men, but the way they've been packing 'em in lately, she probably had more like twelve hundred."

"Think any of 'em made it?"

The crewman put his chin on his chest and shook his head negatively.

"Holy Jeez."

"Amen to that, brother."

I made my way aft. Stooping along the railing, I put my head on my folded hands. Before I could get comfortable, a much larger force rocked the boat. Another Liberty ship had struck a mine—only a hundred yards away (5).

Jostled from this vulnerable perch, I lurched forward, but my motion abruptly stopped. Someone had grabbed me from behind. It was Jack Spring.

"You've seen enough naval battles for one night, Donnybrook. Let's get the fuck below before we both get toasted."

I barely heard him. I was a deer in headlights, transfixed at the sight of the blazing vessel. It seemed near enough to touch (5). Finger-like projections of light and gunfire dotted the sky (5). After much cajoling, Jack was finally able to pull me away. We climbed down into the hold.

Meanwhile, on the bridge, Captain Mortimer B. Jones was having a spirited discussion with Captain Steven Frye. Jones, the 888th Fighter Control Squadron's assistant commander, had been an undistinguished flyer during World War I. Frye, the LST's skipper, was a career naval officer. Friendly rivals, both were wiry, greying men in their fifties. I have reconstructed their conversation from a written history of my outfit and informal discussions I later had with higher-ranking sergeants in the 888th who were close to Captain Jones.

"Come on, Morty! You know I can't turn this boat around any more than I can stop it for a man gone overboard."

"Well, we've gotta do something, Steve. You saw those two ships go up. Thousands of casualties and we're not even at the drop-off point. My men are lightly armed technicians, not combat troops. If they go in now, they'll be slaughtered."

"Try telling that to the heavily armed men who went in yesterday. Or the families of those who died. They didn't get any special treatment, and, frankly, I don't see why your people should, either. Yes, you may take some casualties. You might even lose some men. That's war.

"Look, Morty, we've both been through this before. You know as well as I do that sooner or later, every commander has to take risks. You might think this is a dumb one, but I've got a schedule to keep. Besides, Intelligence says Omaha's quiet now."

"I don't give a crap what Intelligence says," barked Jones. "Intelligence didn't say we'd lose transports, and look what just happened. There's so much gobble-degook coming out of there, it's enough to make anyone crazy. I'm not gonna trust my men's lives to a bunch of smart-assed punks who couldn't tell the difference between an artillery shell and a hand grenade."

Frye's face lit up with a mischievous smirk. "You know, Mort, I think you've gotten a little too comfortable behind that desk of yours."

"Quit clowning, Steve."

"I don't think you ever got over that time your plane went down over France twenty-five years ago. Admit it, Mort. You just don't wanna go back to the scene of your demise."

Jones shook his head and chuckled. "Listen, old man. The only difference between you and me is a couple of lucky shots. Besides, I wasn't anywhere near Normandy." He paused and then icily intoned, "Now what about my request?"

"If it was up to me, I'd grant it, but I can't. I've got my orders."

"At least take it up with headquarters," Jones hotly protested. "You know some people. Call in a marker."

"Mort, who do you think I am? God? I don't have a private line to Admiral Ramsay."

A young ensign approached. "Excuse me, Skipper. An urgent message for you."

Frye sighed wearily. "Another urgent message. I've been up with urgent messages all night. Believe me, Mort, you don't want this job. Okay, son. Who's this one from? President Roosevelt?"

"No, General Eisenhower's headquarters, sir."

"Eisenhower? Gimme that!"

Frye ripped the paper from the ensign's hands. He read it in silent disbelief.

"Well, Steve, what is it?"

Frye read: "Severe enemy action near Grandcamp.[184] Stop. Deploy infantry. Stop. Return to port with radio men. Chief, Naval Intelligence, Headquarters of the Supreme Allied Commander, General Dwight D. Eisenhower."

We were going back to England and would not see Omaha for another nine days.

June 7, 1944

Dear Mom, Dad & Ethel,

As soon as you get news from Joe, let me know, as I am just as anxious as you. Am in excellent health and couldn't feel better.

Love,

Don

I hadn't received a letter from Joe in over six weeks. This occurrence in itself wasn't unusual, given the volatile nature of the army postal system. However, there were other factors, which, when coupled with the lack of communication, made me worry. Joe was a signal corpsman attached to an infantry outfit, and it occurred to me that he might have been sent to Omaha at the start of the invasion. Always the optimist, I quickly brushed this thought aside.

At first, I was confident that he was fine, but then doubts began gnawing at me. So I started making inquiries, meeting with the squadron chaplain, even working up courage to talk to First Sergeant Abatelli, the top kick who'd handed me my head when I went AWOL eighteen months earlier. They had no information for me, but I kept checking back with them.

In January of 1943, I had desperately wanted to visit Chicago. After D-Day, that longing seemed so trivial. All I wanted now was to see Joe. With the dangers I imagined him facing, I considered the possibility that our next meeting—if it ever occurred—would be our last.

The odds of my finding him anytime soon were slim. Units were constantly on the move, and there was much confusion in the early days after the invasion, but I was determined to see my big brother. Where was Joe? Where was he?

Back on the British side of the Channel, things settled down for a while. I had resumed my routine of playing ball, going to dances, and working eight-hour radio shifts. There were many air raids, but no bombs fell nearby.

In southeast England on maneuvers, I was preparing to depart again for France. There were hundreds of different outfits getting ready to cross the Channel.

As during the previous winter, it was extremely muddy. Once again, we put steel mats down to avoid sinking into the sloppy ground.

Still, there was humor amidst adversity. A man sleeping in his tent in the early morning was awakened by several buddies. In loud, cheerful voices, they sang, "You'll be late, you'll be left. Next stop, New York. Today's menu: fresh, hot bacon and eggs."

The eager soldier jumped out of bed and raced to the mess hall, only to find the usual powdered eggs and bad coffee.

June 10, 1944

Dear Mom, Dad & Ethel,

Today I did something I had promised myself for quite some time. I got one of those real short haircuts, with about one-half inch of hair remaining on my head. It looks terrific.

In good condition and have no complaints. Have you heard from Joe yet?

Love,

Don

Not only was I concerned about Joe, I was worried about myself. I had just seen two thousand men get blown up in the Channel, and now the 888th Fighter Control Squadron was making a second attempt to cross it.

June 16, 1944 was my D-Day. On this date, I boarded an LCI bound for Normandy. After passing a pile of combat veterans, I entered my compartment. Our group of about twenty radio men occupied ten staterooms with comfortable mattresses. The beds actually had springs. These accommodations contrasted starkly with those of the infantrymen, who slept sitting up on deck.

I shook my head in astonishment, uncomfortable with the special treatment my outfit had received.

Why did we get it? The only answer I could ever come up with was that the Control Net System must have been hot stuff, an explanation which never satisfied me.

At dawn, about two hundred members of the Seventy-Ninth Infantry, outfitted with impregnated clothing and full packs, huddled outside. My buddies and I emerged from our quarters sporting Class A uniforms with nifty jackets and pleated pants.

"Where do you people think you're going?" barked an intelligence officer. "To a dance?"

"Guess we got our wires crossed somewhere, sir," I joked.

The officer was not amused. "You guys may think your outfit's fucked up, but let me tell you, you're the cream of the crop."

He instructed us to put condoms on the sights of our carbines. This was a precaution to prevent rust.

On line for the latrine, I struck up a conversation with an infantryman.

"Where are you from?" I asked.

"Chicago."

"I've been to Chicago. Had a good time there on furlough."

"Oh yeah? What's your hometown?"

"The Bronx, New York City." I paused uneasily. "I guess you must hate our guts."

"Nah. We always figured Air Corps for glamour boys. It wasn't surprising when you showed up looking the part."

"I'm glad there's no hard feelings."

"Couldn't be steamed even if I wanted to. Got a lot more important things on my mind."

"Yeah, I suppose you do."

"Actually, Omaha's pretty quiet now. It'll get a lot rougher when we start moving toward Paris. But that's not what's buggin' me."

"What is it, then?"

"You know, this bathroom's pretty good. Not like the shitholes in the last ship we were on. They were fuckin' nasty, like some of the whorehouses I've been in... What's buggin' me? Well, I've got this girl back home. Her name's Heather. She's a swell kid. Got everything. Beauty, brains, the whole works. We've been engaged since before I joined up. Now she wants to get married, but I'm not so sure.

"Don't get me wrong. I wanna marry her as much as she wants me. It's just that she's so fuckin' impatient. You know, one of those gals that can be sweet and tough at the same time. But I guess that's one of the things that I always liked about her.

"You see, Heather's got this crazy idea. She wants to get married in Paris after it's liberated. Of course, she's assumin' we're gonna take Paris, and that I'll get there in one piece. I keep tellin' her it's too dangerous, and that we should wait 'til the war's over, but she's dead set on comin'. Nobody can talk her out of it, not even her parents, who, by the way, are not in the best of health. Her mother's a diabetic, and her father's got a fuckin' heart condition. She hates to leave 'em but says she's worried about me all the time. I know she is, but I still can't help thinkin' she wants to check up on me, if you know what I mean.

"Still, I've gotta admit, the idea's kinda romantic. Fuckin' crazy, but romantic. Sometimes I can see us taking a moonlight cruise on the Seine. Or going for an afternoon walk along the Champs-Élysées with millions of French people. Won't that be one helluva of a parade!

"So whaddya think, Corp? Should I send for her in Paris, or wait 'til I get home?"

Nonplussed, I scratched my head. "Gee, I dunno, pal. I suppose you'll have to see what's doing farther down the line and take it from there."

"Well, thanks for listenin'." The infantryman hesitated, and then added, "Hey, Corp! If you're ever in Chicago again, and meet up with a girl named Heather Michaels, do me a favor and don't mention the whorehouses."

"No sweat. It'll be our little secret," I replied with a wink and a smile before entering the latrine.

I overheard the following exchange on the other side of the door:

"Hey, Chuck. That sounded like a pretty serious conversation. Who was that guy? A chaplain or something?"

"Beats me."[185]

Dropped into neck-high water, members of the Seventy-Ninth Infantry waded ashore without incident. The beach had long been taken, and there was no visible fighting.

We remained on board until we reached a pontoon bridge. There, we disembarked, arriving on Omaha without so much as getting our trousers damp. Once again, I was perplexed by the special treatment.

At first, I thought it best not to tell my family that I was in France. I stopped writing for a little while and mulled things over. After unusually careful reflection, I concluded that my parents and sister would worry even more if they didn't hear from me. Thus, I decided to resume my correspondence.

June 19, 1944

Dear Mom, Dad & Ethel,

I guess there is no use in hiding anything from you folks, and I know you will react sensibly to what I have to tell you. Otherwise you will make me awful sorry that I am being honest with you.

This letter is being written to you from somewhere in France. I am in excellent condition. I am getting enough to eat, and although this life is a far cry from a tourist's, I have no complaints.

I hope you are well, and keep the mail rolling. If you can, kindly send me fruit juices: pineapple, orange, grapefruit.

Love,

Don

June 21, 1944

Dear Mom, Dad & Ethel,

Today is the first day of summer, but the only proof of it would be the calendar.

I guess you notice that the contents of my letters since arriving here have diminished. The reason for this is the strict censorship which is enforced.

The main interest and concern of you people, I know, is how I am. Therefore, I want you to know that I am well and in good health.

Love,

Don

June 23, 1944

Dear Mom, Dad & Ethel,

Received another package from Uncle Eddy today. It was a nice, large box of cookies.

Yesterday, when I took a stroll to a French café, I found out what little French I knew. They jabber the words in lightning-like fashion.

It's funny the way things happen. The French people are trying to learn English, and we are trying to master French. Here's the outcome:

An American unwraps a candy bar and presents it to a French youngster. The Yank says, "Bonbon," which is French for "candy." Whereupon the little tot answers in a newly formed tongue, "Tank you."

Love,

Don

June 24, 1944

Dear Mom, Dad & Ethel,

Occasionally we tune in on a German news broadcast, but their bold assertions are too ridiculous to consume. They serve as entertainment and furnish us with many a laugh. There are a few radios around here, so we can keep up with the news.

Love,

Don

France
June 25, 1944

Dear Mom, Dad & Ethel,

Today our morale jumped to soaring heights. A nice batch of mail arrived, and I received six letters: two from you dated the 2nd and 8th of June, one from Joe, one from Ethel, and two from Normie. With mail beginning to come in and keep us informed at home, things are beginning to take shape once more.

Joe didn't say outwardly that he's in England (why, I don't know), but that's where he is. Am feeling fine and hope you are all well.

Love,

Don

At about the same time I received Joe's letter, the chaplain told me that he was somewhere in England. What a relief! The censors had probably prevented Joe from revealing his location. Though I didn't know his exact whereabouts yet, my main fear was put to rest. My brother was okay.

The Normandy campaign was starting to wind down. It would be over before summer's end. Allied casualties on D-Day were estimated at between 10,000 and 12,000 (303), some 6,603 of them American (303). The latter included 1,465 dead, 3,184 wounded, and 1,928 missing (303). On Omaha alone, there were about 2,500 dead, missing, or wounded (291).

Eisenhower's forces responded in kind. By the end of June, Rommel had reported over 250,000 casualties for the month (303).

CHAPTER 8

▼

A NEAR MISS

We were in a five-truck convoy speeding through northern France in the wee hours of the morning. An officer and a driver sat in the enclosed front cab of each vehicle. Exposed to the elements, the rest of us stood crammed in the rear.

For the last several weeks, we had been making rapid progress. Maintaining a distance of about five to ten miles behind advancing front lines, we deployed our mobile antennas to direct air support for ground troops.

Several agitated figures rushed onto the moonlit road. They were local citizens, frantically gesturing and screaming at us.

"*Le pont est cassé! Le pont est cassé!*" they kept shouting.

At first, we ignored them. We were exhausted. Many of us didn't know the language, and few knew it well. We figured it was just a bunch of French people jabbering. The lead driver, annoyed at having to slow down, impatiently blew his horn.

The group scattered, but was undeterred. One man banged his hand against the side of the truck. Another attempted to leap onto the back of it. Finally, their cries were heard by Technical Sergeant Stan Firestone.

Bald and muscular, thirty-five-year-old Stan was a take-charge type of guy. A father figure among us, he was popular and well-respected. His judgment was unimpeachable.

Stan pounded on the back of the cab.

"Hit the brakes, Smitty. They're saying the bridge is broken!"

"What, Sarge? Can't hear with all this noise."

"I said stop! The bridge is broken!"

Amidst a chain reaction of screeching rubber, the convoy came to an abrupt halt.

The bridge was more than broken. It was gone. The previous night, two men in a jeep traveling the same route had plunged into the water and drowned. Anxious to avoid further tragedy, the villagers were warning all Allied motorists. This latest caveat saved hundreds of American lives.

"*Merci, Français. Merci beaucoup,*" we all cheered.

Daylight. I was in the lead truck, which I had occupied the night before. Bang! The vehicle slammed into the thick branches of a massive tree, forcing several dozen of us in the back to duck for cover.

"Driver, stop!" commanded a young lieutenant in the front passenger seat.

The officer nervously jumped out to investigate. Heavy, wooden tentacles rested against the top of the cab. This was his responsibility, and he feared the worst.

A few soldiers were bruised and bleeding. Jack and I escaped with minor grazes. Although we were all shaken up, none of us was seriously injured.

"Was the truck damaged?" inquired the lieutenant.

Jack Spring piped up. "The truck! Who gives a shit 'bout the fuckin' truck? What 'bout us? Did ya look to see if any of us was hurt?"

Ignoring the challenge, the lieutenant surveyed the scene in stony silence. After he saw that there were no dents in the vehicle, he returned to his seat and ordered the driver to continue.

*   *   *   *

Toward the end of July, our squadron had an oral examination. Although it was no picnic, most of us found it more tolerable than a visit to the dentist. In addition to answering technical questions, each soldier had to demonstrate proper transmitter and antenna adjustment in his assigned van. About sixty percent of us were promoted. Jack and I made sergeant.

July 22, 1944

Dear Mom, Dad & Ethel,

The war must be coming to a close. Instead of "Sgt. Don," I accidentally started to write "Mr. Don." Good omen, I'm told. Here's the clincher: the first sergeant was actually seen with a grin on his face. When we first got to this new place, we had to work extremely long hours and got little sleep, but now things have quieted down.

Love,

Don

July 24, 1944

Dear Mom, Dad & Ethel,

Today was a day of days. Quite a number of things were accomplished.

I took a shower, the first one in several weeks. You can't stay under the shower longer than a few minutes because water isn't plentiful.

Next, I brought a pair of shoes and a flight jacket into supply and had them salvaged. I should get replacements in a few weeks. (They claim that means a few months.) Next, I handed out my laundry to be washed.

And last, we played two softball games with the officers. We lost the first game and won the second. Losing to the officers is a disgrace, and I hang my head in shame. I made several errors in that game, along with the other fellows. However, in the second game, it was my triple that tied things up. We went on to win in the following inning.

It was sure swell playing ball again. It serves as an excellent diversion. Aside from its actual enjoyment, you get so engrossed in the game that your mind relaxes, and the tension of being here in France is somewhat eased. I am fine, but the sooner this affair is over, the better. Well, I guess I'll say, au revoir.

Love,

Don

During my next ball game, I almost died in blissful ignorance. Little did I know that a sniper had me in his sights. Dead center. He pulled the trigger and fired.

I was playing deep center field, with the forest about a hundred yards behind me. To this day, I do not know why I chose that instant to move slightly. Maybe it was an involuntary yawn, or my reaction to the batter's stance. I was too far away to hear the bullet exploding out of the rifle chamber, but a couple of seconds later, I heard a whizzing sound in my right ear.

I reflexively jerked away from the buzz, and, unperturbed, idiotically continued to play.

Sixty years later, I imagine the gunman did a double take. "*Dummkopf Amerikaner,*" he must have muttered, while hightailing deeper into the dense foliage. He would have assumed that I'd eventually alert the others and start a full-blown search.

Over the next few moments, I was confused. Then it dawned on me: I had almost gotten my head blown off. I visually scoured the field. Nothing.

The other players didn't react. They were too far away to hear anything.

Confiding in no one, I dismissed the incident with a shrug. *Oh, they must be having target practice a few fields away.*

One hot night, about a month later, I woke up in a cold sweat. I had finally realized that the bullet, which I thought had come from an American firing range, actually belonged to a German sharpshooter. I scolded myself before drifting back into an uneasy slumber. *Better get with it, pal. There's a war going on.*

CHAPTER 9

▼

HUNGRY MEN

I hungered for many things: the end of the war, my parents, Ethel, Joe, and, of course, women. But now I was just plain hungry.

That deprivation lasted only a short time, but, man, did it hurt. For the soldier out in the field, meals are often the highlight of the day. Poor ones are hell on morale. Hunger was a topic I couldn't positively spin when writing to Mom and Dad. Sometimes I would discuss it openly, but usually I just chose another subject. Cheerleading for the Air Corps was a ready standby.

July 26, 1944

Dear Mom, Dad & Ethel,

Back home, both verbally and in print, I've heard and seen heated arguments by musically minded individuals as to what symphony was the greatest ever created. Over here we have no such doubts. There seems to be no difference of opinion whatsoever. Our decision is unanimous. They can have their Beethoven and Bach on the home front, but we'll take that humdrum, continuous drone of hundreds of bombers and fighters filling the skies. You don't see apathetic expressions on the faces of these onlookers. Everybody understands this music, and there is nothing more reassuring. It is truly the greatest symphony ever.

Love,

Don

July 31, 1944

Dear Mom, Dad & Ethel,

Received your letter dated the 12th of this month. Sorry to learn of your illness and hope you are better at this time. Anytime you don't feel right, Dad, leave the letters go for a while and take it easy.

Received a letter from Joe and was very much surprised to learn that he was here in the land of "Bonjours" and "Oui's." The war must be practically over when they permit green troops like his to come over. Upon seeing his letter, I went to see a chaplain close by, and he will try to find out Joe's location.

The war news continues to be very good, and we don't see how a country as hopelessly lost as Germany continues to wage war.

Love,

Don

Aug. 2, 1944

Dear Mom, Dad & Ethel,

The mosquitoes have eased a great deal in the last few days. Perhaps I'm not as tasty now as I was before.

Some of these French towns really took a pasting. They are really leveled down. Pillaging the ruins, and grabbing remnants still in good condition, was a fad in season up until recently, whereupon the French government began to clamp down real hard. I saw French signs on a billboard which indicated that civilians who were found guilty of obtaining articles illegally will be given stiff punishment. In some cases, civilians who steal insignificant items will be punished with 10 years' imprisonment. A lot of stuff was stolen from wrecked homes, and those who get caught will suffer bitterly.

Occasionally in the newspapers, and on the radio, you hear a comment from statesmen who warn against over-optimism, yet many dignitaries are the ones who make statements leading to such a propitious feeling.

In England, a flashlight was an absolute necessity. Here in France, it is a useless item. No lights are allowed anyplace on the Continent after dark.

In good health.

Love,

Don

Aug. 4, 1944

Dear Mom, Dad & Ethel,

I'm afraid that my first attempt to locate Joe has resulted in failure. However, I'll try again, and I'll get to see him.

Ethel's letter about recent engagements and marriages shocked me. Things certainly happen quickly.

Take care, Dad, and give everybody my regards.

Love,

Don

At this time, my emotions alternated between concern for my family and my own lack of nourishment. My barter excursions produced mixed results: a couple of loaves of bread here, a few vegetables there, and some rejections. Most Normans were sympathetic to my situation, but there were occasional sourpusses who didn't seem to give a damn whether the Nazis or the Allies were in their area. With the loud imprecation *"merde"*—French for "excrement"—they'd slam doors in my face. Then my luck changed.

Aug. 7, 1944

Dear Mom, Dad & Ethel,

Last night, after finishing what was supposed to be supper, I was still hungry as a wolf. This was supposed to be the biggest meal of the day. We had a little canned meat, some corn, and black coffee. A lot of guys dumped the meal in the garbage can.

However, I had met a French lady whose husband is a butcher, and I bought 10 steaks from her—believe this—for $2.00! Some fellows got potatoes, onions, a frying pan, and some grease. Then we ate. Some cider was also tossed in.

Today the meals were a little better, but far from what they should be. As you pass other outfits on the road, and you get whiffs of good food and see their mess kits full of good food, you know something is wrong somewhere. However, a lot of fellows are now managing to buy eggs, but when I produced steaks, their eyes almost popped out of their sockets.

Please send some fruit cocktails.

Love,

Don

Aug. 8, 1944

Dear Mom, Dad & Ethel,

The food this week has been "C" and "K" rations, and we're getting fed up with it. There appears to be no excuse for it. I'm sure if we had an officer here punching for us, we'd be getting good chow. Outfits all around us are eating well.

If the Army won't feed us properly, we'll find some food on the outside. I've managed to eke out nine eggs from French people. They're reluctant to sell us eggs, but occasionally you strike it lucky. The little French I know is coming in mighty handy. Tonight I may be able to obtain more steaks.

Feeling fine.

Love,

Don

On my first visit, the Frenchwoman generously sold me ten steaks for the incredibly low price of two dollars. The scarce meat was her donation to the war effort, and a token of appreciation for the Americans liberating France.

A week later, I returned to her for another helping of the coveted beef. She lived in a small house just outside Villedieu-les-Poêles, a village in Lower Normandy known for its copper kitchenware. The woman was on her porch, facing me at a distance of about thirty feet. She was having a bitter argument with a guy in a blood-spattered apron who, I surmised, was her husband. The man had his back to me, and, therefore, did not see me approaching. Although the kind lady was enduring a severe tongue lashing, she managed to give me a message. Moving her head ever so slightly, she non-verbally told me to get lost.

Now the husband was screaming. He had grabbed a pitchfork and was jabbing it at an imaginary enemy, presumably me. Then one of those chunky little black-and-white mutts that you'd see on RCA "His Master's Voice" records flew out of nowhere and began angrily pulling on the man's trousers. The dog was obviously pro-American. With my stomach growling, I quietly left this theater of the absurd and never returned.

A pang of guilt seized me. Although I realized that the harsh scolding the woman suffered was a result of her own generosity, I still felt indirectly responsible for her misfortune.

Generosity is, of course, a relative concept. It all depends on who is doing the giving, and under what circumstances. A man with a full cupboard, handing out produce to strangers, is deemed a selfless benefactor, while another with a hungry family who takes the same action is considered irresponsible. I was among a small group of men in the 888th Fighter Control Squadron who witnessed the reckless greed of our brethren.

On a muggy afternoon in Villedieu, a crowd was converging upon a heavily loaded American convoy truck from another outfit. MP's surrounding the vehicle kept order while the soldiers inside sold groceries to civilians. In less than fifteen minutes, the truck was barren. The vendors had just made a tidy profit on the black market. At this time, we weren't getting enough to eat, and we were disgusted by the sight of fellow GI's bootlegging food.

Aug. 10, 1944

Dear Mom, Dad and Ethel,

I am happy to report that today the food has gotten tremendously better. I guess our regular rations are arriving properly now, and the food should be comparatively good.

Received a letter from Jerry, and he is in Arizona pursuing a gunner's course. Jerry's brother Murray is now in a bomber squadron in China.

I once told you that I had handed in film to the Army Pictorial Department. Today they came back with an apology, "We no longer do such work. Bring said film into the local P.X." I'm afraid I'm not in any mood to go swimming across the English Channel to find a P.X.

Another fellow has a new source for obtaining meat. We have some more steaks promised to us. Cliques are usually no darned good, especially if you are on the outside of them. However, I'm in on this one, and we are an eating group to make up for the deficiencies on the part of the mess personnel.

I managed to get six eggs yesterday for the price of 15 francs or 30 cents.

Took a shave today and washed up a bit. I haven't been able to take a shower in a couple of weeks, but showers should be set up shortly.

A while ago, I went through the town of St. Lô.[186] It is the most battered and bruised town I have ever seen. You can count on your fingers the homes that are still standing there.

Love,

Don

We were eating better now, but French civilians continued to suffer. Our worst nourishment-related discomforts were modest in comparison to theirs.

Aug. 12, 1944

Dear Mom, Dad & Ethel,

The meals continue to be reasonably good. Although we are sick and tired of "K" rations, the French seem to love them. I gave two French kids two "K" ration tins, and their faces lit up. They wanted to kiss my hands. Some of these people were close to starvation. You see civilians with bedding and other belongings always on the move.

Love,

Don

Aug. 13, 1944

Dear Mom, Dad & Ethel,

Today I had some free time and went swimming in a nearby river. Boy, the water was cold, but it was refreshing nonetheless.

You have a misconception of things. There are no Red Cross Clubs near here. These towns have only recently been liberated.

The chaplain is working on it, but it will be a stroke of luck if I bump into Joe. Everybody moves so frequently that it is difficult to locate an outfit and still find it there when you arrive.

Love,

Don

Aug. 16, 1944

Dear Mom, Dad & Ethel,

In talking with the French people now, we find them friendlier than the groups of people we originally met in France. They told me the Germans took everything they could lay their hands on. They stuffed themselves with food, leaving the French family little for their own needs. In talking with a lady of 65 years, I found her eyes brightened like diamonds when we began touching the subject of the conclusion of the hostilities.

Feeling pretty good and hope you are all fine. Take a chance in shipping the salami. I've seen other fellows receive it okay.

Love,

Don

Aug. 17, 1944

Dear Mom, Dad & Ethel,

Received wonderful packages from you, one containing underwear and handkerchiefs, and the other had sardines and juices. The packages are swell. Thanks so much.

This afternoon two fellows and myself went out on a barter deal. I took soap, cigarettes, and candy along, and returned in an hour with 20 eggs, butter, and a frying pan. Tomorrow morning, instead of powdered eggs, we'll have fresh eggs, juice, coffee, crackers, and jam. Feeling trim.

Love,

Don

Aug. 18, 1944

Dear Mom, Dad & Ethel,

Well, today I had one of those French favorites. I traded soap and ciga-rettes for more eggs, and then the lady gave me some cognac. I had two shots. It is colorless and has quite a kick to it. The French say, "C'est fort" (It's strong).

This morning we made our own breakfast: two eggs, French-fried potatoes, juice, marmalade, and crackers. Yes siree, we don't stand short now.

Love,

Don

Aug. 21, 1944

Dear Mom, Dad & Ethel,

Received two letters from Joe yesterday, and he sounds pretty good. I also
spoke to an M.P. yesterday, and he had some information on Joe's location, but it was so vague that it has little merit.

Had a substantial meal this afternoon and ate heartily. It's peculiar, but we
had something staring us in the face and didn't know it. The apple trees
are plentiful, and now the cooks started cooking the apples and adding a
little sugar, making a delicious dessert. I am still trading some items for
eggs and butter, and thus faring nicely.

Love,

Don

About a week later, a few buddies and I got passes to visit Paris, which the
Germans formally surrendered on August 25.[187] Eager to buy some French
bread, we were glad to find a bakery. However, our smiles soon turned to frowns
when we learned that we needed ration coupons to make a purchase. A patron in
the store intervened and gave us his for free. Thus, we happily left with three
crusted loaves. A man in the street asked us how we got the bread.

"*Comment pouvez-vous acheter du pain?*"

When we explained that a generous civilian gave us coupons, he was flabber-
gasted. Such generosity was rare.

The French bread was *merveilleux.* Together with some beer, it was one of the
most delicious meals we had ever eaten.

But we had a hard time finding the Eiffel Tower, the largest structure in Paris.
Doggedly, we stopped passersby and kept asking the same question: "*Où est* Eiffel
Tower?" Nobody seemed to understand.

A crowd formed. Dozens of people gathered in a ring, talking and gesticulating wildly. It looked like a scene out of a French comedy. Suddenly, one bright fellow exclaimed, *"Oh, monsieur, c'est La Tour Eiffel!"*

In French, noun and adjective are reversed, making the landmark's literal English translation "Tower Eiffel." The French pronounce it "Tour Eff-el." We had the name backwards and compounded our error with poor pronunciation.

When we finally found the famed tower, we learned that it was built by Alexandre Gustave Eiffel in 1889 and stood 1,056 feet high. Since my friends and I were in excellent shape, we decided to walk to the top. There, we beheld a glorious view of the "City of Light."

CHAPTER 10

▼

AN ARREST IN
VERSAILLES

Versailles was the historical seat of the French monarchy, and my stay there quickly became a royal pain in the butt.

Shortly after arriving, I secured passes for myself and a few buddies. Brimming with enthusiasm, we immediately set off to explore the city. Alas, my impromptu tour was cut short.

Somewhere between the palaces and downtown coffeehouses, I managed to get separated from the group. At first, I wasn't particularly worried. Although lost, I welcomed the break from the noisy bars and cafés.

Though a stranger to Versailles, I was sure I would soon find my way back to my new lodging, the Louis Pasteur House. All I had to do was ask someone where I could find the Louis Pasteur House.

Off I went, gallivanting around town, snooping here and there. Then it got dark, coal black, and I couldn't see a foot in front of me. Now I started getting nervous.

I finally found my way to a tavern—not by sight, but by sound, following a trail of tipsy laughter, clanging glasses, and boisterous music. The saloon's windows were boarded to protect against air raids, and the interior was dimly lit. I dashed up to a portly man in a suit and asked for directions. To my dismay, I learned that there were six buildings in different parts of the city which had the name I sought. A customer with guilefully gleaming eyes interceded and offered me lodging. Something didn't smell right about him, so I declined the invitation.

It was now 11 p.m., and I was walking the tenebrous streets. Undaunted, I still believed I could somehow find my way back to headquarters. I walked about aimlessly for another five minutes. Then a startling, authoritative voice called out.

"*Arretez!*"

I froze. One wrong move, and I was dead.

"*Qui est là?*" the voice demanded.

"*Soldat Américain,*" I replied, doing my best to remain calm.

"*Avancez.*"

I approached, and two flags shot up from the side of a building. I couldn't see them, but I could hear them loudly fluttering in the mild breeze. I was in front of a French police station.

With my limited language ability, I explained my situation to a tall, mustached gendarme on duty. "*Je suis perdu* [I'm lost]," I began. After a brief conversation, he decided it was best for me to remain at the station overnight.

"*Vous pouvez dormir ici* [You can sleep here]," he said, gesturing toward a straw mattress in a small holding cell.

"*Ça va bien,*" I gratefully replied. I knew I was much safer in jail than on the street.

The mattress had just the right amount of firmness, and my heavy jacket cushioned the rough surface. I slept soundly.

Rising early the next morning, I thanked my jailers for their hospitality and left. Unfortunately, the gendarmes were unable to provide me with directions, and I continued to wander.

After an hour of walking and guessing, I flagged down an American staff car. Lady Luck smiled upon me: the officers inside were from my outfit.

"I got lost," I sheepishly explained. "Had to sleep in a French police station."

"Yeah, right. What was her name?" asked a sarcastic lieutenant.

"No kidding, sir. I was lost. It was late, and I didn't know how to get back."

"All right, Sergeant," interjected a sympathetic captain. It was Mortimer Jones. "Hop in."

They treated me to a scrumptious steak in a fine restaurant and then drove me back to the correct Louis Pasteur House.

I had missed my radio shift in the transmitter van. I was AWOL again, but at least this time I had a legitimate excuse. My master sergeant was understanding.

"It's okay," Master Sergeant Kelly assured me. "Captain Jones told me what happened."

Thus I was pardoned. For the second time in a year, I had escaped the harsh judgment of a military court. Though relieved, I didn't get off scot-free.

I had to live with the fact that I had screwed up royally. Someone had pulled my shift, and I would have to make it up.

In addition to the chagrin and double workload, fate inflicted another penalty upon me. Shortly after coming off duty, I felt an itchiness in my right wrist. At first, I dismissed it as a mosquito bite. Within minutes, however, I knew that my initial assessment was wrong. I carefully examined myself. Something was literally crawling underneath my skin. Using my pocket knife, I exposed a pair of multi-legged insects.

"Oh shit," I muttered. "Hope they don't have any relatives." Then I dashed off to the infirmary for delousing.

Ever resilient, I returned to downtown Versailles a few days later. It was a bright, sunny morning, and German prisoners of war were being given an airing on the main square. Hundreds proudly strutted through the streets. Goose-stepping in precise formation before the French people, mingling defiance with skill, they seemed immune to the humility of defeat. It was the physical equivalent of saying, "We may be POW's, but we're part of a powerful army, and you'll never conquer us."

They were impressive in their arrogance. An unenlightened visitor from another planet might have taken them for victors. Then something unexpected happened.

Tanks began rolling in from around the bend. First ten. Then twenty. Then fifty. Then a hundred. Then another hundred, moving neatly, one behind the other, with a perfection that human feet could not duplicate. Haughty German pageantry wilted before the burgeoning cornucopia of American military might.

I described the events I had witnessed on the square to Corporal Neil Olson, a fellow member of the 888th who operated a Midwestern newspaper.

"Can you write something up about it?" Olson asked.

"I'm not an author, but I'll give it my best."

"I'm sure it'll be fine, Sarge."

I wrote the article, and Olson said he'd wire it to his paper. He never gave me a copy of the story, nor did he thank me for my effort.[188] Although annoyed and disappointed, I wasn't surprised: the newsman was a disgruntled individual.

Corporal Olson was short and heavyset, with dark brown hair greying at the temples. At forty-five, he was one of the oldest soldiers in the outfit. He was still fuming over a ruling that went into effect shortly after he landed in Europe. The regulation prohibited American men over forty from being shipped overseas, but did not authorize the repatriation of those already stationed abroad.

My anger has cooled with the passage of time, and today I'm inclined to give Olson the benefit of the doubt. It is quite possible that he innocently misplaced my article or was unable to wire it in a timely manner. We were traveling frequently during this period.

Aug. 30, 1944

Dear Mom, Dad & Ethel,

I haven't written for quite a few days, but this will happen every so often when things are moving at the pace they are now. Don't get the impression that anything is wrong, because I am really feeling swell.

I've managed to see a few things I never expected, but it is in the continuous life of the opening and closing of barracks bags. Wherever you go, it is convoy after convoy of trucks pouring into or past towns. The French wave and shout enthusiastically as we pass by, tossing us apples and tomatoes. We, in turn, toss cigarettes and candy. I've seen German prisoners marching through the streets while the endless stream of traffic goes by.

A good many women are well-dressed. However, the Frenchmen generally wear trousers that are all patched up.

It is surprising to find as many things available in stores that were unobtainable in England. Some Frenchmen told me that "Americans are liked more than the English." Why? He didn't know. My own feelings are that it is mostly personality. The Englishman is disciplined to such an extent that his thoughts and actions go just so far. He appears to be anything but an individualist. The American is a gay, cocky, brash, independent soldier. Therefore, it appears that he is more aggressive and interesting. Of course, my assessment may be incorrect.

Love,

Don

Sept. 2, 1944

Dear Mom, Dad & Ethel,

Yesterday I had one helluva good time. I went into town and started walking about. The first thing that happens on such a tour is that people start running up to you and shaking your hand. A guy feels like a celebrity after awhile. From a three-year-old tot to a guy supporting himself with a cane, the French show their friendliness by shaking hands. Now I know why those Hollywood stars shy crowds so much. The first few times it's fun shaking hands, but later on, you've had enough. And the worst part is that I don't deserve their appreciation because I have not been engaged in any really dangerous situations. The infantry, the artillery, the pilots, the navigators, and the bombardiers are entitled to this warm treatment. Not me.

Well, anyhow, I start handing out cigarettes, and, before long, there is a queue on my right waiting for the stuff. We receive enough cigarettes, but if you don't hand them out sparingly, you'll find yourself completely empty. And, remember, that's my bargaining tool when I want to trade for fresh eggs.

Later they took me out to supper. We had spaghetti, ham, bread, and an apple. We also topped the meal off with a few glasses of wine.

I was feeling pretty happy when I got a lift from a jeep and rode back to camp. Those people gave me their card and told me to come and see them any time I go to town. They sure treated me swell. It was one terrific day. Mesdames, monsieurs, merci beaucoup, vous êtes très gentilles.

Lots of Amour,

Don

Sept. 17, 1944

Dear Mom, Dad & Ethel,

Today was a quiet day—up until 1 p.m.—when mail call was announced. This was the first time in over a week, so you can imagine the excitement. I did very well. I received 12 letters and a package from Uncle Eddy.

Incidentally, the other day I celebrated my first anniversary overseas.

Love,

Don

▼

CHAPTER 11

BELGIUM

Moving eastward in a convoy under cover of darkness, we anxiously crossed into Belgium. Several minutes later, the trucks stopped, and everyone spilled out onto the dirt road. Pursuant to orders, the non-officers immediately set to work digging foxholes.

"Stop groaning and move your asses," barked a young lieutenant. "I want these five feet deep by 2300 hours."

Shoveling was a distinct possibility whenever the outfit was mobile. It was an occasional chore that made everyone edgy because it meant that the enemy was nearby. A voice blared over the PA system: "Don't get out of your digs tonight. The guards have instructions to shoot anything that moves."

This time I was unlucky. It was my turn to pull guard duty.

It is important to understand the difference between temporary guard duty and permanent guards. Sooner or later, every enlisted man, regardless of his primary responsibilities, had the unenviable task of protecting the base. Guard duty could be tense, especially during the lonely, dark, wee hours, but usually it was just boring. The rank and file uniformly hated the job and made all sorts of excuses to avoid it. By contrast, those who scored lowest on the Air Corps's aptitude test became full-time guards and cooks. These positions were filled by privates and offered little chance of promotion. Of course, anyone who successfully defended the outfit, or prepared a particularly tasty meal, would have been promptly dubbed a genius.

Tense and tired, I struggled to stay awake. The post-midnight moon and stars were my only companions. Occasionally, distant dog barks and owl hoots caused my heavy eyelids to pop wide open, triggering nervous, back-and-forth pacing. Then I saw something.

It was a strange aircraft. Although it was only flying at about a thousand feet, I couldn't identify it as either friend or foe. There were no distinct markings, and the shape was unfamiliar. From my vantage point, it resembled a giant bullet with wings.[189]

I started to doubt my senses. Squinting, I scratched my head. Then I rubbed my eyes and looked again. This was no ordinary plane. It had a peculiar growling sound and was moving very fast. An exhaust mounted atop the rear of the fuselage belched an orange-yellow flame.[190]

Dumbfounded, I watched the mechanized firefly disappear into the night. I had just spotted my first V-1.[191]

The Nazis had unleashed this revolutionary new weapon upon England on June 13, 1944, one week after D-Day.[192] Powered by a small jet engine,[193] these pilotless aircraft terrorized London for the next nine months.[194] By summer's end, they had killed over six thousand British civilians and destroyed seventy-five thousand buildings.[195]

They were colloquially referred to as "buzz bombs." The British called them "doodle bugs," a term coined by New Zealand fighter pilots after the noisy insects of that country.[196] Whatever its name, the V-1, raining death and destruction wherever it landed, quickly became synonymous with terror. Its appearance in the sky was an unsettling sight with which we and the Belgians were about to become intimately familiar.

With the source of excitement gone, my weariness returned. Twice, I abruptly stifled a yawn and raised my carbine, only to find that I had mistaken the rustling autumn leaves for enemy footsteps. At last, the merciful crowing of a rooster greeted the dawn, and my watch was over.

*   *   *   *

Historically, Belgium is something of a paradox. Forged in the heat of battle, she is an orphan of war with a long and distinguished pedigree.

One of the smallest countries in Europe,[197] modern Belgium is bounded by the Netherlands on the northeast, by Germany on the east, and by France on the south and west (420). Originally a northern province of the "Low Countries," it was part of Charlemagne's empire in the early ninth century A.D. (420). Between

the sixteenth and nineteenth centuries, it was ruled by Spain, the Austrian Haps-
burgs, France, and the Kingdom of the Netherlands (423). Although Holland
and Belgium first became separate political entities in 1609 (420), Belgium did
not gain full independence until after the Revolution of 1830 (423).

Due to the numerous cultural absorptions, sharp linguistic divisions remain to
this day. The northern half of the country is primarily Flemish- and
Dutch-speaking, while southern residents are Francophones (421, map). The
area around the nation's capital, Brussels, is bilingual (421, map), and a small
area east of Liège Province near the German border is German-speaking (421,
map). However, a 1947 census found that nearly twenty percent of all Belgians
spoke two languages (422).

At the start of the First World War, Belgium was unprepared for military conflict (428). The guarantee of the five great powers of the day (Britain, France,
Prussia, Russia, and Austria) to safeguard her neutrality (428) could not deter
German aggression. On August 4, 1914, Germany invaded Belgium, and four
years of occupation ensued (429).

Amidst vigorous civilian opposition, Belgian workers were forced to aid the
German war effort (429). Over 57,000 able-bodied men between the ages of seventeen and sixty were rounded up to work on railways and trenches near the
French fronts (429). An approximately equal number were shipped to forced
labor camps in Germany (429). Some 2,531 died of maltreatment (429).

A quarter-century later, history repeated itself. On May 10, 1940, only a few
days after Germany's ambassador promised that his country would honor Belgian
neutrality, Hitler invaded Belgium (430-1). Great Britain and France went to the
aid of the Belgians[198] but were no match for the Nazi war machine.

Only eighteen days later, on May 28, 1940, King Leopold surrendered unconditionally,[199] and another four years of German occupation followed. The Allies
reached Belgium on September 3, 1944.[200]

*   *   *   *

Throngs of happy civilians cast bright shadows along the cobblestone streets
of Verviers on the afternoon of September 9.[201] Tanks of the Eighty-Third
Reconnaissance Battalion were rolling into town (29). There, they were united
with the Third Armored Division and Seventh Corps of General Lawton Collins
of the American First Army (30, photo caption). Elated mobs surrounded these
forces, greatly slowing their advance (30).

Verviers was a small city with a population of about 41,000[202] along the Vesdre River in Liège Province. On September 14, 1944, the town had a big liberation party.[203] It was a grand, egalitarian affair with enormous columns of brass bands and local resistance fighters parading along streets that included the rue Spintay.[204] Male and female *partisans* proudly strode together (99). Children marched side by side with the elderly (104). There were youthful American soldiers (104) and aging Belgian veterans of the First World War (98).

We were among the first Americans to set up headquarters in Verviers. By September 23, my outfit was in foxholes in Stembert, a hamlet of 5,770 souls[205] just east of the city.[206] This *très petit village* appeared on only the most detailed of Belgian maps, where it was designated by a mere pin dot. Stembert mostly consisted of small farmhouses spread over sloping fields. They were plain, white, one-family structures, the homes of poor country folk.

Immediately upon arrival, we planted our stakes. We erected tents and positioned our equipment on the high ground overlooking the area.

Though smaller than the festivities in Verviers, Stembert's celebration was equally spirited. Joyously shrieking townsfolk ran out of their tiny abodes to welcome us with Belgian specialty dishes. We were quite startled.

"*Bonjour, Américains. Soyez le bienvenu!*"

The 888th Fighter Control Squadron was the first unit to bed down in Stembert. Outfitted with helmets, light carbines, and daypacks, we were probably mistaken for battle-hardened troops by the people who showered us with blessings and kisses. "*Buvez du vin*," offered a generous man passing out bottles of wine. "*Mangez du gâteau!*" exclaimed a stout woman distributing pastries.

I walked past these modest farms on the outskirts of town, embarrassed and thrilled by the unexpected adulation. Alongside me was Sergeant Eric "Bobby" Liter, who had been transferred from a London-based unit three weeks earlier. Liter had spent so much time in England that he spoke with a British accent. It was only fitting that we nicknamed him "Bobby," the slang English term for "policeman."[207]

Bobby was a broad-shouldered six-footer with a cherubic face. At age thirty, he was already a bit paunchy. Although good-natured, he tended to take things too much to heart. When Bobby first joined the 888th, he nearly came to blows with a few soldiers who teased him about his accent. But Stan helped smooth things out, and Bobby quickly became an accepted member of the squadron.

Amidst slow-moving military traffic and jubilant *Stembertois*, Bobby and I discovered a minor calamity. Two guards were interrogating the occupants of an overheated car which had broken down on the dirt road. The driver, a short boy of seventeen, was accompanied by a girl of similar age. Both looked frightened. Stan was interpreting, and placating the guards who had been giving the teenagers a hard time.

The guards were within their rights. This was no time to be driving around town. The region had just been liberated, and despite the celebrations, martial law was still in effect.

Less than two weeks earlier, on September 11, Radio Belgium had confirmed the liberation of Verviers.[208] A gas pipeline serving Liège and Verviers ruptured, leaving the latter town without fuel (42). Although intercity trams had been running since the twelfth, there was still no telephone or postal service (43). The whole area was suffering prolonged electric power outages (47), and with the exception of military and food-bearing vehicles, automobiles were banned from the roads (40). Travel was limited to 6 kilometers (40), about 3.7 miles.

"All right, that's enough," Stan interjected. "Don't persecute the kids. These people have gotten enough shit from the Germans. Besides, this is supposed to be a happy day. Let's not ruin it for 'em."

"But they're breaking the law, Sarge," protested a guard. "Regulations say we've gotta bring 'em to the police and confiscate the vehicle."

"You really wanna arrest this boy for partying? Yeah, he shouldn't have been driving around the whole night fucking his girlfriend in the middle of a war zone. But he's only seventeen. If I was in his shoes, I probably would have done the same thing."

"He smells like a still."

"So he got bombed. Hell, the whole country's probably crocked by now. I know I'd be if mine was just liberated."

"But—"

"Look, soldier, my job is to keep this traffic moving. I'll take care of the car. You're done here. If Captain Jones ever found out we arrested a coupla Belgian kids and impounded a broken-down car, he'd have a fit. It would be a public relations nightmare and a waste of our time. Besides, there's an exception to the regulations: discretion of the man in charge. I'm in charge, and I'm exercising my discretion. That's all."

The guards dutifully retreated.

"Bobby. Just the man I need."

"What's up, Stan?"

"I gotta get this car running so these kids can go home and stop blocking traffic."

"Sure thing. Haven't tinkered around since I went into the service." Bobby admiringly glanced at the vehicle's green body. "Wow! A 1934 Sit-troy-yen 7 CV."

"Citröen," corrected the fluent Stan.

"Whatever. I may not know French,[209] but I know my automobiles. This one's a classic. She pioneered front wheel drive, has torsion bar suspension, hydraulic brakes, and a low center of gravity. Grips the road beautifully."[210]

"Gee, Bob, I'd love to chat all day about the 1,303 cubic centimeter engine and rubber motor mounts,[211] but we've gotta get this car off the road. Now."

"Okay. Let's have a look."

A cloud of white vapor greeted Bobby as he opened the hood.

"Jesus F. Christ! This baby's hotter than a Turkish bath. How long has she been sitting here?"

"A coupla minutes."

A moment later, the smoke cleared, and my two friends were peering over the vehicle's innards. Out of my element, I silently looked on from a respectful distance.

"She's got a busted hose," Bobby observed.

"And a frayed belt," added Stan.

"Where you gonna find a belt out here?"

"Just take care of the hose, Bobby. I'll worry about the belt."

Bobby took out his pocket knife, deftly pruned away the small amount of rubber beyond the rupture point, and reconnected the hose. Stan reached into his jacket and produced a different kind of hose: a pair of women's stockings.

"Was she pretty?" needled Bobby.

Stan wryly crinkled the corners of his mouth. "Shut up and see if anything else needs fixing."

"I'm on top of it, boss," replied a smiling Sergeant Liter.

Stan removed the worn belt from its pulley. He tied the stockings together and wrapped them tightly into place.

"That'll get 'em home. They only live about a mile away. How's the rest of her, Bobby?"

"Radiator's okay. The plugs and points look good. The oil's fine, but the water's low."

"Got any water, Donnybrook?"

"Sure thing, Stan. Here."

Stan caught my canteen with one hand. Calm under pressure, he had a way of making everything look easy.

Stan added the water and turned to Bobby. "Anything else?"

"Nope. The rest of her looks good. Ten years old, and this baby's still built."

The boy and girl returned to the car.

"*Tournez*," Stan commanded.

The boy turned the ignition key, and the engine started smoothly.

"Runs like a top," marveled Bobby.

Stan addressed the boy. "*Attendez* [Wait]. *Si vous êtes arrêté, présentez cette lettre* [If you're stopped, show this letter]. "

He pulled out some military stationery, and, in a neat hand, quickly wrote:

September 23, 1944

To Whom It May Concern:

The occupants of this vehicle were detained and duly reprimanded by me on the outskirts of Stembert this morning. They are returning home following a medical emergency. Please allow them safe passage.

Technical Sergeant Stanley Firestone
888th Fighter Control Squadron

"Where'd you get the fancy paper?"

"Don't ask, Bobby."

"You're sticking your neck out pretty far for these kids."

"Yeah. Hopefully nobody'll stop 'em. If they do, well, *c'est la guerre.*"

The teenagers got out of the car. The boy warmly shook the hands of both men, and the girl planted wet kisses on their cheeks. The couple then re-entered the Citroën.

"*Merci, liberateurs*," they shouted, flashing the "V" sign as they drove off.

"Nice kids," observed Stan.

"Yeah. I think you did the right thing."

"Good. Gotta go. Catch you two later."

Bobby and I resumed our walk.

"Jeez. When you two get together, it's like you're speaking a foreign language."

"The only language I know is English, Donnybrook."

"I mean when you talk about cars."

"Cars are either in your blood, or they ain't. It's something you grow up with. My grandfather used to have a body shop. My dad always hung around there. So did I."

"I don't know a damned thing about cars."

"Donnybrook, there's three great things in life: cars, women, and sports. They don't call a car 'she' for nothing. A good car's better than a good woman."

"Oh, come on."

"It's true. A good car is dependable, puts out, and doesn't talk back to you."

"I'll still take the woman."

"Donnybrook, you've got a one-track mind."

"There's something I still don't understand about those kids. Fuel's in short supply, so how do these people have enough gas to drive around?"

"The farmers can make it in their backyards."

"How?"

"Haven't you ever heard of ethanol?"

"Nope."

"Man, you've led a sheltered existence! It's an alcohol you mix with gas, so you use less gas and oil. You can make it from just about any grain—corn, barley, potatoes—as long as it's a starch.[212] If you're a farmer, it's easy.[213] All you need is a still to ferment it and take out the water."

"Like beer?"

"You got it."[214]

"Is it safe?"

"Sure. A few carburetor and engine adjustments, and she's good to go.[215] If it wasn't safe, they wouldn't be using it all over Europe."

Alcohol fuels were used in the earliest internal combustion engines.[216] In the 1890's, they powered farm machinery, trains, and automobiles in both Europe and the United States (1). During the 1930's, there was a drive to introduce "power alcohol" blends, similar to today's gasohol, in Midwestern service stations (1). U.S. companies Texaco, Ethyl, and Esso all marketed foreign alcohol blends (23). However, by the end of the decade, the movement had failed due to a propaganda campaign by the American Petroleum Institute (1).

Across the Atlantic, things were different. In contrast to the United States, most European governments had few domestic oil reserves and therefore encouraged the development of fuels from farm products (9). By 1939, forty nations had either enacted legislation making alcohol programs mandatory, or subsidized alternative energy to make it more competitive with imported gasoline (27).

Between 1930 and 1937, power alcohol consumption on the Continent increased from 59,000 to 540,000 tons (27).

The German government had a particularly well-developed program (9). Not surprisingly, it was emphatically militaristic (27). Believing that lack of oil caused Germany's defeat in World War I, Adolf Hitler was determined to make Germany energy self-sufficient by the end of the 1930's (27). He nearly succeeded. In 1937, a year before Hitler invaded Austria, gasoline alternatives comprised 54.7 percent of Germany's light motor-fuel consumption (28).

Although ethanol has yet to catch on in this country,[217] the American military enthusiastically embraced it as an additive during World War II.[218] The U.S. government even commandeered whiskey distilleries in order to boost its alcohol production.[219]

Once again, Bobby and I were detained. A ten-year-old boy had run up to us and was tugging at Bobby's jacket. Smiling paternally, Bobby got down on one knee to greet the child.

"And what can I do for you, my fine fellow?"

The boy breathlessly replied: "*Monsieurs Soldats Américains, Grands Soldats Américains, venez à ma maison. Je vous en prie! Mes parents veulent vous rencontrer. Vous pouvez manger avec nous et—*"

Laughing heartily, Bobby threw his hands up in mock exasperation. "Slow down, partner. I don't understand a bloody word you're saying. What's he talking about, Donnybrook?"

"I think he's inviting us to his house for lunch to meet his family."

"Fine by me. Anything else?"

"Yeah. He says we're great guys."

Bobby gently squeezed his large paw around the boy's small, thin hand. "Thanks, kid. I've never turned down a free meal before, and I'm not gonna start now."

The puzzled boy turned to me for help.

"*Merci beaucoup, mon ami,*" I haltingly began. "*Vous etês très gentil. Nous sommes très heureux à manger avec vous et votre famille.*"

"What did you tell him, Donnybrook?"

"I accepted."

We resumed our victory stroll. The dirt road remained unnaturally clogged with the outfit's trucks and effusive local citizens. GI's doled out candy to small children, and their mothers enthusiastically embraced the Americans. A brass trio played festive music while thin cattle quizically looked on from an adjacent field.

"You know we don't deserve this, Bob."

"I don't know about you, but I've earned my lunch. I fixed that Belgian kid's car."

"You know what I mean. We didn't do any of the fighting."

"So what? I intend to enjoy my meal. You should, too. Just lose that guilty conscience of yours."

"I don't have a guilty conscience. I think this is swell. The parade, the invitations from the people, everything. I just wish we'd done more to earn it."

"You should have been a chaplain, Donnybrook."

"Haven't stepped foot in a temple since I was thirteen."

"Well, maybe you should start going again. You're one of the most moralistic fellows I've ever seen. Most of the guys I know wouldn't give a shit. I don't. I'll take whatever good fortune comes my way. The infantry has their parties, and we've got ours. Loosen up and enjoy the fun."

The boy began tugging at my jacket. "*Tirez le fusil! Je voudrais voir,*" he insisted.

I stopped walking and looked doubtfully at him.

"What's up, Donnybrook?"

"He wants me to fire a round, Bob."

"In this crowd? I don't think so."

"Why not? Soldiers shoot in celebration all the time."

"You can do what you bloody well please, but if I were one of these folks, small arms fire would be the last thing I'd wanna hear. Some of 'em might like it, but all you need is to scare one old lady or spook a horse, and then you've got a panic."

"Yeah, but I don't wanna disappoint the kid. After all, he's feeding us."

Bobby grinned playfully. "Just itching to pull that trigger, are you? Know what your problem is? You're a frustrated infantryman."

"Bull shit. I just want the kid to have a good time. Guess I'll just wait 'til we hit some open space." I turned to my young host. "*Plus tard, mon ami.*"

We walked another two hundred yards to a tiny farmhouse about a quarter-mile from our drop-off point. Bobby and I removed our carbine clips, put them in our pockets, and left our guns at the door. Inside, six people were huddled in an eight-by-ten-foot room. They looked old and haggard. We shook the leathery hands offered to us.

More welcomes and wine were followed by a modest spread of bread and cheese. The main course was *la soupe populaire*, a broth of potatoes, meat, and vegetables which the municipal government had first mass produced during World War I.[220] The practice was revived when the Germans occupied the country in 1940.[221] For one Belgian franc (2.27 American cents)[222] and a ration coupon, a person could buy a daily serving of six deciliters (2 ½ cups).[223] During the occupation, local authorities estimated that twenty-four thousand liters (100,000 cups) a day were needed to feed the Greater-Verviers area.[224]

Although food was still very scarce, that didn't prevent the anxious-to-please family from adding some extra legumes to the mixture. Unlikely guests of honor, Bobby and I sat down at a rough-hewn, rectangular wooden table for six. A small wizened man, who appeared to be the family patriarch, sat at one end of the table, and an elderly woman sat at the other. Two slightly younger men sat opposite us. The others would have to eat in shifts.

We nodded appreciatively at the small, encircling crowd. We knew that things had been spruced up for us. A middle-aged woman with missing teeth hovered over the table, which was covered with a brand new pink-and-white checkerboard cloth. Bright red napkins were placed near delicate wine glasses. I sampled the cooking.

"*C'est bon*," I remarked.

"*Bon, bon,*" echoed Bobby between greedy slurps. "But I like the wine better."

The patriarch refilled his glass.

"Hey, he knows English. Better watch what you say around here, Bobby."

"I speak little," the Belgian explained in a heavy accent.

There was much merry making and good cheer. I struggled valiantly with my French, while Bobby, who was more inebriated, pantomimed expansively.

The farmers were interested in our carbines. Shortly after I began explaining the firing mechanism, startled gasps and murmurs arose among my hosts. The boy was darting around the room with my gun, stopping occasionally to point it at his relatives.

I yanked the firearm from his grasp. "*Jamais, jamais,*" I scolded. "*Ce n'est pas pour jouer. C'est pour tuer. C'est très dangereux.*"

Bobby, who had been slow in realizing what was happening, became enraged.

"You crazy tyke," he roared, violently shaking the ten-year-old by the shoulders. "What do you think you're doing?"

"Let him go, Bobby."

"No. He could have killed three people with one bullet in this closet. And we'd be bloody well court-martialed for it."

"Lighten up, will ya! The kid feels bad enough. Besides, he couldn't have shot anyone. We took out the clips, remember?"

"That's not the point. He shouldn't be fuckin' around like that."

Mom and Dad, undated photo.
Courtesy of Eli Ellison.

Ethel, Phelan Place, Bronx, New York,
June 1943. Courtesy of Eli Ellison.

(Left to Right) Radio cadets Al Daitch, Julie Isman, and Eli Ellison, Truax Field, Madison, Wisconsin, 1943. Courtesy of Eli Ellison.

Radio men Sal Neri (left) and Eli Ellison, England, April 1944. Courtesy of Eli Ellison.

In preparation for the Normandy invasion, artillery equipment is loaded aboard LCT's at the English port of Brixham. Public domain image courtesy of U.S. Army Military History Institute, WW II Special Collection, Navy-Ships-Landing Craft-LST# 2 206438.

June 6, 1944: British troops landing on Sword Beach. The fellow at the upper right seems quite out of it. Image No. B5114, Imperial War Museum Archive, London. Reprinted with permission.

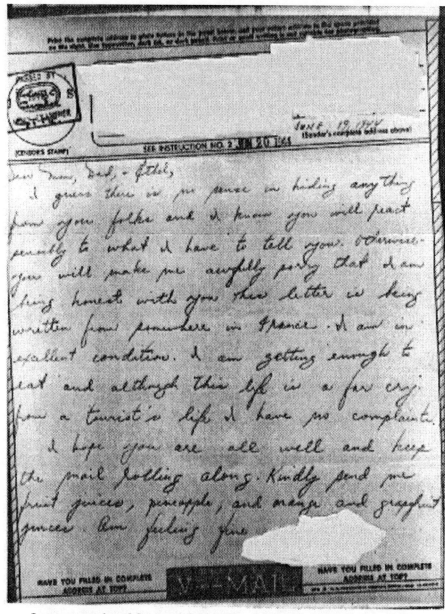

Image reproduced from original letter of June 19, 1944. Courtesy of Eli Ellison.

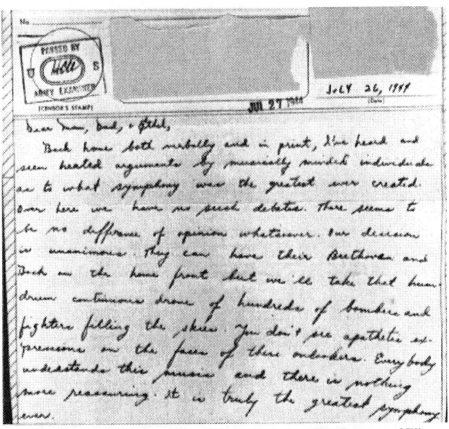

Image reproduced from original letter of July 26, 1944. Courtesy of Eli Ellison.

Life in London during the war. View of a V-1 ("buzz bomb") in flight circa 1944. New York Times Paris Bureau Collection, War and Conflict No. 1323. Public domain image courtesy of National Archives, College Park, Maryland.

Verviers, Belgium, September 1944: Recently-liberated civilians greet American GI's in their Stuart M5 tank on the rue Crapaurue. From Ruwet, A: Vues d'une Occupation et d'une Libération Verviers 1940-1945, 92, Andrimont-Dison (Belgium), 1994, Éditions Irezumi. Reprinted with permission.

The place Verte in celebration, Verviers, September 1944. From Vues d'une Occupation, 96. Reprinted with permission.

Fanfare on the rue Spintay, Verviers, September 14, 1944. From Vues d'une Occupation, 98. Reprinted with permission.

Casualty of War: the l'Athénée, a secondary-school-turned-army-barracks-turned-hospital, became a rubbly tomb for dozens of American soldiers in late December 1944. From Vues d'une Occupation, 110. Reprinted with permission.

Last Gasp: the V-2 rocket, one of Germany's most terrifying technological innovations developed late in the war. Image No. BU10769, Imperial War Museum Photograph Archive, London. Reprinted with permission.

Normie and Vivian Friedberg on their wedding day, April 1945. Courtesy of Eli Ellison.

Eli Ellison, Frankfurt, Germany, August 28, 1945. Courtesy of Eli Ellison.

"He knows. I've explained it to him already. Come on. Cut him some slack." My voice softened as I cocked my head dismissively. "C'mon."

Fatigued and chagrined, Bobby released the frightened boy. His big arms lay limply at his side. "My father was a cop," he quietly began. "He kept his gun locked up in the bedroom. My brother and I, we figured out a way to get to it. We were just a coupla kids horsing around. Next thing I know, my brother's lying in a pool of blood, and my mother's screaming into the phone for an ambulance. He died at the hospital."

Bobby walked up to the boy and gently tousled his hair. "Sorry, kid."

Anxious to smooth things over, I stood up and put a paternal arm around the youngster. Then I walked him to an empty corner of the room.

"What the fuck are you doing, Donnybrook?"

"Cheering everyone up."

"How?"

"I'm gonna show these nice people how an American carbine works. They all wanna see it, so you're outvoted."

"Oh, what the hell. Let's entertain the Belgians with an empty gun."

"Thank you for that ringing endorsement, Sergeant Liter."

"Shut up and shoot, infantry man."

I put on my best showman's voice. "*Maintenant, mes amis. Voilà!*"

Anticipating a soft click, I pointed the carbine toward the ceiling and pulled the trigger. Instead I was greeted by a loud boom. The bullet blasted a tiny hole in the ceiling.

With hot tears streaming down my cheeks, I stared at the aperture above me. Sweat began pouring down my forehead. If I hadn't fired upwards, I probably would have produced the tragedy Bobby described.

While my hosts looked on in shocked silence, I struggled to get a grip on myself. *My God, I could've fuckin' killed someone! I can't understand it. I took out the clip. How could this have possibly happened?*

Then the answer hit me.

Whenever a soldier goes on guard duty, he must throw a bullet into the chamber of his carbine to have it ready for action. After being relieved, he is required to remove the round, a procedure which I had neglected to perform. For over a day, I had been walking around with a live gun, which could have accidentally discharged any time.

The boy stared excitedly at the ceiling. His happy grin had returned. "*Regardez. Un souvenir Américain!*"

The tension was broken. Everyone had a good laugh, and, apologizing profusely, Bobby and I made a quick exit.

If you ever visit Stembert, Belgium,[225] ask for a white-haired farmer about seventy years old. He owns the house where a crazy American sergeant left a souvenir bullet hole shortly after the liberation. The site has been a regional landmark and a topic of conversation for many years.

Somewhere In Belgium
Sept. 23, 1944

Dear Mom, Dad & Ethel,

The Belgian people surpass the French as far as kindness and friendliness are concerned. They cannot do enough for us, and we get all sorts of invitations. In fact, there are so many invitations that we are in a quandary over which ones to accept.

Have had some Belgian beer, and it has considerable sugar added, which gives it a very sweet taste. A little too sweet, but it isn't bad at all.

Signs are posted in all Belgian towns reading: "Welcome To Our Allies," and the flags of every Allied country are visible.

We are encountering a little monetary difficulty because the Belgian and French currency differ in value: 88 Belgian francs are equal to 100 French francs.

The people here speak mostly French, and I can converse reasonably well with them. Flemish and German are spoken a bit also, but only by a very small percentage. The women and girls wear knitted, white stockings in place of the silk ones they can no longer get.

The Belgian people greeted us by running toward us with arms laden with cake, bread, beer, plums, and apples. Unlike many French cities, damage to their buildings appears slight, and they, no doubt, want to show their thankfulness for the good fortune of not having suffered much during the liberating process. Belgium is a beautiful country, with numerous farms everywhere you look.

Lots of Love,

Don

CHAPTER 12

▼

FRIENDLY FIRE

In every war there are needless casualties, those logistical errors that cause armies to attack their own people. Cold statistics can never fully convey the horror of unsuspecting lives snuffed out. The potential of those who died will forever remain unrealized; those who have witnessed such events are doomed to remember them.

Inevitably, there is that nagging "why?" For the grieving widow or orphan, the answers are always unsatisfactory: bad judgment; confusion in the heat of battle; collateral damage; technical problems. The *Verviétois* had their first lesson early.

On May 11, 1940, the day after Hitler invaded Belgium, artillery fire aimed at destroying a railway line instead hit buildings on the rue de la Banque and rue du Palais in central Verviers.[226] The blasts killed seven people and injured fifteen others (110).

Although no structure was completely leveled, there was substantial property damage (107): roofs blown off; windows shattered; walls pierced (107). Forty years later, houses in the area still bore traces of the attack (110).

Belgian historian Jacques Wynants cogently argues that the shelling came from a nearby fort. He notes that on the previous evening, May 10, a Belgian intelligence officer in the Valley of the Vesdre incorrectly reported that a motorized German column had arrived in Verviers (115). Another miscommunication asserted that the *Wehrmacht* had stationed men and matériel in adjacent Stembert (115).

There were several area forts capable of hitting central Verviers: Battice, Barchon, Chaudfontaine, Fléron, Evegnée, and Tancrémont (113). Wynants is convinced that the culprit was Tancrémont (113). To support his conclusion, he cites eyewitness interviews and Joseph Bronckart, a prominent wartime newspaper editor and former city councilman in Verviers (113 nn. 33, 34). Fire from Tancrémont also demolished a textile factory in the nearby town of Pepinster.[227]

Wynants acknowledges that firing on one's own city to dislodge an invader would be entirely justified from a military standpoint.[228] I agree. War is a tragic business in which human lives are often viewed with clinical detachment. Some are considered expendable. In much the same way as a vaccine may destroy healthy cells in order to save a patient, judicious use of artillery can cause civilian casualties but cure dreaded enemy occupation.

A similar situation existed when French naval guns fired on Normandy during D-Day.[229] By contrast, observes Wynants, on May 11, 1940, there were no Germans in Verviers.[230] Thus, seven people needlessly died.

Americans were not immune from making such mistakes. When I was attending radio seminars during my early days in London, several buddies and I struck up a friendship with Private John Soames, an RAF fighter control technician. Soames often visited the 888th and swapped humorous stories with us. He had a favorite joke: "When the Brits bomb, the Gerries duck. When the Gerries bomb, the Brits duck. But when the Yanks bomb, everybody ducks."

*   *   *   *

By late September 1944, the 888th was firmly ensconced in the Verviers area. It is important to remember that although some three-hundred-strong, my outfit wasn't concentrated in one place. Our trucks were dispersed in clusters around Verviers and its suburbs. Commanders had many to choose from, including Stembert, Spa, Dison, Heusy, Andrimont, Petit-Rechain, Lambermont, Wegnez, Pepinster, and Ensival.[231] This arrangement facilitated communication and helped ensure survival of the unit. If one cluster was damaged or destroyed, another could quickly replace it, and the 888th would continue to function.

Jack, Bobby, and I were now among fifty radio men billeted at the l'Athénée Royal, a Belgian secondary school located at 1 rue Thil Lorrain in Verviers. We were very close to the Vesdre river, and only a few blocks from railroad tracks running through the center of the city. However, we continued to work in Stembert, which was only a twenty-minute walk from the l'Athénée.

Stembert was on higher ground than Verviers, making it a better location for positioning equipment. As in England and France, my shift in the transmitter truck began with a telephone call instructing me to tune my radio to a specific frequency. I would then change the crystal in my set and manipulate my dials. The controller in the operations block could now converse with a lead pilot in a group of fighter planes. As new squadrons became airborne, a new frequency would be used. When the next phone call came in, I would insert a new crystal and make the necessary adjustments.

We didn't use this procedure in receiver trucks, where radio conversations were monitored and transcribed. Recall that transmitters allowed controllers to speak with pilots, while receivers allowed controllers to listen to them.

Although Fighter Control also gave tactical support to American ground troops, its primary functions were to keep a close eye on our fighter planes, to be their guardian and director as they flew, and to place them on target.[232] Fighter control squadrons directed U.S. planes toward the enemy and assisted damaged aircraft in returning to base (63).

If a pilot was hit or lost, we needed three receiver trucks to pinpoint his location. A man in each truck would provide a controller with the angle of the plane relative to his vehicle. That angle was determined by taking a bearing on the voice of the lead pilot. The controller, who had a map of all truck locations, would then plot the three angles on a graph. The intersection point was the aircraft's position.

Determining angles could be tricky. The fighter control technician, usually a corporal or sergeant, would turn a wheel attached to his truck's antenna until the pilot's voice reached the "null" or softest volume. Because the difference in loudness between the voice at the correct angle and at one 180 degrees distant was subtle, it was critical that the radio man listen carefully. An error in judgment could cause the pilot to fly out to sea, where death was almost certain.

The pilots, in turn, would radio the controllers information about where they were and what they saw (7). They often destroyed columns of enemy tanks and bridges. Sometimes they would be given an important target; at other times, they were told to locate their own (63). If an infantry division was pinned down by enemy gunfire, the flyers were directed toward the German hardware and instructed not to deviate from that assignment (63). In those instances, only air power could do the job (63).

Complete with air warning personnel, American Fighter Control was originally designed to protect the coast of the United States in the event of hostile air attacks (63). Controllers were well-trained in weather, navigation, and aircraft capabilities (63). On a typical day, fighter-control-directed fighter bombers destroyed over 900 trucks and 775 pieces of horse-drawn equipment (63).

In the radio vans, each buck sergeant supervised two soldiers on his shift, usually a corporal and a PFC. The corporal would perform clerical duties. In receiver trucks, he would also monitor radio broadcasts while the PFC produced a verbatim transcript of all aerial conversations. Higher ranking sergeants were responsible for entire trucks, or small groups of vehicles.

I checked in early one afternoon and found Corporal Clayton Zeke on the phone reciting the following variation of an old schoolboy ditty: "One, two. Unbuckle my shoes. Three, four. I close the door. Five, six. She gets in her licks. Seven, eight. Don't be late. Nine, ten. We'll do it again."

Once aware of my presence, Zeke stopped chattering. "Oh, hi, Sarge," he said with a sheepish grin. "We were just having a little fun. You know how it is." A few seconds of uneasy silence. "Say, aren't you a little early?"

"Yeah," I coldly replied. I felt like punching the little corporal in the nose—or at least dressing him down. But Zeke wasn't under my command. The only other person in the truck was a PFC reading a copy of Life Magazine. I paused momentarily to cool off.

"Who's in charge here?" I inquired.

"Sergeant Spring," replied Zeke.

"Jack Spring?"

"Yeah."

"Jack's a buddy of mine. Where is he?"

"Went to take a leak. Should be back any second."

"I'll find him."

"Look, Sarge, things were slow, and I was just letting off some steam. It won't happen again. Just, please, don't report me, okay?"

"Zeke, whether you're reported or not is up to Jack."

Uninterested in the corporal's reaction, I stormed out of the truck. I hadn't walked very far when I saw Jack's lanky figure striding up the hill. I trotted down to meet him.

"Hey, Donnybrook. Ah didn't know you were on the next shift heah."

"Greenjeans, we've gotta talk. It's about Corporal Zeke."

"Dayem! That guy's an asshole. What did he do now?"

"I caught him horsing around on the telephone."

"Cussin'?"

"Someone was probably testing the frequency and asked him to count from one to ten. He didn't curse, but he was babbling dirty chit-chat between the numbers. Probably wouldn't have stopped if I hadn't walked in on him."

"Ah'll talk to 'im."

"Look, Jack. I'm not a fuddy-duddy, and I hate being a rat. But I just couldn't let this one go. I figure it's your shift, and you should know about it."

"Ah'll read 'im the riot act."

I was climbing back up the hill when Jack called out to me. His voice had a mischievous tone.

"Hey, Donnybrook."

"Yeah?"

"You mean to tell me you was never tempted to hoss around on the phone?"

"Sure I've been tempted. But I never did. Listen, I like a joke as much as the next guy, but whenever I get the urge to act like Zeke, I ask myself, 'What if some bigwig's listening in and decides to have me court-martialed? What if some poor Johnny pilot gets blown up because I'm too busy fuckin' off on the phone?' I couldn't live with that."

"Ah agree. It's dangerous an' dumb. But, ye know, lots of guys do stuff like that all the time."

"Yeah, but most of them don't get caught."

I always took my job seriously. That was a bright line I never crossed. Doctoring passes was one thing; jerking around at work was an entirely different ball game.

A few minutes later, I was working my shift with Corporal Otis Blank. Blank was a balding, pudgy fellow with a perpetually taut facial expression. Happiness seemed to have eluded him. He never smiled. I never saw him with a girl, and you didn't have to be Clark Gable to snare one in Verviers. We were emotional opposites and couldn't stand each other, but we had enough maturity to put our feelings aside while on the job.

A growling buzz bomb passed overhead. To Blank, the drone of the V-1 must have been torture. He tried to smoke a cigarette to calm his nerves, but his hands were shaking so frightfully that he couldn't put a lit match in contact with the tobacco. Blank was a heavy smoker, and he started to panic. Frustrated, he threw the cigarette and matchbook to the floor. I silently picked them up, lit the cigarette, and returned it to him. The corporal took a drag and settled down.

The buzz bomb was barely out of earshot when the radio picked up the screaming voice of an infantry captain: "For Christ's sake, stop your bombing! You're bombing your own troops!"

How he managed to get on a fighter control squadron frequency was a mystery. Front lines were constantly changing, and sometimes it was difficult for pilots to distinguish enemy from American soldiers. Blank's hands started trembling again.

I lowered my head in dismay. Re-tuning the set, I pictured a mass of angry ground troops, some wounded and dying, cursing up a storm while a squadron of errant B-17's dropped its lethal load.

Three days later, Blank was sent to a Paris hospital where he was diagnosed with "battle fatigue." Although I disliked him, I felt sorry for the guy. I was also fascinated by his former occupation. In civilian life, Blank drove a dynamite truck.

It seemed ironic that someone who drove a vehicle full of explosives would crack up so easily. I figured that Blank probably got the shakes whenever he was behind the wheel; fear was constantly building up inside him; and with his nerves shattered, that last buzz bomb and "friendly fire" broadcast finally did him in.

Everyone was concerned about the buzz bombs, but most of us learned to live with them. It was part of the job. Numerous invitations from Belgian civilians were an effective diversion from our occupational hazards, and their exceptional kindness warmed our hearts.

Sept. 26, 1944

Dear Mom, Dad & Ethel,

Today I accepted another dinner invitation. As usual, the meal was good. Meat is lacking in these meals because it is virtually unobtainable. However, that doesn't prevent them from making a good spread. Beer is the favorite drink in Belgium, but they also drink some wine.

In general, the people you talk with are as optimistic as the people back home, and the complete capitulation of Germany is expected to be not far off. Here's hoping it will be real soon.

Love,

Don

Belgium
Sept. 27, 1944

Dear Mom, Dad & Ethel,

In our present location, everything continues to be just about perfect. You cannot imagine just how grand these people are to us. They do our laundry, mend our clothes, and press them, too.

They come to us and ask for laundry. When they return our bundle, they refuse money. The Belgian people may think that we are trying to flatter them when we explain that we have never known such kindness from total strangers before.

Lots of Love,

Don

Sept. 28, 1944

Dear Mom, Dad & Ethel,

I guess we have just about the neatest clothes in the entire Army. Every day, women and children come and plead with us to give them some laundry to do. As a result, our garments couldn't be more immaculate.

After washing the clothes, they iron them for us. If they find a button or two missing, they replace them. They refuse to take money for their services. Then, as if that weren't enough, they insist that you have dinner with them. They aren't just nice people—they're saints.

I have met a nice bunch of Belgian fellows, several of whom speak English. Some speak Flemish, and some speak German.

There is one fellow who is 20 years old and intends to be a writer. He is a medium-built fellow, slightly shorter than me. He already has a desk crammed with stuff he has written. He has written a play for a theatre and is anxious to learn English. He has never studied it in school. I help him in English, and he helps me with French.

His father is an old Belgian army man. His mother is a sweet woman, and he has some younger brothers and sisters.

Everything continues to be just about the best possible. The English say "smashing;" the Belgians say "magnifique;" and I say "terrific."

Love,

Don

War can try even the patience of saints. There are times when the best of citizens can become violent. Tempers flared early in the German occupation of Verviers.

By September 1940, civil unrest had reached a fever pitch. Potato prices skyrocketed, infuriating an already hungry population.[233] A mob of women demanding relief stormed the Office of Food Control (239). The tense standoff continued until the next day, when Communist alderman Henri Lambert was able to calm the crowd (239).

Four years later, the people of Verviers remained malnourished. The situation was particularly bad in the summer of 1944, and was very slow to improve, even after the liberation. Between June 20 and September 17, each *Verviétois* was rationed less than 1,200 calories a day.[234] By September 2, the retreating Germans had taken whatever provisions they could get their hands on (6). There was no meat in the butcheries, and flour was rare (6). Official Allied documents indicate that Belgian food rations did not exceed 1,461 calories until after December 16 (142). Even optimists had to admit that a person could not obtain an adequate diet without recourse to the black market (142).

Meat distribution, in particular, was hindered by local Allied operations (42). Potatoes and butter were hard to find (42). Although bread was regularly delivered (42), a flour shortage kept consumption low (142). Because of high transportation expenses, the cost of bread here was higher than elsewhere in Belgium (144). In November 1944, Verviers went nearly fifteen days without bread, although it was plentiful in the central part of the country (144).

Making matters even worse, the local government responded very slowly to a coal crisis (136), exacerbating existing shortages of electricity, steam, heat, gas, and trains. In short, the region's economy was paralyzed (136).

These circumstances made hospitality in and around Verviers all the more remarkable. Unfortunately for us, this Belgian generosity was about to be curtailed.

Belgium
Oct. 2, 1944

Dear Mom, Dad & Ethel,

Recently we received a disturbing order: we are not to eat with civilians, enter their homes, or stand and talk with them. We are not allowed to enter any civilian shops of any kind, any theater, or anything not military. Naturally, this just about knocks all hell out of any plans we had here.

Orders are orders, but we sure hope they rescind this one soon.

Love,

Don

Though now forbidden, we still managed to have some contact with the locals. Our best conversation partners were young women and children. These encounters were brief and usually occurred when we were walking to and from work.

Oct. 3, 1944

Dear Mom, Dad & Ethel,

The Yanks have left certain vestiges which will always remain here. G.I. Joe has been an excellent English instructor. The first two expressions that are prerequisites and cardinal to the language are "Kiss me quick" and "I love you." Naturally, it requires demonstrative action to make these lessons sink into the female pupils' minds.

The kids here are like anywhere else. They like their bonbons and chewing gum.

Hope you are all well.

Love,

Don

A week later, tragedy struck. While preparing for my shift on the afternoon of October 11, 1944, I was in the courtyard of the l'Athénée when I saw a squadron of American P-38's overhead. Twelve planes were flying in three groups of four.[235] I'll never forget the hour. It was 3:20 p.m.[236] The weather was mild and sunny,[237] which made it easy to recognize the horizontally stacked, "double queue" shapes of the aircraft.[238] Cheerfully waving, I visually followed their flight path. Nothing could have prepared me for what happened next.

A flash of light emanated from one plane. Then another. And another. My smile abruptly changed to an ashen expression of horror. The P-38's were bombing Verviers.

Forty years later, historian Wynants remarked: "The most embarrassing event for the Americans was, without doubt, the bombardment of the city by their own air forces on Wednesday, 11 October 1944, around 15h 20."[239]

The P-38's hit Verviers with seven or eight bombs over several minutes.[240] With air raid sirens wailing, people poured into public shelters (9). Fearful passersby ducked into nearby houses (9), while the more adventurous pressed up against walls outside, looking to see what was falling from the sky (9).

Casualties were heavy. Sixteen civilians were killed (10), including two women and a girl who were found alive but later died at the hospital (10). One of the women, Mrs. Louisa Adam, was pulled from the rubble and received an on-the-spot blood transfusion from a U.S. Army doctor (10). Also recovered was the body of Mrs. Koll, a thirty-three-year-old housekeeper (11). By a stroke of random good luck, the family who employed her was not home when the bombs landed (11).

Four African-American GI's were killed in their jeep, which was hit at the intersection of the rues Biolley and Stembert (12). They were near a school and a railway line approximately eight blocks southeast of the l'Athénée.[241]

In addition, forty-seven other *Verviétois* suffered injuries serious enough to require treatment, including twenty-three sent to a Red Cross facility,[242] and twenty transported to the hospital (12).

Property damage was extensive. The *Magasin Binet*, a store with a vast inventory, was completely destroyed (10). Part of it crumbled into the Vesdre (10). The cost of rebuilding the *Simonis* wool and dye factories was estimated at over twenty million Belgian francs (11), about five hundred thousand dollars. All houses on the left side of the rue Stembert were rendered uninhabitable (11).

The Verviers press did not report any of this information during the war.[243] Under Allied censorship, stories detrimental to military or civilian morale were suppressed.[244] Such incidents were rare, but when they occurred, their impact was devastating. Despite the news blackout, word of the catastrophe soon spread. Many frightened *Verviétois* spent the night of October 11 huddled in cellars (12), waking frequently to the sound of explosions (12).

At least this time there were no mistakes. German bombers and Allied ack-ack were at it again.

✳   ✳   ✳   ✳

Major General E.R. Quesada was in charge of the Ninth Tactical Air Command, which operated throughout Belgium and was headquartered in Verviers. Outraged by the tragedy, Quesada grounded all twelve blundering pilots for the rest of the war.

The bombers had probably mistaken Verviers for the German city of Aix-la-Chapelle,[245] also known as Aachen. Located on Belgium's eastern border, it finally fell on October 20, 1944.[246] Aachen was the first large German city captured by the Allies.[247]

Major General Quesada was someone you never saw unless you worked at Ninth TAC Headquarters. He had flown many combat missions and was a very decorated pilot. In 1942, at age thirty-eight, he became one of the youngest generals in the Air Corps.

Although I never met the major general, I was well-aware of his hard-nosed reputation. If Quesada heard that a soldier hadn't mastered his job, or wasn't performing in the best possible manner, he was history.

While U.S. pilots occasionally mistook friends for foes, they were sometimes fooled by the enemy's benign-looking camouflage. I was monitoring a radio conversation one afternoon when I heard a distressed flyer shout, "Stay away from the hospital! They're shooting at us from the roof!"

U.S. pilots had been given strict instructions not to target anything resembling a medical facility. Meanwhile, the Nazis had mounted anti-aircraft guns on top of those buildings and were taking down Allied planes.

On the evening of October 13, two days after the P-38 disaster, I received a call in my van. The squadron's code name was "Sweepstakes." GI's were most likely to kid around on the telephone when things were slow. That night, I didn't have much to do.

"Okay, Sweepstakes. Give me a count of one to ten," the caller requested.

I'd had a couple of beers shortly before going on duty. I was in high spirits and was going to make a wisecrack. But then I remembered how angry I had gotten with Corporal Zeke for engaging in similar antics.

"One, two, three, four, five, six, seven, eight, nine, ten," I dutifully intoned. "Sweepstakes, over out."

Thirty seconds later, the phone rang again.

"Know who you were just talking to?"

"No. Who?"

"Major General Quesada. He was just checking up on you fellas, to make sure you're on the ball and not screwing around."

That was the only time I was ever tempted to horse around on the job. Wally Cleaver had won an important battle with Eddie Haskell, but the struggle would continue.

CHAPTER 13

▼

DENISE, VERVIERS,
AND THE V-WEAPONS

In a small l'Athénée classroom packed with buck sergeants, Bobby sat down and farted. The two radio men on either side of him instinctively recoiled. A loud burst of belly laughing followed.

Actually, no intestinal gas had emanated from Bobby's body. Some prankster had placed a whoopee cushion under his seat. Sergeant Liter eyed his fellow supervisors with deep suspicion and angrily flung the trick pillow onto the floor. He was in no mood for jokes.

"You step on a duck or somethin'?" Jack needled.

"So it was you, wasn't it? I've had it with your goddamned, bloody bullshit. Now I'm gonna kick your ass."

Spreading my arms eagle-style, I immediately jumped between the two of them. On my left was Bobby, red with anger; on my right, Jack, red with laughter. There was no doubt in anyone's mind that Bobby, who outweighed Jack by about seventy pounds, was quite capable of murdering him.

"Hey! We're all friends here. Let's cool it, okay?"

"Get out of my way, Donnybrook. I don't wanna go through you, but I will if I have to."

Jack grew serious. "Back off, Donnybrook. Ah'm perfectly able to defend mahself." Raising his hand in a conciliatory gesture, the Georgian continued,

"Now, just a second, Bobby. You said you was gonna kick mah ass. Well, Ah'm afraid you can't do that."

"Why the hell not?"

"'Cause Ah don't have an ass."

Another chorus of laughter arose among the men.

Jack paused, and then enthusiastically added, "But Ah've got a mule."

That brought the house down. By now, we had all seen or heard the buzz bombs, and there were rumors that the Germans had a few more surprises in store for Verviers. Tension in the outfit was high, and we welcomed anything that helped get our minds off it.

Then there was Jack himself. His excellent comic timing rivaled Ken's. He was good enough to pacify even the moody Bobby, who quickly exchanged his grimace for a smile. The two men shook hands. Nobody could stay mad at Jack for very long.

"Sorry, Greenjeans. I just pulled a double shift, and both my corporals didn't show up. Guess I'm a bit grouchy."

"No sweat, big fella. It's okay to be grouchy once in a while. Jus' try not to make it a habit."

Stan, unobtrusively standing in the doorway, had seen all. "If you guys are through making love, I'd like to get started," he intoned. Stan had one of those soft, resonant voices that naturally attracts attention. Toting a clipboard, he gestured toward the three of us to sit down. We promptly complied.

Greetings of "Hi, Stan" followed him to the front of the room. Always informal, he possessed an air of quiet competence. Stan sat down on the edge of the teacher's desk and gently placed his clipboard on the hard wood. He grinned. Then his face grew sterner.

"Now listen up, people. The reason I called this meeting was because of all the complaints going around about scheduling. Just the kind of stuff Bobby was talking about. Corporals and PFC's bitching about hours. Sergeants complaining about being short-handed. Some of this has gotten back to First Sergeant Abatelli and Captain Jones. Needless to say, they're ticked off. And they told me to straighten things out, so now I'm ticked off. During our chat, the captain said, 'I don't give a flying fuck how the men arrange their shifts. Just make sure the radio vans are in operation twenty-four hours a day.'"

Angelo, my old tent-mate from basic training, piped up from the back: "Old man Jones really say that?"

"His very words."

"That's some spicy meatballs."

"What do you expect, Angelo? This is the United States Army, not Sunday school." After a momentary pause, Stan continued, "Bottom line: you can arrange your shifts any way you want, so long as the trucks keep running. But whatever the hours are, people have gotta show up for work. Get your corporals and PFC's in line. I don't care how you do it. Just do it."

Up until now, each sergeant had worked one of three eight-hour shifts: either 8 a.m. to 4 p.m.; 4 p.m. to 12 a.m.; or 12 a.m. to 8 a.m.

"Ah've got an ideah."

"Jack, this better not be another gag."

"No, Stan. Ah'm serious. Lookit. Since there ain't much doin' aftah dark, why not work a double night shift? We could rotate 'em. Whenevah you work from 4 p.m. to midnight, you stay in the van 'til eight the next mornin'. Now, mah math is not the best, but Ah reckon this way we'll each have a day and a half off 'bout every three days."

"Jack, you're a bloody genius," Bobby praised.

"Absolutely," I concurred.

"Count me in," added a third sergeant.

"Wait a minute," Stan cautioned. "It sounds good in theory, but I'm a little concerned that with all the rotating, someone might screw up. Will anyone find this confusing?"

"If I get a day and a half off every three days, I will make it my business not to be confused," Angelo retorted. "And I don't think you'll be getting any lip from the corporals and PFC's. Not on this deal."

"All right. Raise your hand if you're in favor of Jack's proposal."

Every man's arm in the room shot up. Now all eyes were on Stan.

"Okay. You're gonna have to work out the details among yourselves and your lower-ranking noncoms. As long as the vans are working around the clock, it's fine by me. Meeting over. Have a nice day."

While the room was clearing out, Stan took Bobby aside. Their voices carried, and I heard them in the hallway. Though uncomfortable with the conversation, I stopped to listen.

"Bobby, you've gotta learn to control your temper. Sooner or later, it's gonna get you into big trouble."

"Look, I was tired, and Jack's stupid trick was just a bit too much."

"Greenjeans pulls stupid tricks on everybody. Sure, he's a bit of an oddball, but he means well, and he works hard. Everyone else laughs him off. You're the only one that blows up. You sure you're okay?"

"I'm fine, Stan."

"You need anything?"

"Yeah. A good night's sleep and a lay."

"You're gonna have to get those on your own, pal. Anything else?"

"Nope."

"I hope so. Everyone who works the vans—and I mean everyone—knows about your temper. So far, your fellow radio truck operators haven't been talking to higher-ups. But if you don't calm down, it's only a matter of time before word gets back to Jones or Abatelli, and then I won't be able to help you. So cool it."

"Okay."

"Listen. If things are getting tough and you ever wanna shoot the breeze over a coupla beers, I'll be around."

"Thanks."

"Get some sleep, Bobby. That's an order."

Happily for Sergeant Liter, a lull in aerial activity[248] allowed him to catch up on much needed rest. On October 12, Verviers began gruesome excavations over areas damaged by the accidental bombing (12). Funerals for victims were held on the thirteenth, while work crews continued their unpleasant tasks (12-3).

But the respite was short-lived. Over the next several months, the skies over the city were very busy. Allied aircraft regularly flew day and night bombing missions into Germany (13), while numerous explosions rocked the region (13). Then there were the V-1's, which appeared on an almost daily basis (13-58), and often arrived in bunches (13-58).

Oddly enough, the origins of the "flying bomb" can be traced to an Englishman.[249] Sir Hiram Maxim performed the first unmanned flight experiments in 1891 (15). Work on military prototypes in the UK and the U.S. began during World War I, but they were considered impractical and eventually abandoned (15-8).

German scientists succeeded where the British and Americans had failed. The first *vergeltungswaffeneins* or "vengeance weapons one" (a.k.a. "buzz bombs") reached England on June 13, 1944 (61). Some 6,725 V-1's would cross the Channel before their delivery vehicles were finally silenced on March 29, 1945 (174).

Their effectiveness could be summed up in two words: inaccurate and deadly. As their name suggested, the "vengeance weapons" were primarily instruments of terror designed to intimidate civilian populations rather than destroy military targets.[250] Powered by noisy pulse-jet engines, they were crude by modern standards.[251] They always reminded me of the "putt-putt" of a slow motorboat.

But sounds can be deceiving. The V-1's attained a maximum speed of 400 mph (165), equal to the fastest conventional fighters of the day (28). These cruise missiles[252] would inflict ten percent of all British civilian casualties during the war.[253]

The key to their fearsomeness was unpredictability. The Germans deployed several versions of the V-1. In earlier models, the engines would cut off about ten seconds before impact, giving people time to take cover.[254] The length of each buzz bomb's flight was determined by rotations of a small propeller, monitored by an internal counter.[255] When the counter reached a certain number, the vehicle would automatically adjust its controls from flying to diving mode.[256] This change would stop the flow of fuel.[257] However, the on-board robot didn't always work properly.

Sometimes the engines would cut and then restart.[258] Occasionally, V-1's would turn around and go back toward the Channel (66). To make matters even more confusing, later versions would continue droning right up until impact. Witnesses would say that these more advanced bombs seemed to have minds of their own, sadistically mesmerizing observers by flying in coiled patterns toward their quarries (84).

Realizing that it was only a matter of time before the Allies would capture their ground sites, the Germans began developing an air-launched V-1 in the winter of 1943 (123-4). They decided that the best aircraft for the job was the Heinkel HE-111H-21 (124), a descendant of the errant plane I saw caught in the searchlights over London. The buzz bomb flew tucked under the Heinkel's starboard wing root, between the plane's motor and fuselage (124), before being released at fifteen hundred feet (124). Supplementing Hitler's arsenal of ground-launched vengeance weapons, air-launched V-1's began terrorizing Europeans on both sides of the Channel in September 1944 (126). The attacks ended on January 14, 1945 (131), shortly before the end of the Battle of the Bulge.

Regardless of their method of delivery, V-1's were always tough targets for countermeasures (101). Most flew at between two thousand and three thousand feet (101), a range above the capability of light anti-aircraft artillery, and below that of heavy (101). In addition, radar was least effective at those altitudes (101).

The Royal Observer Corps, who taught Fighter Control to American squadrons such as the 888th,[259] would fire rockets to attract the attention of RAF pilots toward incoming V-1's.[260] Because of the buzz bombs' great speed, the British used their fastest aircraft to intercept them, including the Hawker Tempest 5, Spitfire, and North American Mustang (102).

The role of new technology and experience cannot be overstated. In July 1944, the British deployed their first jets (105). With a maximum speed of 410 mph, the Gloster Meteor Fighter could overtake a V-1 and fly above it (105). There is the famous story of 616 Squadron jet pilot "Dixie" Dean, who, after intercepting a buzz bomb, found that his guns had jammed (104). Flying along-side the V-1, he tipped it with his wing, causing it to crash before it could do any harm (104). Pilots of propeller aircraft soon adopted this method (104). Another favorite technique was to have the fighter plunge past the missile (104). The resulting turbulence caused it to go prematurely into dive mode and explode harmlessly into the water or countryside (104).

Further defensive developments included an improved fuse mechanism in anti-aircraft guns which dramatically increased the number of V-1 kills in the UK (117-8). The timing was fortuitous: at least eight ack-ack batteries were trans-ferred from England to Belgium in the fall of 1944, just when the people of that newly liberated country needed them most (131).

At this time, the average *Verviétois* was filled with joy in the daytime and fear at night.[261] He basked in freedom from Nazi occupation but was still afraid of visits from the *Luftwaffe* and its robotic friends. Although bombings occurred at all hours, darkness always intensified the terror.

On the first night I arrived in Verviers, I was greeted by frequently wailing police cars and fire engines racing toward splintered edifices throughout the city. A few V-1's were coming over every hour, setting off a cacophony of ack-ack, air raid sirens, and emergency vehicles. Each time, frightened civilians rushed into the town's many air raid shelters.

Twice I got caught up in mobs streaming off the streets. A middle-aged woman got her dress caught under a departing tram. Several citizens struggled in vain to free her. I cut her loose with my pocket knife. A moment later, I found myself being ushered into a wine cellar. The panicked owner slammed the door so hard that he broke nearly every bone in an unfortunate customer's hand. A couple of hours later, I was hunkered down in the basement of a private home. The crowd here was smaller than in the wine cellar, but with less room, it was equally uncomfortable.

I had it out with myself. *This is crazy. There's a lot of buzz bombs flying around, but very few seem to be landing in town. If I'm gonna run to a shelter every time I see one, I'll wind up in a strait jacket. So when they come, I'm just gonna stay put. Wher-ever the hell I am.*

Things were tense, but we still had our diversions, and Belgian civilians con-tinued to be incredibly friendly, despite their financial hardship.

Belgium
Oct. 12, 1944

Dear Mom, Dad & Ethel,

Whenever our vehicles drive down the street, the people, especially children, rush to their windows and shout, wave, and make all sorts of motions to herald our passing.

Yesterday I went to the public bathhouse and had one of those refreshing showers. In France and in Belgium, a bath in one's home is something which only a privileged few have. Thus the average man is compelled to go to the public bath for body cleanliness.

When I went there, the lineup wasn't particularly long, and I was inside the enclosed shower in about 30 minutes. The water was nice and warm. It was worth a million times more than the two-and-a-half francs (6 cents) that was charged.

Civilians in these countries queue up for numerous things, and it resembles the G.I.'s chow lines. They line up for bread, meat (when it's available), newspapers, the bathhouse, etc. It's always lines and more lines.

Last night I went to a G.I. movie. The theater was a beauty, with excellent sound effects. For awhile we almost felt like civilians. But we soon learned our mistake. When the projectionist put the alleged third reel on, it turned out to be the same as the second reel. They had shipped us two #2 reels, instead of #1, #2, and #3. An apologetic announcement came over the loud speaker, and the show was discontinued.

Love,

Don

Belgium
Oct. 16, 1944

Dear Mom, Dad & Ethel,

Our new club for the enlisted men of the outfit has already opened, and this letter is being written in the club. One of our men, who is a carpenter by trade, built a bar, and, right now, drinks are being sold here.

We have a ping-pong table, a piano, a phonograph, a radio, and lots of reading and writing tables. The club is only for enlisted men, and we should have a successful place for recreation and relaxation. Just a few minutes ago, two G.I.'s jumped up and started to jitterbug to the music. One of the two has worked up quite a sweat and has pulled off his shirt.

This evening I went to the G.I. theater and saw Eddie Cantor in "Show Business." I haven't laughed so long and hard in quite some time. Some of the gags and slapstick comedy had us roaring.

Attendance at the theater has been so high that tonight, for the first time, two performances were held. Everybody had been starving for entertainment, and now that word of the show has gotten around, the place is always packed to capacity. An exception was made to allow a few lieutenant nurses to attend the show. These girls were the only ones present, and during the change of reels, the fellows embarrassed them by concentrating hundreds of flashlights on their faces.

Received a letter from Joe the other day, and he says he has only received one package since coming to France. I can't understand why he is getting such tough breaks on mail, while I am getting a continuous flow of stuff. I think you should send Joe more packages than myself, since I am receiving them and he isn't.

So Long and Lots of Love,

Don

Oct. 26, 1944

Dear Mom, Dad & Ethel,

This week the town was put on limits. It feels as if we've been given a prison pardon. I can now walk through the streets freely. Have been to a Belgian movie house, and I tried to follow the French conversation. It's odd to see our American actors talking with dubbed-in, French voices.

Love,

Don

Oct. 31, 1944

Dear Mom, Dad & Ethel,

I saw another Belgian show yesterday. The place was mobbed. They are having a lot of trouble with electricity. As a result, the people can only iron their clothes or listen to the radio during certain periods of the day.

The theaters are now closed several days a week. After I purchased a ticket for the 8 o'clock show and presented it at the door, the cashier told me that it was canceled. The manager happened to be there at the same time. He took the ticket from me, rushed to the cashier, gave her a scolding, returned, and gave me back my money.

Saw some actual shots of the liberation of Paris, and they don't hold back any punches. They were gruesome, bloody, and factual.

Love,

Don

Nov. 3, 1944

Dear Mom, Dad & Ethel,

Last night a friend and I ate supper at the home of some people we knew in a nearby village. We had soup, rabbit, potatoes, apple sauce, bread, beer, and a pear. It was a good meal, and we were plenty full. We rode to the village by trolley car. There is no charge for soldiers on these trams.

I met an English-speaking lady the other day, and it certainly was a pleasure to have a lady talking in a good, clear, English voice.

She had lived in Long Island for about seven years. Like everybody else, she would like to return to the United States after the war. However, she is now a Belgian citizen, must be patient, and try and squeeze her name onto the quota list.

You don't realize how foreigners admire America and Americans. They only know the bright side of America, the Hollywood version, and look at you as if you came from heaven.

I am receiving your mail steadily, and you are certainly doing a good job of keeping me informed of what's going on at home. I received your package of crackers and jam, and these foodstuffs are mighty handy when midnight sometimes finds me a bit hungry.

Fruit is plentiful here, and prices are low, probably because this is mostly farm country. We see more meat in the store windows now than when we first arrived here.

All these victuals, however, are still heavily rationed. They have a long way to go before they reach the pre-war quota. Drinks in cafés are very expensive. Cognac is about 20 to 30 francs (50 to 75 cents) a shot. If you are with a few fellows, it really dents the bankroll. Beer sells for about 6 francs (14 cents) in places without an orchestra, and 10 francs (25 cents) in those that have music.

Love,

Don

Nov. 7, 1944

Dear Mom, Dad & Ethel,

I was amused at your microscopic calculation. You people insist on trying to convince yourselves that I am having it rough. Your last letter practically credits me with being a story teller.

However, my work schedule is so variable, yet so pleasing, that I can understand your unbelieving attitude. Sometimes I work mornings, sometimes afternoons, sometimes nights. On other occasions, I work straight through for long periods and am then compensated by having one-and-a-half days off. Thus I am able to have entire days to myself. So please cancel that doubtful attitude. For fact is truth, and that's all you're getting.

Love,

Don

Things really had improved for us, but Dad wouldn't believe me. I was getting enough to eat, had a roof over my head for a change, and, now, a series of happy coincidences were about to transform my wartime experience.

Under the old schedule, I would have been working an afternoon shift on that weekday in early November 1944. Instead, thanks to Jack, I had the entire day off. And with the non-fraternization order recently rescinded, I was able to take in a matinée in the Cinéma Le Louvre, a movie house on the place du Martyr in central Verviers.[262] There, I met Denise Vervier, a textile worker who just happened to be enjoying some free time of her own. We literally bumped into each other while finding seats.

"*Pardon* [excuse me]," I apologized.

"*Non, c'est ma faute* [No, it's my fault]," replied Denise.

"*Tu es*...oh Jeez...*Es-tu blessée* [Are you hurt]?"

"*Non. Ça va* [No. It's okay]."

Denise, no more than five feet two inches tall, was a curvy brunette with smooth, shoulder-length hair. She had a rather large forehead, high cheekbones, and deep-set brown eyes capable of expressing great mirth and sorrow. Her fine, delicate nose curved slightly upwards at the tip, a counterpoint to her strong, yet feminine, jaw line. She was twenty-three, a year older than yours truly, who had just celebrated his twenty-second birthday. She wore a modest, one-piece, brown dress and little makeup. Subdued red lipstick and a white hair ribbon were her only adornments.

"*Et vous, Sergent?* [And you, Sergeant?] *Ça va?*"

"*Oui, mademoiselle. Ça va*...um...*Est-ce que...ce siège est libre* [Is this seat taken]?"

"*Non, c'est tout à vous* [No, it's all yours]."

I sat down next to her. A few seconds of awkward silence followed.

"*Je m'appelle Don Quix* [My name is Don Quix]."

"*Enchantée, Sergent Don* [Pleased to meet you, Sergeant Don]. *Je suis Denise Vervier* [I am Denise Vervier]."

"*Enchanté.*"

A series of scolding hisses closely followed the subdued whirring of the projector. I glanced sheepishly at Denise. With a knowing gaze, she shrugged and demurely smiled at me, gently placing an index finger to her lips as her face faded into the darkness.

"*Nous parlerons plus tard* [We'll talk later]," she whispered.

The film seemed to last forever. For over two hours, I sat there, wrestling with my admiration, lust, and frustration. Already I sensed a down-to-earth, emotional intelligence in Denise far beyond that of any female I'd ever known. I wanted to put my arms around her, hold her with the tight grip of a man drowning in mediocrity, but I'd have to wait. Many thoughts raced through my mind.

Is my French good enough to have a decent conversation with her? Well, maybe it doesn't matter. It seems like we can already read each other's minds. How long should I wait before I try something? She's a nice girl, and I don't wanna blow it. I don't give a damn what Greenjeans says. I think nice girls can be bedded, too. It has to be better with a nice girl. It's so empty the other way.

At last, the projector stopped, and the lights snapped on. A sultry voice whispered into my ear.

"Hey, Sarge. What did you think of the movie?"

Nonplussed, I stared at Denise for several seconds. "Where did you learn to speak English like that? You hardly have an accent."

"I took some secretarial courses at university before the war. The teachers told us that it is important in business to know as many languages as you can. They said English was becoming, how do you say, universal."

"Gee, why didn't you tell me?"

"Because it was so much fun to see you struggling with French."

"Well, I'm glad you had a good laugh."

"Oh, please do not be angry. So few American boys know the language, and even fewer try to speak it correctly. The care you took with our conversation made me feel special."

"You really mean that?"

"Absolument [Absolutely]."

I grinned and tipped my cap with mock formality. "Well, the United States Army always tries to please, ma'am."

"Ma'am? That is for old ladies."

"Sorry. *Mademoiselle.*"

"Much better. You did make one small mistake, though. You used the '*tu*' form instead of the '*vous*' form."

"Well, I figured we're about the same age, and we were sitting together, so—"

"You should only use *tu* when talking to people you know well."

"Consider it an advance."

"I do not understand."

"For when I get to know you better."

"And how do you propose to do that, Sergeant Done?"

"My name's Don. I'm not done, and we're not either." I leaned closer to her and softly continued, "In fact, we're just getting started. Let's begin with dinner."

"Okay. I am sorry I did not pronounce your name correctly."

"No problem. English is a tough language."

"I hope you didn't mind being corrected on your French."

"Honey, you can work on my French anytime."

"*Bon.* Shall we go? I am, how do you say—"

"Starved."

"*Exactement.* By the way, the word for 'honey' is *chérie.*"

"Okay, *chérie.*"

It was dark when we left the Cinéma at 6 p.m. A rising moon illuminated the blacked-out streets as we walked to a small café on the place Verte a couple of blocks away. There, Denise and I ate a hearty meal of soup and sandwiches. The hours flew by. It was already 9 o'clock.

We didn't have to rush. Beginning November 2, 1944, curfews in the City of Verviers varied from 9 p.m. to midnight,[263] but the cafés always stayed open until 11.[264]

"Isn't Vervier an unusual name?"

"*Mais non*, not at all."

"Where I come from, you don't see too many people named after their home-towns."

"What about your first president, George Washington? You have your capital, Washington. Then there was Washington Irving and George Washington Carver."

"*Touché.* You know a lot of American history."

"I pick up some from English language books. You must have learned some French history when you studied French, no?"

"Yeah, but I forgot most of it."

"Where are you from, Sergeant Don?"

"New York. The Bronx, to be exact."

"I've heard of it. The Bronx. It sounds so rugged and American."

"Never thought of it that way, but now that you mention it, I think you've got a point. *Touché encore, mademoiselle.*"

"I have heard of the Bronx Bombers."

"The Yankees? You're kidding."

"I have heard of, let me see, Babe Ruth, Lou Gehrig—and Jolting Joe Dimaggio."

"Congratulations! You're the first Belgian baseball fan I've met."

"I am not really a fan. But I've been listening to shortwave radio broadcasts from the Voice of America and the BBC for years.[265] It helps improve my English, and it's a good way to keep up on the latest war news."

"Is your shortwave a transmitter or a receiver?"

"I do not understand."

"With a transmitter, you can broadcast. With a receiver, you can only listen to stations."

"Oh, it's only a receiver. I do not know much about radios. The Resistance fighters, I think they have transmitters. Why do you ask?"

"Well, it kind of ties in with my job."

"And what is your job, Sergeant Don?"

"I'm a radio truck operator."

"That is very important work."

"Yeah, but it seems easy when I think of all the combat outfits getting the hell beat out of 'em."

"Do not feel guilty, Sergeant Don. You don't have to be good with a gun to be a patriot. Your job is very, how do you say, *technique.*"

"Technical?"

"Yes."

"Yeah, it's kinda technical."

"There is the war of brains, and then there is the war of brawn."

"Well said. But believe me, I'm no Einstein." Pausing for a moment, I was anxious to change the subject. "Say, when did you get your shortwave?"

"I think it was late 1941 or early '42."

"During the occupation?"

"Yes."

"I can't believe the Germans would let you buy that stuff."

"Well, actually, they didn't."

"Then how did you get it? In the black market?"

"No. A friend gave it to me. It's an old model, but it still works very well. I made one mistake, though."

"What was that?"

"I didn't go home with it right away. I took it with me to the store to buy a little food, and there were two German soldiers there. They tried to take it away from me. We had, how do you say, a tug-of-war."

"Who won?"

"I did."

I laughed loudly and banged my fist on the table. "Yeah!" I shouted. "That'll show those Gerry bastards! Good for you!"

Nearby patrons turned toward me. Chagrined, I lowered my voice to a whisper. "Sorry about that. I enjoyed your story so much that I just hadda let loose."

"Don't be sorry. We are used to Americans acting out. It is very entertaining."

"Now you're making fun of me."

"No, not at all. I think European men are a little too quiet. I like the American spirit. Of course, it can be overdone."

"Actually, I'm usually not too rowdy. But you really got me going there. You know, I'd like to see that radio sometime."

Denise smiled. "That can be arranged."

I hesitated uncomfortably. "So. What other sports do you like besides baseball and tug-of-war?"

"Boxing."

"Now, this has gotta be a joke."

"No, it's not. My father was always a big boxing fan. When I was growing up, he would take the whole family to prize fights: me, my mother, and my sister. He used to do a little boxing in the army."

"Me too. Sometimes I think half the world has done a little boxing in the army."

"Well, Papa was never very serious about it. And now he just likes to watch. But I remember when my sister and I were young, he had us put on these big boxing gloves. He said it was important to learn how to defend yourself. I think he was just sorry that my mother didn't have boys."

"Well, I won't be asking you into an alleyway anytime soon. You must be a pretty strong gal. Boxing. Roughing up a coupla Boches."

Denise dismissively waved her hand and giggled. "Don't be silly. But I do enjoy watching the matches. I still go with my parents and sister every now and then. Would you like to go some time? I think there will be a match in a few weeks."

"Sure, I'd love to. In theory, I could be shipped off anytime, but I know my unit's gonna be here at least until the ground troops get into Germany, and I don't think that'll be for a while."

Denise dejectedly looked down at the table for a moment and then stared straight into my eyes. "Are you certain?" she asked. "Because if you cannot make it, I will understand."

"*Chérie*, we both know that nothing's absolutely certain in this life, but I'm as sure as I'll ever be."

Denise's eyes brightened. "That is good enough for me," she said with a warm smile.

"So we're on?"

"We're on. I will give you the details as soon as I know them."

"Swell. Just tell your dad I'll pay for my ticket."

"No. He would feel insulted."

"Yeah, but with you folks struggling and all—"

"Humor us. It makes us feel more patriotic."

"Well, in that case, okay."

"*Bon.*"

"So you live in Verviers?"

"No, I am a seamstress at a textile factory here. I live in Stembert."

"No kidding? I work in Stembert, but my barracks is in Verviers. Just the reverse. I guess you could say we're mirror images of each other."

"Opposites do attract."

"Ever been married?"

Denise's eyes glazed over. "Yes," she softly intoned.

"Guess I hit a sore spot."

"No, it's okay. It was a long time ago. Looking back, it seems almost like a dream. I was very young, and I had just started my first job. That is when I met my husband, Étienne. We worked at the same factory. He was a cutter and made good money."

"Are you divorced?"

"No. When the Germans came to Verviers, they arrested Étienne and a lot of other Belgian men. They were sent to a forced labor camp. The soldiers must have gotten Étienne at work. He just never came home one day, and I never saw him again. Later I heard from, how do you say, the grapevine, that he died."

"Jeez. That's a tough break, especially for a newlywed kid. You must hate the Germans something fierce."

"Well, yes and no."

"How can you say that? They occupied your country for four years, enslaved your people, and killed your husband. How could you not hate their guts?"

"I hate that evil maniac Hitler and his crazy SS. We are not far from the German border, and I have heard the rumors about the concentration camps."

"Me too. I'm Jewish, by the way."

"And I'm Catholic. *Ça m'est égal* [It's all the same to me]. Jews, Catholics, Americans, Germans, Belgians. We are all human beings. Not all Germans are monsters. Many are decent men who got drafted and had to serve in the army.

Most of the German soldiers I saw were very polite. They tipped their hats to ladies, and they always hung up their guns before sitting down to eat."

"To me, they're all the same. Infantry, Luftwaffe, SS, whatever. They can all go to hell."

"I understand why you feel that way. You're a soldier, part of the great Allied forces. Germany is the enemy, and you must defeat her. If you made exceptions, you would not fight well. Hitler is a madman, and for you to stop him, many Germans must die. That makes me very sad because there are many good people in Germany. If you are a soldier, you are not allowed to have these feelings, but many *Verviétois* do."

"What are you telling me? That you've got a soft spot for Germans?"

"Do not mistake me, Sergeant Don. I am no collaborator. In fact, some of my girlfriends joined the Resistance. Still, you must understand that because we are so close to the border, many of us have German family. I, myself, have a few distant relatives in Aix-la-Chapelle."

Ties between Verviers and Germany ran deep. Many *Verviétois* were of German origin, and some Germans were descendants of *Verviétois*.[266] Refugees fleeing Germany began arriving in Verviers as early as 1933 (29). When Hitler invaded Belgium in 1940, most firms in Verviers had business relationships with their industrial counterparts east of the Rhine (29).

"Wow. And I thought life was simple here. Now you're left without a husband, and you've gotta support yourself. I guess you work pretty long hours."

"Before the war, I worked six days a week. Now I work three or four. Work is hard to find, so I'm glad to get what I have."

"It must be tough to manage."

"Étienne had some savings, but it is almost gone now. When I first got married, I had a wonderful fruit and vegetable garden in my backyard. But when the war started, seeds became very scarce, and it was difficult to keep up. I still grow a little, and I try to sell a few pieces whenever I visit my cousin in Brussels. I usually see her once a month, as long as the trains are running. There is more food there, and she always gives me some to take home."

"Aren't there rules against bringing food on trains?"

"There are all sorts of taxes and fines, but it's easy to get around them."

"How?"

"I always travel first class. In first class, the authorities never inspect your bags."

"Only way to ride. Do you have any children?"

"No."

I looked around for a waiter. "Want a beer?"

"I would love one, but I must refuse."

"Why?"

"See that *gendarme* over there?"

"Yeah."

"If he catches a girl drinking after nine o'clock, he will put her in a brothel. It is the law."

"Oh, come on."

"This is no joke, Sergeant Don."[267]

"Well, then, I guess you'd better not drink any beer."

"I usually have lemonade."

I motioned toward the waiter. "Um…*Une bière pour moi, s'il vous plaît, et pour la mademoiselle…*"

"*Une limonade.*"

"*Très bien.*" The waiter, sensing the electricity between us, promptly returned with the order and then disappeared.

"Denise, we've gotta study together. You could teach me French, and I can teach you a few things."

"Like what?"

"Hmm, let's see. Your English is fantastic. A helluva lot better than my French. But you could still use a few pointers."

"For instance?"

"You've gotta work on your contractions."

"I beg your pardon, *monsieur?*"

"No, not those kind of contractions. The grammatical ones. You know, saying 'I'm' instead of 'I am,' or 'I'll' instead of 'I will.' You should use the short version as much as possible in everyday conversation. It's like your *tu* form. It's less stuffy, and it makes things flow more smoothly."

"I will—I mean—I'll try to remember that."

"We'll talk about it more when I walk you home."

"Thank you, but that's not necessary. I can take care of myself."

"I'm sure you can. Just thought you'd want some company."

Denise smiled. "Yes. That would be nice."

It was 11 p.m., and the moon was shining brightly when we started walking east toward Stembert. By now, most of the city had gone to sleep, and we could hear the clicking of our shoes against the cobblestone sidewalks the Belgians called *trottoirs.*[268] Even in 1944, there were many densely packed stores and apartment buildings in Verviers, and a casual walker unfamiliar with the territory wouldn't notice that he had seamlessly crossed into Stembert. The center of the hamlet strongly resembled its more urban big sister. You had to walk a bit farther east to reach the country homes and farms.

"Do you go to temple much, Sergeant Don?"

"Haven't gone in years. You go to church often?"

"Once in a while. Just to keep in touch."

"With the man upstairs?"

"Yes… Do you believe in God, Sergeant Don?"

"Hell yes."

"Then why do you not go to services?"

"Well, when I was a kid, it seemed like everyone was running away from religion. The services didn't have any meaning for me. All I remember is a bunch of old men mumbling prayers I didn't understand. Then, of course, there was the Depression, and my folks were always struggling to get by."

"Some people have stopped believing in God because of the war. I say it's more important than ever to have faith."

"I've got faith. I just don't show it that much. I have faith in myself, and I think most things usually work out. You'll see. Before you know it, this war'll be over, and Belgium will be freer and better than ever. And I know there's a man upstairs, because he's helped me out of some tough jams."

"You're a good man, Sergeant Don."

"You're not bad yourself, *chérie*."

We stopped walking and gazed longingly at each other. With a sweeping motion, I drew Denise smack against me and kissed her on the mouth. Blushing, she backed off slightly and stared down at the dark pavement. I took her in my arms again, this time sealing my lips to hers and tilting her body downward tango-style. We remained glued together for a long time. Finally, Denise pushed hard against my shoulders, breaking the oral connection. I reluctantly raised her upright. Wide-eyed, she took two steps backward and put her hand on her chest.

"*Mon Dieu*! I must catch my breath."

"Lesson One. Never look an American male in the eye unless you mean business."

"You're a very good teacher, Sergeant Don."

Denise lived in a rectangular, two-story dwelling with a handsomely tiled roof, a cross between a townhouse and a country home. A smaller, ugly grey abode stood directly across the road.

"Thank you for a wonderful evening. I would ask you in, but it's half-past eleven, and I have to get up early for work tomorrow."

"Sure, I understand. I've got a morning shift myself, so I'd better be going anyway. Listen, I'll be off on Monday night and—"

"I'd love to. Wait." Denise produced a worn piece of paper from her bag and scribbled quickly. "Here is my address. I don't have a telephone, but even if I did, it would not work.[269] Perhaps I can meet you somewhere?"

"My barracks is at the l'Athénée Royal."

"The l'Athénée?"

"Yeah."

"I know where it is."

"Good. Can you meet me there Monday at eight?"

"*Certainement.*"

"Swell. See you then. *Bonne nuit, chérie.*"

"*Bonne nuit,* Sergeant Don."

Denise had just turned away when I stopped her. "Wait a minute," I whispered. "Your door's open a crack. You usually leave it like this?"

"No. Something's wrong. Listen."

"I think someone's inside. You have a light switch?"

"When you first enter, on your right. It turns on a bulb directly above you."

"Okay. Wait here."

I put down my knapsack and gingerly tipped open the door with my carbine. Denise, disregarding my instructions, followed stealthily behind me. I saw her out of the corner of my eye, but I didn't want to take the time to argue with her.

When I flicked on the switch, a heavy fire poker came flying at me. I ducked, and it grazed Denise's arm.

A large man, dressed from head to foot in black, darted past the pantry. I pursued him, and he bolted through the back door. The thief was disappearing into the darkness when I was about to fire.

"No, don't shoot!" Denise pleaded. "He is, how do you say, an acquaintance."

Mouth agape, I dropped the firearm to my side. "You know this guy?"

"Not really. A friend of a friend. He was in the *F.I.*"

"The what?"

"*Front de l'Indépendance.*"

"What's that?"

"Part of the Resistance."

"I thought they were on our side."

"Most of them are. But some have turned bad. Many people are frightened of them."

After the liberation, the Belgian government had great difficulty in getting the Resistance to disarm (66). Eisenhower had ordered all weapons turned in by October 3 (66). The *Armée Secrète* began complying in mid-October (66), but the *Front de l'Indépendance* and others held out until late November (66). During the occupation, there had been a proliferation of resistance movements. Some had unsavory reputations and included former collaborators (68). A few of their members became robbers (68) whose favorite target was farm country (68).

For weeks, the national government in Brussels remained awkward and indecisive (71). First, it announced that forty thousand Resistance fighters had been integrated into the armed forces (71). Then, on November 13, it decreed that all arms should be turned over to the police within five days (71). The order was ignored. During a strike later that month, *F.I.* fighters menaced tram operators with machine guns and refused to let them out of their depots (71, 71 n. 11). The group finally disarmed, not to Verviers police, but to Allied forces (71).

I touched Denise's shoulder. "Here, let me take a look at that."

Denise took off her coat, revealing a small, swollen cut on her right arm. "It is not serious."

"Have you got some gauze and peroxide?"

"I'm okay. Don't trouble yourself."

"Let me help you. It'll make me feel more patriotic."

"Thank you, Sergeant Don. There's some iodine in the medicine cabinet on the second floor, to your right."

I dashed up the rough-hewn stairs and returned a moment later to minister to Denise.

"Smallest damned bottle I ever saw."

"That's all I have. Medicine is very scarce here."

"You're running out of gauze and bandages."

"They are also in short supply. Even the hospitals don't have enough."

"That hurt?"

"No, it feels very nice."

"Jeez. I go to have a quiet dinner with a girl, and then I find out she's a Resistance fighter."

Denise laughed. "I'm not dangerous, Sergeant Don."

"I was hoping you were."

The seamstress smiled knowingly.

"But, seriously," I continued, "this guy's—"

"It's okay. Nothing was taken."

I put down the gauze and iodine. "But he broke into your house!" I protested. "You could've been hurt. At least let me file a report."

"That will be fine. Thank you."

"I hate paperwork, but for you, I'll make an exception." I took out a pen and small notebook from my hip pocket. "What's his name?"

"Jacques."

"Last name?"

"I don't know."

I scribbled a few notes. "Tall man dressed in black. Name Jacques. Ex-Resistance fighter, F.I. Nothing taken." I wryly crinkled my lips. "This'll probably be filed in an army wastebasket, but it's better than doing nothing."

After putting away my writing implements, I wrapped a small bandage around Denise's arm. "Okay. All done. You'll probably be a little sore tomorrow, but you'll live."

"You should have been a medic."

"I wouldn't know a scalpel from a pen knife." I yawned. "Boy, what a day. I'm bushed."

"You're welcome to the sofa."

"The sofa!? It looks a little small."

I was crestfallen, but not quite ready to give up. Another long, mutual stare and intense kiss.

"That was very nice, but it's still the sofa."

"Oh Jeez."

Denise walked me to the door. "Be safe, Sergeant Don."

"Keep your door locked. *Bonne nuit, chérie.*"

"Until Monday."

A few yards from the house, I stopped and turned around. Denise was still standing at the door, smiling. She waved goodbye. I reciprocated, and went on my way.

My first attempt to make love to Denise was unsuccessful, but it didn't seem to matter. She was so wholesome that just being out with her was very satisfying. In contrast, I only wanted sex from other European women. With Denise, it was different. She had reinforced my affection for the Belgian people, and I did my best to ease her distress.

Nov. 7, 1944

Dear Mom, Dad & Ethel,

It certainly is too bad they can't transport some of these European people to the States, where they could alleviate the pressing need for civilian workers. You'd be surprised at the number of unemployed in town. Due to the lack of material and restricted electricity, a large number of men and women are without work. It's too bad that they can't work out some system of providing jobs for them when workers are needed back home.

Love,

Don

Verviers had been in rough economic shape for years. A textile center since the mid-seventeenth century,[270] it reached its zenith in the nineteenth (25) and began declining in the early twentieth (25). During the Great Depression, the city was hit hard by strikes and unemployment (25). Although it had recovered somewhat by 1939 (26), the war once again plunged Verviers into turmoil (26).

By the time the area was liberated, its railway stock had been decimated by bombings.[271] Its auto industry, pilfered by the Germans, was skeletal (136). Gasoline was rare (136).

Salaries were low and unemployment high. A national labor conference held in Brussels on September 16, 1944 fixed the minimum wage for women at 6FB (about 12 cents) an hour (126). The rates for unskilled and skilled male labor were 8 and 10FB, respectively (126). By the end of 1944, only a minuscule portion of the region's thirty-thousand-plus laborers had gone back to work.[272] Some thirty-two hundred *Verviétois* were unemployed,[273] and eighty-four hundred were on relief (137). At the beginning of 1945, unemployment in the textile industry was ninety percent (137 n. 5).

The joyous liberation ceremonies had been quickly tempered by strike threats (50). C.O.T.B.,[274] a national textile workers union, demanded a fifty percent pay hike.[275] A walkout began on September 25, 1944 (127).

By modern standards, worker demands were modest. They included representation and unemployment insurance (127). Representation was a major stumbling block. At first, management refused to even sit down with shop stewards

(127). Finally, on October 3, the employers relented and negotiations began (127-8).

*   *   *   *

Councilman Bronckart believed that most American GI's were *"de bons garçons."*[276] There were, however, several sources of resentment.

Uncle Sam requisitioned everything in sight, from industrial establishments[277] to private homes.[278] In Verviers, Spa, and Eupen, 879 properties housed 56,140 men.[279] The schools, already disorganized from enemy bombings, suffered terribly.[280] The Americans occupied them from mid-October 1944[281] until April 10, 1945.[282] In a typical arrangement, one institution held classes half a day each week at two private locations on the place du Martyr (139 n. 3).

In the midst of this privation, U.S. Army Major Lund pressured textile industry and labor leaders in Verviers to make workers produce five hundred thousand meters of quilting for American troops (128-31). The controversial request was widely reported in the local press (128-31). Belgian authorities eventually refused on the grounds that inadequate stocks couldn't cover current civilian needs (130).

Another sore spot involved a favorite GI pastime. While shivering *Verviétois* struggled with severe coal shortages, American dance halls were always well-heated (155-7). During the Battle of the Bulge, the U.S. military would impose Draconian curfew hours on the citizens of Verviers, but at the same time, successfully induce Belgian officials to make exceptions for young women attending dances in the city and two suburbs (170 n. 5). Although frequently considered great liberators, Americans were sometimes viewed as extravagant, undisciplined, sex-obsessed lushes.[283]

My feeling is that members of the 888th Fighter Control Squadron deserved neither lavish praise nor insults. Since we weren't combat soldiers, we didn't actually "liberate" anyone. For the most part, we were moderate drinkers. Although we didn't hesitate to spend money, especially when we were out with women, few of us could be called wasteful.

For our second date, Denise and I returned to the site of our first. There was dancing in most cafés, and this one was no exception. We hadn't been out on the floor together, and I was anxious to remedy that situation.

Denise was wearing a form-fitting, dark-blue-sequined dress. We spoke endlessly in a mélange of English and French, but whenever our eyes met, we established an almost telepathic contact. By the time I asked her to dance, we were already on the floor, swaying to the music.

"You look beautiful tonight."

"Thanks."

"Where'd you get that dress?"

"I made it."

"Wow. Not on my account, I hope."

Denise warmed to the teasing. "Do not flatter yourself, Sergeant Don. I made it before the war. I would never be able to do it now because materials are so expensive—if you can get them at all."

"You must be quite a seamstress."

"I like to think so."

We sizzled when the band began playing "In the Mood." Denise was no Ginger Rogers, but her rhythm was good, and she wasn't a show-off. She had a subtle, pleasant smile that made me more comfortable than I had been since I entered the service.

War accelerates everything. Courtships are brief because men and women caught up in military conflict live for the moment. Once Denise and I were on the same wavelength, there was no stopping us.

"Do you want to—"

"Yes, Sergeant Don. Let's go."

It was early, and we arrived at her house before 10 p.m. While Denise was unlocking the door, I noticed that the woman in the house across the street was staring at me. When I returned her gaze, she shut her window and drew her curtains.

"Who was that?"

"A busybody. Don't bother with her, Sergeant Don."

"Okay."

"It's cold outside, *n'est-ce pas?*"

"Oui."

"I'll make us some *café au lait.*"

"That'll be swell."

We were sitting on the sofa and had only taken a few sips when Denise asked, "Are you tired, Sergeant Don?"

"Quoi?"

"When you want to ask a question, you should say *'comment?'* It, too, means 'what?' but it's more polite."

"Merci beaucoup, Mademoiselle Professeur."

"If you don't want me to correct you, I won't."

"*Chérie*, you can work on my French anytime." I slid over to her and rolled my tongue deeply inside her mouth.

"That wasn't very nice, Sergeant Don."

"Yeah, but did you enjoy it?"

"I'm not sure."

"Then let's try it again so you can make up your mind."

"Wait. You never answered my question. Are you tired?"

"Nope. You?"

"No. Would you like to see the upper floor?"

"I saw it last time."

"I mean, everything."

"I thought you'd never ask."

Within a week, we were virtually inseparable. We ate and slept together whenever our schedules permitted. It was the most natural thing in the world.

Denise and I went dancing in Verviers twice a week. Before each rendez-vous, I would get in the chow line at the l'Athénée for a second helping of food. Then I'd transport the duplicate meal to a very grateful girlfriend. On those days, I would sleep over at her place.

Typically, I'd get up early the next morning and begin the twenty-minute walk back to the l'Athénée in Verviers. After passing the church in Stembert, I traversed the *trottoirs* with houses on either side of me. I then began the descent toward the army barracks on my left, where the ground dipped sharply. Because the terrain was very steep, there were no houses on my right for the next hundred meters. Then I saw the railway tracks at the bottom of the hill. I continued between the homes until the rails appeared on my left. Finally, I crossed a small overhead bridge leading to the center of Verviers.[284] Each time, the same train would roll by, and I would wave to the same genially smiling motorman, who always waved back.

My relationship with Denise usually revolved around nightlife: cafés, dance halls, and boxing matches. But once in a while, we were able to get together during the day. Denise would then treat me to an informal tour of Verviers.

On a brisk afternoon in mid-November, we met at the l'Athénée for a stroll. The sky was almost evenly split between sun and clouds.

"What would you like to see?" asked Denise.

"Let's just walk around," I replied. "Make believe we're up in the air. You're my lead pilot."

"Are you ready for takeoff?"

"Yes, ma'am, I mean, *mademoiselle*."

Off we went, hand in hand, down the crowded streets of central Verviers. Walking was our sole mode of transportation. Neither she nor any of her immediate family owned a car, and I, preferring the exercise, never bummed a ride to work.

With limited public transportation, most people in the city got around on foot. I saw quite a few bicycles, but with gas in short supply, and military restrictions on vehicular traffic, there were relatively few cars.

Beginning November 20, gasoline trucks were in operation only four hours a day.[285] The schedule was inconvenient for consumers because it conflicted with their mealtimes (142). Still, a sizeable number of motorists overcame these obstacles, prompting one alderman to wonder how so many young men were able to drive about, sometimes without license plates (142).

No one could walk the streets during business hours without noticing the lines. People queued up around the block, waiting for the most basic items, everything from bread[286] to milk (38) to cigarettes (22). The lines for tobacco were especially long (22), a fact which did not concern us, since we didn't smoke.

Although disturbing to me and my fellow radio men, the suffering of Verviers was not unique. It couldn't compare to much of the devastation elsewhere on the Continent, such as the pounding of Saint Lô during the Normandy invasion, or the aerial firebombing of Dresden in 1945.[287] Most dwellings and commercial properties, typically no more than a few stories high, survived intact. People calmly went about their business.

Still, reminders of war were everywhere. The shattered glass crackled noisily under our feet as Denise and I passed the occasional storefront or apartment building destroyed by bombing.

A growling V-1 rattled windows a block or two from the l'Athénée. The rue du Collège was a wide, commercial street with tightly packed buildings, tram tracks, and plenty of people.[288] A small boy, pointing in the sky with excitement, tugged at a woman's skirt. *"Maman. Regardez. Un robot!"* he shouted. His sister began crying, and the distraught mother pulled her two children against a brick wall. Some people took cover. Most just glanced up and moved on. We visually followed the flying bomb until it was out of sight.

I put my arm around Denise and gently caressed her shoulder. "Kinda close, wasn't it?"

"Oui."

"You okay?"

"Ça va."

"Helluva thing for kids to grow up with."

"They're young. Perhaps they won't remember it."

"Oh, they'll remember it. They're seeing it practically every day. This stuff has a way of staying with you, even when you're little. I was about their age when I was attacked by a German shepherd on the street. That was a one-shot deal, and it still seems like yesterday."

"Were you hurt?"

"No. The owner came running out of a store and pulled him off me just in time. Ever since then, I've never looked a strange animal directly in the eye."

"That is wise, Sergeant Don." Denise peered up apprehensively. "I hope that bomb does not explode."

"You know, the first night I was here, I ran to shelters every couple of hours. That was it. I just couldn't live that way, worrying all the time."

"Oh, I never went to the shelters. I have a small cellar, but it is not deep, and I don't think it would protect me. I try not to think about it much, but I still worry sometimes."

"You're only human, *chérie*."

Denise looked up at me and gave me a playful nudge. "I thought you said I was out of this world."

"Don't hold me to anything I say when I'm lying down."

Under Denise's tutelage, my French was improving by the day. I, in turn, taught her more about America and its slang. We read the notices plastered along the rue du Gymnase (20), and at the kiosk on the place Verte (20-1), where the municipal monument's leonine heads and dragons stood watch over patrons (20). Here, I got hold of an issue of *La Presse verviétoise*, the only newspaper in Verviers.[289] There was a paper shortage, and copies were scarce (47), but, at least on that day, we were able to read about the latest developments.

"Were you here for the celebrations in September?" Denise asked.

"No," I replied.

"Oh, it was wonderful. There was music and all kinds of fun. It was very crowded, and we were very happy. Not like when the Germans were here. They used to have these stupid concerts that nobody went to."[290]

"Can't imagine why," I facetiously retorted.

Denise smiled sensuously. "You were dreaming in French last night, Sergeant Don."

"How do you know?"

"You were talking in your sleep."

"Really?"

"Yes. It shows you were, how do you say, troubled, but your French is getting much better. You are thinking in French when you are asleep. Just like a Belgian."

"What did I say?"

"I don't remember, but it was very nice."

"You ever talk in your sleep?"

"You should know the answer to that by now, *mon amour.*"

"Haven't heard you yet."

"Perhaps you have heard me in your dreams."

"Then I wouldn't remember, or I wouldn't know that you were really talking, would I?" I looked at Denise quizzically. "You trying to play with my head?"

"Mais non, you are doing a very good job of that all by yourself."

"You know, sometimes it's hard to tell if I'm dreaming or awake when I'm with you."

"Are you awake now, or are you dreaming?"

I drew her close and planted a warm kiss on her lips. "Dreaming, *chérie.* Definitely dreaming."

That was a magical and dangerous moment, and I wanted it to last forever. A hundred buzz bombs could have flown over my head, and I wouldn't have cared.

We walked over to the rue de Bruxelles and paused by the railing overlooking the gare centrale. Denise thoughtfully pursed her lips.

"A few years ago, we had anti-German graffiti here," she observed.

"Really?" I rejoined, my eyebrows rising with surprise.

"Yes. They said things like '*A Mort Hitler* [Death To Hitler],' '*Vive deGaulle,*' and '*Vive RAF.*'"[291]

"During the occupation?"

"*Oui.*"

"Gutsy kids."

"Anger makes people do foolish things."

"What's foolish about it? The Germans took over their country, and they were resisting the only way they could."

"It's not worth getting shot over."

"Maybe not, but I still can't help admiring them. Normally, I hate to see people messing things up, but—"

"These are not normal times."

Working our way back toward the center of town, we stopped in front of the Statue of Chapuis on the place du Martyr. Shielding my eyes from the sun, I glanced upward in admiration.

"Who's that?" I asked.

"Oh, he's a very important person in our history," Denise explained. "His name was Grégoire-Joseph Chapuis. He was a real, how do you say, man of the people. He founded a night school for workers,[292] performed the first *césarienne* in Verviers (14), and promoted civil marriage (152)."

"Civil marriage? What's so unusual about that?"

"It's not unusual today, but Chapuis lived in the late eighteenth century (12). A religious government was in power. The French revolutionaries occupied Belgium for a short time, but when they were kicked out, the Church was again very powerful. Chapuis was a…What is that word for a wild horse?"

"Maverick?"

"Yes. Chapuis was a maverick."

"He bent the rules."

"*Oui.*"

"Sounds like my kinda guy."

"Yes, but he got his head chopped off during the French rule."[293]

"I'm not that brave."

"That's okay." Denise affectionately leaned her head against my shoulder. "I would rather have a live man of ordinary courage than the memory of a dead hero."

"Baby, you are deep!" I looked at my watch. "Hey, I've gotta get ready for my afternoon shift."

"Don't worry, Sergeant Don. We're very close to the l'Athénée. I'll walk you back."

"*Chérie*, I'd be lost without you."

*   *   *   *

The next morning, my buddies and I were sleeping on cots in the l'Athénée, where PFC Paul Carter was harboring a dog he had befriended near the French border. For months, he had somehow managed to conceal the canine from the CO's, but now his luck had run out.

"Carter, I want that mutt gone today," snapped Captain Jones. "Dump it somewhere in town. I don't give a damn where. Just get rid of it."

"Yes, sir," Carter mournfully replied.

That night, he tearfully let the dog run loose in the center of Verviers. Paul departed quickly, hoping that the heartbreak wouldn't linger. Then he walked back to the l'Athénée.

He had been on his back sulking for only a few minutes when he heard strange noises underneath his mattress. Without a road map, compass, or radar, the rejected pooch had beaten his master back to base.

*   *   *   *

At age twenty, Timothy Gordon, a blonde-haired, blue-eyed PFC, was one of the youngest members of the 888th. Small, thin, and fast, Timmy was always checking things out. If there was a fistfight, he'd be the first spectator. If a luscious babe was sunning herself on the sidewalk, he'd catch the earliest glimpse.

Sometimes he'd run laps around the courtyard of the l'Athénée with Corporal Zeke, who had become a close friend. Zeke had better stamina; Timmy was more of a sprinter.

He worked with Sergeant Lance Pierce and Corporal Miles Thompson. Lance was another friend of mine. Brown-haired and freckled, he was a big lug of a guy with a puppy-dog face and large ears. We had some wild times together, but, on the job, he was all business. Lance once told me about a bizarre incident that occurred in his radio truck. I've reconstructed it to the best of my ability.

Lance was in his van, working the 8 a.m. shift with Timmy and Thompson, when their transmitter stopped working. Then the phone rang.

"Sergeant Pierce here. Yes, sir. It just went dead. I don't believe I have the expertise…Yes, sir. I understand."

"Who was that?" asked Thompson.

"Who do you think? Captain Jones. Seems that a storm knocked out some of our antennas last night. I have to go outside and look things over. Listen, we've had a lotta V-1's coming over today, so stay put, and for Chrissake, keep that door shut."

Lance had only been gone a moment when a buzz bomb flew over. Its loud growling suddenly grew silent. The corporal and the PFC braced themselves for an explosion. Nothing.

"Psst," whispered Timmy. "I'm gonna see where it landed."

"Sarge told us to stay put," protested Thompson. "And he said not to open the door."

"Aw, c'mon. I'll just take a peek. Nobody'll get hurt."

"Well…"

It was too late. Timmy was already peering out of the van. He had only opened the door a crack, barely enough for him to see outside, when—Boom!—the bomb exploded. Fortunately, the blast didn't damage any radio trucks or their occupants. That is, except for poor Timmy, who, as a result of his compulsive curiosity, suffered a punctured eardrum.

Civilian casualties also occurred in odd ways. At an Armistice Day celebration on November 11, 1944, a V-1 came down in a meadow between la route Henri Chapelle and the cemetery in Andrimont.[294] The blast instantly killed a farmer where he stood (18). There were no apparent wounds on his body (18). Ten people were hurt (18). The roof of the undertaker's house was ripped off, and a farm was damaged (18).

*   *   *   *

Winter came early to Belgium in 1944, and the inclement weather put a dampener on my sunny spirits. But word from Joe helped restore my chipper outlook.

Belgium
Nov. 13, 1944

Dear Mom, Dad & Ethel,

Received a letter from Joe this week, and he is now bragging about the good chow that has suddenly commenced. He still complains about not receiving his quota of mail, though.

Snow, miserable wet snow, has now cast some of her white barrage on us. I don't mind dry snow, but everything is now just a blanket of slush and mud.

Have met another extremely nice family and spent some pleasant hours with them.

Lots of Love,

Don

Nov. 15, 1944

Dear Mom, Dad & Ethel,

Received your Nov. 1st letter. You state you haven't been receiving mail lately. However, I'll alibi out of that one by clinging onto the vines of St. Nick's Christmas tree. No fooling. The flood of Christmas packages will, without doubt, slow up mail considerably.

You're probably wondering why you haven't received any war bonds in a long time. Some months ago the Army canceled all bond allotments that weren't designated to be taken out in full. It's either complete bonds each month or none at all. I let it ride for awhile, but now I've increased my regular payment: starting in December, you'll receive $50 per month.

Love,

Don

Nov. 16, 1944

Dear Mom, Dad & Ethel,

The one thing I can't understand here is the old-fashioned sanitary conditions. The majority of toilets are outside the house. Very few of them can be flushed. They're just holes that drain into some miserable sewage system. How these people live under these conditions, I don't know.

I've heard of one house here that has a bathtub. The old guy must be at least a duke to rate a luxury like that. Most people have no sink to wash their dishes in. They heat up water until it is scorching, then pour it into a pan. Then they clean their dishes with a wooden stick about a foot long, on the end of which a rag is fastened. Thus, they don't have to put their hands in scorching water. A refrigerator or stove is something about 500 years ahead of them. They live very simply, but they are nice, generous people.

Lots of Love,

Don

Nov. 19, 1944

Dear Mom, Dad & Ethel,

They really put their animals to practical use here. I saw several heavily loaded carts being tugged up steep hills by grunting dogs. It seemed quite a load for a dog. They can't last long, being taxed like that.

Frequently I would see lines forming outside of a building. I figured some kind of ration was being handed out. Later I learned that it was for the afternoon paper, and there aren't enough to go around. So the people have to line up if they want to get the day's news.

Feeling fine.

Love,

Don

On the evening of November 22, there were no queues at the Café du Tank, at 50 place Verte,[295] but the place was really jumping. It was packed with American infantrymen who had just returned from the front lines. Verviers was a three-day rest center for battle-hardened troops,[296] providing them with a well-deserved respite from the shelling. I, Denise, and her married sister, Josephine, decided to drop in.

We'd just come from a boxing match, which we enjoyed with Denise's parents. I grabbed a table, and we ordered refreshments: a beer for me, and lemonade for the two ladies. The three of us were in high spirits.

"That Dupin had one helluva right hook," I began.

"And, *mon Dieu*, what footwork," added Denise.

"But, you have to admit, both fighters had great skills. Dupin just found an opening and took it."

"Yes. It was, how do you say, a good, clean match."

"Yeah. I'm glad it was clean."

"I've never seen a dirty fight, Sergeant Don. There are rules against that, no?"

"Yeah, but they're not always enforced. There's a lot of places in the States where things can get ugly, especially if they're small time. The ref's looking the other way, and all hell's breaking loose: head-butting, hitting below the belt, hitting after the bell."

"That's horrible. The matches we see here are always clean. The fighters are young and, how do you say—"

"Up-and-coming."

"Yes. And they want to make a good impression, even when they don't win."

"Well, your folks certainly made a good impression on me."

"They liked you, too."

"Glad it's mutual." I glanced over at Josephine.

From the neck up, the two sisters looked nearly identical, but Josephine was several inches taller and had a thinner body. She was five years older than Denise and lacked her sibling's liveliness.

"Josephine's pretty quiet tonight."

"She's not much of a talker. *Elle est très réservée* [She is very shy]."

"Yeah, like my brother. *Comment ça va, Josephine* [How are you doing, Josephine]?"

"*Ça va.*"

"*Avez-vous aimé la lutte* [Did you like the match]?"

"*Ça va.*"

"Now I know you're sisters. You've both got the same favorite expression."

Denise shrugged. "Americans say 'okay,' and Belgians say *ça va.*"

I moved my chair closer to my girl and put my arm around her. Then I resumed my playful interrogation of Josephine. "*Que pensez-vous de Denise et moi* [What do you think of Denise and me]?"

"*Ça va.*"

"Can't you say anything besides *ça va*?"

Josephine cracked a smile. "*Oui.*"

"*Ça y est* [Gotcha]!"

"*Oh, Don, ce n'est pas gentil* [Don, that's not nice]," chided a blushing Denise.

"Well, I did get her to say something else." I turned to the older sister again. "And with English no less. You know English?"

Josephine put her right thumb and index finger together. "*Un petit peu* [A little bit]."

Denise whispered something in Josephine's ear, and the two of them burst out laughing.

"Mind letting me in on that?"

"I told her that you're great in bed, but your table manners leave something to be desired."

"Gee, thanks."

"Come on, Don. Let's dance."

Before we could get up, the band began playing a waltz. I loved to dance, but this wasn't my cup of tea.

"No, *chérie*, I think I'll sit this one out. Why don't you go up there with your sister?"

They had only moved a few steps on the floor when an infantryman tried to cut in. Denise rebuffed him. Another try. Same answer. A third attempt and refusal.

I was quite willing to let my girl dance with a battle-weary soldier, but this fellow had crossed the line. Even placid Denise was getting annoyed.

With mounting fury, I approached the infantryman. The interloper looked about thirty-five, and had a stubbly, weatherbeaten face. There was a thick scar on his right cheek. Although he was a husky six feet four inches, I was not intimidated.

"Why don't you leave them alone?" I scolded. "Don't you see she doesn't want to dance with you?"

Assuming the matter was settled, I returned to my seat. When the waltz was over, Denise and Josephine joined me.

"I think that soldier is coming after you, Sergeant Don."

"Don't worry. I'll handle this."

Still seated, I calmly stared back at the large man. A tense silence ensued.

"Can I help you, pal?"

Without saying a word, the infantryman punched me in the chin, moving my head back a couple of inches. Overturning the table full of plates and drinks, I violently sprang from my seat and was about to return the blow when a middle-aged lieutenant interceded.

"Hey!" the officer shouted, pointing an index finger at each of us. "You're guests in this country, and this is a place of business. You wanna fight? Go outside."

"Fine by me, Lieutenant," grunted the infantryman. "I'll be waiting for you, Sergeant."

"I'll be out in a minute," I snapped.

"Do not go," Denise pleaded, grabbing my right arm with both hands. "*C'est trop dangereux.*"

I broke her grip with a gentle firmness. "I don't care if it's dangerous. I've gotta go, *chérie. Il s'agit de l'honneur.*"

"No, this isn't a question of honor, Sergeant Don. To fight—maybe die— over a dance? This is *fou*, crazy. Please do not go. Please."

I took a deep breath, and my head began to cool. It was pitch black outside. I knew that infantrymen carried long knives. All this guy had to do was pull out a six-inch blade in some alleyway and use it. A quick, underhand thrust to the belly, and that would have been the end of me. This realization, and Denise's entreaties, convinced me to back down. With the exception of a small cut to my lower lip, the only injury I suffered that night was to my pride.

Following my usual custom, I stayed over at Denise's house. She was dabbing my lip with a cold cloth to stanch the trickle of blood from my mouth. I felt no physical pain, but was still upset with myself for not retaliating.

My emotional injury soon receded in the wake of Denise's cool caresses. Then came the final, delicate touch: she sealed the cut with a soft kiss.

Although insufficient by American standards, Denise's home was superior to that of the average *Stembertois*. It was rather tall for a two-story dwelling, and the exterior was a pleasant chestnut color. The facade featured a lightly varnished oak door and four tiny black-curtained windows.

Unlike many of its neighbors, this place had indoor plumbing. There was no bathtub, but, upstairs, a very small room housed a toilet, sink, and medicine cabinet. In a nearby closet, there was a shower.

Most of the ground floor was composed of an area no larger than fifteen by twelve feet which served as living room, dining room, and kitchen. A large, black, coal-burning stove was connected to the hearth by a rusty pipe. Two hand irons and a tarnished copper kettle sat atop this ancient appliance, while pots and cooking utensils sat on side racks.

The red-brick hearth was of more recent vintage. A Nativity statue dominated the mantelpiece, framed by smaller likenesses of a Walloon cock and a Celtic warrior.

A few feet from the fireplace stood a worn mahogany table covered with a white linen cloth. It had six matching chairs, whose white upholstery had long faded to pale beige. A couple of bald patches of hardwood floor were covered with Oriental rugs.

Diagonally opposite the fireplace was an alcove containing a pantry which boasted a small porcelain sink. Above the sink was a cupboard usually low on food. Parallel to and behind the pantry was a narrow foyer leading to the back door. Perishables, when available, were stored in the natural refrigeration of a cellar which was only accessible from outdoors.

Closer to the entrance, a coffee table stood directly before the small sofa which now doubled as an instrument of foreplay. Two wooden folding chairs stood off to the right near a thin, half-empty, four-foot bookcase. To the left, Denise's coveted shortwave radio rested on a solitary end table. A couple of strategically-placed, frilly floor lamps completed the ground floor furnishings.

Upstairs, in Denise's pale-white bedroom, there was a double bed and a night table just wide enough to support a lamp. Two paintings depicting pastoral scenes of nineteenth century Stembert graced the walls. Years earlier, she had removed all pictures of her husband and stored them in the cellar. Next door was a guest room barely large enough to accommodate a small cot.

There was a certain domestic quality to our wartime romance. Before turning in, Denise and I would listen to BBC or Voice of America broadcasts over coffee. Then she would heat up the two hand irons and put them on the mattress. By the time we got into bed, everything was nice and toasty.

Despite our mostly enjoyable evening on the town, there was great fear in and around Verviers. A large contingent of buzz bombs had been raining down on the city all week.[297] On November 22, a steady stream of V-1's was seen throughout the day and night (21). Most of them exploded in nearby suburbs (21). We somberly stared out the bedroom window.

"They're coming in hot and heavy now," I observed.

"They're so terrible, but when they explode, they sound like fireworks."

"That's only when they're far away. It's different when they're close up."

"Then let them stay far away."

"Come on. The bed's getting cold."

"Just a minute. I won't be long."

I got under the covers. There was a lull in the growling, and Denise stood transfixed at the window, staring out at the stars.

"Sometimes I wish a comet would take me away from here."

"Where would you go?"

"Anywhere that's peaceful. And when I came back, the war would be over."

The growling began again. This time, it was louder, a malevolent force growing fiercely by the second. Then came a nasty, thunderous sound,[298] and the house shook. Denise dove head first into bed.

"Holy Jeez! You almost poked me in the eye."

"I'm sorry, Sergeant Don. Let me take a look."

"No, it's all right. Forget it... Denise, you're shaking."

"I'm cold."

"No you're not."

I held her tightly. Caressing her bare shoulders, I slowly ran my hands down her compact body.

"Okay, it's letting up now," I consoled. "Everything's gonna be all right. You'll see. Before you know it, it'll be springtime. The weather'll be warm, the birds'll be singing, and you'll be out on the square watching real fireworks, celebrating the end of the war."

"That's a nice dream, Sergeant Don."

"It's not a dream. It's only a matter of time. Think positive. *Ça va, ma chérie?*"

"*Ça va.*"

The covers ruffled as Denise rolled onto her side. I could see her silhouette in the darkness. She had her head on her elbow and was facing me.

"You look lost in thought," I observed.

"Don?"

"Yeah?"

"Do you have a girlfriend in the Bronx?"

"Nope."

"I'm surprised. Any American girl would be lucky to have you."

"It's nice of you to say that, but before the war, I was pretty ignorant about women."

"You were a virgin."

"Bingo."

"You don't have to sleep with someone to have a girlfriend."

"True."

"So you were never close to another woman?"

"Since I joined up, I've been close to lots of women. Real close."

"I meant emotionally."

"Denise, I don't wanna talk about this anymore."

"Why?"

"Because it makes me uncomfortable."

"Most men have trouble talking about their feelings."

"Can we change the subject?"

"Please tell me about your other sweetheart."

"Why is this so important?"

"Because I want to know more about you."

"I'm not very deep, *chérie.*"

"You're deeper than you think, *mon amour.*" Denise playfully tapped me. "Come on," she coaxed.

"Well…I sorta had a girlfriend in the States. Her name was Nancy. I thought her mother was grooming me for marriage, so I broke it off."

"You don't like marriage?"

"I'll get married some day, but right now I don't wanna be tied down."

"Do I tie you down?"

"You could never tie me down." I put my arm around Denise. "You know that if you were anyone else, I'd tell you to buzz off."

"So why don't you tell me to buzz off?"

"Because you're the first girl I can really open up to. I can tell you anything. When I'm talking with you, it's like talking to a buddy, only better. You're my girl and my friend. The others were strictly for good times."

"We've had some good times."

"We sure have, but a little while ago you were almost crying."

"It's okay to cry sometimes."

"I suppose, if you've got something to cry about. Most of the time, I'm happy."

"Thank you, Don."

"For what?"

"For everything."

"You're very welcome, *chérie*. Are we done with this conversation?"

"Done."

As I embraced her, I could feel that she was still shivering. Her interest in me was sincere, but now that I think of it, she was probably also trying to distract herself from frightening feelings. I covered her with tender kisses and felt her quivering torso relax. There was an odd satisfaction in comforting her this way. Denise always excited me, but there was something special about that night. Our lovemaking was particularly smooth and rhythmic. Locked in heavenly transport, we moved toward climax. Our tempo increased—faster and faster—until we reached that oh so golden moment. Then came that delicious, restful sleep.

*　　*　　*　　*

"Ow! Take it easy."

"Okay. I'm almost finished. You don't want to get infected, do you?"

Denise was sitting on the side of the bed, applying iodine to the scratches on my back. Her well-formed breasts peeked out through her open chemise. Fear of the previous night's buzz bombs had made her lovemaking very intense.

"Jeez. With all the girls in Verviers, I had to hook up with a tigress."

"The lion is a national symbol."

"Excuse me. A lioness. Ow! You're enjoying this, aren't you?"

"Not as much as last night. Okay. All done. You'll be sore for a couple of days, but you'll live."

I made a sour face and retorted, *"Touché, mademoiselle."*

In a single, fluid motion, I moved into a sitting position alongside her. Denise drew back.

"I know that crazy smile, Sergeant Don. It usually means trouble."

"You wanna scratch? Then prepare to be bitten."

While Denise let out delighted, girlish screams, I pulled her onto the mattress and began nibbling at her neck. Her hysterical laughter quickly turned her face beet red. After a few more seconds of early morning frolicking, I let her up.

"Gotta go to work." I whipped on my undergarments and tapped Denise on the behind. "And so do you."

"Oui," she groaned, buttoning up her chemise.

For a moment, I thought of the tiny shower in the hall closet. I wanted to squeeze in there with Denise, but I rarely used it because the pressure was poor, and it was very cold. Instead, I usually washed in the sink. It was still much better than a "whore's bath."

I pecked my girl on the cheek. "See you in three days, *chérie.*"

"Until then, *mon amour.*"

✳   ✳   ✳   ✳

The next morning, I was in the l'Athénée, chowing down with my fellow radio men.

"Donnybrook, pass the fuckin' butter, will ya?"

"Here's your fuckin' butter, Jack."

"Hey, Bobby, pass the salt."

"What kind of salt, Lance?"

"The fuckin' salt."

"Now you're talkin'. Here."

"Know where the word 'fuck' comes from?" offered Angelo.

"Pray tell, Father," a leering Lance requested.

"It stands for 'Fornication Under Consent of the King.' In the Middle Ages, the English stamped their marriage licenses 'F.U.C.K.'"

"Sounds like a buncha limey bullshit to me," said Zeke.

"Hey, watch your language," growled Bobby, pointing an admonishing finger at the small corporal. "The Brits are the best."

Jack clasped a friendly hand on Angelo's shoulder. "This boy studied for the priesthood," drawled the Georgian with mock earnestness. "Ya gotta believe 'im, Zeke. Padres don't lie."

Our banter was interrupted by a powerful aerial burst. Plates clanged, forks flew, and everyone ducked under the tables. Then came a whistling sound. Second by second, it grew louder, until it reached a fever pitch. My ears were ringing. Every soldier in the room knew this one was landing in his backyard.

Silence. It was a good minute before anyone dared move.

I was the first person to pick himself off the floor. I peered out the window and squinted incredulously at the trail of white vapor hanging in the sky.[299] "Thank God," I murmured. My words were followed by a soft cacophony of uttered prayers. I looked around the mess hall and saw a roomful of chalky ghosts. Every man's face had been drained of color.

It took us several minutes to recover, even longer for normal flesh tones to return. Stan walked around to every table, checking to make sure everyone was all right.

"Hey, Stan, what in fuckin' damnation was that?"

"That, my dear Jack, was Vengeance Weapon *zwei*."

"Huh?"

Stan walked to the front of the room. "Listen up, people. What you just heard was one of Adolf's latest toys. It's called a V-2. It flies into outer space and comes down ten times the speed of hell."

"Like a rocket chip?"

"Yeah, Jack, like a rocket ship."

"Dayem!"

"So how come we're not all dead?" asked Bobby. "That thing was practically on top of us, and it exploded."

"No it didn't. What you heard was the sonic boom," explained Stan. "When something goes faster than the speed of sound and then slows down, that's what you hear."

Sergeant Angelo piped up. "Stan, if these things are so fast, how does our ack-ack hit 'em?"

"It doesn't."

"Shouldn't there be two bangs?" I asked. "One for the sonic boom and one for the explosion?"

"That's right, Donnybrook."

"So this thing didn't explode. It malfunctioned."

"Right again, Don. We've got an unexploded V-2 out there, and it's under our noses. The bomb people are probably looking for it now. Assume it can blow any time. I love you guys, and I don't wanna see anything happen to you. So watch your backs, and take care of yourselves."

Having lost our appetites, we warily filed out of the mess hall. For the next twenty-four hours, we worked our shifts without any unnecessary conversation.

✱   ✱   ✱   ✱

In contrast to the V-1, which telegraphed it's arrival,[300] a fully-functional V-2 struck without warning[301] and was immune to all known countermeasures.[302] This forty-seven-foot[303] ballistic missile had a maximum speed of 3,800 mph,[304] and a height trajectory of between fifty and fifty-six miles.[305]

It was equally inaccurate,[306] and more lethal, than the first vengeance weapon. V-2's began appearing in London on September 7, 1944.[307] There, the average death rate per bomb was 2.2 persons for the V-1[308] and 5.3 for the V-2.[309] Several factors accounted for the greater deadliness.

First, the V-2 had a larger payload: twenty-two hundred pounds versus one thousand pounds for the V-1.[310] The heavy damage radius for both V-weapons was similar: seventy-five to one hundred percent of houses within seventy-two feet of impact were destroyed by a V-1 explosion;[311] the distance was seventy-six feet for the V-2 (39). But the V-2 created more pulverized rubble, burying and suffocating people who had initially survived (39) the "double bang."[312] V-2's wouldn't only break windows, they'd create flying glass splinters, increasing casualties in zones of lesser damage.[313] In addition, V-2 blasts sometimes caused fires, while V-1's did not.[314]

Like many weapons of war, the V-2 was initially developed with benevolent intentions. Its origins can be traced to *Verein für Raumschiffart* (VFR), the Society for Space Travel, which was founded in Germany in 1927.[315] The VFR conducted pure scientific research on the interplanetary potential of rockets[316] and had international connections.[317] By 1929, it had one thousand members.[318]

Development began in 1930 at the *Racketenflugplatz* or "Rocket Flying Place" (6). At that time, a young scientist named Wernher von Braun joined the group (6). That same year, officers in Germany's Ordnance Department first met to discuss the possible military applications of rockets (6). The Treaty of Versailles, which had strictly limited the size of the country's arsenal, was silent on this subject (6).

In 1932, von Braun began working for the German army[319] in order to complete a doctoral thesis.[320] He eventually became engineering director of the "A" rocket program at Peenemünde,[321] where, by 1936, he had completed his first design of the V-2, then called the "A-4."[322] As late as the summer of 1938, when Hitler was preparing to invade Czechoslovakia, the naïve von Braun still believed that his prototypes would be used for space exploration.[323]

The developers of the V-2 had at least one thing in common with many economically minded Belgian motorists: the need for alcohol fuels. The rocket used a mixture that was seventy-five percent ethanol and methanol.[324] Unlike petroleum, these ingredients were cheap and readily available.[325]

In fact, Germany was literally out of gas. Major General Walter Dornberger, military director of Peenemünde, has aptly described the situation in his book, *V-2*. In a poignant anecdote, Dornberger discusses his visit to an auxiliary airfield at Mecklenberg near the end of the war.[326] There, he observed hundreds of well-camouflaged jet fighters (269). When he asked an air force major why they had not been deployed, the lower-ranking officer replied: "Sir, I've just enough gasoline to get me to a conference tonight two miles away. For my machines, there isn't a single drop (269)."

But there was a much more sinister side to the V-2 than terror bombings or gas-starved Germans. The rocket was mass-produced through the sweat and blood of concentration camp inmates.[327]

In order to carry out this task, the Nazis created Mittlewerk, a state-owned corporation (23), and supplied it with the necessary captives (23). In August 1943, the first group of prisoners arrived at Niedersachswerfen (23). They were housed in tents in a place code-named "Dora," a sub-camp of the infamous Buchenwald (23). I would visit the latter shortly after its liberation in 1945.

SS Brigadeführer Hans Kammler oversaw Dora's construction (23). His appointment created an SS Bureaucracy in the A-4 organization (24) which, up until then, had been run exclusively by the army. Kammler, an architect by profession, had designed the crematoria at Auschwitz (23-4) and played an active role in the destruction of the Warsaw Ghetto in 1942 (23-4). After a failed assassination attempt against Hitler on July 20, 1944, control of the A-4 program was removed from the army and placed squarely in the hands of the SS (34).

When Allied bombings began, V-2 construction went underground (23). Most of the prisoners died in the tunnels from exposure to toxic fumes, malnutrition, exhaustion, and disease (24). With virtually no medical care or sanitation, illnesses such as pneumonia, dysentery, tuberculosis, and typhus ran rampant (24). Although Dora was not an extermination camp, twenty thousand inmates died there (24). Most of these were political prisoners and common criminals (24). Their bodies were cremated, first at Buchenwald, later at Dora itself (24).

During the past fifty years, descendants of the V-2 have compiled a Jekyll-and-Hyde history. Members of the VFR would have undoubtedly hailed American development of the Saturn V rocket, a lunar launch vehicle of the 1960's, as a realization of their dream of peaceful space exploration. They would have been equally saddened by the Soviet Union's construction of the Scud missile, which Iraqi president Saddam Hussein used to terrorize Israeli civilians during the Persian Gulf War of 1990-91. Both the Saturn V and the Scud were based on von Braun's designs.[328]

$$*\qquad*\qquad*\qquad*$$

On a grey, chilly afternoon, I stopped off at the Café du Tank. Today, my shift wouldn't begin until 4 p.m., giving me enough time for both a hot cup of coffee and a long-awaited shower at the public baths. I spotted a familiar figure peering over a magazine at one of the tables.

"Ken?"

"Donnybrook! Long time no see! How are ya?"

Our embrace was warm and instantaneous. Although we rarely displayed such physical affection, it was quite understandable: we hadn't seen each other in nearly two years. We eyed each other's insignia.

"Hey, tech sergeant. Not bad, Ken."

"Not too shabby yourself, Buck Sergeant. C'mon. Siddown."

"I'm gonna get some coffee. How 'bout you?"

"Ordered a few minutes ago. Don't know why it's taking so long."

"How do you want it?"

"Black."

I buttonholed a waiter. "*Un café au lait pour moi, s'il vous plaît, et un café noir pour lui* [A coffee with milk for me, please, and black coffee for him]."

"Your French has gotten a lot better, Donnybrook."

"I'm dating a terrific girl from Stembert."

"That's great."

"With your language skills, you probably have to beat 'em off."

"Nah. I get out now and then, but I'm usually so bushed after work, I don't feel like looking for women."

"That's not like you at all. You even talk different. You were always a little tight-assed, but now you sound like a regular guy."

"People change, especially when they go through a lotta shit."

Ken accidentally brushed against his magazine, and it fell to the floor. I picked it up and discovered a loose page inside. It had been torn from an *Esquire* calendar.

It was an April 1944 Varga drawing of a curvaceous, gravity-defying blonde. She was wearing a see-through, blue-and-white navy-style top, skin-tight black shorts, and a very cute smile.[329] My face lit up.

"Now, that's the Ken I remember!"

"I guess you know I got transferred to a demolition unit after we went AWOL."

"Heard a rumor like that, but I wasn't sure if it was true."

"I've been in a lotta different outfits. They sent me to bomb school for some crash courses. Shells, mines, V-weapons, you name it—I've seen 'em all. Been around a lot, too: Normandy, Italy, Belgium."

I noticed that my friend had aged a great deal over the past two years. Ken was only twenty-seven, but his temples had already gone grey. The lines were etched deeply into his forehead, and there were "crow's feet" around the corners of his eyes. He hadn't shaved in several days and smelled of cigarettes.

"I was in Normandy," I offered.

"Yeah? When?"

"D plus ten. You?"

"H plus one."

"You were on the beaches an hour after the start of the invasion?"

"Yep."

"Holy shit!"

"I was one of the demolition engineers. A bangalore torpedo man."

"Wow. That must've been nasty."

Ken chuckled. "Nasty? That's the understatement of the century. Even now, I can't talk about it much. Not even to buddies like you."

"I understand."

"You can't understand squat unless you've been there. That was around the time the guys started calling me Professor."

"You've gotta admit, the name fits. It sure beats Four Eyes."

"I was really close to the guys in that outfit. Now most of them are dead or permanently disabled. I had this great master sergeant. His name was Butch. He was a real tough guy, but he was a good friend. And he had a very kind heart. He was like a father to all of us. He saved my life. Now he's dead."

"How are you holding up?"

"I'm okay."

"Your job must be nerve-racking. I couldn't do it."

"Donnybrook, you do what you gotta do."

"I once worked with a guy who used to drive a dynamite truck. His hands shook all the time."

Ken proudly held out his palms. "Steady as a rock. In my line of work, we've got this expression for when you're cutting wires: 'black before red, or else you're dead.'"

"I had a little bomb school. Never heard that one."

"It's just a saying to help keep you on your toes. The Germans are always changing their circuitry. It's a new kinda war, Donnybrook. A battle of technology. One day, you insert a probe, and it neutralizes the bomb. The next day, you've got a mechanism that looks exactly the same, and the probe sets it off."

"Tough business."

"Yeah, but either of us could die today or live another fifty years... Hey, I'm up for promotion. Master Sergeant."

"Congratulations."

Ken stretched in his chair and smiled. His poker face had completely melted away. "Should be mostly supervising. Get more sleep. Right now, I always get the toughest jobs."

"There must be a lot of 'em."

"Yes siree. Hitler might be able to hold out a long time."

"No way. We've got mastery of the skies. He's outnumbered and outgunned."

"I wouldn't count him out so soon. He's got some serious shit up his sleeve."

"Those V-2's are frightening."

Ken's eyes narrowed into a cold glare. He leaned over to within a few inches of me and softly deadpanned, "You think the V-2's are scary? Hitler's working on rockets that can hit any place on planet Earth. He's already got Messerschmitts that can best five hundred miles an hour[330] and chew through anything the Air Corps has."

"You're worrying about nothing, Ken. Germany's on its last legs. We'll take Adolf out before any of that stuff becomes a real threat."

"It already is."

"Man, you're such a pessimist! I like to look on the bright side."

"Well, I like to look on the real side. Donnybrook, I hope you're right, and that the war's over in a few months, but I wouldn't bet on it. This thing could go on for years, and we'll be just a coupla little gears grinding away in a giant machine."

"I guess, in the overall scheme of things, we're pretty insignificant."

"I said 'little,' not 'insignificant.' What every guy does matters, but I have this awful sense of being trapped on a huge ship bound for nowhere."

"You'll get home all right."

"I envy you, Donnybrook. I hope. You believe."

"If you don't believe, then life really is a crapshoot... Have you made any plans for after the war?"

Ken's face brightened. "I wanna settle down. Get hitched with my girl. Didn't I ever tell you about Kimberly?"

"You said you had a girl, but you never told me her name."

"Kim's been writing me for months about tying the knot, and I'm ready for some clean living. With the GI Bill, I'll be able to go to college and study engineering, so I can focus on building things instead of blowing 'em up.

"A friend of mine back home has the inside scoop on the housing market. He says that in a few years there'll be tons of cheap houses on Long Island. Maybe I'll go there. Under the Bill, I can get a low-interest mortgage. On the other hand, maybe I'll go out West. I hear it's healthier there, more open space. Better for kids, which I'll eventually get around to having. Hey, what about you?"

"Don't have a clue."

"How's Jack?"

"Fine."

"Still driving people crazy?"

"As always."

"Tell him I said hello."

"You come here often?"

"About once a week."

"Maybe we can get together sometime. Double date or something."

"Sounds super."

I lingered alone a few minutes over coffee and then began making my way to the public baths. I found a street along my usual route blocked off. A stony MP stood guard.

"This is a frozen zone, Sergeant. You need to go three blocks down if you want to pass in this direction."

"What's going on here?"

"You hear about that unexploded V-2?"

"Yeah. It passed over my mess hall."

"Well, there's a bomb disposal unit here trying to defuse it."

Just then, a loud explosion rocked the ground. I hit the pavement and curled myself into a fetal position. Time seemed to slow down, then reverse. I was back in high school, running the half-mile. It was the final stretch, and I was far behind. Desperately sprinting toward the finish line, I could feel my heart pounding heavily inside my chest. I was afraid I wasn't going to make it.

Pieces of shrapnel flew over my head. Silence. Then I was back. I looked up and saw a large cloud of dark brown smoke angrily billowing above me.[331] I had small nicks on the backs of my hands, and a curious pins-and-needles sensation in my palms. I slowly removed my helmet.

Thank God. No holes.

Regaining my composure, I ran up to the MP. "Hey, I think a buddy of mine was working in there. He's a tech sergeant. His name's Ken Jackson."

The MP's expression softened. "The Professor?"

"Yeah. He's a very good friend of mine. Is there any way I can find out if he's okay?"

"Listen, I'm not supposed to do this, but if you come back here tomorrow, I'll have some news for you."

"Thanks."

✳   ✳   ✳   ✳

About thirty hours later, I was sipping coffee at Denise's table. I had to take it straight because there was no milk in the house.

"Black before red, or else you're dead."

"Don, you've been mumbling that all evening. What's wrong?"

"I lost a buddy of mine yesterday."

"Oh, I am so sorry."

"We trained together in the States. Yesterday was the first time I'd seen him in two years. Less than an hour later, he was dead. Killed trying to disarm a V-2."

Denise reached over and squeezed my hand. I slowly pulled away. "I'll be all right, *chérie*. Just need a little time alone."

I stood outside for half an hour with moist eyes, struggling with my loss.

Ken was a terrific guy. Maybe a little moody, but he was so smart and funny. And tough enough to survive Normandy at H plus one. Jeez! To go through all that hell and die, just when he was getting his life together. It could've been me. We were both AWOL. It isn't fair… All right, enough. Gotta get back to my girl.

By the time I went inside, my face was dry, and I was smiling. Denise, startled by this change in mood, put four fingers on my forehead.

"Are you all right?"

I lifted her hand and gave it a warm, tender kiss. "Never felt better, *chérie*. Don't you know by now that nothing can keep me down for long?"

"You must be tired. Perhaps you want to go to sleep."

"Baby, I didn't come here to sleep." I enthusiastically scooped Denise up and carried her to the sofa.

"Are you sure you're okay?"

I kissed her on the mouth, working my way down her neck and shoulders before pausing. "Positive. And you know what? I just got a great idea."

"What's that?"

"I had a shower in the public baths yesterday but didn't get all the dirt off. Need another one right now. Care to join me?"

"You know the shower doesn't work."

"Maybe we can coax her. Why not give it a try? Let's just make believe those two knobs are roulette wheels, and we're going for the big hit. What've we got to lose?"

"You have a very active imagination, Sergeant Don."

"It helps get me through the day, especially when you're not around."

"And what if the shower doesn't work?"

"Think positive, *chérie*! That's half the battle. If you don't try something, sure, you won't lose, but you can't succeed, either. And if doesn't work, we can make believe that it does, and still have a good time."

We hit the jackpot. The shower performed splendidly, and we were very happy.

*   *   *   *

My time with Denise consisted of much more than shacking up. We weren't married, but we had made a voluntary commitment to each other. It wasn't verbal, but it was understood. We confided in each other. When we weren't out on the town, I helped with household chores and made sure she got enough to eat. She, in turn, cooked for me and took care of my clothes.

Dec. 8, 1944

Dear Mom, Dad & Ethel,

I was very glad to learn that you had received the handkerchiefs I sent. I was somewhat skeptical about sending them through the mail in that particular manner. However, since they arrived, I feel lots better.

The girl I go to dances and shows with does my laundry, and yesterday she shortened my trousers. She's okay.

Love,

Don

Dec. 9, 1944

Dear Mom, Dad & Ethel,

Today is salvage day, and I handed in my raincoat for a new one. Whoever sold the Army raincoats since the beginning of the war really was sticking it to Uncle Sam. That's you and I, and, eventually, Joe Citizen.

The raincoats, instead of shedding water, absorb it. Whenever I take my raincoat off, the inside is wetter than the outside. I guess they broke the contracts because now I hear the raincoats are good. I'll have one in a couple of weeks.

Today I played the role of interpreter. A soldier was in town a while back. The other day he received a letter in French from his Belgian girlfriend. I translated it into English, and it will soon be on its way to its intended recipient.

Feeling swell.

Love,

Don

I felt sorry for the serviceman who was separated from his Belgian sweetheart because after a few days away from Denise, I couldn't wait to get back to her. I'd do just about anything to be with that woman.

Every so often, the Army would declare a "sweep day" when no passes would be issued for twenty-four hours. The only GI's on the streets would be those on special duty.

The purpose behind this policy was to catch AWOL's. They, of course, wouldn't be aware of the sweep day. The MP's would round them up, and they'd be court-martialed.

Most of the soldiers in the 888th had steady girlfriends in Verviers. Word soon got around that a clerk in the office had access to blank work passes for sweep day. Refusing to be denied, I got hold of one and set off from the l'Athénée for Denise's house. Eddie Haskell had gotten the better of Wally Cleaver.

I decided that the many small side streets were safer than the usual main roads. Such a route would minimize my chances of being discovered.

Mustn't panic if I get stopped by an MP. That would be the worst thing in the world. I'll just play it cool. If I'm asked for my work pass, I'll show it in a very calm, businesslike way.

I waited until after dark to begin the twenty-minute walk through the blacked-out streets. Navigating by moonlight, I could see no more than three feet ahead of myself. The first five minutes passed uneventfully.

Just when I thought I had it made, a jeep appeared out of nowhere. Barreling down the darkened, dirt road, it came straight at me. I squinted in the path of two blinding headlights. The vehicle raced to my side and came to a screeching halt.

"Where are you going, Sergeant?" barked a burly MP at the wheel. He jumped from the jeep, glowering.

I could feel my heart rapidly beating underneath my jacket, but I had rehearsed well.

"Up the hill," I replied with an outward calmness.

Without prompting, I reached into my pocket and produced a work pass with a forged signature—a document worth at least six months in the stockade.

"What's on the hill?"

"My radio truck."

After closely examining the fraudulent pass, the MP made his decision. "You're okay, Sergeant. Have a good evening." Without further ado, he jumped back into his jeep and sped off into the darkness.

Greatly relieved, I continued my walk at a relaxed pace. My heart slowed, and I began to breathe easier. Finally, I saw Denise's shadowy figure in front of the house.

Thank God. Made it!

I stopped. Someone else was watching me. It was the middle-aged woman in the house across the street.

"Hey!" I angrily bellowed, pointing an accusatory index finger at the meddler. "I'm fuckin' her. Got a problem with that? Well, that's too bad!"

The woman abruptly slammed her window and disappeared from view. Denise grabbed me, and with surprising strength, pulled me into the house.

"What's wrong with you?" she scolded. "You're going to make problems for me."

"Sorry, *chérie.* I know I was way outta line, but I don't like being spied on. Hey, wait a minute. I've seen her before. She's been watching me whenever I go in and out of here, hasn't she?"

"Probably."

"Who the hell does she think she is, a French concierge? I know you want to avoid trouble with your neighbors, but she's got no right to act like that."

"She thinks she does."

"Tell her to mind her own business."

"It's not that easy."

"Why the hell not?"

"She's my mother-in-law."

"Holy Jeez. She's Étienne's mother?"

"Yes."

I momentarily scratched my head and then decisively retorted, "Well, Étienne isn't around anymore. That makes her an ex-mother-in-law, doesn't it?"

"Yes, but around here, family is very important. Once a mother-in-law, always a mother-in-law. She may not have any legal rights over this house, but she thinks she has a moral one."

I felt a chill pass over me. "Do you think she knows what I said?"

"She does not understand English, but I'm sure she, how do you say, got your drift."

"Have you ever thought of selling?"

"Yes. It's been difficult to keep up this place, and there are a lot of memories here. I'd like to move to an apartment in Verviers. It would be much cheaper and closer to work. But I can't do anything until the war's over. There isn't much of a market right now."

"Yeah, I can see you're in a bit of a bind. I shouldn't have blown up like that. Forgive me?"

"It's forgotten. Don't you know I can't stay mad at you for very long?"

We enjoyed each other very much that night, but things were never quite the same. Now there was a ghost between us. Still, we were determined to make the most of our time together.

When I arrived at the l'Athénée the next morning, I overheard two GI's talking in the hall a few feet from my bunk.

"You know what happened to the guys who got hold of those work passes yesterday?"

"No, what?"

"An MP stopped them for questioning and got suspicious, so he brought them back to base."

"No shit?"

"I'm not shittin' you. Honest."

"Okay, so then what happened?"

"Well, the army cops found out that the work passes were phoney. The signatures were forged. Now these mugs are gonna be court-martialled. Heard they could get up to two years."

"Two years? Jesus F. Christ! I don't care how pretty she was. No skirt's worth a coupla years outta my life."

"Mine either. Those guys must've been nuts."

I buried my head in my blanket and cringed. Once again, I had narrowly escaped disaster. I realized that, up until now, I had been extremely lucky in these reckless ventures, and that my good fortune couldn't last forever. With my head pressed hard against the mattress, I silently vowed to curtail my impulsiveness and exercise that all-too-rare commodity known as common sense. Now Wally Cleaver was beating up on Eddie Haskell.

Momentarily humbled, I looked forward to more pleasant happenings. The holidays were fast approaching.

Dec. 13, 1944

Dear Mom, Dad & Ethel,

We've planned a party for several hundred children in the neighborhood for Christmas Day. There will be a Christmas tree, and we'll make up tidy packages for them.

Just received a letter from Joe, and he writes that he is no longer permitted to get into any of the cities.

Yesterday we received another typhus shot, and my arms feel quite heavy. We get one of these every three months.

One thing about prices that's mighty peculiar: when you go to a movie or something of that nature, you are given a reduced rate because you're a U.S. soldier, but when you go to a barber, or to a café, you're given a special increased rate. Although most of the Belgians are more than generous and hospitable, a few entrepreneurs will inflate their prices when dealing with us. Most of the time, though, they treat us royally.

Love,

Don

Belgium
Dec. 16, 1944
Dear Mom, Dad & Ethel,

I received a letter from a fellow I met at radio school. He was part of the first landing on the Philippines. He wrote me a letter a few days before and a few days after the landing. I always marvel at the light censorship that exists in the mail coming from the Pacific. That stuff would be cut out of my letter, and what you would receive would be a paper doll with open circles for eyes, mouth, and nose.

Love,

Don

Despite the loss of Ken and my increasingly complicated relationship with Denise, I was still living a very comfortable life in Verviers. I was always about five to ten miles behind the front lines and, unlike my acquaintance in the Philippines, had rarely experienced serious physical danger. American fighters did the hard work: bombing bridges, enemy convoys, and trains. Meanwhile, in comparative safety, I faithfully worked my radio shifts and had ample time to spend with my lady. Except for a couple of close calls, the V-weapons and air raids had amounted to little more than on-the-job inconvenience.

But all that was about to change.

CHAPTER 14

▼

THE BULGE

Belgium's worst nightmare had come true: the Germans were back.

At 5 a.m., on December 16, 1944,[332] Field Marshal Gerd von Rundstedt[333] began a startling counter-offensive in the Ardennes region of eastern Belgium and northern Luxembourg.[334] It would soon involve over one million men,[335] including six hundred thousand Americans,[336] and become the single bloodiest battle ever fought by U.S. troops.[337]

Amidst snowy, rugged ravines and dense forests,[338] a powerful force of 250,000 Germans stormed through an eighty-five-mile Allied front.[339] The lines were very weak there,[340] and in some places, the Allies were outnumbered ten to one.[341] Worse, they were confused.[342]

Conceived and planned by Adolf Hitler,[343] the campaign was executed against the advice of his top generals.[344] Hitler's ultimate objective was to pierce the Meuse River Line and take the Belgian port city of Antwerp,[345] a vital link in the Allied supply route.[346] For a while, he appeared to be succeeding.

Fog and forest provided a natural cover for the enemy.[347] For three days, the Americans were unable to use their superior air power.[348] On the morning of December 16, the Germans shelled Verviers.[349] A cannon thundered in the distance, and small arms fire was heard on the streets.[350] On Sunday, the seventeenth, over seventy V-weapons were spotted in the skies (28). About forty continued on to the provincial capital of Liège (28), where they inflicted heavy damage (28). A posse of American soldiers and local authorities pursued German parachutists who had landed in the Hertogenwald Forest outside Verviers.[351] One was captured, and another was killed (166-7). These Germans were part of a group later estimated by the Chief of the Second Allied Bureau to be fifteen-hundred-strong (176). Dressed in American military uniforms,[352] they landed in the vicinity of Verviers,[353] where they engaged in various activities of espionage and sabotage, including the cutting of telephone wires.[354] In December and January, fourteen of these spies were killed in the village of Henri-Chapelle and at Huy,[355] one of the four districts of Liège Province.[356]

A massive Allied evacuation of Verviers began on the morning of December 18.[357] Requisitioned schools and factories were hastily abandoned.[358] In the frantic attempt to move many squadrons, traffic jams developed in and around the city.

After traveling a few miles on frosty terrain, our trucks ground to a complete halt. The outfit was in the middle of a four-way intersection choked with gridlock. Horns honked and tempers flared. Nobody was going anywhere for a long time. Soldiers began milling about on the road chatting, bellyaching—even playing catch—to keep themselves occupied and relieve tension. When I got out to stretch my legs, an irate colonel approached me.

"Who the hell is leading this convoy, Sergeant?" he barked. "And don't tell me his name is Smith."

The colonel had put me in a bit of a quandary. My parents had taught me to always tell the truth, but this situation was complicated. To my twenty-two-year-old mind, messing with leave was a mere fib. It was much harder to lie to a high-ranking officer during the serious business of evacuation. On the other hand, I didn't want to get my assistant commander in trouble. Inwardly wrestling for a response, I tried to gather my thoughts, but the words flew out before I could stifle them.

"Captain Jones."

The colonel's eyes narrowed to a menacing stare. "I don't believe you, Sergeant," he icily intoned. Then he turned on his heels and strode off.

With a helpful twist of fate, the problem had solved itself. I had told the truth, and nobody got into trouble because the colonel thought I was a liar. Or did he?

That evening, when we were hunkered down with Mother Nature three miles from Spa, Captain Jones called me into his tent. Because of our haste in leaving Verviers, only a few officers had tents. The rest of us slept outside in snow-covered foxholes. Since our sleeping bags weren't designed for the bone-chilling temperatures, we lined them with blankets taken from our former barracks. For further insulation against the elements, we put silk parachute material underneath our bedding.

The tent, nestled under dense tree-cover, was tall and spacious. Once inside, I drew myself up to my full height. In the weak lamplight, I could barely see the captain's face. As Jones approached me, his shadow danced threateningly against the canvas walls.

I stiffly saluted and began to perspire. I had an urge to urinate.

Oh shit! He knows I ratted him out.

"You wanted to see me, sir?"

"Yes. At ease, Quix."

"Thank you, sir. Begging the captain's pardon, I'd like to explain—"

"Explain? How can you possibly explain anything? You don't even know why you're here!"

"Well, sir, about that convoy—"

"I don't give a damn about the convoy. All I'm interested in right now is this." My captain held up a thick folder. "A while back, I came across your file. You've got quite a checkered past, Quix. I understand you were accepted into gunnery school, but then you went AWOL. You've done pretty well since then, even got a promotion."

"I've tried to make amends, sir."

"I appreciate that, Sergeant, but you're a bit accident prone. What is it with you, Quix? Problems have a way of finding you. I understand that about six weeks ago you were attacked by an ex-Resistance fighter during a date."

"That's correct, sir."

"Weren't you the sergeant I gave a lift to in Versailles?"

"Yes, sir."

"You got lost downtown. Spent the night in a French police station."

"Yes, sir."

"And now this!"

"Sir?"

Captain Jones wiggled the folder under my nose. "I'm mail censor this month, and this is our latest batch of outgoing letters. Yours are absolutely filthy."

I wiped the sweat off my forehead and smiled.

"Do you find that amusing, Sergeant?"

"No, sir," was my sheepish reply. "I had something else on my mind."

"That's your problem, Quix. You're always looking somewhere else and not paying attention to what's going on in front of you. Look at this!" The captain reached into the folder and handed me a letter I had written to a friend in another outfit.

"It's mine all right."

"Quix, your language is unbelievable. I've seen tamer stuff on bathroom walls." Captain Jones eyed me quizzically. "Would you write that way to your mother?"

"No, sir. But I wasn't writing to my mother," I protested. "May I speak freely?"

Captain Jones wearily rolled his eyes. "Go ahead, but make it fast."

This line of questioning had really gotten me thinking. I had been oblivious to the extent to which my speech had coarsened over the past two years. Before entering the service, I rarely cursed, even when I was with my best buddies. My parents didn't tolerate swear words around the house, and they would have been horrified to learn of the casual way in which I now employed them.

"Well, sir, you've gotta realize how it is when a bunch of fellas get together, especially when they're in a strange place far from home. When you're eating or going to sleep, it's always fuck this, fuck that, fuck everything. Sir!"

The captain's taut facial expression loosened, and his lips curved slightly upward. "You may find this hard to believe, Quix, but, once upon a time, I was your age. I entered the Army as a private, so I've been in the mess halls and the bunk houses, and I know the score. By the way, when it comes to foul language, some of the officers are worse than enlisted men. I've been known to occasionally use a salty word or two myself."

"So I've heard, sir."

"I'm glad we're on the same page, Quix, but there's something else you need to know. There's a big difference between talking trash and writing it on official U.S. government stationery. When you're sending V-mail, you're not just speaking for yourself. You're representing the United States of America, and it's my job to help make sure that her reputation isn't tarnished. Understood?"

"Loud and clear, sir."

"Good. Now get the fuck outta here."

*   *   *   *

"Now hear this. Now hear this," blared a voice over the loudspeaker. "Pack up your belongings and get ready to board the trucks. We will be leaving at 0600 sharp. I repeat. We will be leaving at 0600 sharp."

I wearily rubbed my eyes and looked at my glow-in-the-dark wristwatch. It was 5:40 a.m. Overcoming my sluggishness, I wriggled out of my bag in full uniform and whipped on my winter jacket. Shivering amidst my chalky breath, I stamped my feet and slapped my hands together. Since leaving Verviers, I hadn't taken off the woolen gloves Denise had knitted for me.

I quickly packed up my gear. Everyone else did likewise. That is, all except Mack, Lonny, and Charlie.

While we were loading up, this astute trio continued playing poker in front of a lantern. Privates Lonny Wols and Charlie Yardt were cooks. Private Mack Long was a guard. An angry lieutenant approached them.

"Turn that fucking thing off!" he screamed. "Do you want every Kraut in the Ardennes to know where we are? Pack up and get ready to move. You've only got fifteen minutes."

"Yes, sir," replied Mack. With the lieutenant barely out of earshot, Mack turned to his companions and muttered, "What's his problem? We've got some time yet."

"Don't worry about it," said Lonny.

"Yeah," agreed Charlie.

They extinguished the lantern, but kept on playing under small penlights. Now Stan approached them.

"Hey, guys, this isn't a casino. If you're not on one of those trucks in ten minutes, we're leaving without you."

"We'll be right there," Charlie replied.

"In a minute, Stan," said Lonny.

"Yeah, right after this hand," mumbled Mack.

I left with Stan. At the end of the war, in Weimar, I came across a galley of our squadron's history detailing what next befell Mack, Lonny, and Charlie. We couldn't get the book printed before we ceded the area to the Soviets, and they refused to return the manuscript to us. In an abridged version published in the U.S. in 1946, the authors wisely omitted the following events, which were quite embarrassing to the unit.

The trio was still playing. A nervous Corporal Zeke ran up to them. He was breathing heavily.

"Hey, Corp," crowed Mack. "You getting an early start on the '48 Olympics?"

"Are you guys nuts? You've only got a coupla minutes."

"Okay, Corp. We'll be right with ya."

"Well, don't say I didn't warn you."

Zeke ran to his truck, and the casino remained open. Charlie was on a hot streak.

"Well, gentlemen," he happily announced. "I think we should call it quits."

"C'mon, Charlie. Give us another chance," Lonny pleaded.

"Yeah," grunted Mack. "What's fair is fair."

"Okay. This is it. Place your bets and deal."

Charlie wagered his entire stash. Mack dealt the cards. By now, the sun was coming up.

"Hey, it's gonna be a nice day," opined the high roller.

"Not for you it ain't," countered Lonny. "I've got two pair."

"Oh yeah?" Charlie answered. "I've got three tens."

"You're both washed up," Mack triumphantly proclaimed. "I've got three kings."

"And I haf a fool house!" exclaimed a mysterious fourth voice.

Mack slowly turned around and stared into the barrel of a luger. The pistol was held by a smartly dressed German infantry captain. Two massive, heavily armed foot soldiers flanked him on each side. The officer flashed a thin, plastic smile. He cocked his head slightly, and the three stragglers were promptly collected. The lackadaisical Americans paid dearly for their tardiness. Mack, Lonny, and Charlie spent the next four-and-a-half months in a German POW camp.[359]

*   *   *   *

The exodus from Verviers was so sudden that none of us had time to say good-bye to our Belgian sweethearts. I was very worried about Denise, but now I had problems of my own.

Under ordinary conditions, Liège was about a forty-five-minute drive from Spa, but because of the critical situation on the ground, we had to pass through a gauntlet of military checkpoints, and traffic was heavy. After nearly four hours on the road, we arrived at our destination exhausted and dispirited. Our three-hundred-man squadron was quickly dispersed among buildings throughout the city.

Morale continued to deteriorate over the next week. When we reached Liège on December 19, Malmédy was in enemy hands.[360] The First American Army had retreated from several other points, including Stavelot.[361] By December 25, the Germans had opened a fifty-mile bulge into Allied lines, forcing the greatest mass surrender of U.S. troops since Bataan: four thousand men in one day.[362] The Christmas party we had planned for the children of Verviers was canceled. Jack's schedule was scrapped. Sorties were being flown around the clock, and we put in tough, twelve-to-eighteen-hour days. To help relieve the tension, I took up smoking.

At first, the decision to move the squadron to Liège seemed prudent. Verviers was in danger of being overrun, and if a substantial portion of the 888th Fighter Control Squadron had been captured, American air operations would have been severely compromised. Liège was thirteen miles west of Verviers,[363] well away from the front lines. But fickle fate was not kind: we were in far greater peril in Liège than we were in Verviers. Although by December 22, the Americans had retaken Malmédy, Saint-Vith, and Stavelot, the Germans had cut the route from Bastogne to Liège and were within twenty kilometers of the latter city.[364]

Situated along the Meuse River,[365] Liège was an urban center with 156,664 people[366] and a major commercial hub of the Meuse Valley.[367] When its suburbs were factored in, its population swelled to 432,471.[368] With its greater size and industrial base, Liège was an irresistible target for air attacks. In 1944 and 1945, this metropolis suffered 1,586 V-weapon casualties.[369] Some 221 civilians were killed (185), and 937 were wounded (185). On the military side, buzz bombs and V-2 rockets landing in Liège claimed the lives of 92 Allied soldiers (185) and injured an additional 336.[370] However, these numbers pale in comparison to the carnage wrought upon Hitler's primary objective, Antwerp, which sustained 10,145 vengeance-weapon-related deaths and injuries during the same period.[371]

Although comparatively safer, Verviers and its suburbs weren't forgotten by the Germans. Between December 16, 1944 and January 7, 1945, at least 54 people were killed and 126 wounded by V-1 attacks in the city.[372] The l'École des Hougnes became a mortuary (169). Due to extreme cold, bombings, and military traffic, funeral services were performed at the deceased's home (171). From there, the body was transferred directly to the cemetery (171).

Civilian vehicles were banned from the streets (171). A 7 p.m. to 7 a.m. curfew was imposed on Verviers beginning December 19 (170). The starting time was advanced to 6 p.m. on the twenty-fifth (170), allowing units to begin looking for German paratroopers while it was still light.[373] These regulations remained in effect until January 19, 1945.[374]

Dec. 24, 1944

Dear Mom, Dad & Ethel,

Tonight is Christmas Eve, and this is the big holiday of the year in Belgium. New Year's Eve is not celebrated here, and, therefore, the night before Santa makes his popular visit garners the number one spot.

However, Belgium is very serious tonight, as she has been for the past few days. With one eye, the people will be enjoying the gaiety and the festivities, and with the other they'll be watching all the doors and windows for fear that the Germans may return.

The Germans are now in their front yard, and they know it only too well. Atrocity stories are reaching here, intensifying their trepidation. Meanwhile, the parties and dances continue, with cautious people attending.

I recently received a sleeping bag. It is a nice, handy item to have on a cold night, although our rooms are presently well-heated.

Received a letter from Jerry which took an awful long time to get here. He was about ready to go on combat missions, and, perhaps by this time, he has had a taste of it. He praises his pilot, but he's not so keen on the other members of the crew. His brother Murray is doing fine and has been awarded the Distinguished Flying Cross Air Medal and the Second Oak Leaf Cluster.

Jerry is in a Liberator, and I hope he'll be all right. I'll be sweating his missions out with him. I know he'll pull through.

Love,

Don

By Christmas Eve, my buddies and I were heartsick for our Belgian girlfriends. The fighting had reached maximum intensity. Verviers was off limits, but we would not be denied.

In lightly falling snow under a twilight sky, a dozen of us hitched a ride back to the city. Although fatigued from a long shift, our spirits brightened as we approached our destination. The necessary passes had been obtained through the usual back channels. The traffic was cooperative, and the trip took less than an hour. We had just stepped out of the van when the MP's began inspecting our dog tags and started bombarding us with questions.

"What's the Breakfast of Champions?"

"Wheaties," we chorused.

"How'd the Yankees do this year?"

"Shitty," I replied. "Lost the pennant to the Browns."[375]

"Who's the actress with peek-a-boo hair?"

"Hell, even Ah know that," answered Jack. "Veronica Lake. Ask somethin' harduh."

A powerfully built MP got in his face. "Okay, wiseguy. What street is the Park Central Hotel on?"

Wincing with chagrin, Sergeant Spring desperately looked to his fellow radio men for help. I was stumped. Although technically a New Yorker, I lived in the Bronx and seldom traveled to Manhattan. All the other fellows could muster were blank stares. That is, all except Stan, a Manhattan resident, who piped out, "Fifty-ninth Street, and I'll even tell you who the manager is!"

The MP's relented. In his usual cleanup position, Stan had come through. We now had access to Verviers, and our women.

The questions were a very unscientific but effective way of detecting impostors. Although the Army was justifiably concerned about infiltration by German parachutists, we were blissfully ignorant of that threat. Had we known, we probably wouldn't have changed our plans. Wartime romance has a way of bringing out bravery in even the most mild-mannered of men.

Denise rushed into my arms, and we showered each other with warm, wet kisses. Ten days of separation seemed like years.

"This is wonderful, Sergeant Don, but how did you get here?"

"I bummed a ride."

"But the city is closed."

"We got special permission."

"Bull. You boys snuck back in, didn't you?"

"We didn't sneak back in. We just finessed the passes."

"But you could have been arrested, maybe even shot."

"Whaddya want me to tell you, Denise? We did what we hadda do. I couldn't stay away. I was worried sick about you."

Denise relaxed her taut face and smiled. "It was very foolish for you to come, but I'm so happy you're here."

"Glad to see you're working on those contractions, baby."

"What are you hiding behind your back?"

"*Voilà.*"

"Red roses in the dead of winter! *Merci beaucoup*, but how did you get them?"

"Don't ask."

"Here, let me put them in water. Have you been practicing your French?"

"No. I've been kinda busy, so I came back to brush up. How have you been managing, *chérie?*"

"*Ça va.*"

"You must've been scared stiff."

"For the first few days, I was. The news is still very frightening, but it's getting better. I think Hitler will be beaten back."

"That's my girl. Keep the faith." I squeezed Denise's hand and raised it to my lips.

"Your face is freezing, and so hairy," she observed.

"It's cold outside, and I've had no time to shave. Just as well, because the whiskers help keep me warm."

"I like you better with smooth skin."

"Maybe I should leave then."

"Don't be silly."

"I took an open van from Liège to Verviers."

"And you walked from Verviers in this weather?"

"Yeah."

"You must be exhausted."

"I'm okay."

"Are you sure?"

"Yes, *mademoiselle*. I'm sure."

"Here, let me take your coat. I'll make us some *café.*"

"Great. I'll heat up the irons."

After completing these pleasant tasks, we quietly sipped our coffee in front of the fire. We were so comfortable that neither of us wanted to move. Jealously savoring the moment, I let several minutes pass before breaking the silence.

"Listen, *chérie*, I can't stay very long."

"Are those irons hot yet?"

"I think so."

"Then what are we sitting here for?"

*   *   *   *

There are no references to the City of Charleroi in any of the 888th Fighter Control Squadron's surviving records. A frequently offered explanation is that the stop was made under emergency conditions, and the unit was there for less than thirty-six hours. However, the same can be said of a brief stay in Laon, France during early September 1944, which does appear on the outfit's itinerary. Thus, nearly sixty years later, the oversight remains enigmatic.

Despite its modest population of about twenty-six thousand,[376] Charleroi was an important industrial center located on the Sambre River in south central Belgium's Hainaut Province,[377] some thirty-one miles from Brussels.[378] Its name comes from a fortress the Spanish built in 1666.[379] They called it "Charleroy," in honor of Charles II, their infant king.[380] But it wasn't until the advent of the Industrial Revolution in the early 1800's that Charleroi earned its sobriquet "the Black Country."[381] It was here in 1827 that Paul Huart-Chapel built Belgium's first coke smelting furnace.[382] Mining ten million tons of coal a year well into the twentieth century, Charleroi had the nation's largest coal basin.[383]

On the windswept afternoon of December 26, 1944, the radio vans were perched atop the hills overlooking town. I only saw part of what happened over the next eighteen hours. Bobby, who was badly shaken by these events, gave me the full story several days later.

It was a few minutes before 4 p.m., and already getting dark, when he approached his mentor, who had just come off duty.

"I need a big favor from you, Stan."

"Let's go to the canteen truck, and we can talk about it over a cup of coffee."

"I can't. That's down the slope, and my shift's starting."

"Where's your van?"

"Right over there."

"We'll talk inside. No sense in freezing our butts off out here."

"Hey, Donnybrook," Bobby greeted.

"How you doing, fellas?" I replied.

"I've been better," said Stan. "Where you coming from?"

"Just getting off duty."

"Lucky you."

After I left, Bobby and Stan had their fateful conversation.

Stan addressed Corporal Sean O'Malley and PFC Hector Gonzalez, who were on duty inside the van. "Listen, guys, we need a little privacy. Will you excuse us?"

After grumbling about the weather, the noncoms reluctantly complied.

"Okay, Bobby. Let's have it."

"Can you pull my shift for me?"

"Pull your shift? You know I always try to help you out, but I've been on duty since we got here. I'm bushed. Why didn't you come to me with this earlier?"

"I wasn't sure my girl was going to be here until a few minutes ago."

"Look, there's plentya babes in the next town."

"This isn't just a date. I'm gonna ask her to marry me."

"Isn't that a little impulsive? We've only been here for about sixteen hours."

"You don't understand. I met her in Verviers a few months ago. She's British, so there's no language problem. We were seeing each other a couple times a week until we had to leave. I told her I'd meet her here."

"How did you get word to her? Even I didn't know we were gonna be here until yesterday."

"Well, I bunked into Old Man Jones before we left Liège. I mean, really banged into him. He dropped a bunch of papers, and while I was helping him pick 'em up, I saw Charleytown on the schedule."

"Charleroi."

"Whatever."

"You love her?"

"More than life itself."

"Get a ring?"

"Yeah. Here."

Bobby opened a tiny black jewelry box. A small diamond shone brilliantly under the dim wattage.

"Wow. Someone's been winning big at poker."

"Nah. Just been saving up."

"If anyone needed a break like this, it's you, Bobby. I'm happy for ya. So happy that I'll pull your shift tonight."

"You're a bloody lifesaver, Stan. You don't know how much this means to me."

"Oh, yes I do. The day I proposed to Lisa, I thought I'd entered Paradise."

"How are the kids?"

"Funny you should ask. I got this in the mail a couple days ago. With all the confusion and moving around, it's amazing it came through. Here, look. Frances is five, and Justin's gonna be twelve next month."

"Cute little girl. Gee, the boy's getting big. A real bruiser."

"Yeah, but he takes after his mother. Plays the piano a lot better than he can throw a ball."

"Lisa's a pianist?"

"She can play a few instruments, but she doesn't perform anymore. Just teaches."

"You two must make an odd couple. A mechanic and a music teacher, fancy that!"

"Hey, you better get a move on."

"Yeah." Bobby swallowed hard. "Stan?"

"What?"

"I, um, just wanted to tell you what a terrific guy you've been. Not just for this, for everything."

Bobby put his large paws around the technical sergeant, nearly smothering him with an affectionate bear hug.

"Okay. Enough of this sappy stuff. Your lady's waiting."

"I'd buy you a Caddy if I could."

"Just save me a piece of the wedding cake."

The church bells had barely pealed five o'clock when Bobby proposed to his girl in front of the town hall on the place Charles II. Thoroughly absorbed in their own happiness, they strolled by the stately townhouses along the boulevard Audent, barely aware of the V-1 that passed above them.

*   *   *   *

The next morning, Captain Jones was in a foul mood. He was behind schedule, and the convoy was a mess. Jones was walking up and down the base camp, confronting every soldier he saw with the same question: "Where's Stan Firestone?"

Nobody knew.

"Damn it!" bellowed Jones. "He's my right-hand traffic man, and he's never let me down. What's keeping him?"

A young lieutenant approached. "We're missing a truck, sir."

"Wonderful. What other lovely news do you have for me, son?"

"Four soldiers are missing, including Sergeant Liter and Technical Sergeant Firestone. Do you want me to send out a search party?"

"There's not enough time for that. We're short handed as it is."

I had overheard this conversation. "I think I can find them, Captain," I interjected. "I saw them together when I was coming off duty last night."

Captain Jones stroked his chin for several seconds. "All right, Quix," he grudgingly agreed. "Find Firestone. I'll give you an hour."

"Thank you, sir."

"And Quix."

"Yes, sir?"

"If you screw up, I'll have you cleaning latrines for the rest of the war. Understood?"

"Loud and clear, sir."

After twenty minutes of negotiating steep switchbacks, I reached the truck where I had last seen my two friends. There wasn't much left. The radio van was a blackened hulk. A stench of gasoline, rubber, and decaying flesh arose from the mass. Forcing down the rising vomit in my throat, I grimaced and covered my mouth. Sergeant Liter was sitting on a pile of twisted metal, staring out into space.

"Hey, Bobby, what happened?"

No response. I shook him by the shoulders.

"Come on, Bobby. We don't have much time. Talk to me!"

"Leave me alone, Donnybrook."

"Bobby—"

"I said, leave me the fuckin' hell alone!"

"Hey, take it easy."

Bobby clambered to his feet, and, in a fit of rage, rushed at me. I quickly sidestepped him.

"Bobby, what's going on?"

The response was a roundhouse punch to the temple. I ducked. Another. *Man, that was close!* I responded with two quick jabs to the stomach. No effect. Then I followed with an uppercut to Bobby's jaw, knocking him on his buttocks. Though unhurt, the hefty sergeant put his face in his hands and began blubbering uncontrollably.

I shook my bruised knuckles. "Jeez! What the fuck is wrong with you? You wanna kill me or something?"

Bobby's head began to clear. "Sorry, Don," he said between sniffles.

"Is this your truck?"

"Yeah, but I got engaged last night. Switched shifts with him so I could propose. Now he's dead, and it's all my fault."

"Who are you talking about?"

"Stan!"

I stared up at the wreckage. "Oh my God. What about the others?"

Bobby shook his head. "I came up here early this morning to get some gear I'd left behind, and this is what I found. The remains of a radio van and a buzz bomb, courtesy of Adolf Mother Fuckin' Hitler."

For a time, I stood transfixed, paralyzed by the uncomfortable silence. Bobby, still seated on the ground, reached into his jacket pocket and tossed three sets of darkened dog tags at my feet. They clanged eerily against a bald patch of hard earth. Emerging from the daze, I wiped my moist eyes and scooped up the identifications. The names and serial numbers were still visible: Stanley Firestone #13166691; Sean O'Malley #14279583; and Hector Gonzalez #15399774.

"You engaged now?"

"Yeah, but what does it matter?"

"Whaddya mean what does it matter? Of course it matters. It's great."

"I just killed my best friend."

"You didn't kill anyone, Bobby. We all change shifts. It could've been me, Jack, Angelo, anybody. Look. Stan was a great guy. He was just in the wrong place at the wrong time. I know you two were close, but he was a terrific friend to everyone. And I know he wouldn't wanna see you like this. He'd want you to be happy."

"Yeah. He would."

"Come on. Let's get the hell outta here."

*   *   *   *

By the evening of December 27, we were back in Liège. The next day, local radio stations reported that the military threat to the city had been repulsed.[384] The outfit was dispersed among several school buildings, where we remained for the next two weeks.

Over a hundred soldiers showed up for Stan's funeral, which was just about everyone who wasn't on duty. Angelo helped an army chaplain conduct the service. We were all sniffling. Even the hard-boiled Captain Jones was moved. Bobby took it very hard, but with counseling from the clergyman, he got over his grief.

*   *   *   *

The Battle of the Bulge is replete with heroism and tragedy. Doing it justice is beyond the scope of this book. We must, therefore, content ourselves with providing a brief sketch of a few of its major highlights.

For weeks, the front lines were in constant flux. There were times when citizens did not know who controlled their towns.[385] Fear and confusion reigned. Most of the picturesque villages in the Ardennes were destroyed,[386] and their inhabitants scattered throughout Belgium (48). Anxious mothers searched for their children, sons and daughters for their parents (48). Infantrymen fighting in snowy, zero-degree weather often could not see more than twenty yards in front of them.[387] Some froze to death in their foxholes.[388]

Every veteran who participated in the conflict remembers the famous reply of Brigadier General Anthony McAuliffe, commander of the U.S. forces surrounded at Bastogne. When confronted with a German surrender demand, he answered in typically American fashion: "Nuts."[389] By late December, the l'Athénée in Verviers had been converted to a U.S. military hospital. Despite the presence of an enormous red cross painted on its roof, the seventy-year-old edifice became a rubbly tomb for an estimated thirty patients when it was struck by an aerial bomb.[390] An infamous military atrocity was reported on January 1, 1945 by an official Allied communiqué: over one hundred American soldiers taken prisoner at Malmédy had been machine-gunned by German troops.[391]

Less well-known is the story of Sergeant Charles A. MacGillivary, whose company was pinned down in the snowy forests that New Year's Day. With two sub-machine guns and a bunch of grenades, MacGillivary single-handedly wiped out four German machine gun nests.[392] During the assault, he lost his lower left arm to enemy gunfire (18). Unflinching, MacGillivary stuck his stump in the ice, stanching the flow of blood and saving his own life (18). President Truman awarded him the Medal of Honor (18).

*   *   *   *

By the end of 1944, things had improved for us. We were safer, and our routine had returned to near-normal.

Dec. 30, 1944

Dear Mom, Dad & Ethel,

They have one of the finest Red Cross Clubs I've ever seen in this town. They serve doughnuts and coffee all day long. Outside of Uncle Sam's auspices, this is an unobtainable commodity in Belgium. The place is immaculate, and you appreciate the clean spots for entertainment.

Primarily because of its sanitary conditions, the Red Cross is a haven. It is immense. A G.I. walks in like a king and is treated like one.

I received a G.I. issue of a wool sweater. It is long-sleeved and khaki-colored. I knew the government was making them, but I didn't think we'd get them. It's a darned swell sweater and very classy looking. It sure was a pleasant surprise.

Tomorrow is the big morale-booster of the month. That, you no doubt know, is pay day. It comes at a timely moment, for tomorrow is New Year's Eve. The Belgians may not celebrate it, but the Americans sure do. There will be quite a lot of hell-raising, as you can well imagine.

I also bought some ice cream today. It was kinda cold, but it isn't often when you get the opportunity to buy ice cream.

All letters this week have hit a snag, so any day now, I expect to get my back mail. In the meantime, I'll be chasing out the old year and cheering in the new one.

Happy New Year.

Lots of Love,

Don

Actually, the hell-raising began that very afternoon. An incident during one of our periodic day trips to the public bathhouse in Liège provided us with a much-needed diversion from falling bombs. Treated to some fine entertainment, we were both audience and main attraction.

While I and about a dozen other GI's were under the showers, removing the week's grime from our bodies, two maintenance workers sauntered in with squeegees. With exceptional efficiency, they began mopping the floor and directing water into the drains. Ordinarily, such an occurrence would not have been cause for celebration, but these were no ordinary circumstances. The squeegee moppers were about nineteen years old, gorgeous, and female. The two young women eyed our soaked birthday suits with equanimity.

"*Vous êtes tous mouillés* [You are all wet]," one nonchalantly observed.

"Ooh, la, la. Come here, babies!" we unabashedly chorused.

Lewd hoots of hilarity rang out from the stalls. Unfazed, the young ladies continued their chores in front of a bunch of wild-eyed, naked men. It was all in a day's work.

The storytelling surrounding that afternoon lingered well into the night, when the lights were out and the amateur comics were trying to bring the house down.

"Psst! Did you hear what happened at the showers today?" began the first contestant.

"Yeah, we had batting practice," answered a second. "Those Belgian babes had luscious curves."

"But you didn't throw them a slider!"

"Or a breaking ball!"

Soon the nocturnal variety hour was receiving contributions from the whole room. The laughter approached the lofty heights of insanity before everyone grew tired and quieted down. That is, all except Corporal Zeke, who continued on and on. Bobby finally piped up from the darkness.

"Zeke, did you ever get laryngitis?"

"No. Why?"

"Because if you don't shut up and let us get some sleep, you're gonna get a shoe down your big mouth."

*   *   *   *

My desire to reassure my family that I was safe extended to Joe. The Germans were gone from Liège, and it made no sense to tell my brother or anyone else that I had been on the front lines.

Jan. 5, 1945

Dear Mom, Dad & Ethel,

Joe writes that he's worried about my welfare since the recent German push. My letters since then will reassure him that I am nowhere near the advance.

I was complaining to Joe about our chow, which has been going from bad to worse. Then along comes these last few days finding us eating turkey for one meal and steak for another, and, then, the following morning, French toast. Now we're starting to get suspicious. I guess I'm like a typical G.I. When the food is bad, we rightfully complain. When the food is superb, we think something's gotta be wrong: they're treating us too good.

It seems funny writing "1945" on letters. The months seem to pass like days. That is proof that I am moving around a lot. I don't think I'm accomplishing much, but am running around nevertheless.

I went shopping today, and guess what I bought? A pillow! If someone told me that when I started out, I would buy a pillow, I would have thought them nutty. However, when I passed the shop and saw this pillow in the window, I thought, "That's a good idea. I can use that." And I entered the shop and bought a pillow.

I'll bet there's very few G.I.'s who ever thought of buying a pillow. Ludicrous? Nope. It sure beats folding up a jacket.

In spite of snow and rain, we've been fortunate in having decent flying weather.

Am in very good condition, and tomorrow I'll visit the coiffeur and lose a few pounds of hair.

Love,

Don

By the middle of January, the danger was over. Jack's schedule was reinstated, and I stopped smoking. We were back in Verviers, firmly ensconced in several factories in the western part of the city. The accommodations were less comfortable than those in the l'Athénée, and the walk to work was longer, but hundreds of radio men were overjoyed to be reunited with their sweethearts—at least for awhile.

In the end, Hitler's counterattack accomplished nothing. By January 16, 1945, the front lines in the Ardennes were re-established to approximately what they had been a month earlier.[393] Although fighting continued for another nine days,[394] enemy forces were hopelessly stalemated. The cost on both sides was enormous: eighty-one thousand American casualties, including nineteen thousand killed,[395] and one hundred thousand Germans either dead, wounded, or captured.[396]

CHAPTER 15

▼

RUSH TO THE RHINE

Jan. 20, 1945

Dear Mom, Dad & Ethel,

The big news here continues to be the giant Russian offensive which is relentlessly pushing ahead on German soil.

The weather has abated somewhat the last few days. To those without coal, the situation is viewed with grim satisfaction. The people are thinking very optimistically about the war. I don't count on anything anymore until I see it happen. You see so many places and hopes crushed that you become dubious about everything, regardless of how certain its appearance.

Went dancing last night and had a nice time. I had to remind the waiter twice during the night that he failed to give me change after ordering drinks. His excuse was that he didn't have the proper change and was waiting until he accumulated it.

The civilians have been promised better rations of food in several days. From what I gather, their present rations are smaller than when the Germans were here. Thus, our present policy dealing with these liberated countries is not being received too well. The stuff is going somewhere, but just where, nobody seems to know.

The Army apparently has enough coal, and, therefore, we have been able to take care of Old Man Winter.

Chow is fair now. Occasionally, it reaches low levels, and then sometimes, for about a week, it is unusually good. Overall, it's okay.

The civilians are still suffering here. No coal, butter at about $5 a pound, coffee terrible, milk and eggs just for children, scarcity of meat, etc. That's the reason for the huge black market.

Love,

Don

Feb. 2, 1945

Dear Mom, Dad & Ethel,

Talk about lucky breaks. Well, here's one:

Yesterday a meeting was arranged by Joe and me, and we spent the day together. Yeah, I'm not kidding. It was a stroke of good fortune, plus the help and cooperation of several people. A meeting of brothers is so rare and unusual that when the opportunity presents itself, a lot of people are willing to go out of their way to help. I owe a lot of thanks to the adjutant of my outfit, who went to great pains to help me.

Well, Joe looks pretty good. He seems to have gotten taller and a little slimmer. He looks much better than I thought he would. In fact, he is in the best of health. You probably won't receive word from him for a little while, but don't worry. He's fine.

We went scouting around for a photographer to get some pictures taken. Unfortunately, we couldn't find one. The Red Cross couldn't help us either. But one of Joe's buddies had a camera and took a couple of pictures.

We saw a movie while we were in town and also had a few sandwiches and beer. At the Red Cross, we had doughnuts and coffee. All in all, we had a nice time, although the town didn't have much to offer.

Most of the fellows in Joe's outfit that I saw and spoke to were friendly guys. The warrant officer in charge of Joe's group appeared to be a nice fellow and gave Joe the day off. I arrived at Joe's place at noon yesterday and stayed over until the morning.

Joe's job is with signal supply equipment, which is better than I thought. He has some repair work to do but deals mostly with signal company depots.

I doubt if I'll get the opportunity to see him again until the war is over and we're back in New York. Perhaps that won't be too far away.

Love,

Don

Nearly eight months after I started searching for him, I finally got to see Joe. The length of time that had passed made it all the more shocking to receive a call one morning from the chaplain telling me Joe was in my area. Elated, I hitched a ride to his base at the appointed time.

Joe was never much of a talker, but his presence was enough. I saw that he was well, and that's all that mattered. He had said so in his letters, but writing can't substitute for personal contact, especially with a brother who was my only immediate link to pre-war life. Our meeting was timely, because the European campaign was drawing to a close, and the Army was trying to ease us back into civilian life.

Feb. 10, 1945

Dear Mom, Dad & Ethel,

Yesterday I attended one of those army educational talks. The subject was "Propaganda," and the lecturer was a soldier who formerly was an attorney and radio commentator. Lectures will be given regularly now on a variety of subjects connected with the war and problems we will encounter upon turning in those famous and extremely popular articles of clothing.

The first talk wasn't bad at all for the simple reason that it lasted only 3/4 of an hour. If they keep these lectures short and to the point, objections will be slight.

Have had a few days of nice weather this week, and there is that touch of spring. The Russian offensive, plus the attack on Germany's western front, which has just gotten underway, has everybody feeling good.

Love To All,

Don

Feb. 18, 1945

Dear Mom, Dad & Ethel,

To give you an idea of how the food problem is in these liberated countries, I just heard that in Paris, they have already consumed 30,000 cats. They sell for about $5.00 apiece: $2.50 for the skin and $2.50 for the stew. Horse meat is old stuff in this country. They have been eating it for years and love it. However, they can't get horse meat often now due to a shortage.

I've seen an authentic civilian ration list, and I'll give you some of the figures for one month starting Feb. 15:

1.   No butter. Margarine—150 grams

2.   Chicory (for coffee)—250 grams

3.   Sugar—2 pounds

4.   Green Coffee—150 grams

5.   Fresh meat or canned meat—750 grams

6.   Potatoes—2 pounds

There are 500 grams to a pound.

They are still trying to collect rations for January and February on many items which still haven't come in. Because of these shortages, a huge black market flourishes.

Haven't heard from Jerry in quite some time and hope he's okay. I imagine that first flight of his will be the big hurdle.

Had another one of those educational talks this week on "Postwar Germany." Every week we'll have a different subject.

Thank Ethel for the Valentine card. By the way, Valentine's Day is not celebrated by Belgians.

Love,

Don

Feb. 27, 1945

Dear Mom, Dad & Ethel,

You will probably receive this letter about the time Dad is celebrating his birthday. Many happy returns, Dad, and I feel quite certain, on the next one, Joe and I will be back to help you cut the cake.

I've got one pair of brand-new shoes, and I've got my second pair in for repair. I expect a new type raincoat soon, as this old style leaks terribly and is practically useless.

We held our dance Saturday night, and it turned out to be highly successful. The crowd was large enough to be boisterous, yet not rowdy. Sandwiches were served. Coffee and cake was in one room, and, in the large hall, we had dancing to a 10-piece army band.

I was with my girlfriend, who wore a blue satin dress with a yellow lapel. This is a dress she made herself before the war. She enjoyed the dance tremendously.

Chow continues to be very good, and if there is no change along this line, complaints will be nil.

The weather is still good, although we occasionally get some rain.

My girl cooked something for me this week. It was a simple concoction but quite tasty. She took an apple and cut it up in round, thin slices, fried it, and added some sugar. It was a delicious dish.

The new American offensive has the populace abounding in joy once again. It's wonderful that everybody is getting more optimistic.

Regards and Love To All,

Don

Mar. 3, 1945

Dear Mom, Dad & Ethel,

Received a letter from Normie yesterday in which he writes that he and his girl expect to get married in April. That is good news. I am glad to see that rather than shelving the matter, they are making definite plans.

Food continues to be good, and everybody is happy about it. Yesterday they introduced a new item into our weekly rations: Coca-Cola. We got two bottles each. Boy, it certainly is a welcome addition. We must be very careful with these bottles and handle them with care, for if they break, no more Cokes.

We had a basketball practice session today for an upcoming Sunday night game. This is a tournament game, and if we win a series of games here, we will be invited to play in Paris.

However, I personally doubt our chances. A lieutenant is coaching our team, and he has some good ideas. It is quite a problem, though, when you try to whip a team into shape in a few days.

According to the papers and radio, the new offensive is going great guns, and everybody is excited about it. When they start getting across the Rhine River, then I'll start being happy.

Lots of Love,

Don

Mar. 10, 1945

Dear Mom, Dad & Ethel,

We had a squadron dance planned for this past Wednesday night, but for some reason it was postponed until tonight. A good Belgian band entertained us this past week. One girl singer sang English songs and drew tremendous applause from an audience of combat soldiers.

They asked for a volunteer jitterbug dancer to dance with this girl, who was very attractive. It is usually difficult to get volunteers to go up on the stage in this café. In this case, however, you might have thought a riot had broken out because about a dozen guys raced to get up there. The fellows almost killed themselves in the mad dash. They took turns dancing with the girl, and the audience was howling.

The First Army's crossing the Rhine sure was a surprise. Everybody who talked about it heretofore envisioned a tremendous battle. As great as the news is, it has looked swell many times before. And still the fighting goes on day after day.

Lots of Love,

Don

Mar. 12, 1945

Dear Mom, Dad & Ethel,

Yesterday, once again, we were fortunate. Joe had a little time in passing by and dropped in to see me for about an hour. We went into a shop and had an ice cream cone. With the job he has, we might be able to see each other again.

Chow continues to be good. The day Joe was here, we had chicken. This morning we had French toast.

I'm going out to the rifle range today, so we'll have quite a full day.

Love,

Don

Mar. 15, 1945

Dear Mom, Dad & Ethel,

Received a two-page letter from Jerry this week. They have received no further news concerning his brother Murray. You probably know his brother has been missing in action since November 1944.[397]

Jerry writes that he has started going on missions, and that after he finishes his daily run, he has no ambition to go to town. He's just plain tired after the day's work.

We've had some beautiful weather these past few days, and that is exactly what we want to shorten this war.

Today I brought my second pair of shoes into the store to have attachments put on. This does away with the necessity and bother of putting on leggings every day.

The mess section is better than ever. We're getting good chow, and the mess hall is spotless.

Love,

Don

Murray was a bombardier. During a mission, his B-24 was hit. The pilot, fearing the plane would crash, ordered everyone to bail out.

While descending, the navigator and one of the gunners saw Murray's parachute open, but Murray was never found. Remarkably, the pilot, struggling at the helm of a burning aircraft with a mangled wing, still managed to safely land.

Murray's mother wasn't only heartbroken, she was furious. When the pilot visited her to offer his explanation and condolences, she threw him out of her house. For the rest of her life, she blamed him for the death of her son.

I won't second-guess the pilot's decision. I have insufficient facts upon which to base a judgment, and even if I had complete information, my lack of expertise would prevent me from commenting. However, it is interesting to note that while Murray's mother condemned the plane's captain, Jerry, who was regularly exposed to the same dangers his brother faced, did not.

A superbly conditioned airman, Murray had been a physical education teacher in civilian life. A soft-spoken, amiable twenty-five-year-old, he left behind a wife and child.

*   *   *   *

I was curled up on the sofa with Denise, sipping *café au lait* and listening to a BBC broadcast, when I sprang to my feet. With a loud click of the dial, I abruptly silenced the radio.

"What did you do that for? It's early yet."

"*Chérie*, we've gotta talk."

"What's wrong?"

"I'm leaving for Germany."

Denise stared sadly at the floor. "I suppose I should consider myself lucky to have had you this long. There's been talk for quite some time now about soldiers moving out. We both knew this couldn't last forever." She inhaled heavily through her nostrils and looked up. "When are you leaving?"

"In a few days."

"So this is it?"

"It doesn't have to be, *chérie*."

"Do not patronize me, Sergeant Don. Soon the war will be over. You will go back to your Bronx, find a nice, American girlfriend, and forget all about me."

"I can never forget you."

I could feel her slipping away. Denise was standing now, her face contorted with pain and indignation.

"*Chérie*, please don't—"

"No." I grabbed her shoulders, but she pulled loose and turned her back on me, walking a few steps closer to the fireplace. Then, hands on hips, she spun around and asked, "Do you love me, Don?"

"Are the words really that important?"

"*Mon Dieu*, yes!"

"My family and me, we're kinda low-key people. We don't go in much for hugging and kissing. To tell you the truth, I can't remember the last time any of us said, 'I love you.' I guess that's kinda sad, but don't think we don't love each other, because we do. We just express it differently. When my mom or my sis smile at me, I know they love me. I don't have to ask them. The same thing goes for my dad. My brother's a really low-key guy, and he doesn't smile much at all, but sometimes I see a little gleam in his eye, or he gives me a pat on the shoulder, and I get the same feeling. I know it's different with us, *chérie*, but maybe not as much as you think. We finish each other's sentences, do things for each other without having to be told. Denise, before I met you, I didn't know what love was. I went with a few girls back home, but they meant nothing to me. After I joined the Army, I slept with a whole bunch of women I didn't give a damn about. And then I met you. Hell, yes, I love you! You know I've done all kinds of crazy things to be with you, and now I'm gonna do one more."

I got down on one knee. "Denise, will you marry me?"

Her eyes welled up with tears. "I can't."

"Why the hell not? Don't you love me?"

"Of course I love you," she replied through sniffles.

"Then what's the problem? We can get hitched tomorrow. I'll get the day off. After I'm discharged, I'll come back for you. We can probably get an army flight to New York for nothing. Or board an American ship from Antwerp. Everything you've heard about America is true—and more. You have no idea how many opportunities there are."

"Don—"

"Let's face it, no matter how good my French gets, I'd still be a klutz here. But you'll have no problem. Jeez, you already know more about America than I'll ever know about Belgium. In New York, you can get a top-notch university education for free. Maybe you wanna study acting. Or be a teacher. Or a scientist. We've even got a few women who play professional baseball. No kidding. You can do, or be, anything you want. The sky's the limit. Please say yes."

"I'd marry you in a second, but it's impossible."

"Why?"

"I wasn't going to tell you this until tomorrow because I didn't want to spoil our time together."

"Tell me what?"

"That Étienne is alive." Tears began streaming down Denise's cheeks. Gathering herself, she pulled out a handkerchief and wiped her face. "Everyone thought he was dead, but somehow he survived, and he's coming home." Another pause. "I didn't expect you to say you loved me."

"You don't really mean that."

"No, but I was hoping you wouldn't. It would have been much easier. Instead you proposed. Now I have to choose between the two of you."

Emotionally spent, I rose to my feet. An awkward silence lasted several seconds.

"I'm not good at this," I began.

"Nobody is."

More silence.

"When is Étienne due back?"

"A few days. Maybe sooner. It all depends on how fast the authorities can process him."

"You love him?"

"I don't know. It's been so long."

"Then leave him. He'll be all right. He's got this house, and he'll get his job back."

"I would never do that to Étienne. He's my husband. I don't know what people do in your country, but here we take marriage very seriously. We don't just abandon people, especially after what he's gone through."

"What about us? What about me? I've been with you as long as you were with him."

"That is a big problem."

"Look, you don't have to make any decisions right now. We've still got a few days. At least think it over. I know what I said sounds cruel, but when it comes to you, I'm a selfish bastard. I want you all to myself."

Denise sidled up to me and hesitated. It was obvious she wanted to kiss me on the lips, but instead she rose to her tippy toes and gave me a peck on the forehead. "You're a good man, Sergeant Don."

"And you're better than gold, *chérie*. Listen, I think I'll go back to base tonight. You've got a lot on your mind, and I'd only be in the way."

"I don't feel like thinking tonight. I just want to be with you."

"I can't, *chérie*. A little while ago, you were a wartime widow. Now you're a married woman. I can't sleep with a man's wife under his own roof, especially when he's coming home in a few days. It's not right. You yourself just told me you don't want to hurt him."

"He'll know if I leave him, but he won't know if we make love tonight."

"But I'll know. Sleep on it, and you'll thank me in the morning."

"I'll curse you in the morning."

"No you won't. You love me too much."

Denise's expression softened. "You have gotten wiser these past few months, Sergeant Don."

"I had a good teacher."

"Don?"

"Yeah?"

"Perhaps we can meet somewhere else, in a place that's, how do you say, more neutral. Josephine is having a little get-together at her house the day after tomorrow. Can you make it?"

"Just fill me in, and I'll be there. I'll pull a triple shift if I have to."

Denise took out a piece of paper from her purse and wrote down the particulars. "Here."

"*Merci, mademoiselle.* See you in two days."

"*Ça va.*"

"And keep working on those contractions!"

"Yeah."

Things were bad enough for poor Denise, but what made her dilemma even more vexing was the fact that, for the past several months, her mother-in-law had a bird's-eye view of my comings and goings. At this point, it is interesting to note that the literal translation of the French term for mother-in-law, *"belle-mère,"* is "beautiful mother." Ancient French linguists must have had a wicked sense of humor. Given half a chance, Denise's *"belle-mère"* would not have hesitated to tell her son a sordid tale of his wife's infidelity, forever branding her with the proverbial scarlet "A."

During our rendez-vous at Josephine's house, Denise told me about her solution to this difficult problem. She wanted to snag her husband first and explain conditions from the viewpoint of a wife who had been informed by a friend that he was dead. She would tell him that she hadn't heard from him in over four years, and, therefore, assumed that the information was correct. Such an explanation would put an entirely different spin on things.

Denise was betting that her pen was sharper than her *belle-mère's* tongue. Although she hadn't expected him for several days, Étienne could have arrived home at any time. Not leaving anything to chance, she got up early the morning after receiving the news about him, and, before heading off to work, wrote a note to Étienne explaining all. She attached it to the front door, where he was sure to see it if he arrived home before her.

Denise was haunted by many disturbing questions. Did she still love her husband? Did she miss him? How much had they changed over all these years? Could they ever trust one another again?

And what about me? We had lived a happy life together these past few months, and now I was leaving for Germany. Denise was very angry with me, and very worried about my safety.

I knew what she was thinking because, when it came to communicating with each other, we were practically telepaths. Still, it would be a long time before I had the answers to these questions because Denise did not have them herself.

CHAPTER 16

▼

GERMANY

Things would never be the same again.

In Britain, France, and Belgium, we had enjoyed mingling with civilians, but once the squadron crossed into Deutschland, fraternization was strictly prohibited. Violators were severely punished. The war was still on, and this was Hitler's backyard. As far as Uncle Sam was concerned, all Germans were considered potential enemies.

Previously touted as liberators by the French and Belgians, we were now unwelcome conquerors. There were no cheering crowds lining the streets, no happy children bearing gifts, and no home-cooked meals.

The war in Europe was rapidly drawing to a close, but we were still working our daily shifts. For recreation, there were plenty of ball games, movies, and dances on base. While pleasant, these activities were less enjoyable than they had been elsewhere. The dances were a bit dull, partly because the supply of females was limited to American WAAF's and WAVE's. In the other countries, local girls had added more spice and variety to these events.

Even after the anti-fraternization rules were relaxed, we generally kept our distance from German civilians. I preferred the solitude of the woods and only occasionally ventured into nearby towns.

When I did, I was disappointed. In Belgium, I had enjoyed watching the slow, relaxed strides of people going about their business. I even found the French walk reasonably pleasant, but on the streets of Brühl, an industrial city seven miles south of Cologne,[398] my spirits were dampened by the rapid gait of Germans pounding the pavement. It reminded me of those goose-stepping POW's in Versailles: so rigid, impersonal, and mechanical.

That's another reason for me not to like them.

My antipathy was returned in Marburg, a university town sixty miles north of Frankfurt.[399] I was playing tennis one afternoon with some friends in the municipal stadium. Untouched by Allied bombing, the courts were excellent by standards of the day, and we were working up quite a sweat. The warm weather had enticed many people outdoors, and dozens of informal matches were being played. About a hundred German civilians looked on from the stands. Everyone was reveling in the early spring. Well, almost everyone.

Before beginning play, I had placed my gym bag in a holding area near the courts. Inside the satchel was a U.S.-Army-issued German vocabulary booklet from which I studied. When I returned to pick it up, I found the text ripped to shreds. The locals had made their point.

*   *   *   *

Shortly after the Japanese attack on Pearl Harbor, the United States Army produced a short film entitled "Kill or Be Killed." It was required viewing for every American soldier. In a major scene, a supposedly wounded German is lying on the ground, gasping for air and motioning to his mouth for water. Taking pity on the man, a compassionate GI reaches for his canteen. Then the German pulls out a pistol and shoots the American dead.

The moral was clear: don't feel sorry for your enemy. It may cost you your life.

I remembered the film well but failed to heed its warning. Instead, I chose to give new meaning to the expression "screwing the enemy."

Now don't think I had forgotten about Denise. She still hadn't decided about Étienne before I left Stembert, and thoughts of her were constantly with me. She was the first subject that popped into my head when I got up in the morning, and the last I remembered before bedding down at night.

When we first crossed the Rhine, most of us were living in field tents. We were placed in ten rows, twenty tents to a row. I was paired with Lance Pierce.

Early one morning, the officers decided to conduct one of their surprise inspections. I hated inspections. To me, they were just an excuse for superiors to throw their weight around.

The previous evening, Lance and I had gotten friendly with two eighteen-year-old fraüleins. When the hour grew late, the girls decided to spend the night with us. Lance latched on to the looker. I wound up with the plain one, and my misfortune was compounded by the fact that my partner was a lousy lovemaker.

"Psst! Lance."

"Yeah?"

"Wanna switch?"

"Not on your life, Donnybrook."

"Oh Jeez."

By sunrise, I was anxious to evict my unsatisfying female companion. I knew that I'd be a strong candidate for prison or worse if an officer found this young woman sleeping with me. I threw on my olive drabs and woke her up. Using my spotty German, I told her to get dressed and leave. Then I took a short walk. When I returned, I found her snoring.

"*Schnell, schnell!*" I commanded. "No more *schlafen*. Get the hell up!"

The girl murmured something inaudible and turned onto her side. Infuriated, I wanted to throw her out, but that would have caused too much disturbance.

The lieutenant was already walking down my row, peering into each tent. My luck was wearing thin.

Fuck this!

I bolted from the canvas and trotted away but stopped at the end of the row. From this vantage point, I spied the lieutenant examining the tent directly opposite mine.

I'm dead meat.

For the umpteenth time, I was taking a huge gamble. And for what? A good time? I hadn't even enjoyed this girl. Even before the incident in Marburg, I knew that plenty of German civilians hated Americans. Maybe if this one had been in a bad mood, she would have killed me in my sleep.

The lieutenant was now in front of my tent. The officer hesitated. Then, with a sudden impatience, he bypassed the bivouac and began spot-checking every second one.

My mouth dropped open in astonishment. The angels were still out there, turning the odds in my favor.

I knew that the danger I had put myself in was of my own making. Sex, when you could get it, substituted for night life, which was meager in Germany. It was a risky form of entertainment and a way to avoid thinking about Denise. She had provided me with a well-balanced diet of emotional and sexual sustenance. Other girls were peanuts by comparison, but peanuts can be very tasty, and hard to resist.

Additionally, they were a good diversion from the usual tensions of being in a war zone. By this time, I had seen enough suffering to put small problems in perspective, and I had very little toleration for people complaining about trifles, even when it was my sister.

Germany
March 29, 1945

Dear Ethel,

I am really surprised at what you wrote in your last letter dated March 13. You state that you are angry with me for not answering your mail but have calmed down. In the first place, I figured you had better sense than to think the two of us are in the same category when I'm still wearing khaki. I do hope you have shown more consideration to Joe because, as you know, he works much harder than myself. Occasionally, his outgoing mail may stop for short or long periods, but that is no reason for you to stop writing. However, I am not entirely innocent here, and I shall make an effort to do better in the future.

I thought you could stop and do a little more thinking before you let hurt emotions run away with you. Besides, you get a record of my doings in my regular correspondence with Mom and Dad.

Stay well.

Love,

Don

Mar. 30, 1945

Dear Mom, Dad & Ethel,

Am still stiff in the legs from two days ago, when we played softball. It is not only me, however, but everybody else who played that day.

The war news is exceptionally good. There are breakthroughs on practically all western fronts. Read about the peace rumor in the States, and it is a lesson to you folks not to believe things too quickly.

Normie wrote me a letter announcing his coming marriage. Lots of luck to the two of them.

Love,

Don

Apr. 13, 1945

Dear Mom, Dad & Ethel,

Received a letter from Joe dated March 21. This gives you an idea of how erratic the mail system can be. Joe mentions that he has tried to get in touch with me several times, but, unfortunately, without success. Movements are so frequent now, that another meeting seems unlikely.

The food lately is not that great. We are getting lots of "C" rations. Although the English and Europeans go wild over them, we G.I.'s don't like them. We are getting enough to eat, but meat is generally in that hashed form.

Not all the meals are bad, though. Today they surprised us at breakfast. We had fresh eggs, cereal, and coffee. Yesterday at noon we had good roast beef, but decent meals are rare.

I am in good condition and hope everybody at home is able to report the same.

Love,

Don

Germany
Apr. 25, 1945

Dear Mom, Dad & Ethel,

Two nights ago I saw a celebrity. Mickey Rooney stayed at the building adjacent to ours. He was there for several days, and we got wind of it before he left.

He didn't put on any show for us. Four of us went up to see him, though. He was there with several musicians.

He looks exactly the same as he appears on the screen, except perhaps a bit smaller. He looks like a 15- or 16-year-old kid. He wore a Special Services uniform. If you didn't know anybody in the room, and you were looking for a fellow who had a few million dollars, he would be the last person you'd choose. He appears no different than the ordinary person.

There was no fuss made over him. In fact, he was here for several days, and some fellows who slept across the hall from him didn't even bother to go in to see him.

Love,

Don

During this period, we were living in a university dormitory, a palatial facility by army standards. There were latrines and running water. I could actually wash my face and hands before eating. Occasionally, stars entertaining troops in the area would bed down with us.

When Jack, Bobby, Angelo, and I entered Mickey Rooney's room, we found the diminutive actor clutching an open book of Shakespeare. Mickey was busily pacing up and down, softly reading aloud to himself. Interrupting his soliloquy, he excitedly exclaimed, "This is a masterpiece!"

Absorbed in the bard's sonnets, Mickey ignored us. He resumed his murmuring. We felt a bit slighted and quietly left without exchanging a word with him.

Our thoughts of Mickey vanished when the entire outfit fell silent, as did millions of soldiers and civilians throughout the world. America had lost its greatest leader.

May 1, 1945

Dear Mom, Dad & Ethel,

The death of the President was a terrible shock to us. I understand all liberated countries displayed symbolisms to mourn his passing. All flags are at half-mast.

If you walk down a street in town, you see just about every nationality in the world. You'll see Belgians, French, Russians, Poles, Mongolians, Germans, Czechs, English, and others I'm not familiar with.

I've seen a concentration camp with many of its horrors. But the place is cleaned up now, and I didn't get a true picture. I hope everybody at the San Francisco Conference sees the photographs that were taken at this notorious place.

Love,

Don

Buchenwald. Even today, mere mention of the name evokes images of smoke-belching crematories, trucks overflowing with corpses, and barbed-wire fences.[400] Over fifty thousand people were exterminated there between 1937 and 1945 (1).

A few miles away and a world apart is Weimar, the cradle of German intellectualism. It was here in the late eighteenth and early nineteenth centuries that Goethe and Schiller began Germany's "Golden Age" of literature (6).

In 1942, Weimar mayor Otto Koch began blurring the lines between these forces of darkness and light.[401] He ordered Buchenwald inmates to build reproductions of the furniture in Schiller's house (6). At the same time, he had the prisoners construct protective boxes for the author's works (6).

By the time I visited the camp, the bunkhouses had been sanitized, the ovens cleaned, and the bodies buried. I did, however, get to meet a few of the former inmates occupying a very large American Red Cross tent. Although they had been receiving food and medical treatment for several weeks, the skeletal survivors still had sunken faces and shattered bodies. Many of the beds were empty: some of the ex-prisoners had died, others had been discharged. A relief worker in khaki dispensed a meager meal of bread and thin soup. An attractive army nurse took vital signs.

"That's all you're giving them to eat?" I incredulously asked.

"We have to start them off very slowly," the nurse explained. "They've been starved for a very long time. If we give them too much too soon, they can die."

I pulled up a chair alongside the bed of a very thin, pale man. His hair was snow-white. Years of torture had etched lines deeply into his forehead. Discounting the emaciation, one side of his face appeared quite normal. The other was hideously mangled: purple eyelid swollen shut; puffy lip curled upward in a snarl; missing teeth; deep scars. His left arm was attached to an I.V.

"How ya doin'?"

"As well as can be expected, Sergeant," replied the man in a soft, erudite baritone. "Once upon a time, I was a very good fencer. Now I can't even stand."

I grinned at the nurse. "Well, you're in good hands," I cheerily intoned. "I'm sure you'll be up and about in no time."

The nurse shook her head and scowled at me. Realizing the seriousness of the man's condition, I pursed my lips in a mixture of chagrin and sadness.

"You speak very good English, old timer. Where'd you learn?"

"Oh, many places, Sergeant," he replied between dry coughs. "Before the war, I was a professor of languages at the University of Heidelberg."

I tried to smile, but the best I could manage was a half-wince. I patted the man's hand.

"Take care of yourself, sir."

"Goodbye, Sergeant."

My brief brush with the Holocaust kindled within me an outrage and sorrow of which I had not thought myself capable. Although the news of Stan and Ken's deaths had been very painful for me, I took comfort in the fact that they did not suffer. But now I had just met a dying man, one of millions who had experienced unimaginable torment for years.

I was very quiet for several days. Then came the best possible news.

Germany
May 7, 1945

Dear Mom, Dad & Ethel,

Today German Radio announced that the war is over and that the Germans have unconditionally surrendered. At this writing, the word hasn't been verified from S.H.A.E.F. (Supreme Headquarters, Allied Expeditionary Force) yet, but we all know it to be true. So far, there haven't been any terrific celebrations here, but tonight at the club there'll be lots of drinking on the house.

It's hard to believe the war is over, and when all the shouting dies down, and it's quiet, and you're alone, it'll be a time for reflection. Then you can try and figure out what it was all about. One can imagine how the boys up front feel. Of course they're jubilant, and, at the same time, they must be crying their eyes out. It sure is quite a happy occasion. Two of the boys just came in the room, and they are pretty well tanked up. Merrymaking will really be underway in a short time, and I don't want to miss it.

Love,

Don

On May 5, 1945, Germany's Army Group G, the remnants of Hitler's forces in Austria, yielded to the Allied Sixth Army Group.[402] The formal surrender didn't come until 2:41 a.m. on May 7 in a schoolhouse in Rheims (557). General Eisenhower refused to attend (557). Instead, he sent emissaries (557). To symbolize unity among the victors, the Allies repeated the ceremony the following day in Berlin, where Marshal George Zhukov signed for the Soviet Union (557). Thus, May 8, 1945 was enshrined as V-E Day (557).

Now that the European war was over, we were mainly concerned about what the Army was going to do with us.

Germany
May 8, 1945

Dear Mom, Dad & Ethel,

Today I was interviewed along with the rest of the fellows. We were asked how much schooling we have had, what our pre-army jobs were (salary, etc.), and what we expect to do after the war. Most of us are in doubt as to what we'll do because nobody knows yet just what will happen to us. There are rumors that air force personnel will go to the Pacific, so don't be shocked if it happens. If we're lucky, we'll stay in Germany a while.

Today a Red Cross truck came and served doughnuts and coffee. It was pretty nice.

Love,

Don

May 10, 1945

Dear Mom, Dad & Ethel,

Tomorrow we are supposed to see "Movie of The Year." The film may give us some information on what happens to us now. So perhaps in my next letter, I will have a little more definite news for you. We've already had another lecture on "Postwar Plans."

Love,

Don

May 13, 1945

Dear Mom, Dad & Ethel,

You, no doubt, are reading lots of stories about furloughs and discharges. Rather than have you build up false hopes, I'll explain what I know about these regulations. The Army specifies that 85 points makes a soldier eligible for discharge. From my own tabulations, I find myself with a mere 66 points thus far.

Each branch of service will have its own quota and act accordingly. Here's what can happen to me:

My points are too low for discharge. Therefore, I can either remain here with the Army of Occupation (probably the best deal) or go to the Pacific by way of the United States.

The fact that a lot of fellows have over 85 points does not guarantee them discharges because if the Army deems them essential, they may wind up little better than the fellows with less than 85 points. They may even share foxholes alongside one another on some island in the Pacific.

Air Corps personnel will be in great demand in the Pacific in order to begin large scale bombing there. Very few will be released from duty for some time to come.

Exactly what is going to happen to us, we don't know. As soon as I have that information, I'll pass it on to you.

Something happened to the water supply in the buildings around here, and it has been difficult to obtain water for the past two days. That makes it somewhat uncomfortable in this extreme weather, but the C.O. claims that everything will be running again today.

Today we had some fried chicken for lunch, and they fixed it up swell this time. I just about ate it, bones and all, it was so delicious.

In playing ball for the past few weeks, I've brought myself around to good physical condition, whereas before, I tended to feel a little sluggish. I feel in real good trim now, but I feel sorry for those fellows here who don't take an interest in sports and just mull around from day to day.

Love,

Don

The point score for discharge consisted of many factors, including length of service, time overseas, and participation in a significant battle zone. Naturally, it was of great interest to us and our families.

May 24, 1945

Dear Mom, Dad & Ethel,

Received a letter from Joe this week, and he writes that he is fine. Also received a letter from Jerry. All three of us have no definite information on our future status. Something is bound to be stated soon. I'll relay whatever it is, pronto.

The point system was slightly altered recently. They split the German Campaign into three sections. As a result, my count will either remain the same or increase by five or ten points. It will take time before scores are recalculated for each unit.

Three men who were over 42 years of age left the unit for the States yesterday. I guess they weren't happy. Yeah, we tried to sneak a ride on that vehicle, but, alas, it was in vain.

Well, this war is over, and here we sit and wait for some of the top brass to decide what they are going to do with us. Meantime, our operation continues, but instead of the real thing, as before, everything is on a practice basis.

They are scheduled to start different educational courses in a short while, but nothing has actually gotten underway yet. Things will be popping in several weeks, and when they start, it won't resemble a firecracker. It'll probably be more like a gigantic explosion.

Ethel, if you don't appreciate what you have in the United States, take a trip abroad.

Love,

Don

CHAPTER 17

▼

ALICE IN WUNDERLAND

Oh, the things you see in a forest.

When I took solitary walks exploring the German hinterland, I was rarely alone. Even when I didn't bring my buddies, I usually met other GI's on the trail. The war in Europe was over, and on the outskirts of Weimar, everyone was coming down with a bad case of wanderlust.

It was a heavily wooded area, studded with mighty oaks and pines. The ample foliage provided plenty of cover from the elements. When the June sun toasted the town, the forest remained comfortably cool. It was on such a day that I decided to commune with nature.

The non-fraternization rules were still in effect, but twenty minutes into my walk, I saw a line of several dozen GI's patiently waiting to break them. They were taking turns with a couple of German prostitutes. Their fee: a chocolate bar.

Oh Jeez, that stuff's too rich for me. Never went with a hooker before, and I'll be damned if I'm gonna start now. Who knows what those girls have? But I sure understand the urge. God, I wish Denise was here.

A mile down the path, I spotted a small female figure in the distance. She was wearing nothing but a bra and panties. At first, I thought she was in her early teens. She had very short black hair and was less than five feet tall. But when I got closer, I could see that this was no child. She had a well-developed body and the face of a thirty-five-year-old woman. I put my hand over my eyes and turned away.

"Oh, don't bother," she said in perfect English.

"You startled me a little," I uncomfortably replied. "It's not every day that a guy finds a girl modeling lingerie in the woods."

She threw on an olive-colored, form-fitting tee shirt. "How's this?" she asked.

"Fine," I answered, stealing an admiring glance. "What are you doing out here?

The woman calmly lit a cigarette, took a puff, and exhaled. "Oh, just fucking around."

I noticed a ladder propped against the side of a tree directly behind her. It led to a well-constructed shelter.

"Nice house," I remarked.

"Thanks."

"I'm Don. What's your name?"

"You wouldn't be able to pronounce it. Just call me Alice."

"Where are you from, Alice?"

"Estonia."

Our conversation was interrupted by heavy footsteps above us. A very large male figure dressed in full military uniform emerged from the tree house. He carefully descended the ladder, his boots scraping loudly against each rung. I stared at him in disbelief.

Alice's companion was an American brigadier general. He was seven feet tall, and, with his white hair and wizened face, looked at least seventy years old. Eyeing me suspiciously, he sidled up to the Estonian woman, stooping over her. She whispered something in his ear. The general straightened himself to his full height and gave me a civil nod. I responded with an awkward salute.

"Smoke?"

"No thank you, sir."

"Enjoy your hike, Sergeant."

"Yes, sir."

The general lit a cigarette and vanished into the greenery.

"The old man's pretty fast, isn't he?"

"He can move when he wants to."

"Why are you here?"

"I was in a Soviet refugee camp with a bunch of other girls. We ran from the Russians to the Nazis."

"Why?"

"Because it was so horrible. The Soviets treated us like pigs. We couldn't even wear makeup or lipstick. At least the Germans let us be women."

"Jeez. And I thought the Russians were good guys."

"You'll see. Soon Stalin will take over half of Europe, and America will have to fight him."

"Listen, my base isn't far from the trailhead. Why don't you stop by some time?"

"I don't give lessons, honey."

"I'm not asking for any. I've been around."

"I'll bet you have," replied Alice, looking me over with a prurient glance. "Happy hunting, Sergeant."

"Yes, ma'am."

A few miles later, I spotted three soldiers from my outfit engaged in a conversation with a comely, well-endowed fraülein who looked about nineteen years old. She had picked up a little English and was asking for Richard, a private attached to the 888th Fighter Control Squadron.

I positioned myself behind a broad bough, obscuring my body while keeping my eyes fixed on the unfolding spectacle. From the young lady's embarrassed demeanor, and the colorful translations of the male trio, it was obvious that Richard had been having intimate relations with her.

The three radio men began crowding the girl. Giggling nervously, she disappeared into the greenery. Actually, she hadn't gone very far, but the trees concealed her well. After several minutes of fruitless searching, the GI's gave up.

Soon the fraülein reappeared. She aimlessly walked about for a moment before sitting down on a crude bench which had been hewn from a large log. The others were gone; now it was my turn.

I knew that almost any female would seem attractive to sex-starved soldiers who'd been overseas for a year and a half, but this lovely young woman was extraordinary. In an age long before implants, she had perfectly shaped breasts that stuck out nearly six inches from the sides of her chest, straining her form-fitting white blouse to the bursting point.

I sat down and scooted to the opposite side of the seat, about five feet away from her. Then I recalled an acting class in high school where the teacher made everyone communicate by pantomime. Holding my hands up, I motioned for her to sit as far away from me as possible. The fraülein gave me a puzzled look. Three guys had just tried to box her into a corner, and now I was trying to push her away.

It was a masterful performance. The more I backed away, the closer she came. I made sure that my retreats were much shorter than her advances. Soon she was smack against me, clutching my fingers. I wondered what Mickey Rooney would have thought.

She stood up and led me by the hand to a quiet spot away from the path. Then she motioned for me to lie down. With a mischievous smile, she slowly undid the buttons of her blouse and tossed the garment to the ground.

She was a tall, big-boned girl, and her gargantuan bosoms shook violently as she unclasped her bra. They were amazingly firm. Her areolae were nearly the size of my fists.

The fraülein charmingly shimmied out of her tight skirt, revealing a curvaceous tummy, shapely hips, and dancer's legs. I always thought German women were very prudish, but this girl wore no panties.

At last, she was beside me. With the enthusiasm of a child in a chocolate factory, I gleefully reached for her. She couldn't wait to have intercourse on a bed of leaves and sand.

My libido spent, I brushed myself off and headed back to base. I'd had enough exercise for one day.

CHAPTER 18

▼

THE HOME STRETCH

Once the war in Europe ended, the Army eased its censorship restrictions. When writing home, I could now reveal my exact location and more details about my situation. While I had no bombshells to publish, I welcomed the ability to speak more candidly when putting pen to paper. That was a freedom I would never again take for granted.

Weimar, Germany
June 1, 1945

Dear Mom, Dad & Ethel,

Received a score of packages from you this week. Thanks a lot. I'm well-stocked in every imaginable item, so hold off on any future shipments.

Joe writes that he's swamped with packages also. While he appreciates their thoughtfulness, he hopes people will stop sending him things. I guess we sing a different tune every six months.

All through the European Campaign, we were in the First Army Sector, giving support. When Joe read that the First Army was home on furlough, he naturally thought we would be following them. However, the fact that we gave support to First Army troops during these campaigns doesn't mean that we cannot be transferred to another army.

I don't know if I mentioned this to you before. On this point system, the Air Corps critical scores will probably be much higher than the 85 points needed by other forces for discharge eligibility. This is due to flying personnel who receive lavish decorations—which they deserve—but which will necessitate a higher score for the rest of us, since each decoration they've earned has a five-point value. Therefore, whatever points I have will be equivalent to about 10 points less in a non-air force unit. I know this is no morale builder, but it is cold fact.

They started giving us drills today. We had marching for an hour. This is the beginning of the program that is in store for us.

Right now we are fairly fancy free and can use our time according to our discretion. This will probably come to an end shortly, and we may get a rehash of our basic training all over again. I hope not, and they have made some promises to try and avoid it, but it is slowly creeping up on us.

Lots of Love,

Don

Weimar, Germany
June 9, 1945

Dear Mom, Dad & Ethel,

Received your letter of May 28th and a letter from Normie in which he apologizes for not being able to visit you because of his father's illness, a new wife, and passes being cut down. He just couldn't spare the time. I told him to make sure he doesn't neglect his wife.

The G.I. schools are supposed to open in a few weeks if nothing intervenes. However, we are expecting to move shortly because this zone will undoubtedly be Russian occupational territory. So we'll have to go westward.

A lot of letters I receive now contain complaints about G.I. food, but ours continues to be okay. Feeling fine.

Love,

Don

Fritzler, Germany
June 24, 1945

Dear Mom, Dad & Ethel,

Well, we finally moved, and for the last two days, we've really been working. Now that we are settled in our new quarters, we can heave a sigh of relief. We are several miles away from Kassel and are on an air base.

Yesterday we had 17 truckloads to take down and store away. We also put up 15 tents for a mess hall and section supply. The outfit has accumulated so much material in the past few months. The whole trouble is that the top brass keep acquiring stuff at every opportunity because "it may come in handy some day." However, they're never around when it comes to loading and unloading the trucks. It really was a workout. We have showers in the new building, though, so when the day's work was done, we felt pretty good.

I came down with the first echelon. Another group is due to come in today, and the remainder of the outfit will arrive in several days. School has been interrupted and is supposed to recommence on July 2nd.

I'm in a nice, small room with one other fellow. We'll probably take in one more entry when the other fellows get down here. We have carpets on the floor, spring beds, and a clothes closet. They hooked up electricity yesterday. We also have a latrine, a washroom, and showers on each floor.

There is a Red Cross Club on the post here, where we can get doughnuts and coffee. Opposite the club is a ballfield with a backstop. In deep field, there are quite a few stones, but with a little work, we can probably make it a first-class facility.

There was another outfit housed in our building, but because we had a higher priority, they were compelled to move out. This has caused hard feelings on their part, and these other fellows who were evicted are still in the vicinity. They hold their dispossess against us, but we've experienced the same treatment on numerous occasions. It's just one of those things that can't be helped. As the French would say, "C'est la guerre."

The place is all cleaned up now, and we had our first good meal just a short while ago. It consisted of roast beef, potatoes, vegetables, peaches, and coffee. There are Italian prisoners who help us in cleaning up our area every day.

There have been articles in "Stars and Stripes" (the army newspaper) about how difficult it is for some discharged soldiers to get civilian clothes.

We have a bingo party scheduled for tonight. We have several hundred dollars in our club fund, and, according to army regulations, we must dispose of it. Through bingo parties, we are managing to get rid of our capital.

This place should prove to be good once the finishing touches are added to it. It just started to pour, and it's just as well because there has been a water shortage due to dry spells.

Love,

Don

Arnheim, Germany
June 27, 1945

Dear Mom, Dad & Ethel,

My outfit is still located in the same place, but four of us, including a cook, moved to this village, which is about 20 miles southwest of Fritzler. It's a snap here. We eat extremely well. We are operating a repeater station, and the only work is to keep a power unit operating 24 hours a day.

We are living in two tents. One is for our food and cooking appliances, and the other is for sleeping. Every few days we drive into Fritzler for rations and anything else we need. There is a roving patrol of G.I.'s around here, and we befriended them on the first day. They drop in every day now and bring us a copy of "Stars and Stripes." They have a theater in their unit and told us to come anytime we desired. We are left alone, and this detached service is a pretty nice deal.

Love,

Don

Actually, it was a great deal. On this extended detached service, I was teamed with Corporal Zeke, PFC Dan Tarwater, and Private Calvin Potts. Each of us had a cot.

Since there were no officers around, we rarely bothered getting out of bed before noon. Potts, a short, portly cook, always made an enormous brunch. The rest of us took turns driving with him to Fritzler each week, where we'd buy enough groceries to feed twenty people.

Improving on this sweet situation with yet another female find, I met a young blonde woman on the road overlooking town. She was nearly six feet tall, slim, and drop dead gorgeous.

"My husband was a German officer killed in the war," she explained in very good English.

"My condolences."

"It was a long time ago, but thank you."

"What's your name?"

"Greta."

"Listen, Greta, I'm running a radio truck with three other soldiers here. Feel free to stop by sometime."

"Where are you?"

"Right over there." I pointed to two bivouacs about a hundred yards from the bottom of the hill.

Oh, I'll never see her again. But at least it was worth a try.

Early the next morning, when everyone was in a deep slumber, I felt something against my cheek. Wearily opening my eyes, I saw Greta bending over me, running her satin hands gently across my face.

No, this can't be real.

I shook my head and blinked. Greta was still there. She smiled invitingly.

"Come on in," I whispered, moving over in my cot to make room for this most welcome visitor.

When the others in the tent awoke, they, too, thought Greta was a mirage. Before them was the newest member of their troupe, a splendid example of feminine pulchritude, curled up with their sergeant.

Greta wasn't just an overnight guest. She stayed for almost two weeks. To avoid having sex in front of an audience, we moved into the food tent.

My bedding consisted of a biscuit mattress designed for only one person, but it had two separate sections. Instead of placing it on the bed lengthwise, I turned it sideways to accommodate my new sleeping partner. We were very comfortable and very happy.

When it came to radio work, we functioned pretty well together, but we were an odd quartet. Zeke and I had similar athletic interests, but we didn't like each other very much. Potts was a pleasant fellow, but no smarter than the three privates captured near Spa. Tarwater, a lanky American Indian of indeterminate age, kept mostly to himself.

But after a time, I grew closer to Tarwater, and often took walks with him into the woods, where he was more talkative. He was always whittling, making small wooden statues of various animals.

"Was making those figures your job back home?"

"No. I've been thinking of setting up a little shop, but right now it's just a hobby."

"You're really good."

"Thanks. Want me to make you one?"

"That'd be swell."

"There is a belief among my people that every human being possesses the spirit of an animal. I want to choose one that's right for you."

"What did you have in mind?"

"An eagle."

"Why?"

"Well, you always wanted to fly."

"You married?"

"Yeah. I've got a wife and two kids."

"Really?"

"Why is that strange?"

"I dunno. You just seem the bachelor type. I bet you've got a sqaw hidden in some cave around here."

"Sqaw is a very offensive word. Please don't use it again."

"Sorry. I didn't know." I paused uncomfortably. "You ever unfaithful?"

"Not recently."

"Then you must have a lot of self-control."

"Why do white people always think Native Americans are either holy men or horny savages? We're just folks with ordinary strengths and weaknesses like everyone else. I'm no shaman, just a shoe salesman from Seattle."

"Gee, you don't have to get so sore about it."

"I'm not sore. I'm just tired of hearing the same things over and over again."

We approached a small stream. I picked up a stone and skipped it halfway across the water. It momentarily lingered on the surface before disappearing.

"Isn't it a little unusual for an American Indian to be selling shoes?"

"No. Why do you ask?"

"It's just that I read somewhere that you guys run hundred-mile races barefoot."

Tarwater chuckled. "I've got news for you, Donnybrook. These days, most of us wear something on our feet."

"You have sports growing up?"

"Didn't have much equipment."

"All you need are a coupla bats and balls."

"We were lucky to have one."

"Hey, you work with what you've got." I paused uneasily. "You still live on the reservation?"

"Moved off years ago."

"Why?"

"No work."

"It's so beautiful here. I wish I could show this to Denise."

"You talk about Denise a lot."

"Can't get her out of my mind."

"You two gonna get hitched?"

"It's complicated... She's married. We thought her husband died in a forced labor camp four years ago, but then he showed up alive. Before I left Verviers, I met her at her sister's house. We were supposed to settle everything then, but we kinda left things up in the air. I'll have to get in touch with her."

"Don't wait too long."

"I've written her. What else can I do? I can't call her because she doesn't have a phone, and we don't either. Even if I had a pass, there's no way to get back to Belgium from here."

"Figure something out, Donnybrook. Take it from an old, married man: an untended wound of the heart is bound to fester."

I looked up at the late afternoon sky. "Let's get going. I don't wanna be walking in the dark." I put a friendly hand on Tarwater's shoulder. "Don't forget about that eagle now."

"Don't worry. It's already taking shape in my mind."

Back at camp, Potts had the fires burning. It was dusk, and a full moon was rising.

"This is good stew," said Greta between mouthfuls. "Can I have some more?"

"Sure, honey," obliged Potts, ladling out another bowl. "Take as much as you want."

"Better watch him, Donnybrook," joked Zeke. "I think he's trying to steal your girl."

"I'm not worried. I've got her well-trained. Besides, if you don't have faith in your cook, who can you trust? Right, Potts?"

"I don't double-cross nobody."

"See. I knew he was an honest man."

"I think we're getting low on grub."

"I'll go into town with you tomorrow, Potts." I put my arm around Greta. "This woman has one hell of an appetite, doesn't she?"

"The word 'appetite' has many meanings," Tarwater observed.

I laughed and reprovingly shook my finger at him. "Now, this one I don't trust."

In the distance, a wolf let out a loud howl. Potts was so startled that he spilled his beer and knocked over several empty pans.

"What's the matter, Private? You afraid of the dark?" teased Zeke.

"No."

"Yes you are. You're always curled up in bed at night, shivering with the covers around your face, even when it's warm out."

"Screw you, Corp. Maybe you wanna make your own dinner tomorrow night."

"Hey, cool it fellas," I interceded. "We're stuck with each other out here, so let's make the best of it."

"Oh, all right," the corporal reluctantly agreed. "Sorry, Potts. I was only kidding."

"Okay, you're back on the meal plan."

"Be careful, Corp," joked Tarwater. "He might put you on the menu."

"Potts would never do that. But if you were the cook, I'd be worried."

"I'm an American Indian, Zeke. Not a cannibal."

"Yeah, but you always seem to have a knife in your hand. What are you doing now?"

Tarwater had the end of a long piece of wood in his lap, and was honing it to a fine point. He threw some shavings into the fire.

"Making a spear."

"Wh—"

"Don't even think it, Corp."

"Think what?"

"You know."

"Boy, are you sensitive."

"Calm down, guys," I admonished.

"All right," Zeke assented. "Look, Tarwater. I wasn't trying to be a wiseass. I was just wondering what you need a spear for. You plan on going hunting?"

"No," the Native American stonily replied.

"Then why bother?"

"There are many dangerous animals in the forest. A weapon like this might come in handy some time."

"We've got carbines," I observed. "If we're attacked by something, we can shoot it."

"I never liked guns," Tarwater countered. "They can misfire. And ours use a very small caliber bullet. They might not be able to stop a large creature."

"Shoot it in the head, and it'll be dead," said Zeke.

"Tarwater, do you really think it's dangerous out here?" asked Potts.

"There is much violence in nature, but as far as I'm concerned, man is far more brutal. Take the horrors of this war, for instance. Animals can't go to the store. They have no choice but to hunt for their food. There's nothing evil about it. They're just trying to survive."

"I'm going to bed," announced Greta. She caressed my leg. "Don't stay too long."

"I'll be there in a few minutes." I turned to Tarwater. "Did you hunt much when you were a kid?"

"A little. Some of my people say it's a rite of passage, something you have to do to become a man, but I never really bought into that." Tarwater admiringly looked up at the stars. "It's nice out here, but we're still pretty close to civilization. If I were really out in the wild, I'd kill for food and self-defense. I'd never kill for sport."

Potts eyed the unfinished spear with fascination. He reached for the sharp tip.

"I wouldn't do that if I were you," Tarwater cautioned.

"Ow! Shit."

"You were warned."

"Well, I didn't think it was that sharp."

"Here, let me take a look," I offered. "Oh, it's just a little cut."

"But it's bleeding," Potts moaned. "I can't stand the sight of blood, especially when it's mine."

I rolled my eyes. "Hold on. I've got a first aid kit in my tent."

When I returned, I laid it next to Tarwater. "Can you finish this up?"

"No problem, Donnybrook. I always wanted to play medicine man."

I stretched my arms and yawned. "Okay, fellas. I'm gonna turn in. Pleasant dreams."

"Tarwater, am I gonna need stitches?"

"Relax, Potts. All you need is a little iodine and a bandage."

"No Purple Heart, huh?"

"I'm afraid not. You'll have to tough it out with the rest of us."

*   *   *   *

Shortly after I returned from an afternoon trip to Fritzler, Zeke took me aside. "I've got a confession to make."

"What's that?"

"I tried to fool around with Greta."

"Really?"

"Yeah, but she wouldn't let me. She said you'd get mad."

I slapped my hands together and burst out laughing. "Hah! Didn't I tell you I had her well-trained? Can't blame you for trying, though. But I can't believe you told me. You're not exactly the type of person that suffers pangs of guilt."

"Tarwater talked me into it. He said it would be better if you heard it from me instead of her."

Curious, I approached Tarwater. "Zeke just told me everything. You have anything to confess, PFC?"

"No, Sergeant, but I can't say that I wasn't tempted. You leave a couple of hungry men around a full refrigerator, and sooner or later, someone's bound to go looking inside."

I facetiously furrowed my brow. "I think I'm gonna have to start keeping Greta under lock and key. Listen, Corporal, I'm glad you fessed up. Just don't do it again," I half-seriously intoned, punctuating each of my last five words with a jab of my index finger.

"Quit pointing at me," snapped Zeke.

"Hey, don't get sore at me," I replied in surprised anger. "A lot of guys would've kicked your ass." A light went on inside my head. "Wait a minute. You're still mad at me for ratting you out to Jack Spring, aren't you?"

"Well, now that you mention it—"

"Oh, we can't have that. We're living too close together to have any bad feelings. I'll tell you what, Zeke. We'll have a foot race, and if I lose, you can move in with Greta."

"Your challenge may not be wise, Don," Tarwater opined. "Zeke is a very fast runner."

"I'm aware of that, PFC. Well, Corporal? Is it a deal?"

"Deal."

*   *   *   *

It was all set. The four of us got up bright and early the next morning for the big event. After examining a topographical map, Zeke and I settled on a path that was approximately three-quarters of a mile round trip. Tarwater was standing at the halfway point, while Potts stayed back at camp to call the winner.

Greta was still sleeping. I had told her about the race but never informed her of its purpose.

"Good luck," she had said the previous night. "Let me know how you make out."

"You're not gonna watch?" I disappointedly asked.

"No, it's too early for me. But I'll be rooting for you in my dreams."

Zeke and I were at the starting line. We were ready. "Take your marks," shouted Potts. "Get set. Go!"

We both began with a strong, steady pace, but I hung back slightly, in line with my usual strategy. After a quarter-mile, I was exactly where I wanted to be, about a yard behind Zeke. Up to this point, our running resembled the inner workings of a finely tuned machine. The sounds of our rhythmic breathing and chugging footsteps were nearly identical. Then things fell apart.

Rounding a narrow curve, I tripped on a tree root. I tumbled off the trail, skinning my knee. Upset with myself, I quickly got up and broke into a determined sprint, but before I could close the gap, the peacefulness of the forest was shattered by a terrifying scream. I skidded to a stop.

"Zeke!" I yelled.

The scream had now become a continuous wail. I frantically ran another ten yards and then froze in my tracks. A large black bear was holding Zeke by his belt, shaking him in midair as if he were a rag doll.

I knew that if I didn't do something fast, my corporal would soon be dead. "Haw! Haw!" I hollered, in an effort to distract the ursine aggressor. The bear ignored me, so I picked up a large stone and heaved it at his right flank. The animal released his grip, and Zeke dropped to the ground with a heavy thud. He was unhurt, but still sobbing with fear.

"Shut up and get up, or we're both dead men."

"I, I can't."

"You can, and you will. Do it now, Corporal. That's an order."

"But I'm scared."

"Make believe you're not. It's the only chance we've got."

I was betting that the bear would sense that he was outnumbered and back off. Momentarily confused, the creature now turned menacingly toward me. He straightened himself to his full height and snarled. I gulped hard and wiped the cold sweat off my forehead. Zeke stood up.

"For Chrissake, make some noise!"

"Ha! Ha!" complied the corporal.

My seat-of-the-pants strategy began to take hold. The bear stopped, turned toward Zeke, then back to me. Seized with a sudden change in mood, he dropped to all fours, and, with a parting grunt, bounded off into the distance.

Tarwater arrived. "You guys okay?" he asked.

"A bit shaken up, but we're all right," I answered in a relieved tone.

But that wasn't the end of it. Tarwater looked down the trail and saw the bear heading straight for Potts. My cook fired several shots.

Tarwater put his hands to his temples. "Oh, that idiot!" he exclaimed. "Take cover. He's coming back."

All of Potts's shots had missed, and the bear, now more frightened and angry than ever, was running straight back toward the three of us. I climbed up a thick oak.

"Come on. Give me your hand!" I shouted to Zeke.

Instead of accepting my assistance, he began running in circles and shrieking madly. Tarwater stood his ground and raised his spear.

Unfortunately, the bear's boundings had loosened a five-hundred-pound boulder perched on a nearby incline. It began rumbling toward my PFC at rapid speed. Tarwater flung himself out of the way, and the spear slipped out of his hand. The massive rock crashed against the oak with such force that it broke in half and knocked me from my perch. Tarwater played dead.

For several horrific minutes, I watched the enraged animal turn Tarwater over, move away from him, and then return to repeat the procedure. Satisfied that he was dead, the bear now focused his attention on Zeke, who was cowering behind a fallen tree trunk. Urine began dribbling from his pants.

The beast reared up before him with a vicious roar. For an instant, it stood motionless on its two hind legs. Then, with an eerie moan, the bruin collapsed lifelessly into the dirt. At the moment the bear was going to rip Corporal Zeke to shreds, I had plunged Tarwater's spear into the base of its skull.

I staggered away and exhaled loudly. Drained, I put my hands on my knees and let out a nervous titter.

Tarwater slowly rose from the ground and brushed himself off. "You all right?"

"Yeah."

"You showed great courage, Don."

"Does this mean we're blood brothers?"

"No, but maybe we're kindred spirits."

"I'll settle for that." I approached Zeke, who still hadn't moved. "You okay?"

"Y-yeah, Sarge." He looked up at me in awe. "Thanks."

"Forget it."

"How can I forget it? You saved my life."

"Well, we Americans have gotta stick together, especially when there's German bears around."

Zeke extended his hand. I grasped it and pulled him to his feet.

Aside from a few minor scratches and bruises, none of us were hurt. Exhausted and dirty, we trudged back to camp. Potts already had brunch on the griddle.

"I came running as soon as I heard the growling," he explained. "When the bear ran away, I figured I'd scared him off, so I came back here. I scared him off, didn't I?"

The three of us gave him an icy stare.

"I guess not," Potts surmised.

Greta emerged from the food tent looking fresh and magnificent in a nifty pink outfit. She had slept through everything.

"Hello, boys," she intoned in a chipper voice. "So who won?"

Zeke and I perplexedly turned to each other.

"We decided to call it a draw," I finally answered.

"Oh well," replied the beaming fraülein. "Maybe you can do it again some time." She was completely oblivious to the three blank faces staring back at her. "So what's for breakfast?"

From then on, Zeke constantly sang my praises, complimenting me on everything from my choice of reading material to my taste in women. We agreed to nullify the contest and remained on friendly terms until the end of our service. None of us ever discussed the race or the bear again.

That evening I found a necklace on my bed. It had a wooden charm depicting a soaring eagle. With it was the following note:

For My Sergeant, the bravest man I have ever known.

Your Friend,

Tarwater

Because the incident was never reported, I considered the necklace a very personal trophy. I never tired of telling its story, and wore it proudly for many years.

*   *   *   *

A few days later, the four of us were called back from detached service, and I left Greta behind. She was a fantasy come true, but I never really missed her. It was time to move on.

My main interests were the disposition of my squadron and Joe's impending discharge. In the field, I had thought often about Denise. I still couldn't get her out of my mind. However, at this point, all I could do was keep my eyes and ears open for furloughs and transportation to Belgium. My radio duties were very light now, and I signed up for some French and business courses being offered on base.

French was a mixed bag. I had forgotten many grammar rules and needed a review, but mere study of the language reminded me of my Belgian love.

My thoughts were so jumbled that I dared not share them with my family, but even if I had been more clear-headed, details of my relationship with Denise still would not have appeared in my letters. As a general rule, people in the World War II era were far less open about their feelings than today's generation, and I was no exception. It was much easier to discuss Joe, the Pacific Campaign, and my other class.

Fritzler, Germany
July 9, 1945

Dear Mom, Dad & Ethel,

I resumed my advertising course, and it is still holding my interest. The number of G.I.'s attending is three, sometimes four. We are still trying to keep this thing going. We're moving at a more rapid pace, and the small number of students is to our benefit.

Just read a piece in the paper which indicates that Joe's outfit is slated to leave this theater of operations around September. He'll probably tell you more about that.

Love,

Don

---

7 Kilometers from Kassel, Germany
July 23, 1945

Dear Mom, Dad & Ethel,

Received a letter from Joe yesterday, and he wrote the best news I've heard in ages. He wrote, "I'm in Rheims, France, awaiting shipment back to good old U.S.A."

I was sure tickled to hear that.

It continues to be pretty nice out here. The meals are good, which is unusual because most outfits in Europe have been complaining bitterly. They have some swell cooks here. One was with me at Felixstowe, England.

We had a tent inspection this morning. It was scheduled to begin at 10 a.m., and, therefore, I decided to take a walk to the Red Cross at five minutes to ten. I returned a little after eleven and found to my dismay that the inspection had just begun. How lucky can a guy get?

The C.O. is a young man, about 27 years old. He's tall and slim. I've seen him on the ballfield back in Fritzler. Fortunately, it was a cursory inspection, and it went okay.

Last night I pulled my first radio shift here. The night shift isn't bad at all because about 10 o'clock, and sometimes before, they shut down, and a vehicle takes you back to camp.

When the war was still on, the radio vans were in operation 24 hours a day.

Love,

Don

Near Kassel, Germany
July 26, 1945

Dear Mom, Dad & Ethel,

We got a treat today. Bob Hope and his troupe, including Jerry Colonna, arrived in Fritzler and put on a show for us. We sent five trucks, fully packed with G.I.'s, to see the performance. Soldiers for miles around showed up. Altogether, there were several thousand soldiers watching the show. They were everywhere: sitting on the ground, hanging from trees, perched on top of roofs. It was a swell performance, and we enjoyed it immensely.

Nothing new on our status. In a month we should be told something definite. I know I told you this several times before, but we just keep getting stalled off. If you get any more news on Joe, let me know.

Love To All,

Don

July 30, 1945

Dear Ethel,

The calendar says it is summertime, so I guess we'll get a break in the weather soon. That will improve things a lot after all this rain.

Read about the news of that plane crashing into the Empire State Building, and I must confess, I'm a little worried and anxious to hear from you, Mom, and Dad soon.

I'm getting loads of sleep here. I hardly ever get up for breakfast. What a wonderful feeling when I don't have to work mornings! When I hear others rolling out of bed with regret, I merely chuckle to myself, pull the covers over me, and go back to sleep. So if I come home a lazy individual, you'll understand. Lots of luck, Sis, and let me hear from you real soon.

Love,

Don

Aug. 3, 1945

Dear Mom, Dad & Ethel,

We still have no news on our status. Fellows are still getting transferred from one outfit to another. Last night an official said, "The critical score will remain at 85 points for quite some time."

However, this critical score evaluation is not working out to satisfaction. Many fellows with over 100 points are in outfits slated for direct shipment to the Pacific. It seems if you're in an outfit that has orders to go to the Pacific, and you have more than 85 points, it's just too bad. There are some outfits that have more than 50% of its members with over 85 points, and they have been given orders from this theater to go directly to the Pacific. "So why in hell," they ask, "did the government make a point system?"

There is no use in kidding myself and you. I may be in this army for quite a while yet. I'm afraid I was overly optimistic in one of my previous letters. It's still a question of waiting and seeing who's going to be among the lucky ones. My point count has now been increased to 71 on a recalculation.

Love,

Don

Aug. 7, 1945

Dear Mom, Dad & Ethel,

I received a letter from Joe and one from you yesterday. Joe was finished processing and awaiting shipment to Le Havre, France, and then to good old U.S.A. He's naturally pretty happy about it, and I guess you are overjoyed knowing that he's coming home soon. It's hard to believe, but you should be seeing him shortly.

This afternoon I went swimming over at the air base. They have a classy little pool there. It is painted an aqua color.

However, the water was cold, and we didn't stay in long. They recently filled the pool, and that's the reason for the low temperature. You work up quite an appetite, though. The coffee and doughnuts at the Red Cross tasted swell.

Love,

Don

Near Kassel, Germany
Aug. 10, 1945

Dear Mom, Dad & Ethel,

Wow! What news! Let's hope the war will really end now. I guess we all felt the same way when the announcement came over the radio. It was difficult to believe what we had just heard. The boys are gathered around the radio right now—and it looks like in a week's time, we'll actually be hearing the authentic, heart-warming news.

It looks like just matters of procedure remain to render this thing complete. Although everyone here is inwardly excited, there are few outward emotions expressed. In the Army, one experiences disappointments and knows not to trust any possible happenings until they actually occur. Therefore, with unexpressed words, we await the wonderful news. Nothing else seems very important now.

Lots of Love,

Don

My jubilation was in reaction to the announcement that on August 6, 1945, the aircraft *Enola Gay* dropped the first atomic bomb on Hiroshima.[403] Statistical workers initially said that it killed 78,150 civilians.[404] Investigators later estimated the death toll at 100,000 (81), explaining that multiple causes of death prevented them from obtaining precise figures (81). Approximately twenty-five percent died from burns; twenty percent from radiation sickness; and fifty percent from other factors (81). On August 9, a second bomb was dropped on Nagasaki.[405] The devastating results provided the world with a somber introduction to the Nuclear Age.

In contrast to recent revisionist views, the morality of using "the bomb" on Japan was never an issue among us. The wisdom of President Truman's decision seemed so axiomatic that it was rarely discussed, let alone questioned. The vast majority of American men and women in uniform were war-weary. We all wanted the conflict over as soon as possible. Most of us had been overseas for at least two years and were anxious to reunite with our families. We would have welcomed anything that hastened the process.

We also had a lot of enmity toward the Japanese. Had you raised objections to the use of the A-bomb with me in August of 1945, I probably would have said, "Tojo and his crowd started this. Let them suffer the consequences. I'd take a hundred thousand dead Japanese civilians over a million dead American soldiers any day."[406]

The world of 2004 is very different from that which existed during my days in the service. Japan is now a staunch American ally, and my hot anger has long cooled. Still, nearly sixty years later, I continue to support Truman's use of nuclear weapons to end the war in the Pacific.

In 1945, many Hiroshima residents would have backed me up. They raised no ethical objections to the dropping of the bomb[407] and spouted fatalistic platitudes about the evils of war (89). This attitude seems especially remarkable given the widespread hatred of Americans in the city at the time (89).

Near Kassel, Germany
Aug. 16, 1945

Dear Mom, Dad & Ethel,

Well, the seemingly impossible happened. The most optimistic person wouldn't have believed there could be such a speedy victory in the Pacific. It's still difficult to comprehend that the war is over. There's no celebrating here because we haven't had the opportunity.

I am living in a different spot. I'm in a fairly nice room with two other fellows. I have a spring on my bed, which is swell sleeping. The food is bad, however, but that doesn't matter now. One's dreams are sweet and mellow, and you keep reminding yourself that the war is really over.

We are still in operation, manning our radio sets. However, it rains all the time here, and, therefore, intensive aircraft activity is impractical.

Last night I went to Kassel and saw the G.I. version of the opera "Carmen." It's in burlesque style, and one of the best G.I. shows I've ever seen.

I keep hoping that Joe will get that break of being shipped to the States. Now that the war is over, there is a difference of opinion on whether to send outfits like his, that have already been processed, back to the States, or to hold them back and re-form outfits of high-point men to get priority shipment. The papers hint that most officials are in favor of sending them on to the States because they have already been processed and they are practically set for sailing. I'm keeping my fingers crossed that he'll get the break.

The ball hasn't actually started rolling on getting men home in any substantial numbers, and, until it does, don't get over-optimistic. There are still plenty of men here that have over 110 points. There are supposedly 550,000 men with over 85 points that are still in the Army.

The present program releases 170,000 per month. The program now to be accelerated has 500,000 men per month as it's objective. If they achieve that goal, it shouldn't take too long. However, commencing this stepped-up program requires time to get the machinery in operation.

The only sour note is that the Russians and the Japanese are still fighting in Manchuria.

Lots of Love,

Don

Japan surrendered to Allied Forces on August 14, 1945.[408] However, August 15 is generally recognized and celebrated as V-J Day (618). It was then that millions of Japanese wept tears of sorrow when Emperor Hirohito went on the radio to announce the capitulation (618), but many more millions of people around the world cried tears of joy. Church bells chimed, crowds filled the streets, and strangers hugged (618). In San Francisco, two young women were so overcome with patriotic fervor that they bathed naked in a public fountain (618).

A formal signing ceremony took place on September 2 aboard the battleship *Missouri*, which was anchored in Tokyo Bay (620). There, two doleful Japanese representatives signed the surrender document accepted by generals and admirals of the armies and navies of the following nations: The United States, Great Britain, China, Russia, the Netherlands, New Zealand, Canada, France, and Australia (620). Shortly after making a speech on deck, General Douglas MacArthur began his duties as ruler of Japan (620).

Aug. 29, 1945

Dear Mom, Dad & Ethel,

The ball is rolling, and I'm glad. Here is what they're up to now: 112-pointers and above left the fighter control squadron yesterday to begin processing to go home. So my newly calculated 76 points are still diabetic-looking.

With all this moving around, it will take some time before my mail catches up with me. I still don't know if Joe is on his way home and am anxiously waiting to hear about him.

Lots Of Love To All,

Don

Dornheim, Germany
Sept. 8, 1945

Dear Mom, Dad & Ethel,

The redeployment program seems to be gaining momentum. According to all reports, it has far exceeded expectations. With additional points added on, I now have 84 points—which are enough for discharge. The Army is really revved up now, and I don't want to make any definite promises, but from all appearances, I should be home eating Christmas dinner with you.

The one thing that keeps me thinking is the fact that we are still operational and still manning radio sets. High-pointers have left here, but no replacements have as yet come in. Thus we are continuously getting smaller in number.

We are still not working hard at all, but our points are around the lowest here, and if we don't get replacements when our time comes around, I don't know exactly how we'll be able to leave. You say, "Surely the Army has that all planned out." I hope you are right. However, I've seen them pull bigger blunders, yet, at the same time, they are capable of mastering the most difficult tasks. Although this thought rests on my mind, I do honestly believe that everything will turn out okay.

Meanwhile, I'm feeling fine, eating very well, and working very little. The weather has been excellent—in fact, too good. This seems to make for a social get-together for pugnacious mosquitoes, for they attack me with vigor. In the evening, if you try to shave, you need about ten hands to keep them away from you.

Then we have another kind of pest: German kids. Most of them are good kids, but you've got to watch them because they're always around the tent bothering you.

Despite the fact that both wars are over, the Army is still the Army, and today is inspection day. I expect the "metal men" here very soon, so I'll sign off now with lots of love.

Perhaps it won't be too long now. We're coming down the home stretch.

Love,

Don

Dornheim, Germany
Sept. 9, 1945

Dear Ethel,

Hiya doing, Sis? There's been lots of good news lately, and lots of fellows have been fortunate enough to be sent home already.

I read in the paper that Joe's outfit sailed on the Queen Mary on Sept. 6th. It's a five-day voyage on that ship, and by the time you receive this letter, he should be back in the United States. I guess he'll have to wait a short while for discharge, but I imagine that the points needed for discharge will be lowered again in a few weeks.

This setup here is very good. We are still eating like royalty because we only have a small group of about 40 men.

I expect that within several months you'll probably have the misfortune of seeing me again. I know life has been pretty sweet without me, but what can I do? Orders are orders, and if Uncle Sam commands, a poor soldier like myself must obey. So, although it's a little tough, bear with me, and if it's too distasteful, I'll go away and come back some other day.

All kidding aside, I feel fine and hope to be home before the year's out—or sooner.

Love,

Don

CHAPTER 19

▼

DENISE

I had sent Josephine many letters for Denise while I was in Germany, but I never got an answer. Knowing something was wrong, I wrote Josephine directly, and she replied that Denise had decided to stay with Étienne. Shocked, I fired off a note to the sister saying that I was coming anyway. Josephine wrote back begging me to stay away.

Disregarding her warning, I finally arranged a trip on two days' leave. Furloughs were easier to get now, and I timed mine to coincide with a westward-bound supply convoy that was passing through Dornheim. I sat with the driver of an ordnance truck, the same type of vehicle that had so terrified Corporal Blank. If I was afraid, I didn't notice. My thoughts were focused on Denise.

The convoy took me over the Belgian border. From there, a kindhearted civilian picked me up and drove me to Stembert. I offered him fifteen dollars, but he refused to take any money. That's how I showed up on Josephine's doorstep one morning in mid-September 1945.

She said that Denise wasn't home, and that even if she were there, she wouldn't have been able to see me. Where was she? Josephine didn't know. I had every reason to believe her. Josephine's personality was very similar to Joe's: quiet and honest. If I'd had the slightest doubt, I would've run right over to Denise's house. I had taken great risks to see her before, and I wouldn't have hesitated to do so again.

Josephine explained that she had given Denise my letters, but that she was too distraught—and preoccupied with her recently released husband—to answer them. She urged me to write Denise after I returned to the States and assured me that Denise would respond.

Though in great emotional pain, I knew it was time for me to face reality, and my love for Denise compelled me to honor her wishes. Shaking with sorrow, I wiped my moist face, got up from Josephine's couch, and departed. I would never see Denise again. We were done.

It was pouring outside, and I let loose with a torrent of expletives. Paroxysmally sobbing on my knees, I cursed the Army, Europe, God, Creation—everything and everybody except Denise. Even in my blind rage, I couldn't say anything bad about her.

I started out not wanting to be tied down to anyone and ended up willing to make the ultimate commitment, but fate got in the way. *C'est la guerre.*

Outwardly, I recovered quickly. Mushiness was not considered manly, so I returned to my post in Germany a slightly more subdued version of my usual, upbeat self. Inside, I was bitter for a while. Time would heal that wound, but a scar would remain.

Did I wait too long to return to Stembert? Had I arrived earlier, I'm sure the outcome would have been the same. Denise's feelings about her husband were one group of thoughts that I couldn't read. She was a strong-willed woman who made up her own mind, at her own pace, and without any pressure from me. Besides, I couldn't have done anything differently. Making the trip back was no small undertaking, and I traveled at first opportunity.

I continued writing Denise for several years after my discharge. I addressed my letters to Josephine, who would hand deliver them to her sister when they were alone together. When Denise wrote back, she would reverse the process, giving her letter to Josephine, who would then mail it.

July 2, 1948

Mon Cher Sergeant Don,

I am so happy that you continue to write to me. All the other soldiers have stopped writing to the girlfriends they had when they were here, and the girls are very sad about this. But you continue to be "mon cher," and I thank you from the bottom of my heart. Je t'aime beaucoup.

I will always remember the happy evenings, nights, and mornings we spent together. I will never forget how we made love while the bombs were falling, and how we could hear the sound of the anti-aircraft guns pounding against the windows. The sight of those big searchlights lighting up the sky, and the sound of those sirens wailing, were very scary, but somehow, they made love-making a lot more fun. Perhaps it was because I was so frightened, n'est-ce pas? But you always made me feel safe. For this, I will always love you. And for the simple things, too. Your politeness, the way you worked so hard on your French. I suppose we cherished each moment so much because we always thought it might be our last.

Even though we are no longer together, we still have these beautiful memories that nobody can take away. Oh God, but we had such wonderful times! You were good and kind to me. I needed you then, and I need you now.

But, of course, it cannot be. Étienne is back. He went through a lot, and he, too, is a good, kind man. He is hurting inside, and I am his wife.

As much as I might have wanted to, in all honesty, I could never have gone to America. I am a Belgian. I love my country, and I have roots here.

At first, my husband was very angry with me for spending time with you. But after awhile, he understood that these things happen in wartime. And guess what? I'm pregnant!

And now that the baby's on the way, he is in a much better mood. And soon I will have a real family, and I am very happy and excited about that. I hope you will be happy for me, too.

I hope to hear from you again soon. You will always be my darling. Tears are running down my cheeks as I write this. I remember that while those were hard, troubled years, we had something wonderful together.

Tu me manques de tout mon coeur.

Ta Chérie Toujours,

Denise

July 14, 1948

Ma Chérie Denise,

I see that you have taken my advice to work on your contractions quite literally. Mes Félicitations! I am very, very happy for you. Maybe the baby will be the bridge you need to heal the rift between you and Étienne. Then you can really get on with your lives.

Still, it makes me very sad to know that I can no longer see you or be with you. It all seems like the end of a beautiful dream. I can't believe all the things we did really happened. I can't believe I was in Belgium during the war years. It just doesn't seem real, and now it's all over.

War is hell, but I was lucky. I got sent to England, France, Belgium, and Germany. I met a lot of people who were very kind to me, but the months I spent in Verviers were the happiest days of my life. It was as if I was living in a glorious fairy tale. I guess I was hoping I'd be there forever, and that time would stand still, but you can't hold back the ticking of the clock.

As wonderful as our loving times together were, our fairy tale ended sadly. In all probability, I can't see you again. I can no longer hold you tightly, kiss you, and make love to you. I can no longer say, "Gee, I'm going to Denise's tonight."

We did simple things. We went to cafés. We danced together. We went to boxing matches. We ate together. We slept together. We made love, and loved every minute of it.

When I left you in the morning, I couldn't wait to come back to see you in a few days. Because of my good fortune to be in Verviers, and because of my wonderful schedule in the radio van, I was able to see you two or three times a week.

We acted like we were married, but, in a way, it was good that we weren't. Not being married gave us time away from one another, and that made me want you all the more.

Every moment had to be lived to the fullest, because any day, without notice, I might have received orders to pack up and move on to a different city. That's what happened during the Battle of the Bulge at Christmas time, when I was sent to Liège. Even though Verviers was off limits, I managed to sneak back in again and take my chances because I longed to see you so badly.

I couldn't bear to be away from you, and when you told me that Étienne was coming back, we got together at Josephine's house, where we made love one last time. It was dangerous, but all the more beautiful. Just like when the bombs were falling, right? Yes, chérie, it did make the lovemaking more fun!

Then Étienne, probably suspicious, rushed over to the house looking for you. We were making passionate love in your sister's bedroom, and he was in the adjoining room talking to Josephine and your brother-in-law, Gerard. Stifling our heavy breathing, we made love very quietly and lay on the floor, so there would be no creaking sounds from the bed.

When your husband left the house, we breathed easier. I never told you this, but when we came out of there, I asked Gerard what he would have done if Étienne had opened the bedroom door. Without batting an eyelash, he answered, "My home is my castle. If he had put his hand on that doorknob, I would have killed him."

I'm glad he didn't. You said you never could have left Belgium, and I'm as much a New Yorker as you are a Stembertois.

Still, part of me wants you here with me right now, but that wouldn't be fair to either of us. We never could have built a life together when one of us was deathly homesick. I'm a little older and wiser now, and I love you too much to allow my selfishness to cause you so much pain.

Chérie, this will be my last letter to you. It's not that I don't want to write you anymore, it's just too dangerous. The slightest slip-up by you or Josephine, and Étienne could wind up reading our letters. Then all your efforts to rebuild your marriage would be jeopardized. This is a risk to which I can no longer, in good conscience, subject you.

Think only good thoughts, Chérie. Those were delightful and dangerous times, and now only beautiful memories remain. But we can still call upon them whenever we want to brighten up a rainy day, turn a frigid night into a sunny morning, or a sad thought into a happy one. Nobody can take that away from us.

I'll always be with you, if not in body, then in spirit. You can find me in a Voice of America broadcast, or in a gentle breeze caressing your cheek on the place Verte, at a boxing match, or a ball game. Just think of me, and I'll be there.

Please, for your sake, read this letter twice, so you'll always remember the love we shared. Then light a match and burn it. God bless you, sweetheart, for all the happiness you've brought me.

Je t'aime à jamais,

Sergeant Don

EPILOGUE

▼

Shortly before his death in 1961, Dad gave me an old box of Havana cigars containing the letters I had sent him during the war. That correspondence is reproduced in this book.

Mom died in 1981 at age ninety.

At the time of this writing, Joe resides in Florida.

Ethel married shortly after the war. She had two children, two grandchildren, and was married for fifty-five years. She died in Atlanta in 2001.

Normie built a successful wallpaper business and was happily married to Vivian until her death in 1990. He is now retired and resides in Boca Raton, Florida.

These days, my gambling is limited to occasional trips to Atlantic City.

*   *   *   *

Ten years after I returned home, I received the following letter:

November 23, 1955

Dear Sir:

I am the widow of Jack Spring. I found your name and address on the back of a picture you took with my late husband.

Jack left three children and myself. He went to work one day and suffered a fatal heart attack.

I am in great difficulty financially and would like you to go with me to the Veterans Administration to substantiate a widow's claim for service-connected disability. I would appreciate this very much. You are my last hope.

Mrs. Bonnie Spring

I sent the following reply:

November 29, 1955

Dear Mrs. Spring,

I am shocked and saddened by the news of Jack's death. He was a close friend of mine during the war years. We spent considerable time together and went to shows and the Red Cross Club frequently.

However, I regret to inform you that I cannot comply with your request. To the best of my knowledge, Jack was never hurt or injured—or even sick— in all the time I knew him. Therefore, it would be impossible for me to testify before the Veterans Administration that he was incapacitated from any wartime sickness, bullet, or bomb. It would not only be unethical, I would be committing perjury, thereby exposing myself to criminal prosecution. Therefore, I cannot help you in this regard.

However, I'm enclosing a small check. It's not very much, but it's all I can afford.

I know you'll need a lot of courage for the difficult burden of raising three small children without a father. I wish that I could be of more assistance, but what you are asking is impossible for me to do. Please forgive me.

Sincerely,

Don Quix

I felt awful about Jack's family, but committing perjury was another bright line I never crossed. I wouldn't have done it at any age. Taking an oath before a judge is a sacred act. You don't put your hand on a Bible when you show an MP a pass.

To help clear my thoughts, I wrote this note on a piece of paper:

To Jack, wherever you are,

You know I would go to bat for you if I could, but your wife's asking something that's unthinkable for me. You were a fun-loving guy with a quick laugh and a lust for doing wacky things.

I remember when we were on a ship together, and you took a dollar bill and flung it into the ocean while giant waves smashed against the boat. You laughed. This was kicks for you. You were saying, "Dollar bill, you are nothing."

I was stunned by your extravagance, but I understood. I'm horrified by what happened to you. You were a bit rough around the edges, but deep down, you were the best friend a guy could ever have. I will truly miss you.

So long, Greenjeans. God bless your earthy soul.

I tossed the sheet of paper into my fireplace and watched it slowly disintegrate. Mrs. Spring never contacted me again.

*   *   *   *

In the midst of global conflict, I found love and friendship, but the war did not create those relationships. They did not flourish because of the war, but in spite of it, and that's why I'm optimistic about the human race.

If I could go back in time, would I still do the same crazy things? Some of them, sure. When you're young and brazen, you take all kinds of risks. All of them? Probably not—except the ones for Denise. She will always occupy a special place in my soul. I would have died for her.

Back in the States, I avoided discussing Denise. It was too painful. In rare instances, however, I did speak about other aspects of my wartime experience. One of these candid moments occurred shortly after I returned to the Bronx.

After three years and twenty-five days of service in the Air Corps, I was discharged on November 20, 1945. Joe had received his separation papers on November 4.

I arrived home just in time for Thanksgiving dinner. The living room furniture had been pushed aside to make space for a large, laminated, cherry-wood table reserved for special occasions. We had about two dozen family and friends over, including Normie, Vivian, Seymour, Wally Gold, Jerry, Uncle Eddy, and Cousin Claire.

When Mom opened the door and laid eyes on me for the first time in years, her knees buckled. "Oh my goodness!" she exclaimed while throwing her arms around me in a tearful embrace. During my absence, Mom's salt-and-pepper hair had turned snow white, and she was stouter than I remembered, but to me she was more beautiful than ever.

Dad absent-mindedly removed the pipe from his mouth. His hand went limp, and the smoking implement fell to the brown-carpeted floor. "We didn't expect you so soon," he softly intoned as we awkwardly shook hands. "Good to have you back, son." Then, with uncharacteristic energy and emotion, Dad flung himself at me, and we hugged each other tightly. Ethel and Joe followed in similar fashion. All physical barriers among us had finally broken down.

At the table, I was immediately supplied with food and a place befitting a guest of honor. Thrilled and chagrined, I felt transported back to that tiny farmhouse in Stembert shortly after the liberation.

"Gee, this is swell, but I wish everybody wouldn't make such a fuss over me," I finally said.

"It's only natural," Dad replied. "You were gone a long time."

"But I didn't do any of the fighting, Pop. If you wanna heap praise on someone, Jerry's your man. He flew combat missions."

"Right now all I care about is you and Joe. Your mother and I fussed just as much over him when he came back two weeks ago. And as far as I'm concerned, everyone who served overseas is a hero."

"That's a nice speech, Dad."

Pop's brow furrowed. "How do you feel, Don?"

"Swell."

"Come on. Who do you think you're kidding? For years I've been reading your letters about partying, dancing, and ball games. It must have been a whole lot rougher than that."

"Marvin, please," Mom pleaded. "The boy just got home."

"Michelle, I usually don't make demands, but I have a right to ask this question of my son. Don, how do you really feel?"

All eyes were on me. I cleared my throat. "Dad, I really don't wanna talk about it, but I suppose I owe you an explanation because you're my father and I've been away for awhile. A few years ago, I was a dopey kid who took a lot for granted. I'm still no sage, but now I'm more thankful for what I have, like seeing all you folks and friends here tonight.

"People who've never been in a war zone blow stuff way outta proportion. You've got a bad cold, your boss chewed you out, your car broke down, whatever. Sure it's upsetting, but just remember that no bombs are falling and nobody's shooting at you.

"I went into the Army looking for action and adventure. I found a smidgen, and it was more than enough.

"You wanna know how I really feel, Dad? I'm happy to have a roof over my head because I've slept outdoors for months on end in all kinds of weather. I'm glad to be in a solid building because I've walked in the rubble. In an hour or so, I'll enjoy taking a shower because I've lived without running water. I appreciate this meal so much because there were times when I was hungry. And, for the rest of my life, I'll savor every moment of peace because I've had a taste of war."

REFERENCES

Allin, John and Arnold Wesker. *Say Goodbye: You May Never See Them Again.* London: Jonathan Cape, 1974.

"The American Troops in the Attack to the South of Soissons," trans. John Roberts. Club Internet (France) [online]. Date unknown [cited 4 January 1999; 03:45 EST]. Available from Internet: <http://perso.club-internet.fr/batmarn2/us187eng.htm>.

"Antwerp X: The AAA War Against the Buzz Bombs" [online]. Skylighters, Updated 28 January 2000 [cited 8 June 2000; 19:40 EST]. Available from Internet: <wysiwyg://1/http://www.strandlab.com/buzzbombs/>.

"Aperçu historique de Charleroi" [online]. Ville de Charleroi. Date unknown [cited 4 October 1998; 17:58 EST]. Available from Internet: <http://www.charleroi.be/histoi_1.htm>.

"Baseball: New York Yankees Year-by-Year" [online]. The Sporting News, 1998 [cited 29 October 1998; 18:50 EST]. Available from Internet: <http://www.sportingnews.com/archives/baseball/yankees-yby.html>.

"Battle of the Bulge Facts" [online]. Veterans of the Battle of the Bulge. Date unknown [cited 6 October 1998; 00:43 EST]. Available from Internet: <http://www.battleofbulge.com/facts.htm>.

"Battle of the Bulge: About the Program." In *The American Experience: Guts and Glory* [online]. PBS, 1998 [cited 29 October 1998; 17:41 EST]. Available from Internet:
<http://www.pbs.org/wgbh/pages/amex/guts/about_bulge.html>.

Bebie, Jules. *Manual of Explosives, Military Pyrotechnics and Chemical Warfare Agents*. New York: Macmillan, 1943.

Bermant, Chaim. *London's East End: Point of Arrival*. New York: Macmillan, 1976.

Bernton, Hal, William Kovarik, and Scott Sklar. *The Forbidden Fuel: Power Alcohol in the Twentieth Century*. New York: Boyd Griffin, 1982.

British Adventures. "The Story of British and Irish Money" [online], 1997. Updated 21 May 1997 [cited 28 April 1999; 15:06 EST]. Available from Internet: <http://www.britishadventures.com/britmony.htm>.

Bronckart, J[oseph]. *Bombes, Obus et Robots: Ce qui troubla la quiétude des Verviétois du jour de la libération à la fin de la guerre*. Verviers, Belg.: n.p., 1945.

Chapuis: Textes de Charles Roger-Claessen, Théodore Bost et Félix de Grave. Edited by Michel Bedeur and Paolo Zagaglia. 1847, 1874, 1894. Reprint (3 vols. in 1), with a forward by Michel Bedeur and Paolo Zagaglia, Dison, Belg.: Irezumi, 1999.

Chicago Fact Book [online]. Chicago: City of Chicago, 1997 [cited 26 November 1998; 19:40 EST]. "Geography/Climate." Table of average temperature citing National Climatic Data Center. Available from Internet: <http://www.ci.chi.il.us/WorksMart/Planning/ChgoFacts/Geo.html>.

Chicago Historical Society. "Al Capone." Chicago Historical Society [online]. 1998 [cited 28 November 1998; 10:24 EST]. Available from Internet: <http://www.chicagohs.org/history/capone/cpn2.html>.

———. "The Black Sox." Chicago Historical Society [online]. 1998 [cited 28 November 1998; 10:56 EST]. Available from Internet: <http://www.chicagohs.org/history/blacksox.html>.

———. "What George Wore and Sally Didn't." Chicago Historical Society: World's Fairs [online]. 1998 [cited 28 November 1998; 11:09 EST]. Available from Internet: <http://www.chicagohs.org/treasures/world.html>.

Churchill, Winston S. *Triumph and Tragedy*. Boston: Houghton Mifflin, 1953.

City of Chicago. "Chicago: A Brief History." Chicago Mosaic [online]. 1997 [cited 27 December 1998; 17:49 EST]. Available from Internet: <http://www.ci.chi.il.us/Tourism/PressReleases/History.html>.

————. "Chicago Building." Chicago Landmarks [online]. 1997 [cited 26 November 1998; 18:16 EST]. Available from Internet: <http://www.ci.chi.il.us/Landmarks/ChicagoBldg.html>.

Cooksley, Peter G. *Flying Bomb: The Story of Hitler's V-Weapons in World War II.* New York: Scribner's, 1979.

Covent Garden Market Authority. "A Short History of the Market from the Middle Ages to the Motorway" [online]. London: Covent Garden Market Authority, 1998 [cited 2 March 1999; 16:10 EST]. Available from Internet: <http://www.cgma.gov.uk/history.htm>.

"Distances from Liverpool to Major U.K. Ports" [online]. Liverpool: Sanchez On Line, 1997 [cited 29 June 1999; 17:35 EST]. Available from Internet: <http://www.sanchez-uk.com/distance.htm>.

"Dollar-Pound Exchange Rate, 1800-1998" [online]. Alhambra, Calif.: Global Financial Data, 1999 [cited 28 April 1999; 15:34 EST]. Available from Internet: <http://www.globalfindata.com/tbpound.htm>.

Dornberger, Walter. *V-2.*Translated by James Cleugh and Geoffrey Halliday. With an introduction by Willy Ley. New York: Viking, 1954.

"Ethanol-Powered Vehicles" [online]. California Energy Commission, Updated 3 November 1998 [cited 26 December 1999; 17:56 EST]. Available from Internet: <http://www.energy.ca.gov/afvs/ethanol/ethanolhistory.html>.

Federation of American Scientists. "R-11/SS-1B Scud-A, R-300 9K72 Elbrus/SS-1C Scud-B" [online], date unknown. Updated 29 July 2000 [cited 2 August 2000; 17:34 EST]. Available from Internet: <http://www.fas.org/nuke/guide/russia/theater/r-11.htm>.

"The First U.S. Division at Cantigny, 27 April-8 July 1918," trans. John Roberts. Club Internet (France) [online]. Date unknown [cited 4 January 1999; 03:36 EST]. Available from Internet: <http://perso.club-internet.fr/batmarn2/dvcneng.htm>.

Franchi, Francesca. "Mecca Comes to Covent Garden—the Royal Opera House as a Dance Hall." *About the House* (September 1991): 12-20.

Gasohol: A Technical Memorandum. Washington: United States Office of Technology Assessment, 1979.

"Greater Madison at a Glance: Madison Area Facts" [online]. Greater Madison Convention and Visitors' Bureau, 1997 [cited 1 October 1998; 23:03 EST]. Available from Internet: <http://www.visitmadison.com/areastats.htm#wx>.

Hammond, William M. *Normandy* [online]. Washington: United States Army Center of Military History, 1999 [cited 2 August 1999; 18:20 EST]. Available from Internet: <http://www4.army.mil/cmh-pg/brochures/normandy/nor-pam.htm>.

Hersey, John. *Hiroshima.* New York: A.A. Knopf, 1985. Reprint, New York: Vintage Books, 1989.

Historic Madison, Inc. "A History of the City of Madison" [online]. City of Madison Home Page, 1997 [cited 22 December 1998; 10:03 EST]. Available from Internet: <http://www.ci.madison.wi.us/Parks/madhist.html>.

"History of the BBC: 1920's" [online]. BBC, date unknown [cited 27 July 2000; 18:07 EST]. Available from Internet: <http://www.bbc.co.uk/info/history/1920s-1.shtml>.

"History of the World Series: 1944" [online]. The Sporting News, 1998 [cited 29 October 1998; 18:23 EST]. Available from Internet: <http://www.sportingnews.com/archives/worldseries/1944.html>.

Insiders' Guide to Madison, Wisconsin [online]. Helena (Mont.): Falcon Publishing, 1995-98 [cited 22 December 1998; 10:38 EST]. "History." Available from Internet: <http://www.insiders.com/madison/main-history.htm>.

Ivey, Mike. "Madison's Hom-Pak Goodness: Schoep's Going Strong at 70." Madison Newspapers Archives [online]. Madison Newspapers, 8 July 1998 [cited 2 October 1998; 01:03 EST]. Available from Internet: <http://newslibrary.krmediastream.com/cgi...ocument/md_auth?DBLIST=md98&DOCNUM=20722>.

Jackson, Alan A., and Desmond F. Croome. *Rails through the Clay: A History of London's Tube Railways*, London: George Allen & Unwin, 1962.

Jaeger, Richard W. "Forgotten Heroes of Truax Field: Street Names Only Hint at Lives of the Soldiers." Madison Newspapers Archives [online]. Madison Newspapers, 27 May 1996 [cited 2 October 1998; 00:23 EST]. Available from Internet: <http://newslibrary.krmediastream.com/cgi...ocument/md_auth?DBLIST=md96&DOCNUM=16288>.

Katsiavriades, Kryss. "The Piccadilly Line" [online]. Personal site, date unknown [cited 5 October 1998, 23:48 EST]. Available from Internet: <http://www.ultisoft.demon.co.uk/piccline.html>.

Kennedy, Gregory P. *Vengeance Weapon 2*. Washington: Smithsonian Institution, 1983.

"Landguard Fort" [online]. Landguard Fort Trust, 1997 [cited 5 October 1998; 21:33 EST]. Available from Internet: <http://www.landguard.com/landguard/one.htm>.

"Landguard Peninsula—Management Plan" [online]. Landguard Fort Trust, 1997 [cited 5 October 1998; 21:35 EST]. Available from Internet: <http://www.landguard.com/landguard/archaeol.htm>.

Marshall, S.L.A. "First Wave at Omaha Beach." *Atlantic Monthly* 206, no. 5 (1960): 67-72.

Milfred, Scott. "Life on the Porch: From Downtown to the Suburbs, the Front Porch and a Culture of Neighborly Relaxation Are Back." Madison Newspapers Archives [online]. Madison Newspapers, 26 May 1998 [cited 2 October 1998; 01:09 EST]. Available from Internet: <http://newslibrary.krmediastream.com/cgi...ocument/md_auth?DBLIST=md98&DOCNUM=16126>.

Mondadori, Arnoldo, ed. *100 Years of Automobiles, 1886-1986*. New York: Gallery, 1985.

Murphy, S. Sgt. Mark, USAAF. "Fighter Control: Nerve Center of Battle." *Air Force* (October 1944): 6-7, 63.

National Railway Publication, *Official Guide of the Railways and Steam Navigation Lines of the United States*, no. 5, October 1943.

New York Post, 13 November 2005.

New York Times, 2, 11 October 1940; 2 January 1941; 25 November 1998; 3 January, 3 August 1999; 30 June 2000.

Newman, Scott A. "Bohemian Chicago." Jazz Age Chicago [online]. 27 April 1997 [cited 29 November 1998; 18:46 EST]. Adapted from John Drury, *A Century of Progress: Authorized Guide to Chicago* (Chicago: Consolidated Book Publishers, 1933). Available from Internet: <http://www.suba.com/~scottn/explore/scrapbks/bohemian/bohemian.htm>.

————. "Union Station." Jazz Age Chicago [online]. 27 May 1998 [cited 28 November 1998; 14:16 EST]. Available from Internet: <http://www.suba.com/~scottn/explore/sites/transpor/union_1.htm>.

Ohart, Theodore C. *Elements of Ammunition*. New York: J. Wiley & Sons, 1946.

Omaha Beachhead (6 June–13 June 1944) [online]. Washington: United States Army Center of Military History, Pub. 100-11, Facsimile Reprint, 1984 [cited 2 August 1999; 18:19 EST]. Available from Internet: <http://www4.army.mil/cmh-pg/100-11.HTM>.

Phillips, Bob. "History." Veterans of the Battle of the Bulge [online]. Date unknown [cited 5 January 1999; 17:21 EST]. Available from Internet: <http://www.battleofbulge.com/History.htm>.

Pyle, Ernie. *Brave Men*. New York: Henry Holt, 1944.

"Reading and Resource List: Making and Using Your Own Ethanol" [online]. United States Department of Energy, Updated May 1997 [cited 26 December 1999; 19:23 EST]. Available from Internet: <http://gils.doe.gov:1782/cgi-bin/w3vdkhgw?qryLGAVeG99_;doecrawl-010957>.

Record of the 327th Fighter Control Squadron. N.p.: privately printed, [1946?].

Royal Opera House. "History and Heritage" [online]. Cable & Wireless, date unknown [cited 5 October 1998; 22:48 EST]. Available from Internet: <http://www.royalopera.org/house/archives/archives5.htm>.

Rutishauser, Andreas. "A Short History of the Citroën Traction Avant" [online]. Personal site, 26 December 1995 [cited 15 May 2000; 18:41 EST]. Available from Internet: <http://www.traction.ch/tahiste.html>.

Ruwet, Armand. *Vues d'une occupation et d'une libération: Verviers, 1940-1945.* Andrimont-Dison, Belg.: Irezumi, 1994.

Ryan, Cornelius. *The Longest Day: June 6, 1944.* New York: Simon and Schuster, 1959.

"A Short History of Charleroi" [online]. Ville de Charleroi. Date unknown [cited 5 October 1998; 16:40 EST]. Available from Internet: <http://www. charleroi.be/ehisto_1.htm>.

Smithies, Edward. *The Black Economy in England since 1914.* Dublin: Gill and Macmillan; Atlantic Highlands (N.J.): Humanities Press, 1984.

Suicide Missions: Dangerous Tours of Duty—Ball Turret Gunners, Vol. 1, prod. and dir. Rob Lihani, 50 mins., A&E Television Networks, 1999, videocassette.

Sulzberger, C.L. *The American Heritage Picture History of World War II.* [New York]: American Heritage Publishing, 1966.

Times (London), 11 October, 13, 16 November 1940.

United Nations (Population Division, Department of Economic and Social Affairs). "Countries with a Population of 50 Million or More: 1950, 1998, and 2050." United Nations [online], 1998 [cited 2 March 1999; 18:46 EST]. Available from Internet: <http://www.popin.org/pop1998/5.htm>.

United States Air Force History Support Office. "Evolution of the Department of the Air Force" [online], date unknown. Updated 30 December 1998 [cited 5 January 1999; 18:18 EST]. Available from Internet: <http:// www.airforcehistory.hq.af.mil/soi/evolution_of_the_departmen.htm>.

Virtual Felixstowe. "The Port of Felixstowe" [online]. Eastern Counties Network, date unknown [cited 5 October 1998; 20:55 EST]. Available from Internet: <http://www.felixstowe.gov.uk/history/port.htm>.

————. "Town History" [online]. Eastern Counties Network, date unknown [cited 5 October 1998; 20:51 EST]. Available from Internet: <http://www.felixstowe.gov.uk/history/history.htm>.

Voice of America. "1942-2000: 58 Years of Broadcasting Excellence" [online], May 2000 [cited 26 July 2000; 04:17 EST]. Available from Internet: <http://www.ibb.gov/pubaff/voafact.html>.

"Walgreens Soda Fountains Served Up Decades of Success." Walgreens [online]. Date unknown [cited 27 December 1998; 14:10 EST]. Available from Internet: <http://www.walgreens.com/hist/sodafountain/sodafountain.html>.

Williams, Allen. "The Twenty-Ninth Infantry Division" [online]. Normandy Allies, 5 September 1999 [cited 18 September 1999; 12:16 EST]. Available from Internet: <http://www.normandyallies.org/29hist.htm>.

Wilson, Capt. Barbara A., USAF (Ret.). "World War Two Women." Military Women Veterans: Yesterday, Today, Tomorrow [online]. May 1996 [cited 5 January 1999; 16:51 EST]. Available from Internet: <http://userpages.aug.com/captbarb/femvets5.html>.

Wynants, Jacques. *Verviers libéré: De l'allégresse à l'inquiétude, septembre 1944– janvier 1945.* Verviers, Belg.: Librairie dérive, 1984.

————. *Verviers 1940: Contribution à l'étude d'une ville et d'une région au début de l'occupation allemande.* Brussels: Crédit communal de Belgique, 1981.

Notes

CHAPTER 1: JUST THE THING TO DO

1. During World War II, the United States Air Forces existed as a semi-autonomous branch of the Army. In passing the National Security Act of 1947, Congress created the Department of the Air Force, and within it, the U.S. Air Force, a fully independent organization. United States Air Force History Support Office, "Evolution of the Department of the Air Force" [online].

CHAPTER 3: MADISON

2. Wisconsin license plates began bearing this slogan in 1940. *Insiders' Guide To Madison, Wisconsin* [online], "History: Mining and Agriculture," 3.

3. Historic Madison, Inc., "A History of the City of Madison" [online].

4. *Insiders' Guide To Madison, Wisconsin* [online], "History: Mining and Agriculture," 3.

5. Ibid.

6. David Savageau and Richard Boyer, *Places Rated Almanac: Your Guide to Finding the Best Places to Live in North America*, all new ed. (New York: Simon and Schuster, 1993), 369. The Madison Convention and Visitors' Bureau reports that the contemporary average high temperature during winter is 28.4°F. "Greater Madison at a Glance: Madison Area Facts" [online]. The latter statistic has probably increased over the past sixty years due to the "greenhouse effect." See Savageau and Boyer, *Places Rated Almanac*, 335.

7. The average daily low for January is 7°F. Savageau and Boyer, *Places Rated Almanac*, 369, table of average temperatures. Temperatures as low as -37°F have been recorded. Savageau and Boyer, *Places Rated Almanac*, 369.

8. Savageau and Boyer put the average annual snowfall at thirty-nine inches. Ibid., diagram of seasonal change. The Madison Convention and Visitors' Bureau reports forty-two inches. "Greater Madison at a Glance: Madison Area Facts" [online].

9. *Encyclopaedia Britannica*, 14th ed. (1973), s.v. "Wisconsin," population table citing 1940 census data; all subsequent citations to same edition.

10. The University of Wisconsin-Madison was founded in 1848. WHA, the world's oldest continually operated radio station, began broadcasting on campus in 1917. *Insiders' Guide To Madison, Wisconsin* [online], "History: University Crisscrosses the State," 3.

11. The first rail line arrived in 1852. By 1887, Madison had become the hub for eight others. Ibid., "History: Early Economic Development," 3.

12. Ibid., "History: Industry and Technology," 3.

13. Ibid.

14. Rayovac, *Time Line* [online], Madison: Clotho Advanced Media, date unknown [cited 7 June 2001; 13:22 EST], available from Internet: <http://www.rayovac.com/about/info/tim_lin.shtml>.

15. The base continued to operate until 1968. Today it is the site of Dane County Regional Airport. Jaeger, "Forgotten Heroes of Truax Field," Madison Newspapers Archives [online].

16. Ibid.

17. Ivey, "Madison's Hom-Pak Goodness: Schoep's Going Strong at 70," Madison Newspapers Archives [online].

18. The premier local brand of ice cream. It was established in 1928 by E.J. Schoephoester in the back of his East Side Madison grocery store. In 1997, Shoep's was the leading ice cream manufacturer in Wisconsin, producing 8.5 million gallons annually. Ibid.

19. Ibid.

20. Historic Madison, Inc., "A History of the City of Madison" [online].

21. *Insiders' Guide To Madison, Wisconsin* [online], "History: Early Economic Development," 3.

22. Ibid.

23. Ibid. The other two lakes are Kegonsa and Waubesa. Ibid., "History," 1.

24. Milfred, "Life on the Porch," Madison Newspapers Archives [online].

25. Ibid.

26. These qualities are discussed in Milfred, "Life on the Porch." Today, homes of this type still exist downtown near the University of Wisconsin-Madison and West Washington Avenue. Ibid.

27. Ibid.

CHAPTER 4: HIGH-PRICED FUN

28. The schedule was reconstructed from National Railway Publication, *Official Guide of the Railways and Steam Navigation Lines of the United States,* no. 5, October 1943, 924.

29. Newman, "Union Station," Jazz Age Chicago [online].

30. Ibid.

31. A picture of the station during this period can be found in Newman, "Union Station."

32. Ibid.

33. *Encyclopaedia Britannica*, s.v. "Illinois," population table citing 1940 census data.

34. Although the specific percentage of passengers that were in the military is unavailable, it was "significant." Newman, "Union Station."

35. Members of the Women's Army Auxiliary Corps. In July 1943, President Franklin Roosevelt signed legislation making these women full-fledged army personnel. Thereafter, they became known as WAC's (Women's Army Corps). Wilson, "World War Two Women," Military Women Veterans: Yesterday, Today, Tomorrow [online].

36. Female navy personnel. The acronym stands for "Women Accepted for Volunteer Emergency Service." Wilson, "World War Two Women."

37. In February, the average daily temperature in Chicago is 25.4°F. *Chicago Fact Book* [online], "Geography/Climate," table of average temperature citing National Climatic Data Center.

38. The Chicago Building is part of a group of structures including the Carson Pirie Scott Building and the former Mandel Brothers Store, which collectively earned this epithet. City of Chicago, "Chicago Building," Chicago Landmarks [online].

39. Walgreens had been operating a drugstore in the Loop since 1922. To attract customers, the store began serving soup and sandwiches during the winter months, when demand for its soda fountains typically declined. "Walgreens Soda Fountains Served Up Decades of Success," Walgreens [online].

40. Walgreens invented the milkshake in the 1920's. Before then, malteds were made with milk, chocolate syrup, and a spoonful of malt powder. Fountain Manager Ivar "Pop Coulsen" decided to add two scoops of vanilla ice cream, which made all the difference in the world. "Walgreens Soda Fountains Served Up Decades of Success," Walgreens [online].

41. The South Side, home of Chicago's African-American community, had some of the city's best and "hottest" night life. The so-called "Black Belt," between Twenty-Sixth and Sixtieth streets, was filled with jazz clubs, theatres, ballrooms, and restaurants frequented by both races, although whites returned to "their" part of town toward morning. Newman, "Bohemian Chicago," Jazz Age Chicago [online].

42. The fire began in a West Side cowbarn owned by Patrick O'Leary. It killed three hundred people, left ninety thousand homeless, and destroyed property valued at two hundred million dollars. City of Chicago, "Chicago: A Brief History," Chicago Mosaic [online]. The story, familiar to every Chicago schoolchild, that

the fire started when Mrs. O'Leary's cow kicked over a kerosene lamp, is considered legend.

43. Also known as the World's Fair of 1893. The Ferris Wheel is named after its inventor, George Gale Ferris. Chicago Historical Society, "What George Wore and Sally Didn't," Chicago Historical Society: World's Fairs [online], 2.

44. Eight members of the Chicago White Sox were linked to several financiers who conspired to fix the World Series of 1919. Afterward, the team was nicknamed "the Black Sox." Sadly, Jackson, who refused to participate in the corruption, is forever associated with it. Chicago Historical Society, "The Black Sox," Chicago Historical Society [online].

45. Al Capone masterminded the killing of six members of a rival gang and an unlucky friend. Chicago Historical Society, "Al Capone," Chicago Historical Society [online].

46. One of the highlights of the "Century of Progress Exposition" in the 1933 World's Fair was Sally Rand's fan dance. Ms. Rand used two seven-pound fans to conceal her nude body. Chicago Historical Society, "What George Wore and Sally Didn't," Chicago Historical Society: World's Fairs [online], 1.

47. The "hottest" jazz was primarily the province of African Americans. Newman, "Bohemian Chicago," Jazz Age Chicago [online]. However, although they were less famous than greats such as Louis Armstrong and Duke Ellington, a number of white musicians were also known for playing on the "cutting edge." These included cornetist Bix Beiderbecke, trombonist Jack Teagarden, and the Jean Goldkette Orchestra. Richard M. Sudhalter, "A Racial Divide That Needn't Be," *New York Times*, Sunday, 3 January 1999, sec. 2, p.1, col. 1.

48. See note 28, above.

49. Formed in 1790, the Marne is a *département* of northeastern France covering 3,168 square miles. The Marne River, crossing southeast to northwest, traverses most of its area. *Encyclopaedia Britannica*, s.v. "Marne." The Second Battle of the Marne marked the turning point of World War I. In the first of a series of offensives, the U.S. First Division was rushed to the area south of Soissons in July 1918, setting in motion a series of German defeats which led, four months later, to her request for an armistice. "The American Troops in the Attack to the South of Soissons," trans. John Roberts, Club Internet (France) [online].

50. On April 27, 1918, at Cantigny, the United States First Division became the first American fighting force to take up position on an active battle front. The Division held the lines for seventy-three days, sustaining losses of fifty-two hundred either killed, wounded, or missing. "The First U.S. Division at Cantigny, 27 April-8 July 1918," trans. John Roberts, Club Internet (France) [online].

51. During five days of fighting, the United States First Division suffered 6,870 casualties south of Soissons. Three-quarters of the front line infantry officers were either killed or wounded. "The American Troops in the Attack to the South of Soissons," trans. John Roberts, Club Internet (France) [online].

52. See note 28, above.

CHAPTER 5: OVER SEAS

53. See *Suicide Missions: Dangerous Tours of Duty—Ball Turret Gunners*, vol. 1, prod. and dir. Rob Lihani, 50 mins., A&E Television Networks, 1999, videocassette.

54. "Post Exchange," a military canteen.

CHAPTER 6: BATTERED BUT UNBOWED

55. Sulzberger, *The American Heritage Picture History of World War II*, 62-3, map.

56. According to 1951 census data, the population of London was 3,348,336. *The Columbia Lippincott Gazetteer of the World*, s.v. "London."

57. In 1950, the population of Britain (the United Kingdom), which included England, Wales, Scotland, and Northern Ireland, was 50,616,000. United Nations (Population Division, Department of Economic and Social Affairs), "Countries with a Population of 50 Million or More: 1950, 1998 and 2050" [online]. The 1951 population of London, 3,348,336 (see note 56 above), divided by 50,616,000, is 6.615 percent.

58. *Columbia Lippincott Gazetteer*, s.v. "London."

59. Sulzberger, *World War II*, 98-9.

60. David Anderson, "London Shelters 1,000,000 Nightly," *New York Times*, 2 January 1941, late city edition, p. 4, col. 5.

61. Jackson and Croome, *Rails through the Clay*, 303.

62. *Record of the 327th Fighter Control Squadron*, 2.

63. Ibid.

64. Jackson and Croome, *Rails through the Clay*, 305.

65. Franchi, "Mecca Comes to Covent Garden," 14.

66. Covent Garden Market Authority, "A Short History of the Market from the Middle Ages to the Motorway" [online].

67. Ibid.

68. Ibid.

69. Ibid.

70. A photograph of costumed usherettes can be found in Franchi, "Mecca Comes to Covent Garden," 15.

71. Royal Opera House, "History and Heritage" [online].

72. Ibid.

73. Ibid.

74. Franchi, "Mecca Comes to Covent Garden," 13.

75. A photograph of the stairway can be seen in Franchi, "Mecca Comes to Covent Garden," 15.

76. See Franchi, "Mecca Comes to Covent Garden," 12, photo.

77. Chewing gum, an imported American habit, became a major problem at the Opera House because it could not be removed by conventional cleaning without damaging the floor. In December 1944, a circuit engineer would invent an inge-

nious electric scraper that heated the gum and harmlessly peeled it off. Franchi, "Mecca Comes to Covent Garden," 19.

78. The Opera House's daily hours were 3-6 p.m. and 7-11 p.m. Ibid., 17.

79. A 1943 Hollywood musical film tribute to the war effort, featuring a cavalcade of stars, including Helen Hayes, Ray Bolger, and William Demarest.

80. Kryss Katsiavriades, "The Piccadilly Line" [online].

81. Jackson and Croome, *Rails through the Clay*, 307.

82. "Shelter Policy: Contracts for Bunks," *Times* (London), 11 October 1940, late London edition, p.9, col. e.

83. Jackson and Croome, *Rails through the Clay*, 299.

84. "London Names 'Evans of the Broke' to Solve Urgent Shelter Muddle," *New York Times*, 2 October 1940, late city edition, p.1, col. 4, continued on p.4.

85. "Duke of Kent at Tube Station Shelter," *Times* (London), 13 November 1940, late London edition, p. 7, col. b.

86. Jackson and Croome, *Rails through the Clay*, 300.

87. "Feeding the Tube Shelterers," *Times* (London), 16 November 1940, late London edition, p. 6, col. g.

88. British Adventures, "The Story of British and Irish Money" [online].

89. Ibid.

90. The value of the British pound was fixed at $4.032 U.S. throughout the war. "Dollar-Pound Exchange Rate 1800-1998" [online]. If you do the math, you will see that a British penny was equal to about one and two-thirds American cents.

91. British Adventures, "The Story of British and Irish Money" [online].

92. When British soldiers were asked why they resented Americans stationed in their country during the months preceding the Normandy invasion, this was the common answer. *Dictionary of Word and Phrase Origins*, s.v. "overpaid, oversexed, and over here."

93. "Feeding the Tube Shelterers," *Times* (London), 16 November 1940.

94. Ibid.

95. Jackson and Croome, *Rails through the Clay*, 300.

96. Ibid.

97. Churchill first used this phrase in a May 13, 1940 speech to the House of Commons. It was his first public statement since being commissioned by the Crown to form a new government. *Dictionary of Word and Phrase Origins*, s.v. "blood, toil, tears, and sweat."

98. See Anderson, "London Shelters 1,000,000 Nightly," *New York Times*, 2 January 1941.

99. Raymond Daniell, "50 Areas Bombed in Siege of London," *New York Times*, 11 October 1940, late city edition, p.1, col. 5, continued on p. 4.

100. "St. Paul's Bombed," *Times* (London), 11 October 1940, late London edition, p.6, photo caption.

101. Bermant, *London's East End*, 237.

102. Daniell, "50 Areas Bombed in Siege of London," *New York Times*, 11 October 1940, p.4.

103. The first was in 1666 and destroyed eighty percent of the city. *Encyclopaedia Britannica*, s.v. "London."

104. Bermant, *London's East End*, 238.

105. For a collection of drawings capturing the spirit of the East End during World War II, see Allin and Wesker, *Say Goodbye: You May Never See Them Again*.

106. Bermant, *London's East End*, 236.

107. Dogs, cats, and large, exotic birds were common features of the area near the river. Ibid., 245.

108. Smithies, *The Black Economy in England since 1914*, 64.

109. Pubs were frequent sites of black market transactions. Ibid., 75.

110. Because it was a business district, Covent Garden was frequently deserted at night and on weekends, making it a popular black market site. Ibid., 76.

111. "Distances from Liverpool to Major U.K. Ports" [online].

112. Virtual Felixstowe, "Town History" [online].

113. Ibid.

114. Ibid.

115. Ibid.

116. Virtual Felixstowe, "The Port of Felixstowe" [online].

117. "Landguard Fort" [online].

118. "Landguard Peninsula—Management Plan" [online].

CHAPTER 7: NORMANDY

119. Ryan, *The Longest Day*, 59.

120. Sulzberger, *World War II*, 490.

121. Ryan, *The Longest Day*, 58.

122. Pyle, *Brave Men*, 361.

123. Ryan, *The Longest Day*, 28.

124. Ibid., Foreword.

125. See Ryan, *The Longest Day*, map of the assault, inside rear cover.

126. John Keegan, "The Normandy Beachhead, June 1944," in Britannica Online, Encyclopaedia Britannica, 1998-9 [cited 1 August 1999; 16:56 EST], available from Internet: <http://normandy.eb. com/normandy/week2/invasion.html>.

127. Ronald J. Drez, "Omaha Beach," in Britannica Online, Encyclopaedia Britannica, 1998-9 [cited 11 Aug. 1999; 18:17 EST], available from Internet: <http://normandy.eb.com/normandy/week2/Omaha_Beach.html>.

128. Ibid.

129. Ibid. Intelligence Sergeant Herb Epstein of the Fifth Ranger Battalion speaks of a four-foot seawall. Patrick O'Donnell, ed., "The Landing: An Interview with Herb Epstein" [online], Drop Zone Virtual Museum, 1999 [cited 5 Aug. 1999; 13:02 EST], available from Internet: <http://www.thedropzone.org/europe/Normandy/epstein.html>.

130. Ryan, *The Longest Day*, 29.

131. Ibid.

132. Hammond, *Normandy* [online], 27.

133. Ryan, *The Longest Day*, 135-6.

134. *Omaha Beachhead* [online], 42.

135. Keegan, "The Normandy Beachhead" [online].

136. Ryan, *The Longest Day*, 208.

137. Pyle, *Brave Men*, 360. Combat historian and former U.S. Army Colonel S.L.A. Marshall's assessment of Omaha was harsher than Pyle's. Writing sixteen years after the invasion, Marshall charged that earlier accounts whitewashed the beating the Allies took: "The worst-fated companies were overlooked, the more wretched personal experiences were toned down, and disproportionate attention was paid to the little element of courageous success in a situation which was largely characterized by tragic failure." Marshall, "First Wave at Omaha Beach," 67.

138. Williams, "The Twenty-Ninth Infantry Division," [online].

139. *Omaha Beachhead* [online], 42.

140. Rear Admiral John D. Hayes, U.S.N. (Ret.), "Developments in Naval Warfare," in Grolier Online, Grolier, 1998, [cited 18 September 1999; 12:45 EST],
available from Internet: <http://gi.grolier.com/wwii/wwii_12.html>.

141. See *Omaha Beachhead* [online], 42.

142. Ibid., 44.

143. This was standard issue for bangalore torpedo men of the 5th Ranger Battalion, and A and B Companies of the 2nd Ranger Battalion, 116th and 16th Infantry
Regiments. See Patrick O'Donnell, ed., "'Rangers, Lead the Way!' An interview
with Ellis 'Bill' Reed, D Company, 5th Ranger Battalion" [online], Drop Zone
Virtual Museum, 1999 [cited 5 August 1999; 12:50 EST], available from Internet: <http://www.thedropzone.org/europe/Normandy/reed.html>.

144. The message, signed by General Eisenhower, is reproduced in Sulzberger,
World War II, 496.

145. Hammond, *Normandy* [online], 27.

146. Ryan, *The Longest Day*, 225.

147. *Omaha Beachhead* [online], 42.

148. Ryan, *The Longest Day*, 227.

149. See "Interview with Ellis 'Bill' Reed" [online].

150. This appears to have been a common problem. See Marshall, "First Wave at
Omaha Beach," 70-1; Patrick O'Donnell, ed., "A Trip to Hell: An Interview
with Ray Alm, Second Ranger Battalion" [online], Drop Zone Virtual Museum,
1999 [cited 5 August 1999; 13:07 EST], available from Internet: <http://
www.thedropzone.org/europe/Normandy/alm.html>; *Omaha   Beachhead*
[online], 44.

151. Marshall, "First Wave at Omaha Beach," 68.

152. "Interview with Herb Epstein" [online].

153. Ibid.

154. Drez, "Omaha Beach," in Britannica Online.

155. Ibid.

156. "Interview with Ellis 'Bill' Reed" [online].

157. Hammond, *Normandy* [online], 28.

158. Pyle, *Brave Men*, 366-7.

159. *Omaha Beachhead* [online], 42.

160. Omaha's width was probably not uniform. Bill Reed of the Fifth Ranger Battalion estimates it at 100 yards, "Interview with Ellis 'Bill' Reed" [online], while the United States Army Center of Military History puts the figure at "200 yards or more," *Omaha Beachhead* [online], 44.

161. According to Marshall, this is how the majority of soldiers in the first wave survived. Marshall, "First Wave at Omaha Beach," 68.

162. A photograph of wounded soldiers waiting to be evacuated from the Omaha seawall can be found in Ryan, *The Longest Day*, 213.

163. The photographic collection of the Imperial War Museum in London contains a picture of a similar incident which occurred among British troops during D-Day on Sword Beach. See the art section in this book.

164. The 5th Ranger Battalion played a key role in the advance up the bluffs on Dog White. The 5th's bangalore men blew several obstacles, and by the end of the day, the Battalion, together with the 116th Infantry's Company C, had advanced to the strategic area around Vierville. *Omaha Beachhead* [online], 62.

165. *Elements of Ammunition*, 120, 375.

166. Ibid., 375.

167. *Manual of Explosives*, 19.

168. *Elements of Ammunition*, 375.

169. *Manual of Explosives*, 126.

170. Ibid., 114.

171. *Elements of Ammunition*, 367.

172. The hero of Victor Hugo's 1862 novel, *Les Misérables*, known for his immense physical strength and selflessness.

173. *Omaha Beachhead* [online], 60.

174. Sulzberger, *World War II*, 483.

175. *Omaha Beachhead* [online], 58.

176. "Interview with Ellis 'Bill' Reed" [online].

177. E.g., *Omaha Beachhead* [online], 60; Ryan, *The Longest Day*, 288-9; "Interview with Ellis 'Bill' Reed" [online].

178. *Omaha Beachhead* [online], 43.

179. See Drez, "Omaha Beach," in Britannica Online.

180. See *Record of the 327th Fighter Control Squadron*, 5.

181. Hayes, "Developments in Naval Warfare," in Grolier Online.

182. Ibid.

183. *Record of the 327th Fighter Control Squadron*, 5.

184. *Record of the 327th Fighter Control Squadron*, 5, reports that on June 7, 1944, radio men near Grandcamp "had been unable to land because of severe enemy action."

185. While en route to Normandy, perfect strangers would readily discuss the most intimate details of their lives. Ryan, *The Longest Day*, 92.

CHAPTER 9: HUNGRY MEN

186. The fall of St. Lô on July 18, 1944 marked the first massive breakout from Normandy. Allied forces were now able to advance rapidly in France. Up until this time, German opposition had been very stiff. Sulzberger, *World War II*, 486, 511.

187. Ibid., 485.

CHAPTER 10: AN ARREST IN VERSAILLES

188. All efforts to obtain a copy of the article have been unsuccessful.

CHAPTER 11: BELGIUM

189. Descriptions of V-1's varied with the observer. One of the more colorful comments came from a British Home Guard sergeant who said they were "little aeroplanes with a light up their arse." Cooksley, *Flying Bomb*, 63.

190. RAF historian Peter Cooksley describes "spurts of red and orange flame from the jet unit…" Cooksley, *Flying Bomb*, 96.

191. My citing, in September 1944, was unusual but plausible. By then, all of the launching cites in France had been captured, severely hampering the German effort. "Antwerp X: The AAA War Against the Buzz Bombs" [online]. However, air-launched V-1's were fired over Gilze Rijen, Holland during most of that month (missions were suspended between September 5 and 15). Cooksley, *Flying Bomb*, 126. On September 22, a V-1 caused heavy property damage in Ans, Belgium, and several others landed in the surrounding countryside. Bronckart, *Bombes, Obus et Robots*, 7. New launching sites in Holland were operational by October, when attacks on Belgium began in earnest. "Antwerp X: The AAA War Against the Buzz Bombs" [online].

192. Sulzberger, *World War II*, 483.

193. Ibid.

194. The last V-1 to cross the English Channel was fired on March 29, 1945. Cooksley, *Flying Bomb*, 174.

195. Sulzberger, *World War II*, 483.

196. Cooksley, *Flying Bomb*, 69.

197. *Encyclopaedia Britannica*, s.v. "Belgium."

198. See Sulzberger, *World War II*, 60.

199. Ibid.

200. *Encyclopaedia Britannica*, s.v. "Belgium."

201. The local date of liberation. Wynants, *Verviers libéré*, 1.

202. Official Verviers census figures: 40,731 (1944); 41,188 (1945) as reported in Wynants, *Verviers libéré*, 138.

203. Ibid., 43.

204. Ruwet, *Vues d'une occupation*, 98-9, photos and captions; all subsequent citations to photos and captions.

205. 1948 official estimate reported in *Columbia Lippincott Gazetteer*, s.v. "Stembert."

206. Ibid.

207. Named for British Home Secretary Sir Robert Peel, who founded the London Police Force in 1829. He later became Prime Minister. *Encyclopaedia Britannica*, s.v. "Peel, Sir Robert."

208. Wynants, *Verviers libéré*, 40.

209. Although the Citroën was a French car, by the 1930's, it was being manufactured in Belgium, Switzerland, Italy, Spain, Germany, Britain, and Poland. Mondadori, *100 Years of Automobiles*, 162.

210. Rutishauser, "A Short History of the Citroën Traction Avant" [online].

211. Ibid.

212. See Bernton, Kovarik, and Sklar, *The Forbidden Fuel*, 216.

213. It is "technically quite simple to produce ethanol containing 5% or more water on farm." *Gasohol: A Technical Memorandum*, vi. There is a vast literature on home-grown ethanol, e.g., extensive bibliographies in Bernton, Kovarik, and Sklar, *The Forbidden Fuel*, 233-5, and "Reading and Resource List: Making and Using Your Own Ethanol" [online].

214. Ethanol is distilled similarly to beer. Bernton, Kovarik, and Sklar, *The Forbidden Fuel*, 3.

215. Because ethanol is corrosive, cars using it require engine and fuel delivery system modifications to protect parts. "Ethanol-Powered Vehicles" [online].

216. Bernton, Kovarik, and Sklar, *The Forbidden Fuel*, 1.

217. After World War II, a glut of cheap oil helped keep ethanol out of the transportation market. In the postwar era, the U.S. government expressed virtually no interest in alternative fuels until the energy crises of the 1970's. "Ethanol-Powered Vehicles" [online].

218. See Bernton, Kovarik, and Sklar, *The Forbidden Fuel*, 32, and "Ethanol-Powered Vehicles"[online].

219. "Ethanol-Powered Vehicles" [online].

220. Wynants, *Verviers 1940*, 245.

221. Ibid.

222. The exchange rate is based upon information contained in my letters of August 10, 1944 and September 23, 1944.

223. Wynants, *Verviers 1940*, 245.

224. Ibid.

225. In 1976, Stembert and several other suburbs merged with Verviers. They retain their individual names as districts of the current metropolitan entity. Jacques Wynants, letter to Mark Stuart Ellison, 18 July 2000.

CHAPTER 12: FRIENDLY FIRE

226. Wynants, *Verviers 1940*, 107.

227. Ruwet, *Vues d'une occupation*, 15.

228. Wynants, *Verviers 1940*, 115.

229. On the morning of June 6, 1944, an emotional Contre-Amiral Jaujard, aboard the French vessel *Montcalm*, ordered his men to attack their own country. Ryan, *The Longest Day*, 197.

230. Wynants, *Verviers 1940*, 115.

231. In 1976, the following independent municipalities were integrated into a "new single entity" of Verviers: Stembert, Heusy, Petit-Rechain, Lambermont, and Ensival. Andrimont, an independent municipality until 1976, is now part of Dison. That same year, Wegnez merged with the town of Pepinster. Jacques Wynants, letter to Mark Stuart Ellison, 18 July 2000.

232. Murphy, "Fighter Control," 6.

233. Wynants, *Verviers 1940*, 239.

234. Wynants, *Verviers libéré*, 6.

235. Bronckart, *Bombes, Obus et Robots*, 9.

236. See Wynants, *Verviers libéré*, 152.

237. Bronckart, *Bombes, Obus et Robots*, 9.

238. For a photograph of an American Lockheed P-38 Lightning, see Wynants, *Verviers libéré*, 153.

239. My translation of: *"L'événement le plus embarrassant pour les Américains fut sans conteste le bombardement de la ville par leur propre aviation, le mercredi 11 octobre 1944, vers 15h 20."* Wynants, *Verviers libéré*, 152.

240. Bronckart, *Bombes, Obus et Robots*, 10.

241. See Wynants, *Verviers 1940*, 108-9, map.

242. Bronckart, *Bombes, Obus et Robots*, 12.

243. Wynants, *Verviers libéré*, 153.

244. Bronckart, *Bombes, Obus et Robots*, *"Aux Lecteurs* [Preface]."

245. Wynants, *Verviers libéré*, 152.

246. *Encyclopaedia Britannica*, s.v. "Aachen."

247. Ibid.

CHAPTER 13: DENISE, VERVIERS, AND THE V-WEAPONS

248. See Bronckart, *Bombes, Obus et Robots*, 12-3.

249. Cooksley, *Flying Bomb*, 15.

250. See Kennedy, *Vengeance Weapon 2*, 51.

251. Cooksley, *Flying Bomb*, 62.

252. Kennedy, *Vengeance Weapon 2*, 35.

253. Cooksley, *Flying Bomb*, 40.

254. Reports on the amount of warning time vary. Kennedy estimates it at eight to ten seconds. Kennedy, *Vengeance Weapon 2*, 39. Although Cooksley puts the figure at fourteen seconds, Cooksley, *Flying Bomb*, 70, he reproduces notes of early British eyewitnesses who said V-1's fell silent about thirty seconds before hitting their targets. Ibid., 65.

255. Cooksley, *Flying Bomb*, 29.

256. Ibid.

257. Kennedy, *Vengeance Weapon 2*, 39.

258. Cooksley, *Flying Bomb*, 66.

259. See *Record of the 327th Fighter Control Squadron*, 2.

260. Cooksley, *Flying Bomb*, 102.

261. Wynants, *Verviers libéré*, 54.

262. The Cinéma Le Louvre was under control of the United States Army between January 26 and August 20, 1945. Jacques Wynants, letter to Mark Stuart Ellison, 30 September 2000. A photograph of the Cinéma can be found in Ruwet, *Vues d'une occupation*, 144.

263. Bronckart, *Bombes, Obus et Robots*, 15.

264. Ibid.

265. The Voice of America began broadcasting on February 24, 1942—only seventy-nine days after the United States entered the war. Voice of America, "1942-2000: 58 Years of Broadcasting Excellence" [online]. The BBC started daily transmissions on November 14, 1922. "History of the BBC: 1920's" [online].

266. Wynants, *Verviers 1940*, 29.

267. Denise genuinely feared being put in a brothel for drinking after 9 p.m. It seems that somebody really put one over on her because in an email dated 30 November 2003 to Mark Stuart Ellison, Jacques Wynants said that this was indeed a running wartime joke.

268. Jacques Wynants, letter to Mark Stuart Ellison, 30 December 1998.

269. Telephone service was not re-established until November 29. It was interrupted again in December and January during the Battle of the Bulge. Wynants, *Verviers libéré*, 157.

270. Wynants, *Verviers 1940*, 25.

271. Wynants, *Verviers libéré*, 136.

272. Ibid., 137, citing "Le problème du chômage à Verviers," *La Presse verviétoise*, 27-9 December 1944.

273. Wynants, *Verviers libéré*, 138.

274. Centrale des Ouvriers Textiles de Belgique.

275. Wynants, *Verviers libéré*, 50.

276. Bronckart, *Bombes, Obus et Robots*, 51.

277. Wynants, *Verviers libéré*, 135.

278. Ibid., 139, citing *Bulletin communal* (Verviers, Belg.), 22 January 1945, p. 34.

279. Wynants, *Verviers libéré*, 135 n. 6.

280. Ibid., 139.

281. Wynants puts the starting date at October 18, Wynants, *Verviers libéré*, 139 n. 3, but, as previously stated, I had been living in the l'Athénée Royal for quite some time prior to the accidental bombing by American P-38's on October 11.

282. Wynants, *Verviers libéré*, 139 n. 3.

283. See Bronckart, *Bombes, Obus et Robots*, 50-1.

284. Scenic description obtained from Jacques Wynants, email to Mark Stuart Ellison, 30 November 2003.

285. Wynants, *Verviers libéré*, 142.

286. Ruwet, *Vues d'une occupation*, 23.

287. One American and two British raids over Dresden on February 13-14, 1945 killed 135,000 people. Sulzberger, *World War II*, 420.

288. Ruwet, *Vues d'une occupation*, 19.

289. A merger of three pre-war papers: *Le Jour*, *Le Courrier du Soir*, and *Le Travail*. *La Presse verviétoise* ran from 12 September 1944 until 20 July 1945. Shortly thereafter, the three original publications reappeared. Wynants, *Verviers libéré*, 47.

290. Compare photos in Ruwet, *Vues d'une occupation*, 23, 96.

291. Ruwet, *Vues d'une occupation*, 29. The graffiti were written in early 1941 and removed later that year on German orders. Jacques Wynants, email to Mark Stuart Ellison, 30 November 2003. Verviers had three train stations. The West was for shipping only. The Central served passengers, while the East catered to passengers and local industry. Wynants, *Verviers 1940*, 25.

292. Bedeur and Zagaglia, *Chapuis*, 152.

293. He was executed on January 2, 1794. Ibid., 150-2.

294. Bronckart, *Bombes, Obus et Robots*, 18.

295. Address furnished by Jacques Wynants, letter to Mark Stuart Ellison, 30 September 2000.

296. See Wynants, *Verviers libéré*, 135.

297. Bronckart, *Bombes, Obus et Robots*, 21.

298. Witnesses have described the sound of a V-1 explosion as a "roll of thunder." Cooksley, *Flying Bomb*, 14.

299. Cooksley describes a V-2 producing a "white vapour trail hanging vertically in the air." Ibid., 146.

300. See Cooksley, *Flying Bomb*, 74.

301. Kennedy, *Vengeance Weapon 2*, 19.

302. Ibid.

303. Cooksley, *Flying Bomb*, 165.

304. Ibid.

305. Dornberger, *V-2*, xviii.

306. See Cooksley, *Flying Bomb*, 155-6.

307. Ibid., 145.

308. Kennedy, *Vengeance Weapon 2*, 39.

309. Ibid.

310. Cooksley, *Flying Bomb*, 165.

311. Kennedy, *Vengeance Weapon 2*, 39.

312. Normally, a V-2 explosion had a characteristic double bang: sonic boom, closely followed by warhead detonation. Cooksley, *Flying Bomb*, 145-6.

313. Kennedy, *Vengeance Weapon 2*, 39.

314. Cooksley, *Flying Bomb*, 159.

315. Kennedy, *Vengeance Weapon 2*, 6.

316. Cooksley, *Flying Bomb*, 146-7.

317. Ibid., 147.

318. Kennedy, *Vengeance Weapon 2*, 6.

319. Dornberger, *V-2*, 26-7.

320. Cooksley, *Flying Bomb*, 147.

321. Dornberger, *V-2*, 5.

322. Kennedy, *Vengeance Weapon 2*, 10.

323. Cooksley, *Flying Bomb*, 148.

324. Kennedy, *Vengeance Weapon 2*, 10.

325. Ibid.

326. Dornberger, *V-2*, 269.

327. Kennedy, *Vengeance Weapon 2*, 23-4.

328. Ibid., 66 (Saturn V); Federation of American Scientists, "R-11/SS-1B Scud-A, R-300 9K72 Elbrus/SS-1C Scud-B" [online] (Scud missile).

329. A reproduction of the drawing can be found in Shirley Christian, "But Is It Art? Well, Yes," *New York Times*, 25 November 1998, sec. E, p. 1. According to the article, Peruvian-born artist Alberto Vargas worked for *Esquire* during the 1940's. Because his editors thought his name sounded like a possessive, Vargas omitted the "s" when signing his work. Ibid. His drawings of impossibly perfect, voluptuous females were immensely popular among American soldiers, and reproductions graced the nosecone of many an aircraft. Ibid. By the 1960's, Vargas had added the "s" back into his name and was working for *Playboy*. Ibid.

330. The Messerschmitt 262 jet could reach 540 miles per hour. Sulzberger, *World War II*, 420.

331. Cooksley describes the aftermath of a V-2 explosion in which a "billowing cloud of black-brown smoke from the devastation" was visible for several miles. Cooksley, *Flying Bomb*, 146.

CHAPTER 14: THE BULGE

332. Sulzberger, *World War II*, 525.

333. See Phillips, "History," Veterans of the Battle of the Bulge [online].

334. "Battle of the Bulge Facts" [online].

335. Ibid.

336. Ibid.

337. "Battle of the Bulge: About the Program" [online].

338. See Phillips, "History," Veterans of the Battle of the Bulge [online].

339. "Battle of the Bulge: About the Program" [online].

340. Phillips, "History," Veterans of the Battle of the Bulge [online].

341. "Battle of the Bulge: About the Program" [online].

342. See Sulzberger, *World War II*, 525.

343. Sulzberger, *World War II*, 525; "Battle of the Bulge: About the Program" [online].

344. Sulzberger, *World War II*, 525.

345. Phillips, "History," Veterans of the Battle of the Bulge [online].

346. Sulzberger, *World War II*, 485; see Phillips, "History," Veterans of the Battle of the Bulge [online].

347. Sulzberger, *World War II*, 485.

348. See "Battle of the Bulge Facts" [online].

349. Wynants, *Verviers libéré*, 164.

350. Bronckart, *Bombes, Obus et Robots*, 28.

351. Wynants, *Verviers libéré*, 166-7.

352. Bronckart, *Bombes, Obus et Robots*, 43.

353. Wynants, *Verviers libéré*, 176.

354. Bronckart, *Bombes, Obus et Robots*, 43.

355. Thirteen were shot at Henri-Chapelle in December, one at Huy in January. Wynants, *Verviers libéré*, 176 n. 5.

356. *Encyclopaedia Britannica*, s.v. "Liège."

357. Wynants, *Verviers libéré*, 166.

358. Ibid.

359. The capture of American privates near Spa is mentioned in *Record of the 327th Fighter Control Squadron*, 3.

360. See Bronckart, *Bombes, Obus et Robots*, 28-9.

361. Ibid.

362. "Battle of the Bulge: About the Program" [online].

363. See *Columbia Lippincott Gazetteer*, s.v. "Verviers."

364. Bronckart, *Bombes, Obus et Robots*, 31.

365. *Columbia Lippincott Gazetteer*, s.v. "Liège."

366. Ibid., citing 1948 official estimate.

367. *Columbia Lippincott Gazetteer*, s.v. "Liège."

368. Ibid., citing 1948 official estimate.

369. Cooksley, *Flying Bomb*, 185.

370. Ibid. Compare Bronckart, *Bombes, Obus et Robots*, 46, which reports that between December 16, 1944 and January 8, 1945, 525 people in Liège were killed by flying bombs.

371. Cooksley, *Flying Bomb*, 185.

372. Wynants, *Verviers libéré*, 169.

373. Bronckart, *Bombes, Obus et Robots*, 32.

374. Wynants, *Verviers libéré*, 170.

375. The New York Yankees won seven World Series championships between 1936 and 1943. "Baseball: New York Yankees Year-by-Year" [online]. In 1944, with most of their heavy hitters in the service, they lost the American League Pennant to the St. Louis Browns. It was the only time in the Browns' fifty-two-year history that they made it to the World Series. "History of the World Series: 1944" [online].

376. The 1948 official estimate is 26,262. *Columbia Lippincott Gazetteer*, s.v. "Charleroi."

377. Ibid.

378. Ibid.

379. "A Short History of Charleroi" [online].

380. Ibid.

381. "Aperçu historique de Charleroi" [online]. This French version refers to it as "*le Pays Noir*," literally, "the Black Country," but compare the English version, "A Short History of Charleroi" [online], which translates it as "the Coal Country."

382. "A Short History of Charleroi" [online].

383. Although the last mine closed in 1984, the town is still one of the largest glass, iron, and steel centers in Europe. Ibid.

384. Bronckart, *Bombes, Obus et Robots*, 38.

385. Sulzberger, *World War II*, 525.

386. Bronckart, *Bombes, Obus et Robots*, 48.

387. "Battle of the Bulge: About the Program" [online].

388. Sulzberger, *World War II*, 525.

389. Ibid., 485, 524.

390. Bronckart, *Bombes, Obus et Robots*, 36-7.

391. Ibid., 42.

392. Richard Goldstein, "C.A. MacGillivary, 83, Dies; Won Medal of Honor," *New York Times*, 30 June 2000, sec. C, p. 18.

393. Sulzberger, *World War II*, 525.

394. "Battle of the Bulge Facts" [online].

395. Ibid.

396. Ibid.

CHAPTER 15: RUSH TO THE RHINE

397. Murray was actually missing since November 22, 1943. Murray Weiss, "Hero's Honor For My Uncle At Long Last," *New York Post*, 13 November 2005, p. 21.

CHAPTER 16: GERMANY

398. *Encyclopaedia Britannica*, s.v. "Brühl."

399. Ibid., s.v. "Marburg."

400. Roger Cohen, "As Goethe's City Is Honored, Buchenwald Lurks Nearby," *New York Times*, 3 August 1999, late city edition, sec. A, p. 1, cols. 5-6, continued on p. 6; Sulzberger, *World War II*, 566.

401. Cohen, "As Goethe's City Is Honored, Buchenwald Lurks Nearby," p. 6. Weimar was voted the Continent's cultural capital of 1999 by European ministers. Ibid., p. 1.

402. Sulzberger, *World War II*, 557.

CHAPTER 18: THE HOME STRETCH

403. Sulzberger, *World War II*, 590, 616.

404. Hersey, *Hiroshima*, 80-1.

405. Sulzberger, *World War II*, 612.

406. Prime Minister Churchill estimated that a full-scale invasion of the Japanese mainland would have cost an additional one million American and five hundred thousand British lives. Churchill, *Triumph and Tragedy*, 638. Commenting on a U.S. plan to capture the westernmost Japanese island of Kyushu, and from there to launch an attack on Japan proper, Churchill wrote:

> Here stood an army of more than a million men, well trained, well equipped, and fanatically determined to fight to the last… These two great operations…were never required. We may well be thankful. Ibid., 628-9.

407. Hersey, *Hiroshima*, 89.

408. Sulzberger, *World War II*, 620.

978-0-595-66444-3
0-595-66444-X